Into the
Wilderness

W. E. Zazo-Phillips

The Phillips and More Company

Into the Wilderness is a work of fiction. Any names, characters, places, and incidents utilized or described are the products of the author's imagination or are used fictitiously. Any resemblance to actual events, locales, or persons, living or dead, is entirely coincidental.

The Phillips and More Company

Bucks County, PA 19021

phillipsandmore@gmail.com

ISBN 978-0-9882401-0-0

Acknowledgements

The author would like to thank:

- my husband, for his continuous support.

- Ben Schrecengost, for comparing this book to a fine wine.

- Justin Gilmore. "Washing one's hands of the conflict between the powerful and the powerless means to side with the powerful, not to be neutral." – Paulo Freire

- Dr. Irving Goldfarb, DDS, who told me a story once about the pedal-driven dentist drills they used in-country during the Vietnam War.

- the Examiners of Selection Services, whose debates about punctuation and one vs. two-spaced full stops continue to improve my understanding of the writing process.

- Marc Grossman, his wife Gemma, and the monthly Traveller group.

- anyone reading these words.

- all SCAdians, everywhere, who are living the dream.

Author's Notes

To All Who See These Presents, Greetings,

This is the second book of a literary triptych. The first novella is called *Demons Among Us*, which chronicles Infusion and its aftereffects and introduces the government-affiliated characters. If the reader has difficulty finding a copy, please email the author at oocdc2@hotmail.com.

The Society for Creative Anachronism is a real, vibrantly living organization with chapters located worldwide. Anyone who would like more information about the SCA can go to www.SCA.org. Find a local group; maybe I'll see you at an event someday.

To absent friends

Prologue

The Known World
The Middle Kingdom
The Barony of Red Spears
The Marche of the Dusk
(McNerney, Ohio)
Two Weeks after Infusion
10:25 am

<u>Red</u>

The world had gone mad, but at least Sir Karl the Red's family and friends were safe for now. When reports of the virus had first been reported in Cincinnati, Red invited his SCAdian household and squires to come stay at his homestead for the weekend until things calmed down.

Instead, things had gotten worse, and his people had now been in his home for over ten days. Food runs were getting dangerous; there were reports of mob activity not even ten miles away from McNerney.

To be safe, Red had started around-the-clock watchstanding in each direction around his House on the Hill about three days ago, but everyone knew that they couldn't stay there forever—it was only a matter of time before the mobs swung their way.

Red walked through the house, considering their situation. It was getting harder with every passing day to maneuver through his home: since his initial invitation, over a dozen more families from the Marche had found their way to his door, and Elspeth couldn't turn anyone away. He estimated there were about forty people now crammed into his ranch house, and he felt responsible for their well-being. He just wasn't sure where to go from here.

As he sidestepped around children and climbed over couches,

1

his guests would look up and smile at him, gratefulness and fatigue shining in their eyes. As a retired Navy senior chief who spent some time overseas assisting with humanitarian relief, he recognized the look. He also knew that circumstances could change their attitudes in a microsecond, and he and his wife could be the Bastards that Got Them Killed just as easily.

Humans were humans, no matter where you live, Red thought.

Well...until they get Infected, anyway...

Red passed by one of his squires posted by the large picture window on the east side of the house. He was armed with his rifle, looking towards the horizon. Just as Red was at the doorway leading out into the hallway, John said his name.

"Come look at this, sir."

Red returned to John and peered out the window. It was a landscape he was very familiar with: gentle, rolling hills with a patchwork of fields and grasslands with the occasional small herd of cows, or maybe even some horses or dots of sheep. Farmhouses and silos could also been seen, quiet and serene.

Past the hills, however, Red saw what concerned John: tiny pillars of black smoke were rising into the clear blue sky.

"How long do you think we have?" asked Red.

John shook his head. "Hard to say. The horizon ends about fifteen miles from here, maybe?"

Red nodded. "OK. Let's keep this quiet for now. We'll call the squires together in an hour. I'll ask Roderick to relieve you when it's time; I want you there."

"I understand, sir."

Red stood up and continued down the hall. When he approached the second door on the right, he stopped and tapped his knuckles on the doorframe.

"Come in," he heard from behind the door.

He opened it and stepped into the room. It was the master bedroom, large enough for a king size bed, four large dressers, a full antique vanity with a mirror, and a full tapestry loom in the corner. His wife, Elspeth, was sitting behind the loom, working on a wall-hanging based on a fourteenth-century Norman piece. Sometimes he would wake up in the middle of the night to the sound of her shuttle passing through the warps and the *clack* of the petals as they changed the alignment of the threads. She stood as he approached.

"What's wrong, Caleb?"

Red placed his hand on the hardwood loom. He built it for her the first year they moved into their House on the Hill. The peerage was so impressed with his attention to its authenticity and scale that he won the Order of the Silver Oak for his effort that year. The award was tacked to the front of the loom with brass finishing nails.

"We need to run soon, Eileen."

Elspeth gazed down at the floor. "How soon?"

"I think tonight."

Elspeth looked up at him, a sad mix of determination and resignation showed on her face. Red remembered that she often looked like that before his patrols, all those years ago, when he would leave her alone for months at a time. She had hated being a Navy spouse, but she had loved being with him enough to stay and endure it for his sake. Now he was asking her to move yet again.

Actually, now they were fleeing for their lives, but that didn't make it any easier for Red to say the bad news.

"Well, then; I'll start packing up the smaller loom. Do we know where we are going?"

Red shook his head. "Not yet. I have a phone call or two to make. I think west."

Elspeth nodded. "When are you telling our guests?"

"I'm meeting with the squires in an hour. We'll start making preparations for departure then."

Elspeth came around the loom and walked to him, arms wide. Red pulled her into his chest and squeezed her with a hug.

"We'll make it through this," Red promised.

"I know."

They disengaged and Red left the room, leaving his wife to start gathering her things.

Several minutes later, after quietly spreading the word about the upcoming meeting in his study, Red finally arrived at the kitchen and opened one of several junk drawers. About five years ago the previous Baron of Red Spears, Marc of the Resurrection, left Ohio to start a *kibbutz* in Wyoming. That December, he had sent Red and Elspeth a generic holiday card, expressing his mass-produced Seasons Greetings, with Best Wishes for the Coming New Year. At the bottom of the card, Marc had written his new phone number.

Red found the card and pulled it out. That was five years ago—Red had not spoken to Marc since. It was a long shot that the *kibbutz* was still in operation, let alone that Marc was still there, that they could accommodate Red and his refugees, or that they could even *get* to Wyoming. Hell, it would be a miracle if his phone and the Wyoming phone were still working, but it was worth a try.

Saying a small prayer, Red picked up the receiver to the wall phone. He heard a dial tone. He noticed that his hand was shaking as he punched in the phone number, starting with "1," and then the area code.

After several clicks, he heard the phone ringing. After two rings, he heard another click, a pause, and then finally a voice.

"Ramon's Seafood Market and Whorehouse: freshest fish at the freshest prices!"

Red let out a sigh of relief. Marc never could just say "Hello"...

Act One

Chapter One

District Tango Headquarters
Location Classified
Six Years after Infusion
0943

Abby

There was something in Abby's throat.

That was the first thing she noticed. She registered that it was round and smooth, and it ran out from her mouth, and she constantly wanted to gag. She tried to open her eyes, but she couldn't--something was holding her eyelids down. When she tried to take a breath, she found that her lungs wouldn't respond the way she wanted them to. Rather, her breathing was regular, measured, and...controlled.

Abby was finding it impossible not to panic.

What happened? Why am I here!? She screamed wordlessly to herself for a long time.

Finally, she heard someone near her making soft, muted noises. She made her right hand move.

"Oh," she heard a female voice say. "You're awake. Hold on, Abby, I'll remove the tape from your eyelids."

She felt the pressure, and then the pulling as the woman removed the medical tape. The attendant managed to do it carefully enough that only a few eyelashes and eyebrow hairs went with it.

Abby opened her eyes. She supposed she was in a hospital room--it looked like one. She nudged her head over and saw a middle-aged woman with dark brown hair wearing Spongebob Squarepants scrubs.

"How are you feeling?" the woman asked.

Abby tried to give the attendant her best glare, and then

looked down near her chest.

"We had to ventilate you—you were a real mess when you arrived. Do you remember what happened?"

Abby managed to jerk her head a little sideways in a *no* gesture.

"That's OK. I'll let the doctor know you're awake, and he'll be in to talk to you."

A short time later, one of the residents came in to see her. She thought he looked familiar, but she never really paid attention to him because...well, he was a resident.

"Hi, Ms. Burgess, I'm Dr. O'Malley, and I'm assigned to your case. Are you feeling up to a short conversation? One blink for yes, two blinks for no?"

Abby blinked once.

"The nurse told me you don't remember what happened. Is that true?"

Abby blinked once.

"We're not sure exactly what happened, either, but you were found in your office about a week ago. You were unconscious, you had traces of codeine in your mouth, and a stun gun burn on your chest."

Abby's eyes widened. That nudged something in her memory. Something bad. She refocused her attention on the doctor.

"Are you still with me, Ms. Burgess?"

Abby blinked once.

"So, the good news is that all of your organs are still functioning--your kidneys were being ornery, but they straightened themselves out--and from what I can observe with you right now, you didn't suffer any cognitive brain damage, though we'll have to do some tests to be sure.

"Unfortunately, we think you suffered a stroke. Your left side was unresponsive to painful stimuli while you were unconscious. I'd like to re-evaluate now, are you ready?"

Abby blinked once. Even during the initial Infusion, when the entire world was falling apart around her, she was never this scared.

Dr. O'Malley took out a small, spiky wheel attached to a stick. He showed it to her and demonstrated how it spun. "I'm going to run this up and down your limbs, Ms. Burgess. When you can feel it, I want you to blink. OK?"

Abby blinked once. For the next few minutes, she blinked as instructed when she felt the wheel. To her dismay, she didn't feel anything on her left side, even though the doctor kept making "Good, good" and "You're doing great!" noises.

At the end of the assessment, she felt tears running down the right side of her face.

Dr. O'Malley had the decency to look uncomfortable. "That's it for now. I know this seems hopeless now, but we'll have you go through some physical and occupational therapy--you might get some function back--we'll just have to see."

Abby blinked, and then closed her eyes until the doctor left the room.

Time passed without measure for a while--maybe two or three days. Eventually, the breathing tube was removed. As soon as Abby got her voice back, Dr. Donald Hart came to see her.

He walked in with that fake, reassuring smile that he wore when he was working with the demon-Infected. Abby had never thought about it before, but it was a good thing Infected people were insane and oblivious to their surroundings: that smile was damn annoying.

"Hi, Abby! It's good to see you."

Abby did an approximation of a nod. It still hurt to talk, and she wanted to conserve her voice as much as possible.

"So, you were told you were attacked. Do you remember anything about the incident?"

Abby jerked her head to the left. "Nuh."

Don sat down next to Abby's bed. "The last appointment you had before we found you was with Elizabeth Townsend."

When Don said that name, some things started to come back. "Wh...whu?"

"Petty Officer Townsend--one of the strongest Sensors we have. You set a trap for the demons to attack here at Headquarters. It worked—not only do we know now that they have evolved to the point that they demonstrate critical thinking and some degree of problem solving, but Townsend made an entire pool of holy water. We only had one casualty—her Officer in Charge, BM2 Phillips. She was destroyed by the holy water, do you remember?"

Abby was starting to remember. "Gu ohn."

"You had Townsend woken up the next day, and then you had

8

a meeting at 1000. Some people heard you two arguing..."

They both came in a rush: the memories and the adrenaline. Townsend didn't want to cooperate; she was whining that she didn't want to do more tests and "kill people." Abby had lost her patience with the worthless little bitch and...and...

What did *happen next?* Abby remembered yelling at Townsend that the world's survival was more important than one person...or, that what was what she was trying to say, anyway, and...

"She tased you, and she fed you narcotics. She didn't kill you outright, but sometime between the incident and the time we found you, you had a stroke. Sorry, Abby.

"Hey, are you OK?"

...and what's a few hundred test subjects compared to the world, anyway? Abby continued with herself, growing more agitated. *Townsend couldn't...or wouldn't...see the greater good. Plus, the subjects would mostly be the ones in Stasis; it's not like they would feel anything. But...first things first.*

"Wh...whresh...shethe?" Abby asked.

"Sorry?" Dr. Hart asked, bending closer.

Idiot!

"WHR ESH SHEE?" Abby shrieked, and then convulsed as her right side jerked in pain and wrenched around the coughing spasms--*too much, too soon.* It was a few minutes before she could uncoil. Dr. Hart waited patiently for the coughing to subside, and then spoke.

"We're not sure yet. She cut off radio communications here at Headquarters and then ran for the Alpha Laboratory. The guard there said she stopped in and saw her leave again--we haven't found the van yet.

But, don't worry, Abby, we'll find her. She'll answer for what she did..."

Oh, yes, she will, Abby thought. At that moment, she made three promises to herself.

She was going to walk again. Elizabeth Townsend was going to suffer.

Abby was going to watch.

Lizzy

Lizzy Townsend stood watch as Dr. Stella Goddard secured the canvas harness underneath the tractor trailer in the receiving depot of the laboratory. Someone put a lot of thought into engineering an escape space under the trailer: a large metal plate had been welded to various pipes, leaving just enough space for a person to fit, suspended by the harness over the plate. The harness was stretched taut enough to keep the person from swinging around, but slack enough for some give as the truck moved and swayed. There was some thin, squishy-looking blue padding between the harness and the underside of the trailer. After a minute, Stella snapped the last carabineer in place and crawled out of the space. Turning, she reached over and pushed a button on a tool chest mounted to the side of the cab. When the lid popped open, she reached into the chest and pulled out a full-face helmet and a packet of ear plugs. After a quick glace around, she handed them to Lizzy.

"Remember, wait until the driver gets completely out of the cab and you see him walk away—he's only agreed to cooperate if he has culpable deniability." She paused, noticing that Lizzy had fitted the ear plugs in her ears. She spoke louder.

"Then, get yourself out of the harness and get going before he comes back! Leave the helmet in the tool chest! YOU HAVE THE DIRECTIONS!" She helped Lizzy buckle her helmet strap. "MAKE SURE THE LETTER ONLY GOES TO KARL THE RED! ASK FOR HIM FROM STAGGER LEE! GOT IT?!"

Lizzy nodded, her face now obscured by the helmet. For a full three seconds, she was frozen with fear. Her blood ran cold, her knees went weak, and she considered tearing off the helmet and asking Stella if there couldn't be another way.

Then she forced herself to turn around, crouch down, and pull her way onto the harness. She banged on the metal plate twice with her fist, and then she waited in the dimness and the quiet for something to happen. Just for good measure, she made sure her taser was still securely strapped to her thigh.

Though, it probably needs a charge after this morning... She had a rush of dark emotions at the thought, but she forced herself to focus and wait for the driver.

Within a few minutes, she saw a pair of black books walk past her. There were some jostling movements as the driver got into the cab. A few minutes after that, the engine roared to life, and the tractor trailer started rolling over the gravel driveway. In a minute, they were accelerating on the paved, opened road.

Once the truck was fully engaged and speeding towards wherever, the ride wasn't so bad. There were occasional bumps, but the give of the canvas, combined with the cushioning and the helmet, eased the worst of it. Still, Lizzy was pretty sure that there were going to be some spectacular bruises on her back and hips before she was done with her journey.

Lizzy had always liked to travel. Even during her tour on the *Surveyor*, when all the crew really had to look forward to was cutting squares into the ocean, she couldn't help but be excited about getting underway. They always stopped at three or four ports during a patrol, which was fun, and there was always the fact that the sooner they got underway, the sooner they could return to home port. That she even would survive tonight was uncertain, but she was starting to adjust to and even get excited about the fact that, for the first time in years, her destiny was in her own hands.

After what seemed an eternity (and a very tricky relieving of her bladder) she saw the wheels slow down, and then the tractor trailer finally pulled over onto the side of the road. After a minute the engine stopped, and Lizzy saw those same black boots walk past her. She counted to ninety and then pushed her way out and down onto the ground. She unbuckled her strap and pulled the helmet off. Even with the plate and the canvas underneath her, she saw that her coveralls and boondockers got covered in dust. She popped open the lid of the tool chest, placed the helmet inside, and then closed the box with a quiet *snap.* Lizzy then pulled out her compass and oriented herself to a south-by-southwest direction. Finding a point on the horizon, she began to walk. She decided she would shake off the dust and sand when she lost sight of the truck.

The only thing she was uncertain of was how long it would take to go two miles. She knew that she could once run a mile in eight minutes, but she didn't want to run now. So, she just kept walking, stopping after the first ten minutes or so to shake the worst of the dust from her coveralls. Lizzy itched—the dust was also coating the inside of her coveralls, as well—but she figured she'd have to wait to clean up. She also was grateful that she learned basic orienteering as a camp counselor—it was not something an engineer would learn in the Coast Guard. After maybe thirty minutes of walking, she heard a noise to her left.

"STOP!"

Lizzy immediately froze and raised her hands to the back of her head, lacing her fingers. "I'm unarmed!"

She heard some rustling on her nine. She glanced over to see a man rising from a clump of brush, dressed in tan camouflage with sticks of brush in his helmet. In one hand, he was carrying a 9 mm. A dull metal asp was attached to his belt. He had a large, bristly mustache and wore dark sunglasses. Lizzy heard the soft *click* as he disengaged the safety on his pistol. He pointed it at her.

Fuck! I thought there was no military here! Lizzy considered her options, but there weren't too many with a pistol pointed at your head...

"What's yer name?" the man asked.

"My name is DC2/8 Elizabeth Townsend. I'm attached to Commune Ruth, District Tango."

The soldier came forward. "Where the fuck is that?"

"You know I can't tell you that! Identify yourself, soldier!" She looked at his collar. "Where are your collar devices?"

The man was right next to her now, the 9 mm's barrel pointed right above her ear. "I don't have collar devices! I ain't in the military!"

"OK...are you with Karl the Red?" Lizzy was confused and trying not to panic over the muzzle at her temple. She didn't see him cycle the round, though...

The man lowered his pistol a little. "Yeah—who are you again?"

Lizzy took a deep breath. "I am Lizzy Townsend. I've been sent by Do—Stagger Lee to find a guy named Karl the Red in Caradoc."

The man lowered his pistol but continued to stare at her.

"Where did you say you were from again?"

Lizzy now turned to face the man. It was hard to tell how old the man was, but he certainly wasn't younger than twenty or older than thirty. "I'm from a military attachment. Now, do you know Karl the Red or not? 'Cause I've had a hell of a day, and I'd really like to get where I'm going."

Lizzy saw him engage his safety with his thumb. "Sure, I know His Excellency Duke Karl the Red: he's my knight! Come with me, we'll straighten this out." He holstered his pistol. "You're not going to cause trouble, right, chicky?"

She didn't even pretend to understand why Karl was "His Excellency," a "knight," why she was being called "chicky," or even who was stupid enough to allow this guy to have a firearm. Lizzy noted the direction where he was pointing and started walking that way. "Nope. Just trying to get safe."

"Well, if your letter and story checks out, don't you worry about that. There's no safer village in the New Middle Kingdom than Caradoc."

The man continued to chat on, taking about His Excellency-this and tournament-that, until Lizzy felt like she was in one of those conversations with Mike, where he would be explaining his latest hypothesis on Infected-cell mutation, and Lizzy could only smile and nod because she was neither a surgeon, nor did she possess a Ph.D. in microbiology.

With a rush of sadness, she considered Mike and Jessica. They were two of her closest friends, and she'd never see them again. She tried to remember her last moments with Jessica, when her Officer in Charge, Erin Phillips, got Infected, and they all almost died:

Lizzy and Jessica were at the Headquarters pool party when Lizzy felt the demons approaching. Almost at the same time, Jessica rose and also looked towards the door, which confused Lizzy: Jessica couldn't sense the Infected. Then, Jessica had bent down by Lizzy's ear.

"I'm sorry," she had said. "But, I think it will be OK."

Before Lizzy could ask her what the hell she was talking about, Erin and the other girl attacked. When Lizzy was done destroying Erin the guards came, and Jessica vanished.

How *did* Jessica know what was coming? Did she know about Abigail's plan? Maybe they had discussed it at the lunch table that afternoon with all of their victims sitting around them, laughing and eating spaghetti...

No...that didn't make sense! Jessica would have said something. Lizzy was pretty sure of that.

So...how did she know?

It was then that Lizzy noticed that camo man had stopped talking. He was looking at Lizzy expectantly.

Lizzy tried Mike Response #18: "Sounds difficult."

The man suddenly beamed. "Yeah, it was! Imagine, trying to keep that flank from approaching the guard tower. No shit, there I was..."

Lizzy stopped listening as she noticed the sihouette of a wall coming over the horizon. As they got closer, the shadow gained color and contrast, and Lizzy could hear children playing.

She remembered her best friend Mary's children and the other children of her commune—she'd probably never see them again, either. She felt the tears welling in her eyes; Lizzy looked up and blinked to try to staunch their flow.

Everything she had, everything she had known, was gone. It was like before, when the Infected had taken over the world six years ago, and she had lost her family, her friends, and her husband, Brydan.

*God...*when was the last time she thought of him? Maybe it was when she woke up after being shot by Cynthia, the psychopathic Tracker that went apeshit and killed at least six females.

OK, Cynthia Olin I will not *miss.* At that sobering thought, she managed to gain control of her emotions and consider what awaited her in Caradoc.

Through the opened gate of the wall, Lizzy could see that Caradoc was built to stay. Commune Ruth was designed to transport easily and at a moment's notice. The buildings now in front of her would remain rooted to the earth long after the people occupying them had passed away. The homes she could see through the opened gate were built of a hodge-podge of materials: mostly sand, adobe, and maybe some metal here and there. The fifteen-foot wall surrounding the village was made of the same materials, but there was a lot more metal in the wall—old hulks of cars, steel I-beams, and rebar could clearly be seen through the mud. Watchstations were perched on top of the wall. A man in the closest station leaned over the wall.

"Who you got there, Tex?"

"I found her in the desert—wants to see Baron Duke Red. Says she has a letter."

"Can she write?"

"Now, how in the hell was I supposed to do that? Do I look like I carry around a pad and paper? Besides, she could have jumped me."

Lizzy stifled a giggle. *As if, asshole...*

"All right," the man on the wall called. "What's your name, honey?"

"Elizabeth Townsend."

"OK, Ms. Townsend, Tex here will take you to see Mistress Elspeth for your writing test, and then you can see the baron. It's just a formality—it's easy to see you're not Infected—but it's His Excellency's rules."

"OK," Lizzy called back.

She followed Tex through the gate and down the main street. It was a well-worn dirt path, wide enough for two cars to pass each other, though there were no usable cars in sight. There were plenty of horses, though, and Lizzy noticed two boys carrying buckets and shovels, scooping up any manure that littered the path. The air smelled horsey, and there were cooking smells, but the village was clean and tidy with no refuse to speak of.

"What do you do with your human waste?" Lizzy asked Tex.

"Compost," Tex replied. "Baron Marc would be a better guy to talk to about that, but it gets processed somehow, and we use it in some kinds of farming."

Lizzy nodded. That's what they did at Ruth, too, though it was stored in vats and taken away every month or so on flatbed trucks. She didn't know what the government did with their waste—Lizzy never thought to ask. They'd be getting a pick-up next week, though, she could...

She stopped that thought mid-stream. *Get a grip, Townsend...*

The houses were typically two stories tall, all desert tan in color with chunks of rust and various paint chips enbedded throughout. Their footprint tended to be on the small side— maybe 700 square feet or so. All the houses had chimneys, and most appeared to be in use. The sun was low on the horizon—the evening meals were being prepared. Lizzy then realized that she hadn't really had a meal all day; all she had eaten were those two bananas she took from the cafeteria before she made her escape from Headquarters.

The street was filled with the activities of children and a few women. The children, all dressed in brighty-colored shirts and poofy pants, were running, chasing, and throwing various balls at each other. Lizzy noticed that several pairs of the children's pants had denim patches stitched around knee level; she guessed that they were getting in some last-minute playtime before dinner. Lizzy considered that this was the first time in several years that she had seen any children over six—all of the commune children were six years old or younger. These children ranged from about two years old to maybe fourteen or so. They all looked a little on the thin side but relatively healthy. Some even had dogs with them, yipping and woofing as they ran.

None of the women were walking casually: some carried water buckets, some carried baskets, and some had babies strapped to their backs. One couple was almost running down the lane, a covered casserole pan in the woman's hands that she held with potholders. Some stopped to look at Lizzy, but most people didn't seem to take much interest in the dust-covered stranger.

Tex led her past the town square. In the center, there was a statue of a large-framed man dressed in some kind of medieval costume.

"Who's that?" Lizzy asked.

"That's Baron Duke Karl the Red," Tex replied. "It's actually is a pretty good likeness of him. One of the members of our household, Colin, found a large boulder about a month after we settled here and carved it. He died of the flu a couple of winters ago."

Lizzy paused. Of course these people didn't get annual flu shots like she and the other women and the children did. Then she realized that she wasn't likely to get another one anytime soon. In fact...

"How is the medical care around here?"

Tex looked at her. "Well, we really don't have much. The apothocares and chirurgeons have things, herbs and such. Haven't had much in the way of antibiotics or medicines since Infusion. We also don't have immunizations for the kids, so we have to be very careful when someone gets the mumps or the

16

measles or something. In fact, we had a bad whooping cough outbreak about two years ago—I can't say the p-word for that—and several people died, mostly babies and children."

Tex looked grim as he walked. "That time, Red got some vaccines and antibiotics somehow—sometimes that happens, I guess it's from y'all—but it wasn't in time for everyone." Tex stopped and looked at Lizzy. "Why *don't* you help us? Why is the government so stingy?"

Lizzy was caught unaware, and she was a little bewildered by the question. "I honestly don't know," she said. "Where I come from, we were told from the beginning not to ask where food or anything else came from—a demon might Infect you and locations would be compromised. Honestly, we often wondered what we would do if the trucks stopped coming, because we had no back-up plan."

She over looked at the gardens that covered the ground. "Actually, in some ways, you guys may have a better chance of surviving in the end, being as self-sufficient as you already are. We would be lost."

Tex nodded and walked on. They didn't speak again until they reached the end of the street, where a very large building sat.

"This is Baron Duke Red's house." He walked up to the door and knocked.

A small slip of a girl, not more than twenty years old, opened the door. She peered at Tex.

"Playing soldier again, Tex?"

Tex put his hand on her shoulder and gently pushed her back into the entryway. "I ain't gonna stand in the middle of the desert in garb, announcin' to the demons that it's dinnertime. Besides, it worked—sugar here didn't even see me coming." He gestured with his head towards Lizzy; his chest swelled with pride.

The girl gave Lizzy the once-over, who was still standing outside. She arched an eyebrow. "Be easy to do—you look dead on your feet, ma'am. Are you here to see Mistress Elspeth?"

Lizzy nodded.

"We need to get you cleaned up before you can come into the house. Tex, take her out back and sit her inside the barn—that bench right inside the door will do. I'll come out with some clean clothes and some water to wash with." The girl gave her an appraising gaze. "What are you, about a medium?"

17

Lizzy nodded again, suddenly too tired and too confused to say much.

"I'm Eloise. Tex is crude, but harmless." She grinned at him. "Thanks, Tex."

"OK," Tex replied, frowning. He backed out through the door and started down a stone path that led around the house. "You comin'?" He called back to Lizzy.

Lizzy silently commanded her feet to move, and she followed him. Sure enough, around the back of the large house was an even larger structure. She could hear a variety of animal noises coming from inside.

Tex pulled at the large barn door; a strong smell of manure and animal blew over them as the door slid aside. The inside of the barn was dim, but Lizzy could see various furry bodies shifting around. Tex walked into the gloom. Lizzy hesitated, but then followed him into the barn.

Once she was inside, Tex gestured to a rough bench that was off to the side. Sounds of muffled *mew*ing came from underneath it. Lizzy bent down and looked through the seat slats: she saw a shallow box that contained a white cat and four tiny kittens.

"Awww," she said involuntarily. She began making cooing sounds at the kittens. She hadn't seen a cat in more than six years, and she suddenly felt quite gushy. The kittens were so *cute*, nothing but little furballs of fluff...

Tex walked up behind her and looked down. "Man," he said. "Ghost Cat always got kittens. Well, always makes for good eatin'."

Lizzy straightened up and looked at him. He hadn't bothered to remove his sunglasses or his helmet, so she really couldn't read his face.

Tex grinned. "Just kiddin'."

Lizzy sank onto the bench. She focused her attention on a cow in a stall about ten feet away and did her best to ignore Tex. She considered the taser that was still attached to her thigh.

Tex leaned against the opposite side of the doorway, watching the house in silence. After several minutes, he straightened up and glanced at Lizzy.

"I'll see you back at the house, chickpea." He then took a step forward and disappeared from view. A moment later, Eloise stepped in from the sunlight. She peered at Lizzy over a large bundle of cloth sitting on top of the bucket she was carrying.

"I found some day garb that should fit you. It's a tunic and an overdress, so it should be very forgiving." She grabbed the bundle and placed it next to Lizzy on the bench. "I couldn't find any sandals or shoes, so I'm afraid you'll have to keep your boots for now. I did find some men's socks, so you can change those out.

"No one will be coming in here—I'll be right outside, and most people are getting ready to eat, anyway—so feel free to strip down. There are basic undergarments in there, too. I'll be right back with the water." She reached into the bucket and pulled out a bar of soap and a washcloth. She handed them to Lizzy, and then disappeared back into the daylight.

Lizzy unstrapped her tazer, took off her boots, and then proceeded to take off everything else. She really wasn't self-conscious about nudity—the showers at the commune were communal, and she always had a tentmate—and she figured if anyone was going to rape her, there had been plenty of opportunity before now.

About the time she was removing her bra, a female-looking arm reached through the doorway with a full bucket of water. The arm placed the bucket down onto the ground and then vanished.

Lizzy washed up the best she could, not worrying about getting the ground wet, though she tried to avoid getting water on the box of kittens. When she dried off with the provided towel, she looked at the offered "garb."

The underpants looked a little like men's boxer shorts, but they were a tighter fit. She noticed that there was a flap that served as a crotch piece, attached in the front by velcro strips. She figured that, in a pinch, a woman in a dress could squat, pull the flap around to the back, do her business, and then fasten the pants back up when she was done. Or, if she wore pants, she could just pull the pants down. She pulled them on; they fit well.

The bra was, miraculously, a modern-looking sports bra. She pulled it on—it was loose and a bit dingy, but it did the job. She stuffed her letter of introduction from Stella/Stagger Lee in between her breasts.

The woven cotton tunic was off-white and soft from many, many washings, with a bit of green embroidery on the collar. The overdress was a deep patterned green-on-green with a scooped neckline, no sleeves, and a good deal of wear and staining along the hem and under the arms. It was a bit ill-fitting around the shoulders and hips, but it was acceptable.

The socks, on the other hand, were new, and they were made of a thick, wonderfully soft grey wool. She pulled the socks onto her feet, and then put on her boondockers over them. Her boots were still cruddy as hell, even with a fresh-water wiping, but she figured a real cleaning would have to wait.

Once her boondockers were laced up, she stood and appraised herself. It felt weird to have a dress on—she never, ever wore dresses, even before she was in the military. But, this what was offered, so she figured she would deal. She stuffed her dirty clothes and her equipment in the bucket, picked it up, and then carried it out into the yard.

Eloise was sitting on a porch swing at the back of the house. As Lizzy approached, she saw that the swing was made of metal. Eloise stood.

"You look better! I brought out my comb, if you'd like to go through your hair." She threw Lizzy a black plastic "unbreakable" comb. Lizzy sat down the bucket in the middle of the yard just in time to catch the comb, and then started at the tangles in her hair.

"Thanks. Could you answer a question for me, please?" Lizzy asked as she pulled and teased.

"Sure."

"I don't understand all of the Middle Ages stuff: 'tunics,' 'barons,' the 'knight' reference..."

Eloise looked confused. "How can you not know about the SCA? We're everywhere."

Lizzy winced as she attacked a larger knot. "No...not where I'm from."

"Oh...OK." It was like Lizzy had just told her that gravity didn't apply where she came from. "SCA stands for the Society for Creative Anachronism. Oh, dear," Eloise said, staring into the distance, "this will take some explaining. The SCA is a re-enactment society, like civil war re-enactors, maybe. Did you ever see those?"

Lizzy frowned, thinking. "Like those people that crossed the Delaware River every Christmas, pretending to be Washington and his men, or Ren Faires?"

20

"Yes! Except we were a lot bigger, and our timeframe was from the fall of the Roman Empire to the end of the 16th century. Plus, there was more to do in the SCA, like heavy-weapons fighting, or you could join a guild, or just hang out. Some people were big on authenticity—some people still are—but most people just went to weekend events in medieval clothing and had fun. I grew up in the SCA, so I have a lot of experience with it."

Lizzy nodded. "How did you all get here?"

"I was with my parents when the Infection hit. We were members of Baron Red's household, so we went to his House on the Hill—his big ranch house. After a few days, we were told that we were going to make a run for it and go to Wyoming, where Baron Marc of the Resurrection was with his *kibbutz*. Some people chose not to go—I'm not sure what happened to them—but those of us who went with Baron Red got here fine.

"Baron Marc and his people already had everything set up to be self-sufficient and off the grid, like solar panels and such. We learned what we needed to know, took a lot of what we knew from studying medieval societies, and built our village. There were other SCA groups that came with us or ended up here, so we have a whole network now. We have travelling troubadour/minstrel shows and trade agreements set up with other villages. There's even a map of the New Known World that Baron Red keeps in his study.

"We got really lucky with Baron Marc—sanitation wasn't a strong point back in medieval times. A lot of people have died who wouldn't have before, because we don't have modern medicine out here, but we actually have it pretty good—better than a lot of folks. Where are you from?"

Lizzy was finished combing her hair. "Maybe a few hours from here? I'm not sure." She picked up the bucket and walked onto the porch. She handed the comb back to Eloise.

Eloise furrowed her brow. "Are you from militia country? They don't like to mingle with us too often. How did you get here?"

Lizzy began to tell her, but then Eloise raised her hand. "You know what? Never mind. You really should tell Mistress Elspeth and Baron Red first. I don't want to know before they do." She rose from the swing. "Well, shall we go in? Just leave the bucket out here for now." Eloise opened the screen door, holding it opened for Lizzy as they both stepped inside.

21

The first floor was one big common room that was quasi-partitioned into four sections by furniture. The "living room" corner was made up of a square of couches and sofas, a coffee table, and a fireplace. There was a dining area behind it and to Lizzy's left, with a huge rough-cut dining table and several chairs. The kitchen to Lizzy's right had an aluminum box with a thermometer on the front, a tiny refrigerator, and a lot of cabinets and countertop space. The far right corner contained a large structure made of wood. It looked like a loom, maybe, but it was *huge.*

"When we need to have large meetings, everything gets put into the barn and everyone brings a chair." Eloise explained as they both looked around. Then Lizzy sensed movement to her left, and she saw Tex rise from one of the couches in the living area. He still had his helmet and sunglasses on.

"I'll get Mistress Elspeth, Tex." She walked to the opposite end of the room and passed through a doorway. Lizzy heard her footfalls as she asended unseen stairs.

Tex and Lizzy stood and looked at each other. After a few awkward moments, Lizzy finally said, "My husband was from Texas. Which part are you from?"

Tex frowned. "Ohio."

That did it: Lizzy swore she could feel something snap in her brain as she began to laugh, and then she realized she couldn't stop laughing. She made loud, hysterical cackles that only stopped when she gasped for air. Lizzy managed to pull out a chair during all of this and sit down before she sank to the floor. Then, after a few minutes, the laughter turned to sobs, and she felt huge, fat tears wet her tunic sleeves as she rested her head in her arms and cried and cried and cried. Then, when she thought about Tex saying "Ohio," she laughed out loud again.

Sometime during all of this, she heard a higher-pitched voice ask something. She then heard Tex's baritone voice.

"Ummm...she said her name was Townsend, and that she was in the military." There was a pause.

"I didn't make her cry like this, Mistress Elspeth." Another pause. Lizzy raised her head and, through her tears, she saw a tiny woman glaring at Tex. Tex had removed his glasses and helmet and looked very uncomfortable. He actually was a handsome man when you could see his face, Lizzy noted, even with the ridiculous mustache. He looked back and forth between Lizzy and the woman.

"Ummm...I gotta go, Mistress, please excuse me." Tex finally said. He bowed to the woman, turned around, and then ran out the front door.

The woman then turned toward Lizzy. She was maybe in her mid-sixties, with long, white hair pulled back into a bun and icy-blue eyes. She wore a simple pink homespun dress, and she had the presence of someone who would not be trifled with. However, when she saw the tears on Lizzy's face, tears formed in her eyes, too. "Oh, you poor dear. What did Tex say?"

Lizzy sniffed and chuckled. She really didn't want to wipe her nose on the tunic sleeve: that seemed rude somehow. "He didn't say anything, except...except...that he was from Ohio!" Lizzy involuntarily erupted with laughter at the memory, and the laughing/crying cycle began all over again.

The woman—Lizzy supposed she was Mistress Elspeth—walked over and sat down next to Lizzy at the table. She patted Lizzy on the shoulder. "You've had a long day, haven't you?"

Lizzy could only nod; she couldn't even stop her hysterics to speak.

"I'm Elspeth. Tex said you were in the military. What branch?" Mistress Elspeth's voice was soft and low, like a kindly grandmother's voice.

Lizzy sniffled again. "Th-the Coast Guard."

Mistress Elspeth smiled. "Now, then, Karl was in the Navy for thirty years. I knew a lot of coasties when we were stationed in military housing together. Were you ever stationed in New London, Connecticut? We were there for four years at the sub base."

Somehow, talking about ancient history was having a calming effect on Lizzy. "No, but a shipmate of mine was stationed on the *Eagle*."

Mistress Elspeth nodded. "That was a beautiful ship. We would see it coming and going in the harbor from the Academy."

"I never saw it—the closest I was ever stationed was Patton in Rhode Island."

"Hmm...I never saw Patton. But, it's amazing what a small world we live in. I'm going to get something to eat, would you like something?" She stood.

23

"Yes, please."

Mistress Elspeth walked over to the kitchen area. She rummaged through cupboards until she found a large bowl and a sharp knife. "I have to go down into the larder. Do you prefer pork or beef roast?"

Lizzy's mouth watered. "Whatever you're having is fine, ma'am."

"Could you get some silverware and plates and such out, please? You'll find everything up there. Just for the two of us, though, Karl won't be joining us." Elspeth nodded towards the cupboards, and then disappeared through the doorway.

Lizzy found the items she needed well enough. By the time she had set the table, Elspeth returned with the bowl filled with chunks of meat, some bean paste, and green beans. She sat the bowl on the dining table. "I'll just get some bread."

Lizzy took about half of what was in the bowl. Then she waited for Elspeth to sit, though it was hard not to drool all over her plate. Finally, Elspeth came back. She sat and offered her hand to Lizzy. Lizzy took it, and Elspeth said a short prayer before Lizzy finally allowed herself to eat.

Everything was excellent: the bean paste tasted a bit like refried beans, and it went well with the hard, crusty bread Elspeth offered. The meat was cold but seasoned well; the beans were raw but were surprisingly good that way. There had been a pitcher of water on the table already, so Lizzy helped herself. She couldn't help but note how clean it looked and tasted; she wondered what kind of filtration system they had.

Another surprise was that Elspeth didn't ask Lizzy about her current situation, or how she got there. Rather, she reminised about the past, about being a military spouse and moving with her husband from billet to billet.

"Karl thinks I didn't like it, and it wasn't always nice, but there were some good things about it, too. I always managed to find a SCA group wherever we went, so that was a stable base in my life.

"Plus," she lowered her head and spoke in a half-whisper, "I love Karl, but sometimes he can get underfoot, especially when he gets bored. I can't tell you how happy I was when they elected him Baron of Vagabond Haven—keeps him busy." She winked and took a bite of green bean.

Dessert was a red-looking cobbler dish that Elspeth kept in that tiny refrigerator in the kitchen.

"It's cactus," Elspeth explained. "It's a recipe of mine. I added some fresh fruit in a syrup base. What do you think?"

It tasted strange, but it was OK. Lizzy was still a bit hungry, so she consumed her serving. "Thank you, ma'am."

Elspeth smiled. "You're welcome, dear. It's always nice to have guests. Would you please help me clear?"

Lizzy gathered the dishes and put them into the sink. She started to look around for water to wash them. Elspeth waved her off.

"One of my apprentices will get them. So, I think it's time we got more aquainted, don't you think? Let's sit down, and you can take your writing test and tell me how you got here." She lit the lamp on the table.

For the next two hours, Lizzy was the focus of their conversation. After she wrote out the chorus of *Semper Paratus*—Elspeth was tickled that she still remembered the lyrics from her boot camp days—Lizzy carefully answered Elspeth's questions about her life at the commune and the circumstances that led to her being at Caradoc. She explained about her abilities to sense demons, how she could make holy water, and how sick she got when she was around Infected material. Elspeth nodded at this.

"We have a few people here who can do that, too. John the Younger's son can tell from twenty feet, we figure. No one in the whole barony can make holy water that I know of. In fact, I believe you're the first one I've met."

When she got to the part of the story about tasing Abby and running for her life, she didn't tell Elspeth all of the details; she only said that once she realized that she was about to be forced to kill more people, she managed to escape.

Elspeth pulled her lips thin. "Oh, Lizzy, I wouldn't worry about freeing those poor souls from their torment. Anything must be better than being Infected, as I see it. But I'm not you, and I'm sure the Lord has his reasons for you being here."

Lizzy didn't answer her. She didn't know what to say, so she just nodded and finished describing the ride under the truck and being found by Tex.

Elspeth sat back in her chair, taking Lizzy's story in. "Sounds like quite the thing," she finally said. "I have to admit I have a lot of questions, but you are not the government's representative, so I shall not place those burdens on you.

"But, you do have burdens that are yours, and yours alone. What was your sin?"

Lizzy blinked. Elspeth seemed like such a well-adjusted person until she asked that question. Her guard went up. "What do you mean?"

"To get out of that place, you had to hurt someone. Not the Infected," Elspeth waved her hand dismissively, "they're no longer human. But, to escape, what was your sin?"

Lizzy remembered the smell of burning flesh. "Nothing that I didn't have to do to survive."

Elspeth looked disappointed in her answer. "All right, Lizzy, I won't push. But I want you to think about what I'm saying, that eventually you will have to confess and repent for what you did. Just don't wait too long, all right?" Elspeth smiled.

Lizzy nodded, not really sure what was going on.

Elspeth stood up. "Well, my dear, you must be tired after all that, and Karl will want to talk to you first thing tomorrow. We have plenty of rooms upstairs; you can stay there tonight. Tomorrow, he'll assign you somewhere."

Elspeth picked up the lamp and led Lizzy through the doorway at the opposite end of the room. There were stairs leading up and down, encased in their own space on the side of the house. Elspeth noticed the look of interest on Lizzy's face.

"Back during the mobs, we designed these buildings so that entrances to the upper floors were not within the interior of the dwellings. If a mob came through, the staircase could be quickly detached and destroyed. Thank the Lord that we never had to do it here, but we heard stories that it did save people's lives in other towns. We always keep rope ladders upstairs, just in case."

"Clever," Lizzy replied, impressed. She let Elspeth lead her up the stairs and onto the second floor. She noticed the opened steel door with its hinges on the inside as she went through the entryway and down the hall. Almost immediately, Elspeth opened a door on her right and stepped into a small room with a bed, a chest of drawers, and a washstand. A long nightgown was laid out on the bed, along with a new-looking toothbrush and a towel. The room was illuminated by a candle on the dresser. Elspeth set the lamp on the chest next to the candle.

"Oh, good," Elspeth said. "Eloise left these for you. Please make yourself at home. When you wake up tomorrow and are ready just come down. I'll make sure you get some breakfast before Karl sees you." She took Lizzy's hands in hers and looked into her eyes.

"The Lord bless you and keep you; the Lord make his face to shine upon you, and be gracious unto you; the Lord lift up his countenance upon you, and give you peace. Amen."

After Elspeth left with her lamp, Lizzy dragged her clothes off her body and put them in a drawer. She pulled the nightgown over her head, moved the toothbrush and towel onto the washstand, blew out the candle on the dresser, and then lunged for the bed.

When she woke up the next morning, Lizzy did not remember her head hitting the pillow. The sun was shining full bore into the room; it had to be after ten o' clock. Lizzy quickly washed up and dressed and headed down the stairs, carrying her letter in her hand. When she arrived in the common room, Elspeth was sitting at the loom-looking contraption, pushing a wooden card in-between threads and stepping on pedals on the floor. When she saw Lizzy come through the doorway, she stopped and smiled.

"Well, good morning!" Elspeth said. "Let's get you some breakfast, and then you can see Karl in his study."

After a quick breakfast of tea and bread with cactus jam and almond butter, Elspeth lead Lizzy up the stairs again and down to the other end of the hallway. The last door on the left was closed. Elspeth gently knocked in the door.

"Come in," called a voice from inside.

Elspeth opened the door, and Lizzy saw a room about one quarter the size of the common room below. Indeed, there was a very pretty wall map behind the huge desk in front of her labelled *The Known World*. File cabinets lined the left wall, and several drawers were opened with pieces of paper and file folders peeking out. The wall to Lizzy's right was entirely covered with a beautiful tapestry of a modern-looking ranch house sitting on a hill in the middle of farmland. There were two chairs in front of the desk.

The man writing at the desk looked very much like the statue in the village square, except the man now had a large, bristly mustache and mostly-white hair with some tinges of red. He wore an opened-collar shirt, a vest, and a Hard-Core-Military-Veteran

Presence. As it was supposed to, his demeanor made Lizzy squirm a little. She knew immediately to be courteous, careful, and to speak only when spoken to.

"Karl," Elspeth said, totally at ease. "This is Elizabeth Townsend, the guest we had last night."

Karl the Red looked up and smiled at his wife. The transformation from a grizzled retired senior chief to adoring husband was stunning. "Thank you, sweetheart."

Then he looked at Lizzy, and his smile faded. "Take a seat."

"Would you like something, Karl?" Elspeth asked as Lizzy sat down.

He smiled at Elspeth again. "No, thank you. I'll grab some cobbler after this interview."

Elspeth squeezed Lizzy's shoulder and left the room.

Lizzy expected the baron to immediately ask her questions; rather, he ignored her and went back to writing. Lizzy sat in silence, glancing around the room and waiting for her turn.

After a few minutes, Red signed whatever it was with a flourish. He set it aside, and then looked at Lizzy.

"Before we get started, we need to clear something up first." He reached into a desk drawer and pulled out something black. Lizzy realized that he was holding her taser. Lizzy felt herself pale.

Damn...

"You brought a taser into my village." He stared at her, waiting.

"Yes," Lizzy admitted, "but it probably isn't charged anymore."

Red leaned over and pushed the tazer into the a metal filing cabinet. It made a small *hum*, but that was it. Red leaned back and examined it.

"Was it used recently?"

Lizzy decided to be honest. "Yes...but nowhere near here."

Red continued to turn the taser in his hand. "Something to do with why you're here?"

Lizzy heart sank. "More like something I had to do to get here."

"Will they come looking for you?"

Lizzy considered that. "I don't know," she finally said. "But I did everything Stagger Lee told me to do to make sure no one followed me here."

Red nodded. He put the taser back in the drawer.

"All right. We'll deal with that if it comes up. Do you have your letter?"

Lizzy handed it to him.

Red opened the envelope and unfolded the letter. He glanced at the upper right-hand corner of the paper, and Lizzy saw that about a half-inch of the corner was ripped off. She hadn't even noticed Stella ripping it.

After a moment, Red spoke. He never took his eyes off the paper. "She tells me you're good at maintenance." After a pause, he looked up at Lizzy for her answer.

"Yes, I served as the Damage Controlman/Maintenance Mechanic at my commune for six years. I was a DC for three years before that."

Red grinned. "So, you were a turd chaser?"

"Yes." Lizzy frowned at the term.

Red chuckled and went back to reading. After a pause, he said, "That could be useful. Marc's always looking for help."

Lizzy kept silent.

After another couple of minutes, Red set the letter to the side and sighed.

"OK, Petty Officer Townsend, welcome to Caradoc. First, we need to asign to you a new name and identity." Red reached down and rummaged through a lower drawer. He pulled out a paper and began to write. "We'll say you're a relative of Elspeth's. It's well-known that she had a very large family, so no one will question it..."

"Excuse me...Your Excellency?" Lizzy interrupted. *Was that the right terminology?*

Red stopped writing and looked up. "Yes?"

Guess so... "I told Tex I was from a military instillation. Is that a problem?"

Red stared at her. "You told *Tex* you were from the military?"

Lizzy nodded.

Red paused for a beat, looking into space and shaking his head a little. "Great," he muttered, crossed out something on the paper, and then went back to writing.

Lizzy felt like an idiot, which was the point, but wasn't sure why that was so stupid. It wasn't her fault Tex was dressed as a military man, for Christ's sake...

After a few more minutes, Red finished writing. He read over what he had written, sighed again, and then focused on Lizzy.

"All right," Red began. "You can't stay here. Tex is a good kid, but he can't keep a secret in a bucket, so the village is going to know who you are and where you come from by lunchtime." Red paused, looking lost in thought. Finally, he hoisted himself out of his chair and went over to the file cabinets. He opened a middle drawer and began to thumb through file folders.

"William Plantagenet of the Star-Crossed Travelling Players owes me a favor, " Red said as he pulled out sheets of paper. "I'm going to send you to him requesting that he take you on as an indentured servant for two years."

Lizzy stared. "Like a slave?"

"Yeah, pretty much." Red sat back down and arranged his paperwork in front of him. He reached down and pulled out a fancy-looking pen set from behind the desk. Lizzy saw that the pen was well-worn with an old-fashioned nub. Red used it to write on paper that looked like thick parchment, periodically dipping the nub into a dark green ink bottle. He continued to speak as he wrote.

"Wills has been married for some time, so I wouldn't worry about him asking for sexual favors." Red looked at Lizzy. "He's a honorable man, and his partner Justin wouldn't like it." Red looked back down and wrote some more; Lizzy understood.

"I'm giving you a Writ for Safe Passage, so you can travel from place to place and not be questioned. Your village of origin will be Caradoc, Barony of Vagabond Haven, the New Middle Kingdom of the SCA. Once you get to Wills, though, you'll have to prove to him that you're worth something, or he may not keep you on; I can't force him to do that. Can you sing, play something, act?"

"I can sing, sort of. I play guitar and trumpet, though I haven't played the trumpet in a while."

Red nodded. "Do what you can to stay with the Players. Wills goes all over these days, and you might find yourself dumped in a really shitty area if you screw up too much. Your Writ won't go very far unless you're attached to a group.

"And, I don't want to see you again until your two years are up, unless you're here for an event. Got it?"

30

Lizzy nodded.

Red handed her the first paper he had written on. "This is your Writ. Don't ever, ever lose this." He bent his head and continued writing on the second paper.

She read:

To All Who See These Presents, Greetings:

~~*Let it be known that*~~ *So soon did our esteemed traveller arrive, but so soon did she have to leave. To speed her on her journey and with all good intentions I, His Excellency Baron Duke Karl von Worms, with full authority granted by Their Royal Majesties King Rufus and Queen Mary, do hearby give this Request for Safe Passage to Petunia Pendragon, citizen of the village of Caradoc, Barony of Vagabond Haven, the New Kingdom of the Middle, under the auspices of the Honorable Society for Creative Anachronism.*

Signed,

Duke Karl von Worms
Baron of Vagabond Haven

Lizzy looked up, mortified. "*Petunia Pendragon?!*"

Red shrugged, smirking beneath his mustache. "It was Eloise's favorite hamster. We'll call you Pet for short."

"Oh, no!" Eloise said later as she and Lizzy searched in the basement for suitable clothing. "My *hamster?* I am so sorry."

Lizzy sighed. "It's only a cover name for now, Elspeth told me. I can change it later when I get my Award of Arms, whatever that is."

"Your AoA. It's kind of a formal recognition that you are committed to being in the Society. You even get to submit a design for your coat of arms, like a shield design. Back before the Infection, folks would receive AoAs for being helpful, working in kitchens, doing scrolls, stuff like that. Now it means more: you have to demonstrate that you are a real member of the community, that you'll be staying a while. It helps to apprentice or join a guild.

"Or, get married." Eloise looked wistful. "A Spousal AoA doesn't carry as much weight, but that's the easiest way to get it."

That's what he *said,* Lizzy thought, smirking, but kept the joke to herself.

"Hey, sneakers!" Eloise exclaimed after opening a cardboard box. "What size are you?"

"Seven in female, five in male."

Eloise rummaged around and pulled out a pair of brand-new sneakers. "Size seven and a half—now you don't have to wear those black work boots." She placed the sneakers on the floor as she turned to her left to open a plastic bin. "It's mostly tunics and shirts in here. I think for travelling, pants and shirts are best. We can find you dresses for when you get wherever they're sending you." Red told Lizzy not to tell anyone where she was going, not even Elspeth.

Lizzy grimaced. "Would it be a big deal if I always wore pants? Aren't there women who do?"

Eloise smiled. "Yes, though you may feel out of place after a while, especially during official events. You should pack a couple, just in case."

Lizzy nodded. She placed a box onto the floor and opened the flaps.

At first, all she saw was sparkle. Then she saw that the glittering came from fine glass beadwork on off-white, finely woven silk material. She pulled it out. It was very poofy, and it glistened in the lamplight.

"Wow!" Eloise said. "I've never seen that before. It's not Elspeth's—it's too big. It might fit you. Why don't you try it on?"

Lizzy shrugged, and then stripped out of her overdress and shirt. She loosened the ties in the back of the dress and then climbed into it from the bottom. Eloise walked around and tightened the strings that ran up the dress. She turned Lizzy around to face her.

"It needs hemming, but it looks really good on you!" She pointed over to a corner. "Take a look!"

Lizzy picked up the skirt of the dress and walked over where Eloise pointed; there was a full-length mirror leaning against the wall. She saw that the dress did look good on her. It had long sleeves that were sort of poofy at the shoulders and then tapered down to the wrists. It actually was made of two pieces: there was a main dress of a dark blue fabric, and then the glittery cream overdress was an attached overtop. It didn't look like the Halloween princess costumes that she remembered, but it made her feel like royalty. She turned to Eloise.

"Is there some equivalent of makeup here?" Lizzy asked.

"Sure," Eloise replied. "We have pigments and such. Why?"

"Would you help me out of this, please?" Lizzy felt the strings loosen at her back. "My daddy always said to never miss an opportunity to make a good first impression. I might as well look my best when I get where I'm going."

And, Lizzy thought to herself, as she descended out of the gown, *I do have an audition...*

When Lizzy finally emerged from the baron's house, she was dressed in a tunic and breeches and loaded down with two sea bags, a knapsack full of travel food, three canteens of water, and a belt around her waist with an eating dagger, three small pouches, and her multi-tool. She also wore Elspeth's favor threaded through her belt: a green scrap of fabric embroidered with the images of a sewing needle and a horse reared up, both within a shield shape.

"The horse is *rampant,*" Elspeth had explained to Lizzy when she given it to her. "And," she said, pointing to a particular spot on the shield, "*pizzled.*" Lizzy looked where she was pointing.

"Oh," was all she could think to say.

Now Elspeth gave her a hug at the doorway. "God speed you and keep you safe."

Despite Lizzy's doubts about the existence of a loving, actively-working higher power, she was touched. "Thank you, Mistress Elspeth."

She walked with her gear towards the barn. Ahead, Lizzy could see His Excellency, two men, and a boy about eleven years old or so. They were all standing next to horses.

Lizzy grew anxious. *No one mentioned anything about horses...*

"Ready to go, Pet?" the baron asked.

"Yes, Your Excellency." Lizzy came up to Red and gave a slight bow. "Though, I probably should warn you that I've only ridden a horse once, and I nearly fell off."

Red smirked. "That's OK; you'll have plenty of time to learn on the way." He gestured to the rest of the assembled.

"These gentlemen will be escorting you to Wills' camp. May I present Master Cuthbert of Lewes, Sir John the Younger, and his son, John the Youngest or Little John. Gentlemen, this is Pet."

The two men and the little boy bowed. Lizzy tried her best curtsey, but it was clumsy.

"While you're travelling, Pet, these men will teach you basic heavy-weapons fighting, some heraldry, and SCA history. It is my expectation and command that you do everything they tell you to do." He patted Lizzy's shoulder, and then addressed the men.

"I'll see you when you get back. I'll make sure your homes and lands are tended to. Good luck."

"Thanks, Red, but we'll be fine." Cuthbert said. They all bowed as Red walked back towards the house.

John the Younger looked at Lizzy and gave her a nod. "Well, let's get your gear on Blue here and get going. The rumors are already spreading that you're military, and we want to get you out of here before people start getting ideas."

Lizzy watched Cuthbert and John strap her gear to Blue's saddle. By the time they were done, there was barely enough room for her.

"Will the horse carry all of that and me?" Lizzy asked.

"She's stronger than she looks." John replied. "Do you need a hand getting up into the saddle?"

Lizzy shook her head. She placed her left boot into the stirrup, grabbed the saddle horn, and then managed to swing herself up in one motion. She was very proud of herself.

"Blue is the mare we use to teach beginning riders," the knight explained. "She's very forgiving. Once you get more confidence, we'll let you ride one of the other horses.

"All set?" he asked his companions, who were already saddled. "Let's go."

Lizzy grabbed the reins and gave the horse's flanks a gentle tap with her heels. The horse started forward, and then took a spot in the center of the group.

Little John rode beside her on her right. "Are you really from the military?"

"Yep," she replied. "I was in the Coast Guard."

Little John leaned in a little. "What's your real name?"

Lizzy smiled. In spite of the uncertainty of her future yet again, she was getting that excited-to-be-underway feeling once more. "Ask me again in two years. I'll tell you then."

Chapter Two

The first few hours were spent in awkward silence, save for the quiet clomping of the horses and the sounds of nature around them. John and Cuthbert were constantly glancing around, scanning the horizon. Little John was, too, but still managed to maintain his exuberance.

Lizzy, on the other hand, figured that she was getting saddle sore. Her lower back ached, and she felt pain in places that had never complained before in her life. She wished she could start a conversation to distract her from the discomfort, but Lizzy figured everyone was making sure they got out of Caradoc without stragglers or...

Robbers? Do they have those out here? Lizzy started to glance around herself. All she saw was flat land with some mountains in the far distance. When the sun was a hand-width from the horizon, John raised his hand. The horses stopped. He turned around to look at Lizzy.

"There's an established campsite about a mile from here, Pet. We'll stop there for the night. Once we're there, we'll figure out who's doing what, split up the chores, that kind of thing."

Lizzy nodded in response. A few minutes later, they arrived at a well-tramped patch of ground with a fire pit, a standing charcoal grill, and a few logs scattered on the ground for seating. Lizzy pulled on the reins to stop Blue. The horse stopped; the other horses walked right past her.

"Hey," Lizzy called. "Isn't this it?" Blue started walking again on her own, coming up behind Wind Walker, Cuthbert's horse.

"Nope," Cuthbert called back. "Too obvious. There's another one up here, behind these rocks. More secure."

Sure enough, a much rougher site was found five minutes later. The smell of stale urine hit Lizzy's nostrils—because it was behind rocks away from the road, it must have been where people camping at the nice site went to do their business. She looked at John.

John shrugged. "Once we start cooking, you won't notice the smell." He dismounted and walked towards a clump of weeds in the distance. Cuthbert and Little John also dismounted and followed without comment. Lizzy half-dismounted, half-fell from her saddle and sat with a hard *thump* onto the ground as her legs refused to work. She felt a small mound under her right butt cheek give way under her weight, followed by a *squish* sensation as the mound flattened out beneath her.

Oh, fuck me...

Lizzy sat in the increasingly smelly mound for a minute, massaging her legs. By the time John had returned, Lizzy had managed to stagger to her feet.

"Found a shithole," Lizzy said.

John wrinkled his nose and gave her the slightest of smirks. "Yup, you sure did." He walked to his mount and started untying bags. "Did Mistress Elspeth give you a funnel?"

Lizzy forced her legs to carry her to Blue. She worked her hand into the top of a sea bag and pulled out a green, shallow plastic cup with a long spout. She showed it to him.

He nodded. "Johnny and Cuthbert should be back in a minute. We'll usually dig a latrine, but this site is so nasty I don't think anything we do could make it worse. Do dig a hole if you take a shit, though—at least seven, eight inches; the funnel doubles as a trowel. You might want to take a change of pants, too—you're stained."

Lizzy felt her cheeks grow hot, not because she was covered in shit—she was used to that as a former damage controlman and the commune's engineer—but because John had looked at her ass.

Then again, Petty Officer Townsend, a big brown shit stain on buff-colored pants is hard to miss; calm the fuck down. Without looking at John again, she took a couple of minutes to pull another set of breeches from a sea bag before she walked away in the opposite direction to find a place to relieve herself.

Lizzy hadn't had many interactions with men in the past six years, except Jessica's husband Mike and some passing acquaintances at the lab. Not that there weren't available men at the lab—Bea was *constantly* trying to hook her up—but she never thought it was a good idea. She liked the freedom of being the maintenance officer at the laboratory a lot more than the idea of a prohibited fraternal relationship.

37

Now that she was out and about, however, she was becoming uncomfortably aware of the fact that she hadn't gotten laid in a long, long time, and she wasn't sure what she wanted to do about that. She was fairly sure, though, that it would be prudent to explore these feelings when she was settled down somewhere and safe, rather than on the run.

By the time she returned, the party had unloaded the kitchen bag and was busy making a quick meal of salted chicken and biscuits that Cuthbert had packed. He smiled at Lizzy as she approached.

"My wife Jane packed our first meal," Cuthbert explained. "We also have charcoal for the first couple fires, but starting tomorrow we'll have to start gathering wood along the way, and we have dried provisions and tea for meals for the next few days. Can you cook?"

Lizzy pondered this as she took a plate from Cuthbert and helped herself to two biscuits and a chicken leg. "I really don't know how to cook over an open fire. Could I offer to wash the dishes or something? Dig latrines?"

Cuthbert grinned and looked over at John. "See? I told you she wasn't dainty and useless."

John didn't answer. Little John grinned at Lizzy, his mouth full of biscuit.

The next morning, Lizzy woke up to pain. Her legs hurt. Her back hurt. Her stomach muscles hurt. *Everything* hurt. She groaned. John walked up and stood over her as she lay in her sleeping bag.

"The best thing to do is to get yourself up and walk around. Once you're up and moving, you'll feel better."

Lizzy grunted and rolled herself onto her stomach; her entire body burned in protest. John walked away and gave a pot a stir that sat over the fire ring. Lizzy commanded her limbs to stand her upright, and they eventually complied. Her forearms even complained when she unbuttoned her breeches to use her funnel. At no other time in her life—not in boot camp, not on the ship, not ever—did she feel like such an out-of-shape pussy. She staggered back to the camp, wrapped the funnel back in its rag, and then sagged onto the ground for breakfast.

John was right, though—by the time they were packed and back on the trail, Lizzy did feel better. She also noticed that John and Cuthbert didn't seem so twitchy anymore—they were chatting amongst themselves about people in the village and had a particularly long conversation about Marc's newest idea about an irrigation system that would be better than Isabella's, whoever that was.

She also noticed for the first time that they carried thick, wooden sticks with small cages on the end made of welded, mild-steel round stock. She figured they were play swords for clubbing, but she wondered what else they were for. Why did they need "hilts," if they were just for hitting people?

They rode until a little past high noon. While they ate a meal of pickles, bread, bean spread, and cheese, Cuthbert began to teach her about the SCA.

"The Society for Creative Anachronism began in 1966 as a large outdoor costume party. By the time of Infusion, it was estimated that there were over 60,000 active participants all over the world in almost twenty kingdoms. Kingdoms were mostly divided into baronies, and each barony had a group of officers. Within the Society, there were members—we call them citizens now—and peers. There are three Orders of the peerage: the Order of Chivalry, the Order of the Pelican, and the Order of the Laurel. Both John and I are members of the Order of Chivalry, which means we are experts in armored combat—sword fighting—and have been dubbed at some point by a king, swearing an oath to defend the Known World. Pelicans have been honored for their service and work in the SCA, and Laurels have achieved a master's level in an art or science.

"When the demons came, we quickly figured out that extreme pain exorcised the demons—the government did, too, yes?"

"Sure," Lizzy replied. *And holy water...*

"A well-aimed, quick hit to the knee of an Infected person with a SCA rattan sword or its equivalent can usually cause enough pain to blow a kneecap and force a demon out. Or, at the very least, puts the guy down so you can hit him again, maybe in the groin or something, so you can get away. There are a lot of people out there with messed-up knees, but it's better than the alternative.

"So, that's why today everyone is trained at least in sword and shield from the time they are fourteen years old. If they want to also learn Florentine or pole-arm, that's their prerogative, but all

SCAdians are trained in the basic skills to fend off a demon attack. Are you with me so far?"

Lizzy nodded.

Cuthbert continued, "During Infusion, those SCAdian members who could gathered themselves together and made their way to isolated locations. Sometimes the demons possessed people and we lost a village, but for the most part those who managed to settle here—at least in the New Kingdoms—survived. We already had a hierarchy established with the peers, so there wasn't the jockeying for power that happened with some of the other local towns. We also already knew on how to rough it. The militias also have done well for the same reasons, though I wouldn't want to be in those towns." Cuthbert looked at John, and John shook his head in agreement.

"The militias really treat their people rough," John explained. "They're patriarchal, hard-core military societies, and they don't travel often outside their circles. We keep thinking they'll attack someday to take our supplies, but they never do."

Cuthbert looked at Lizzy, a gleam of mischief in his eyes. "What about where *you* come from? Was it male-dominated, too?"

John began, "Cuthbert, I don't think..."

"It's just us, John," Cuthbert cut him off. "Who cares? I'm not going to say anything; no one else here will say anything, right?" He looked at Little John and Lizzy. They both shook their heads.

John glared at Little John, and then at Cuthbert. "Fine." He looked at Lizzy. "Might as well tell us, then. What was it like on the government side?"

Lizzy paused. "Aren't you guys afraid that the demons could—you know—read your mind if you got possessed, find out everything you know? We made it a point not to know too much because of that."

The rest of the party stared at her, bewildered.

"Find out about what?" Cuthbert finally asked.

"Locations, people, that kind of thing? Mostly locations."

Cuthbert seemed to mull over what she said for a moment, and then he shook his head. "No, we don't work like that. We take our chances, I guess. We couldn't function otherwise. Christ, how would we trade? Travel?" He paused. "Wow, that's a really fucked-up operation."

"Language, Cuthbert," John said.

Cuthbert rolled his eyes. "Sorry," he told Little John. Little John waved him off.

"I think maybe," Lizzy said, considering her logic as she spoke, "that it was really to control us. I mean, we didn't know about any of this, any of you. If we knew..." Her heart skipped a beat at the thought. "I'm not sure if people would leave exactly, but that there would be choices..."

She decided to stop that train of thought for the moment—it was uncharted, and not something she wanted to explore with strangers. She returned to the original question. "Actually, I was in an all-female commune with kids. Lots of kids."

"Really?" asked Little John. "My age?"

"No," Lizzy replied, smiling. "The oldest is my godson, Brydan—he's almost six. We had almost two hundred kids at last count, all healthy, and all five years old and under."

"What were the infant mortality rates there?" John asked. Lizzy noticed that Cuthbert frowned slightly at the question.

"Maybe every six months or so, we'd have a problem with a delivery. The infant would go to Headquarters, and then it was maybe a fifty-fifty chance that the baby returned. It was horrible, not knowing what was going to happen. Anna, our chaplain, had her hands full with the mothers during those times."

"So, maybe two deaths a year?" John asked.

Lizzy nodded. "More at the beginning, but once the equipment came in we were able to handle almost anything. We've never lost a mother, though. Master Chief is really good at emergency C-sections."

John didn't answer. He rose and walked behind Lizzy. His footsteps got softer and then gradually faded away. No one said anything.

"What?" Lizzy finally asked Cuthbert and Little John.

Little John answered. "Momma died in childbirth almost six years ago, trying to have my little sister. Neither of them made it: the baby was too big, and then they tried a C-section, but Momma got sick afterwards and died. My sister wasn't alive when they pulled her out. That's all Dad's told me."

Lizzy felt ill. "I'm sorry, Little John." She looked at Cuthbert. "I really stuck my foot in it, didn't I? I didn't mean to."

"Don't worry about it, Pet." Cuthbert replied after taking a pull of water from his canteen. "You didn't know the situation—he asked and you told him. He loved Regina a lot, and though Red's been on him to remarry for years, he's not interested." Cuthbert looked at Little John and smiled. "It's just been John and Little John, with the rest of Caradoc helping."

"Yeah," Little John replied, wrinkling his nose. "It's like having a whole village of mothers and fathers, always telling you what to do."

John walked back into the gathering; his eyes were red and bloodshot. "Are we ready to go?" he asked no one in particular.

He turned to Lizzy. "We should start going over heraldry this afternoon. When we stop for the night, I'll start showing you basic sword work." Then John turned away before Lizzy could say anything and began to check the straps on his mount.

That evening, after dinner, John unstrapped two wooden swords from his pack. He handed one to Lizzy. She examined the welds on the hilt.

"How do you weld?" she asked. "These welds are good."

"Most of the gear was made before Infusion. When a weld breaks, sometimes you can still find someone with cold weld, or there are a few towns with a portable generator that they run once or twice a year specifically to run welders to repair gear for a fee."

Lizzy nodded. She held the sword in her left hand and looked at John.

"You're left-handed?" John asked.

"Yes. Is that a problem?"

He sighed. "No, it just makes things more difficult for me as your instructor. But, I've trained a lot of lefties." He reached into a pouch and pulled out a gold chain. He placed it around his neck.

"You are now in training to be a heavy-weapons fighter in the SCA, to defend yourself and your people from the Infected and all other enemies of the realm. When you received your Writ for Safe Passage from Baron Duke Karl the Red, you accepted all of our traditions and laws. You have no title, so you are beholden to all lords, ladies, and peers of all kingdoms. From now on, you will address me as Sir John and Cuthbert as Master Cuthbert. Even when you eventually receive your AoA, you will still address us as such until a time that you may become a peer." He held up the chain around his neck and showed it to Lizzy.

"All knights wear a gold chain at events and tournaments; sometimes they also might wear gold spurs. There are other defining accoutrements to identify different peers, much like the devices and striped sleeves in the military—we'll go over them all in the next few days. For now, just know that this is a symbol of authority. Do you understand?"

She nodded. Hell, establishing rank was speaking Petty Officer Townsend's language, though she hoped that didn't mean that he could be a dick to her. Somehow, though, John didn't seem that type. He didn't like her around—that was clear—but he was going to do his duty and train her as Red asked him to. Lizzy could not respect him because he wore a chain, but she could respect him for that.

"Yes, Sir John," Lizzy replied.

"So, the king is the absolute authority in a kingdom?" Lizzy asked later as they sat in the night, their campfire blazing, after a review of the different peerages in the SCA.

"Yes and no," Cuthbert replied, slowly. "He can still make laws arbitrarily—that's still a throwback to pre-Infusion days—but recent kings have been politically restricted for the most part to do so anymore—it can be dangerous and it upsets the barons. Our king is still required to defend the land, though."

Lizzy leaned back, thoughtfully chewing on a sweet pretzel that Elspeth had packed for her. "How often does he have to defend it?" she asked.

"In the beginning, quite often," Cuthbert replied. "There were the demon mobs, of course, but also a lot of skirmishes, fights over borders and food, that sort of thing. In the last three years...eh, not at all, really. These days he appears at local tournaments, greets other members of royalty if they come into the realm, that sort of thing. Things have settled down."

"So...he's a figurehead?"

"For the most part; almost all the power is maintained by the barons." Cuthbert leaned forward. "That's something to remember as you're travelling around. Red's a pretty good baron, but there are some villages and settlements that are ruled by iron fists, even within the SCA. Despotism, if you're familiar with the term."

Lizzy nodded. "So...is Wills Plantagenet a baron?"

"No," John replied, smiling at the thought. "He is a double peer, a Laurel and a Pelican, though the way he carries himself you'd think he was a king."

Cuthbert and Little John nodded in agreement.

"What can you tell me about him?" Lizzy asked.

John leaned back against his log and looked up into the sky; it was a clear, black night, and the sky was full of stars. "I didn't know him before Infusion...did you?" He sat up a little and looked at Cuthbert.

"Sort of," Cuthbert replied. "I had taken a few of his workshops at Pennsic, but I never really talked to him until that incident that time."

John sat in silence for a few moments. "Oh, yeah," he finally said, nodding.

"Incident?" Lizzy asked.

"It was an incident involving a member of his troupe," Cuthbert said. "That's all I can say about it. It was decided that it could be handled quietly, and I negotiated the terms. I'm Red's herald," he added when Lizzy looked confused. "I'm one of his representatives. I announce for him in court, that kind of thing, so I was designated to handle it."

"Oh," Lizzy said, still confused, but not caring enough to ask for clarification. "So, what about Master Wills?" Lizzy remembered to add the "Master" this time.

"Wills was a well-known thespian even before Infusion," Cuthbert began. "Every year, he ran a production at Pennsic— that was a big war in Pennsylvania, I'll tell you about that later— and he did a lot of community theater in his home town. I forget where, but somewhere in New York State.

"After Infusion, he packed up his theater people and came west. I heard a rumor once that he walked into the abandoned Library of Congress and made off with a lot of their archived stuff, but there's a lot of stories about Wills that seems kinda bullshit." He stopped himself suddenly and glanced over at Little John; the boy was asleep in his sleeping bag. Cuthbert sighed and continued.

"At first, it was a struggle for him—everyone was just trying to survive at first, figure out how we were going to live, that kind of thing—but then he met Jonah Goldberg."

"Who's that?" Lizzy asked.

"A dentist, and a very smart one at that—he had vintage tools and contraptions that he had collected as a hobby before Infusion, and he wanted to start a mobile practice. Wills was already starting to travel around, so they came to an arrangement: Dr. Goldberg would travel with the group and give Wills most of the proceeds of his practice in exchange for Wills' protection, food, and the occasional bit part in a production. That was, what, four years ago?"

John nodded.

"So they meander around the kingdom, Dr. Goldberg sets up shop wherever Star-Crossed stops, and everyone wins. He's a pretty good dentist, too—I had to have a tooth filled last year, and it barely hurt. I was just happy he didn't have to pull it."

"What does he use to numb the tooth?" Lizzy stomach clenched a little as she realized that, along with everything else, she had also lost her access to modern dentistry when she had decided to run.

God, this is such *a sucky deal...*

"I honestly don't know," Cuthbert admitted. "All I know is that it smelled strong, tasted awful, but did the job.

"So Wills has charters with all the kingdoms..."

"And some places we probably don't know about," John interrupted.

"True, and has built the Star-Crossed Travelling Players into one of the best troupes out there. He manages to get more and more elaborate every year."

"I think he wants to expand more into non-SCAdian areas," John speculated. "I heard he's already played at Murphy's Place up north and New Covington by Bristol."

"Well, and why wouldn't he? Now that things have stabilized, for better or for worse, the people that are left want to have a little fun—even the militias, I'm sure."

John snorted. "If anyone of his persuasion could go into militia country and live to tell the tale, it's Wills. He could charm the devil himself."

"Yeah—you can't push your luck with him, though. He'll help people, sure, but only as much as he thinks you are worth."

"True...in the end, Wills is all about Wills," John agreed.

Lizzy said nothing, just chewed on her rye stick.

"But, you'll figure him out," Cuthbert assured her as he stretched himself out, the firelight illuminating his face in an unearthly glow.

Alpha Laboratory
District Tango
Location Classified
06 JUN
1520

<u>Stella</u>

If anyone had discovered *anything* about the disappearance of Petty Officer Townsend, she figured, they would not have sent Jessica Donovan to ask her questions. Most likely, they would have just hauled Stella off to never be heard from again.

Stella observed that Jessica still seemed a little off her game, but considering that she witnessed the now-famous Swimming Pool Exorcism Event first-hand, that was understandable. The psychiatrist managed to carry herself with the utmost professionalism as she asked her questions.

"So, you did speak to Petty Officer Townsend that day?" she asked Stella.

"Yes—Townsend told me that soldiers were after her and asked for my help. I explained to her that I was in no position to hide her, she left, and I haven't seen her since."

Mark Twain once said that, "If you tell the truth, you don't have to remember anything." So, while she couldn't always tell the *entire* truth, suggesting a close-enough facsimile had served Stella well over the years. That she wasn't in a position to hide her was entirely true.

Red was, in point of fact, but Jessica didn't need to know that.

"Do you know where she went?"

"No." Also true—she could have gotten off the truck early and went to Montana, for all Stella knew.

"Do you have any other information about Petty Officer Townsend that could be helpful, or any other information about her disappearance?"

Jessica was such a soft sell. She had been sent to question Stella and her people a couple of times before when her operations had gotten periously close to being exposed, but she never seemed to ask the right questions. Perhaps the psychatrist just didn't want to know.

"No," Stella replied. "Has anyone else said anything?"

Jessica shook her head. "The van is gone, and its tracking device was disabled. She could be anywhere by now." She stood up.

"She was your friend, wasn't she?" Stella asked.

"Yes, she was." Jessica paused and closed her eyes for a moment, then looked at Stella. "Mike and I had her over for dinner all the time; he isn't handling this well."

Stella frowned. "How can you tell?"

"I can tell," Jessica said with a dry chuckle. "He'll never admit to it, but he's worried about her, and he misses her. So do I.

"Thank you for your time, Stella." She began to walk out of Stella's office, but then stopped herself. She turned around and took a breath.

"There's going to come a time when you'll want Mike's help for something unusual." She looked a little nervous, and she swallowed before continuing. "All I want to tell you is that he'll be the right choice, and so will Bea."

Stella stopped breathing for a moment. Could Jessica know about their operations? *That* would be discomforting. "OK—could you be more specific?"

"No," Jessica said over her shoulder as she left the room, "just wanted you to know."

Lizzy

By the fifth day of the journey, Lizzy was tired of hitting trees, what John called "pell work."

"When do I get to hit animate objects?" Lizzy asked as she snapped her arm to hit the tree with what she hoped was a "leg shot": *Whoosh-THRACK! Whoosh-THRACK!*

"When you stop using so much of your wrist and more of your shoulder and hip," John said dryly. "Wills' company will train you further, but for right now you need to perfect the basic snaps and moves. Besides, someone might get hurt if we try slow work now, and we can't afford that."

"I'm getting pretty sore now," Lizzy said, massaging her shoulder. "Between my arm and my ass, I feel like a walking bruise."

"Well, take a break," John replied, pointing to a rotten log across from where he was sitting. "We'll work on heraldry while we rest."

Lizzy sank down on the ground, propping her back against the log. "Shoot."

"Hey, Johnny," the knight called to his son. "Come on over and help me quiz Pet, please? We've got plenty of food and water now, thank you."

Little John unslung the water bag he was filling from the well they had found and ran into the clearing. "OK!"

John turned to Lizzy. "Barony of Vagabond Haven."

Lizzy had to think about it. So many patterns and colors and devices and stories had been poured into her brain over the past few days. "White and green checkered background, three yellow griffins triangulated, rampant and pizzled." She was glad Elspeth taught her the word *pizzled* so she wouldn't have to say "erect penis" in front of Little John all the time. A lot of animals in coats of arms were pizzled.

John nodded and turned to his son. "Johnny?"

"Checkey argent and vert, three griffins rampant and pizzled or, two over one."

"Good!" John had told Lizzy that she would have to learn the heraldic way of saying what was on a device eventually, but for now it was enough to recognize the area's baronial devices. John turned back to Lizzy. "Baron?"

"His Excellency Duke Karl von Worms, also known as Karl the Red."

"Disputes?"

"None at the moment." Before Infusion, John had told her, some SCAdian peers were stubborn and quarrelsome, taking their hobby too seriously and flaming each other on list-servs and social networking sites. Those same people, after pushing their way into governing roles after Infusion, continued to squabble over rank and power and food. Sometimes arguments would even escalate into bloody skirmishes, and a Court of Chivalry would have to be called and the matter mediated. However, no one had ever died during these disputes—or, not yet.

"Next, the Barony of the Brandywine."

"Vagabond Haven's neighbor to the west. Blue on top, black on the bottom, with that..." Lizzy drew blocks in the air with her finger.

"Embattled."

"Right—with a keyhole in the center, blue and black counterchanged."

"Johnny?"

"Per fess embattled, azure and sable, a Keyhole counterchanged."

John smiled. "Pet, the baron?"

"Her Excellency Isabella de Castilla."

"Disputes?"

Lizzy frowned and leaned back; sure as shit there were. "OK...there's a wandering nomadic tribe known as El Hajj. About three years ago, there was this whole big thing that a nephew of the leader of the tribe raped the niece of the baroness."

"Oh, for Christ's sake." Cuthbert snorted at that and spit into the cooking fire, adjusting mid-spew to avoid the stew that was simmering. "No one believes that!" He looked at John. "Did you really tell her that?"

John set his mouth into a line. "That's the official story." He looked at Lizzy. "If anyone asks you about it, that's what you say happened."

"What a crock of shit," Cuthbert muttered, picking up a metal cooking spoon. "Sorry," he added, looking at Little John. Little John shrugged.

John sighed. "Then, by all means, tell her what you've heard. I was just trying to make things simple."

"You were trying to be a company man, John—and that's OK, you and Red go way back and he's your knight. She's going to be SCAdian, though, and she should know all of it. Especially when people find out what her home village is and ask her questions, don't you think?"

John's face darkened, but he didn't respond. He merely shrugged, stood up, and walked away towards the freshly-dug latrine.

Cuthbert kept stirring the stew as he talked. "It's fairly well known that Christina, the niece and ward of Isabella, and Zaki, Rohan's kid and the nephew of Maalik, had a serious thing going. They found each other around festivals, they were seen together— it was obvious they were dating each other exclusively. Isabella didn't like this—she's never understood why El Hajj chose the lifestyle they did, travelling without a homeland, and sees them as inferior. It also doesn't help that their leader, Maalik, is untitled."

"But," Lizzy interrupted, "if he's the leader of a tribe, he's like a baron. No one's technically 'titled,' anyway. All these titles are made up, right?"

Little John's eyes widened; Cuthbert *tsked.* "Don't let anyone hear you say that out loud, Pet. The SCAdians have chosen a quasi-democratic form of feudalism and the peers, however they got that way, still hold sway." He paused to taste the stew, and then added some salt before continuing. "Besides, even back in ancient times when the peerage claimed divine right for real, someone along the way made up those titles, too, right? But everyone respected them."

Lizzy nodded in agreement.

"So the point is, it's not what they were in the mundane world—it's what they are now. Most people will do anything they can to keep their power, Pet." He looked up to watch John return from the latrine; he smiled at him.

"I was enlightening Pet with my blasphemous rhetoric, John. I still haven't told her the whole Christina story yet."

John sat back down on his stump and glared at Cuthbert. "All I'm saying is that, for all of your bashing of Red, you'd be drawn and quartered in any other barony by now. And you know it."

Cuthbert grew somber. "Yes, John, I know it. And I know we owe Red a lot for keeping us alive. But he's not goddamn Jesus, John! Last time I checked, we're still in America, even if the government abandoned us out here..."

"Oh, god, here we go..." John muttered to himself, rolling his eyes and burying his head in his arms.

"Is it so wrong to take the best of what we had and leaving the politically-corrupt bullshit behind that was bankrupting this country and doing more damage that the demons ever could? It's only been six years, and look at us! Entire groups of people shunned, people being treated like serfs or slaves or worse, and for what? Politics! Because one woman can't see past herself and everyone's afraid of her!"

John untangled his arms and looked up at Cuthbert. "Ben, why don't you finish the story for Pet? She's probably very confused right now."

Cuthbert turned to Lizzy. He was a bit wild-eyed, but he seemed to focus when he saw that there was a puzzled look on her face. "Oh, yeah, OK. Where was I?"

"Zaki and Christina were an item," Lizzy suggested.

"Yes! So, one afternoon during the Paradiso festival Zaki and Christina were found together in a barn loft by Isabella and her entourage—they were looking for Christina to attend high court or something. Zaki ran away, and Isabella screamed statatory rape. Now," Cuthbert looked over at John, "they were seventeen, right?"

"Yes, though Zaki was turning eighteen that following week."

"So, it was a grey area about age and consent. Plus, again, it was an open secret they were seeing each other. So Isabella wanted him tried for rape, but insisted that the trial be held in her jurisdiction, rather than in a Court of Chivalry."

"Which was technically proper," John interrupted. "The act took place in the Barony of the Brandywine, and El Hajj is not led by a peer."

"But, it would have been a kangaroo court! She could have ruled however she wanted, and you know that boy would have done real time. No, I don't blame Maalik for refusing to turn Zaki over. And that's complete bullshit that it wasn't held in a Court of Chivalry—Maalik is responsible for more people than half the barons in the Known World. And, Timothy was planning to grant him an unlanded title at Twelfth Night before that all happened—that was well-known, too!"

John half-shrugged in acknowledgement.

"So," Lizzy interrupted. "Why did the barons go along with Isabella, if everyone knew Zaki was innocent?"

Cuthbert sighed. "The Barony of the Brandywine has a natural aquifer and boasts the largest hydroponics farm in the Known World, probably anywhere. Isabella employs many people, and the baronies rely on her for fresh food, especially during the cold and the dry seasons. When Maalik refused to turn over his nephew to her, she banished El Hajj from her barony and insisted that the other landed barons follow suit. They did, though I suppose many towns still trade with them under the table.

"What a mess," Lizzy commented.

"Yes, it is," John agreed. "El Hajj, before this happened, was one of the greatest trading tribes in the Known World. They were fair, they left the places they camped better than they found them, and Maalik is a good and competent leader. But... he couldn't turn Zaki over to Isabella. That's the kind of man he is." He turned to Little John, who had been listening quietly the whole time. "Remember, we met him once?"

Little John nodded. "He was nice. He gave me a rock candy stick—I'd never seen that before."

"So," Cuthbert said, "from what I hear, the tribe is surviving on the borders of the North Kingdom, but barely; nothing like before. I hear that Zaki married someone else—or was married to someone else—and Christina still remains under the thumb of her aunt.

"And, seriously, she's not even SCAdian, Pet—there's no way she should be a baroness in the first place. She came out of nowhere, married Baron Rothbert, and then manuveured herself into power when he oh-so-conveniently died. She just plays along so she can keep up appearances. Oh, and legally starve a whole tribe of people because she feels politically embarrassed—can't forget about that."

He walked over to Wind Walker and pulled some bowls and spoons from a saddlebag. "I need to stop—I'm about to lose my appetite. Soup's on, folks."

From the Journals of Maryanne Weber
(Her Excellency Baroness Isabella de Castilla)
September 5th
Third Year of the Tribulation (Infusion)

After all I've done for her...how could my niece do this to me? I have lain awake at night for the past two weeks, asking myself that question.

I have not written yet of the incident that happened a fortnight past—it was just too painful to write about. But now that I am assured by the King himself that my position will be supported, I am confident to tell the story to you, those who are reading these journals: thank you again, those who yearn to know my secrets and my struggle during the early years of the Tribulation. It is a dark time in my life, but through Jesus and his infinite blessings, we will carry on.

Maalik, the untitled leader of El Hajj, was a fool. In a few weeks his tribe will be exiled, I am told, and they will only be a footnote in our history, if even that. He still thinks, because he is a popular merchant and a life-long SCAdian, that he will be supported by the peers. He refused to obey the law—he will soon discover that his thinking was wrong.

During my great festival of Paradiso this year, as every year, I invited the entire Known World (as they call it) to celebrate another good harvest and to share our bounty with our neighbors. As customary, we also invited the nomadic tribes, including El Hajj. When I think of the women and children of El Hajj, it saddens me that they will suffer for their leader's and his nephew's transgressions.

On the evening of High Court I could not find my niece, Christina, and I wished for her to accompany me. I knew Maalik's nephew, Zaki, and my niece had seen each other on several occasions that summer, but I thought nothing of it at the time: I trusted her, and I thought she knew about the sins of the flesh and its consequences. I had hoped that we had taught her to be strong enough to resist temptation. After several minutes of searching that evening, someone mentioned that Christina and Zaki were seen near one of the hay barns.

To my everlasting horror, we all heard the sounds when we entered the barn. You know the ones I mean.

There, in the loft above, we found them rutting. My entourage was with me—there were several witnesses. I screamed, and the boy jumped out of the window when he saw me and ran unclothed towards where his tribe was camped.

Christina, in turn, stood there and attacked me, in front of my people. "They were in love!" she insisted. "I had no right!" she claimed.

What does a seventeen-year-old girl know of love? I covered her and had two of my ladies-in-waiting lock her in her room until we could straighten this out.

Though she had sinned against our faith and God, if I had found them in the privacy of our house we might have managed to keep it quiet. But I was not alone, and I just couldn't take the chance that the wrong kinds of rumors would spread. I filed a formal complaint of statutory rape that night with the Crown. As was my right, I demanded that the boy be tried in my barony. Maalik refused to turn him over. The rest will soon be history.

As I lie awake at night, I wonder: if I knew before what I know now, would I have adopted her? If I knew how much she would change from the sweet little girl that was literally dropped on my doorstep, who performed so adorably at campaign rallies, to this ungrateful child that I don't even recognize anymore...even though people expected their candidates married with beautiful children? I'm not so sure I would have done it.

Why do they have to grow up? If they only could stay little girls—they are so much easier! Keith and I had made sure she went to Sunday school and church, even when we were on the campaign trail. We were a good Christian family, and I had thought we had instilled in her the values we hold so dear: chastity, honesty, and integrity, to name a few.

Fortunately for me, the SCAdians are, at least, not dissenting. They are a more unorthodox crowd than my constituents ever were—I suspect they may even feel sorry for my niece, though considering that she brought this upon herself I cannot imagine why. The people that tend to be SCAdian, I've noticed, are a more...unusual sort. They are more non-traditional than the people I knew in my former life—they are more accepting in many ways.

I think this may have helped them keep a hold of themselves in the transition from civilization to the Tribulation, but I fear most of them will not see the Kingdom of Heaven—they are incapable of that straight and narrow path that leads to salvation. As Isaiah said, which is so true of them, "You will be ever hearing but never understanding; you will be ever seeing but never perceiving." I honestly do not know how these people could go through Infusion (which was the Rapture, of course) and not be changed, not become dutiful and faithful servants of God. But I remain, as Jonah in Nineveh, to serve God and his children until I go to receive my glory.

Christina has made me so ashamed, and she threw her sacred virginity away. I am starting to think she did it on purpose— perhaps she meant for me to find her there? What did I ever do to receive such scorn, that I continue to receive to this day? I rescued her from my drunken whore of a sister, God rest her soul—I was like a mother to her. I saved her from the demons. I kept her safe while I built up this barony.

I can only pray and hope that she will one day cast aside her rebellious ways, that she will be my faithful and obedient companion once again. That I will someday see the beautiful little girl again with the long pigtails I had come to adore.

Until then, I sit and wait for my prodigal daughter to return.

Chapter Three

Lizzy

On the seventh morning, Cuthbert told her that they were about two miles from Diablo's Keep.

"There's a stream that way about a quarter mile." He pointed towards a clump of trees. "You might want to clean yourself up before we go to town."

Lizzy grabbed her sea bag and headed into the trees. When she found the stream and was fairly certain that she was alone, she stripped down and used a sliver of soap Elspeth gave her to wash off most of the road dust. She pulled out the silvery-blue gown that she and Eloise found out of her seabag. It was a little wrinkled, but it had weathered the trip well. Even after she awkwardly tightened the lacings in the back two times, though, it was still somewhat loose in the bodice—it didn't fit as it should. Lizzy hoped Cuthbert or maybe Little John could give her a hand. She used a pocket mirror Eloise gave her to apply some pigments and a comb to brush out her hair. She thought about french braiding her hair, but she didn't have an elastic band or a ribbon to hold the braid, so she decided to keep it loose. She finally put away her supplies and started back to camp.

By the time she arrived on-site, the men had broken camp and were almost finished packing. Cuthbert noticed her first.

"Wow—look at you!" he said.

"That's a really nice dress!" Little John added.

John turned around and stared, frowning. "Where did you get that?"

Lizzy wondered what she did wrong now. "In Elspeth's basement, in a storage bin. What is it?"

"That was Regina's dress," John replied. He started walking towards Lizzy.

"Oh, crap," she said, talking in a rush. "I'm sorry—we didn't know who it belonged to. I can take it off if you want..."

John shook his head as he stopped in front of her. "Turn around, I'll tighten the strings for you."

Lizzy blushed, but she did as she was told. John started with the lacings at her lower back and worked his way up, tightening as he went. Lizzy was impressed at how he seemed to know the right measure of constriction so the gown fit properly but didn't restrict her breathing. She could feel the warmth of his fingers through the fabric.

"This was one of her favorite outfits," he said as he worked. "If she had been SCAdian at the time, I think she would have gotten married in this gown. And yet, if Regina was still alive and she had heard that you were going to see Wills, she would have lent you this dress without question—that was just the kind of woman she was. Someone must have hemmed the gown before we left, though—she was a good head taller than you."

"Eloise," Lizzy said. She felt John make a bow with the lacings at the top to keep them in place.

"That should do it," John said.

She turned around to look at him. His expression was friendly, but reserved. "Thank you."

"You're welcome." He looked over her head to his son. "Ready to go, Johnny?"

It was about midmorning by the time they reached Diablo's Keep. The village was surrounded by a wall fifteen feet tall of thick tree trunks lashed together by large ropes.

"It took 'em five years to build the wall," Little John whispered to Lizzy. "They just got done, so they're having a big party. That's why Master Wills is here."

"Will we be seeing anyone from Caradoc?" Lizzy asked.

"Nah—too far. But I've been here once before, and wait until you see the square! And there was a guy last time that was trying to build a roller coaster in the back, and..."

As Little John chatted away, Lizzy took note that, as grown-up as John the Youngest wanted to be, he was still eleven years old. It made her smile and yet a little sad—listening to him talk reminded her of her godson, Brydan.

For the first time, Lizzy was riding Wind Walker. The stallion was not nearly as forgiving as Blue, but earlier that morning he and Lizzy reached an understanding. He seemed to comprehend her when, after he reared up and almost threw her off, Lizzy threatened to punch his lights out and sell him for glue. He calmed right down after that.

Atop the watchtowers were bright banners of black, red, and gold—the city's colors. After they had stabled their horses in a livery outside the wall, they waited in a line to enter the village. When they arrived at the front gate, they were greeted by two guards with wooden swords at their sides and daggers in their belts. The guards in the towers carried rifles.

"What's yer business?" one asked the elder John.

"I'm Sir John the Younger, seneshal of Vagabond Haven," he replied as he handed the guard their Writs. "This is Master Cuthbert of Lewes, herald to His Excellency Duke Karl von Worms; my son John the Youngest; and Petunia Pendragon," he finished, pointing to each member of the party in kind. Lizzy winced at the mention of her new name.

The other guard looked at Lizzy and chuckled at the expression on her face. "Silly name and no title, in a feast gown before lunch? Must be for Master Plantagenet." He looked at Cuthbert.

"Hrmmm..." Cuthbert grunted. "May we enter?"

The elder guard waved them through. As soon as they stepped through the gate, Lizzy felt a very familiar rush of nausea.

"Oh, no..." she said aloud, swallowing.

Cuthbert came to her side. "What is it?"

"There's demon flesh here," Lizzy said, gulping down saliva and looking around. It was obviously a marketplace—there were tents and vendors everywhere.

Cuthbert looked around and frowned. "Can't be...he'd be on the rampage by now."

"I can sense dead flesh, too," Lizzy replied weakly.

"What's wrong with her?" John asked, coming up behind them.

"She says there's demon flesh around here, and it's making her sick," Cuthbert replied.

John turned to his son. "Johnny?"

Little John concentrated a moment. "Maybe, but not really."

"Look," Lizzy said to Cuthbert, "Either get me to a privy so I can throw up, or let's go that way," Lizzy pointed to the left, "and get away from whatever it is."

Little John took some steps to the right. "I'll go see what it is!" he yelled, merging into the throng.

"I'll go with him," John called while nudging people aside, trying to keep up with Little John. "We'll meet you at Wills' tent later."

"OK," Cuthbert replied in a loud voice, and he and Lizzy walked through the crowd towards the center of town.

A few minutes later, Cuthbert and Lizzy arrived at the town square. Literally from edge to edge a huge circus tent spanned the square, decorated with green and white stripes and patches of assorted colors scattered throughout. A flag with the Diablo's Keep coat of arms could be seen hanging from the top of the main mast. There was a large stage of unfinished soft wood in the center with crude bleachers surrounding it on all sides, allowing for 360° viewing. Behind one column a bright gaslight shone down, illuminating the stage. There were a few people milling around working, but it was mostly quiet and empty.

"Excuse me, please! We're looking for Wills!" Cuthbert called to a man who was setting up a ticket booth. The man looked up and jerked his thumb behind him.

"Back there, by the far corner, small white tent," he said, and then went back to work.

"Thanks!" Cuthbert said as he and Lizzy started in that direction. He looked back at Lizzy. "How are you feeling?"

"Better," Lizzy said, though she was still gulping. "I'm glad I didn't throw up back there. That would have been embarrassing."

Cuthbert nodded. "Now, when we go in there, let me do the talking. Speak only when spoken to, and remember to address him as Master Plantagenet until he tells you otherwise."

Lizzy nodded as they approached the entrance to Wills' tent. Cuthbert felt the canvas side for a pole surface and knocked against it.

"Come," a voice called from inside.

Cuthbert took a breath and walked into the tent; Lizzy followed. The inside was sparse, with a single table in the center and some chairs scattered throughout. There were two men inside—one sitting at the table, the other sitting next to and a little behind him. Various papers were strewn on the table, and a quill pen and ink pot sat off to one side.

Lizzy's gaze was instantly drawn to the man sitting at the desk. He was, without a doubt, the most handsome man Lizzy had ever seen. He was probably in his early forties, with a full head of reddish-brown hair and a slightly squared jaw. The narrow mustache above his well-defined mouth that tapered down into a pointed goatee made him look a little like that guy who played Robin Hood in the 1930's, except Lizzy doubted that guy ever looked this good, even on his best day. The man was plainly dressed in a white shirt, and yet he exuded undiluted charisma just sitting there. His blue-grey eyes narrowed when Lizzy and Cuthbert entered the room.

Cuthbert bowed as Lizzy curtseyed. "Master William Plantagenet, I am Master Cuthbert of Lewes, herald to His Excellency Duke Karl von Worms—we've met before, some years ago. This is Petunia Pendragon."

Wills looked at Cuthbert, then at Lizzy, and then back to Cuthbert again. "Charmed, I'm sure." he purred. He raised his arm with a slight flourish to the man sitting next to him. "May I present to you my husband, Lord Justin Maplewood?"

My god, Lizzy thought, a little stunned as Justin stood and bowed, *even his voice is instant seduction...*

"Lord Justin," Cuthbert said, returning the bow; Lizzy curtseyed again. Justin was also a handsome man, but not quite in the same league as his husband. Cuthbert looked back to Wills as Justin sat back down.

"I am here on behalf of His Excellency Duke Karl von Worms. Please allow me to present this letter." He reached into his jacket and pulled out a green sheet of paper that was sealed with a blob of yellow wax.

Wills took the letter, broke the wax seal, and began to read. Five seconds into reading the message he stopped, lowered the letter, and glared at Cuthbert.

"Red has got to be shitting me." he said. "I have enough mouths to feed, thank you, without another one that I'm supposed to take *for free*," he slapped the paper with his free hand, "and not even with an audition? Really?!"

Wow...even a hissy fit is a performance...

"If you will remember, Master Plantagenet," Cuthbert said, unaffected, "there was that matter a few years back regarding one of your people conducting...questionable business...within the limits of Vagabond Haven. Part of the arrangement, if you recall, was a favor to be paid at an unspecified date."

Wills shortstopped his momentum into another rant to stare at Cuthbert, and then at Lizzy.

"He's handing in *that* favor?" He genuinely looked taken aback. He exchanged a look with Justin before standing up and walking towards Lizzy. He gave her an obvious once-over and arched one perfect, masculine eyebrow. "Let me see your Writ for Safe Passage, please."

Lizzy opened one of her larger belt pouches and pulled out the document. She handed it to Wills. He opened it and began to read.

"He doesn't know you," Wills announced, not looking up. He slowly walked around the tent in a circle as he spoke. "You are running from something...or someone..." He stopped again and looked Lizzy in the eyes.

"You're dangerous," he finished. He seemed to make no judgements about his observations, but simply waited for her response.

"You could tell all that from my Writ?" Lizzy asked.

"You'll learn that barons and other peers speak their own code, especially amongst each other." He held the paper up to the light and looked at it again. "He also made some deliberate edits that suggest some other things. Some people think Red is a dumb hick, but he can be quite sophisitcated when he wants to be." Wills walked over to Justin and handed him the Writ to review, and then sat back down.

"So, where do you come from?" Wills asked.

"My lord, if I may," Cuthbert said before Lizzy could reply. "There were rumors that she is a refugee from the government, though Pet has not confirmed or denied that; she has been quite stubborn about disclosing that information. We found her about a mile from our village."

"OK," Wills said, frowning. "We'll leave that alone for now.

"So...Pet...you're pretty enough, I suppose. What can you do? Can you sing?"

Gee, thanks... "I can play the guitar and sing—I'm an alto. My best instument is the trumpet, but I haven't played one in years."

"How long ago?"

"Before Infusion—twelve years ago?"

Wills frowned. "Hmm...a trumpet player might come in handy down the line, but your chops are probably crap right now, and I have no way of telling how good you were before."

"I was first chair in high school."

"Not terribly encouraging," Wills replied. "Anything else? We could use a violin player, or the string base?"

Lizzy shook her head. "Sorry."

"Any acting experience?"

"Not since junior high."

Wills and Justin shared a look.

"Can you think of any other openings, dear?" Wills asked Justin.

"Not at the moment, unfortunately," Justin replied.

Wills looked at Cuthbert. "I'm sorry, Master Cuthbert, but Red's going to have to come up with another way to repay him. A *pro bono* visit by Dr. Goldberg, a discount on a festival, perhaps, but I just don't think..."

"There is something else," Lizzy interrupted, her heart starting to pound in alarm. "I can Sense demon flesh."

Wills waved his hand in dismissal. "I have three members of my troupe who can do that. Besides, the demons haven't moved in four years, there's not much of a use for that at the moment." He walked over, took Lizzy's hand, and patted it as he would a child's. "Now, I know this much be very disappointing, but I'm sure other arrangements will be made on your behalf...a domestic or something..."

Lizzy stopped listening as he chatted on. She didn't want to use her trump card, but she knew Wills was not going to even consider taking her otherwise—it was her last chance.

"I can make holy water, Master Plantagenet," Lizzy heard herself say.

Wills dropped her hand as if she had suddenly burned him. He paused, and then his lips curled into a snear.

"Nice try," he said. "I don't believe you."

She looked him full in the face. "I'm also the most powerful Sensor you will ever meet. I sensed demon flesh in the marketplace—Sir John the Younger's son is looking for it. Find the demon flesh, give me a bucket of water, and I'll prove it to you."

Wills eyes widened as he pointed at Lizzy like a prosecuting attorney in a courtroom drama. "We'll see about that!" He strode past her and out of the tent, trailing indigation behind him.

Justin made a face at the ceiling and followed him.

Cuthbert and Lizzy stood next to each other in silence for several moments, staring at Wills' empty seat.

"Well," Cuthbert finally said, "I hope you can deliver on that claim you just made. How good are you at making holy water?"

"I don't know," Lizzy admitted. "I've only done it once."

Cuthbert groaned. "Great." He went to the nearest chair and sagged onto it.

Lizzy went to another chair, adjusted her gown, and then sat down to wait. Perhaps five minutes later, Lizzy began to feel sick. A minute after that, she stood up to find something to vomit in. By the time Wills, Justin, John, and Little John arrived back at the tent, Lizzy was holding onto her chair with both hands, trying to fight the vertigo. Little John came bounding through the tent flap first.

"THEY WERE EARS!" he crowed as soon as he stepped inside. "It took me a while to find them, because they were under a booth and they were small, but the vendor had pickled ears in a jar and...hey, Pet, what's wrong with you?"

The rest of the men had filtered in as Little John was making his report. John looked more than grim as he held a mason jar with several rigid lumps of curved flesh.

"Disgusting!" Wills spat as he walked towards the back of the tent. "Why anyone still thinks there's any value to dead possessed flesh, I will never know." He stopped and looked down into the pail he used as a wastebasket. He sighed.

"Well, we're not using *this* bucket," Wills said. He turned to Little John. "John, would you please find one of my people, and ask for a bucket of water?"

"Yeah, sure!" Little John replied as he shot out of the tent. Lizzy swallowed and tried to speak.

"Could you take those away, please?" she croaked. "I only need one to show you." She swallowed again and concentrated on not retching.

Wills nodded. He motioned to John to place the jar on the table. Drawing a knife from his belt, he opened the lid and then fished around with his knife tip until he cornered one of the ears against the wall of the jar.

"Sorry," Wills said to the ear as he stabbed it through. Grimacing, he pulled out the pickled ear and placed it on the table, leaving the knife tip lodged through its upper rim; runny pink fluid puddled around both objects. He then made quick work of closing the jar and passing it back to John.

"The constable said he wanted this back immediately, so he could prosecute the booth owner. Would you please find Stewart Cooper at the pinfold and see that he gets this?"

"Of course," John said. He gave Lizzy a glance of concern, exchanged a pointed look with Cuthbert, and then walked out to complete his errand.

Less than ten seconds later, Little John waddled through the tent's opening carrying a galvenized pail of water. He carried it to Lizzy and then sat it on the ground. Wills gingerly picked up the ear and flicked it into the pail; it floated on top of the water's surface. The men in the tent and Little John gathered around the pail and Lizzy.

"All right, Pet," Wills said. "Showtime."

Lizzy crouched down and slipped her fingertips into the water. Making sure that her fingers were not even close to the ear, she closed her eyes and tried to remember how she made holy water before.

This time, she didn't even have to concentrate. The white geyser came almost immediately, flooding her senses again and shooting that wonderfully soothing energy down her arm and into the water. She heard a small *phoomp!*, and then the column of energy switched off as abruptly as it had appeared. She opened her eyes to see what happened.

The ear was gone—all that was left was a small amount of ash, floating on the water. Then, she was suddenly at the pool at Headquarters, watching the doors open and the soldiers come pouring in. The lifeguard's hook was pulling through Erin's remains, her body crumpled apart...

The smell of burnt flesh...

"I'm going to make a mint," she heard someone say over the scene. She clawed her way out of the flashback and tried to focus on the present.

"What?" she asked to no one in particular. She had to struggle with her gown, but she finally managed to wrench herself into a standing position and look around. She saw that everyone in the tent was staring at her in utter disbelief.

Everyone, that is, except for Wills, who was looking at her like Christmas had come early, and she was the gift he had always wanted.

"You're the real deal," Wills said with wonder. He turned to Justin. "We could advertise exorcisms, demonstrations...it's a little 'sideshow,' but it would bring in a different kind of audience..."

"Fuck that," Lizzy growled, not caring anymore about the SCA, or protocol, or that Wills was supposed to be her salvation. She wasn't nauseous anymore because of the demon flesh; she was sickened for an entirely new reason.

"Did you *see* what I did to that ear? If that was a person, that could happen to them, too, depending on how Infected they were. There is no fucking way I'm going to be a part of your freakshow, Wills. Infected are innocent people, and they deserve better."

Wills grew quiet. Everyone was quiet. Lizzy waited.

"Oh, really?" Wills replied. "I have to tell you, Miss Pet, that it's been quite a few years since someone's talked to *me* like that. But, sure, we can go down to your level." He paused to clear his throat.

"Little John, would you please fetch your father for me?" His eyes never left Lizzy's.

The boy nodded and ran out of the tent.

"Master Plantagenet ..." Cuthbert began.

Wills held up his hand to silence him. "I've got this, Cuthbert." Wills said, throwing a piercing look at the herald.

Cuthbert held his tongue as Wills turned back to Lizzy.

"Listen to me, you haughty government bitch," Wills growled in a low, quiet voice. "I have the distinct impression that you were one of *those* people that got whisked away and shipped off to safe locations, leaving the rest of us to be slaughtered and eaten by those motherfucking demons. Do you even *know* what we went through those first years: running from mobs, waiting for your husband, your mother, your father, to become one of *them* and attack you?" As he spoke, his voice grew louder. This was not the actor speaking anymore, but the man underneath.

"How fucking *dare* you, suggesting that those demons deserve sympathy, deserve *anything! Billions* of people died, and killing them was a blessing; most of those who we managed to exorcise either died of demon poisoning or were permanently crippled. So don't sit there in judgment in your goddamn ivory tower when *we* suffered and starved!"

Well...I just got told, Lizzy thought. To be totally honest with herself, the survivors at Commune Ruth really *hadn't* thought about the civilians during those first few months—they were too busy setting up shop, writing out procedures, and arranging for those first few babies to be born. She took a deep breath, and hoped her response was a good one. Or, at least good enough.

"OK," she began. "You're right, Master Plantagenet: I don't know what you went through. I'm sorry. But while I don't believe in a god, I think this is a powerful gift, and it shouldn't be squandered.

"How about this: when we find possessed people, I will help them. This is new to me—this was only my second time making holy water—so maybe I can refine it, so it's not so destructive? Besides, I hear you want to expand your show—do you really think parlor tricks are the way to go right now?"

Wills looked at her. While she was speaking, his face had returned to its natural, bronzed tone. He turned to Justin. "What do you think, sweetheart?"

Justin studied Lizzy for several moments.

"First off," he said, addressing Lizzy, "When telling my husband that there's no fucking way you'll be a part of his freakshow, it's *Master* Wills." He smirked slightly. "Otherwise, I think she's right, love. I'm not sure drawing attention to a possible military refugee who can disintergrate people is good for business."

Wills nodded and grinned at Justin; the actor was back on stage. "That's why I married you, my darling. You truly are my anchor."

Justin blew him a kiss.

Wills approached Lizzy again, stopping only an inch or two away from her. It was uncomfortable, him being so close, and it was meant to be so. She breathed in a strange combination of vanilla, sandalwood, and sawdust. It was intoxicating, and it had the intended effect.

"I wonder," Wills said, his voice smooth, "why Red didn't have you stay at Caradoc. Why did he send you..." he paused, his look turning suggestive, "to me?"

Lizzy swallowed. Though she completely understood that Wills had no interest in her, he still knew how to work his mojo—the rest of the world slipped away. *God, I need to get laid...*

"There were complications," Lizzy finally managed to say.

"Yeah?" Wills said, smiling, his perfect white teeth gleaming. He moved around her until he was standing next to her. He bent down to whisper in her ear; the scents grew stronger. "Are those complications coming here?"

His breath was warm as it tickled her ear; Lizzy closed her eyes. She remembered the look on Abby's face when she had tased her and grimaced. "I don't know."

There was a long pause. She could feel his gaze on her face.

"Did they deserve what they got?" he finally asked, his voice carressing.

Lizzy was out of sorts. She opened her eyes, but all she could see was Abby lying on the floor in front of her, unconscious and shitting herself. Wills' fragrance vanished as she was almost overpowered by the perceived smell of fresh defecation.

"I did what I had to," she whispered.

The vision and the scent faded away. She blinked rapidly and shook her head, trying to clear it.

What the fuck was that?

Wills straighened up and stepped back. He looked at Justin and nodded.

"OK," he said, turning back to address Lizzy, "just so we all understand each other: I'll protect you, but only until you are a threat to me and mine. This isn't your government Xanadu," he pointed at her chest, "this is the real world, and it can be very dangerous out here. You do what I tell you, when I tell you, or you'll find yourself out on the street, and I doubt you'll last a night. Do you understand?"

Lizzy nodded. "Yes, Master Plantagenet." Christ, all she wanted was a couple or three of Demerol and a six-pack right about now. *Holy shit, what a mind-fucking day...*

Wills nodded in return. "You call me Master Wills—everyone does." He stepped back and turned to Justin, smiling.

"Spread the word if you would, sweetheart: we're having an audition this afternoon after lunch and before teasers. I'll let Bill and his group know that they're up." He turned to Cuthbert. "I'd be honored if you all would stay for lunch. I think we're having shepherd's pie."

Just then, John and Little John came charging through the tent door. They both looked ready for a fist-fight.

"*What the hell is going on here?!*" John yelled. He looked at Lizzy. "Are you all right?"

"Yes," she replied. "I have an audition this afternoon."

"There was some drama, John," Cuthbert offered, "but it's settled now. We're invited to lunch—shepherd's pie!" He smiled at the knight.

John ran his fingers through his hair and sighed. "OK." He looked down at Little John, who looked as confused as he did. "We'll get the whole story later."

There were approximately twenty people in Wills' troupe, not including Bill's group. Lizzy knew this because they were all seated in front of the wooden stage when she went under the big tent after lunch with John the Younger, Cuthbert, and Little John. They applauded when they saw her.

"What the hell is this?" she asked Cuthbert. He shrugged in ignorance.

"Welcome!" Wills called from the stage. "Auditions are always big events for the Star-Crossed Travelling Players. By auditioning in front of us all, we quickly discover how you fare in front of an audience, and everyone can offer their feedback, right down to the last scullery wench.

"Ladies and Gentlemen," Wills announced to the crowd, "it is my pleasure to introduce a mysterious stranger who wishes to join our humble troupe. Please give a warm welcome to... Petunia Pendragon!"

The audience laughed and cheered.

Damn hamster name... Lizzy thought. She walked up the three steps that led to the stage and walked over to Wills' side. She cutseyed to the audience. Wills gestured to an empty chair in the center of the stage with a sheet music stand and a guitar sitting next to it. A group of six musicians sat behind the chair. She lifted her gown a little and arranged herself before sitting down.

"First...do you know anything rote?" Wills asked her. "No singing yet."

She strummed the guitar. Her ear for pitch wasn't the best, but she noticed the high-E string was flat. She adjusted it, and it sounded better. She started to play the Indigo Girls' "Closer to Fine," which was a favorite song at the adult commune sing-alongs. After a minute, Wills stopped her.

"Not bad," he said. He set three pieces of sheet music in front of her. "Please choose one and sight-read."

One of the selections was a song by Bob Dylan that she was quasi-familiar with, so she began to strum and pick the notes. At the bottom of the page, Wills stopped her again.

"Troupe?" he called to the audience.

"She slows down a bit when she has to reach across the neck," a dark-haired man observed in the front. "But it was almost unnoticeable during her first selection, so I don't think it will be a problem."

"Pet, this is Master Paul of Birmingham, one of our best guitarists," Wills said. Paul waved; Lizzy nodded in acknowledgement.

"Now," Wills said, "What can you play and sing along with?"

"A lot of songs," Lizzy replied. "Mostly children's songs."

"Hey," Justin said from his seat off-stage, "we're always looking for that for children's events. Play a funny one."

Lizzy played and sang a song about a rabbit and a frog having a jumping contest. She had to tamp down a wave of sadness and concentrate when she remembered it was her godson Brydan's favorite song, but she plastered on a smile and performed through it. It did cheer her up that, by the end, the mostly middle-aged audience was gamely singing along with the chorus. There was a hearty round of applause at the end.

Wills was clapping, too. "Well done, Miss Pet," he said with a smile. "Now, for the last part." He pointed behind the tent. "Go about thirty feet directly behind the stage, and you'll find a chair and a stand with some sheet music. You have about twenty minutes to read through and practice the guitar part, and then you will be expected to come back and perform with the ensemble." He gestured to the group of stage musicians, who all smiled and waved.

Lizzy gave them a slight bow and descended the stairs to the ground below. As she made her way behind the stage, she heard Wills say, "So, let's talk about tonight..."

Sure enough, there was the chair and stand, right where Wills said they would be. There was a short guitar solo within the piece, but overall the composition was fairly easy. Violin was the main instrument—Lizzy had never accompanied a violin before, even as a trumpet player. Before she knew it, Justin was approaching her.

"It's time," he said, smiling. "It sounds like you have the jist of it."

"It's familiar," Lizzy said, rising and following Justin back to the tent. "Something on TV, maybe?"

"Yes," Justin replied. "It's called 'Ashokan Farewell'—it was played a lot during Ken Burns' Civil War documentary; it's one of Wills' favorites. Even though it isn't even close to being period, he always plays it at the end of the Middle Kingdom's A&S consortium and at Crown Tournament." He opened the flap of the tent and let Lizzy enter first.

The troupe applauded for her as she came in. She walked up the stairs and took her place on the stage once again.

"Are you ready, Pet?" Wills asked.

"Yes, Master Wills."

He grinned. "Bill, it's all yours."

Bill nodded to Wills. He raised his bow, tucked his violin under his chin, and counted softly, "1, 2..."

When she heard the first note of the piece, she realized she hadn't heard a live orchastrated performance since well before Infusion. The melody was beautiful, and Bill played with such emotion and sweetness that she almost missed her entrance. She didn't, however, and played along as the other parts swelled and ebbed around her. She flubbed her small solo, but not horrendously, and continued right on playing as she was taught to do. When the entire group finally joined in multi-part harmony, she felt tears in the back of her eyes as she played—it was so magical. She had forgotten how wonderful playing with an ensemble could be, and she had never performed with quality musicians such as these. She envied their life.

As the audience clapped and cheered, Lizzy stood and bowed to the musicians. They rose and returned her bow, all of them smiling. Wills approached her, bowed, and then raised his hands for silence as he addressed the crowd.

"Thank you, one and all, for attending! Let's give Pet another hand for being such a good sport..."

The troupe applauded one more time and then dissolved into groups to prepare for the afternoon activities. Justin approached Wills and whispered something in his ear. Wills chuckled in reply and gave him a quick kiss on the mouth.

"OK—I'll catch you later," Wills told Justin.

Justin turned to Lizzy and bowed. "I'll see you later tonight. I'm guessing you'll want to see the festivities."

Lizzy's heart sank. *What the hell—am I in or what?!* "Yes, Lord Justin, thank you." She curtseyed in return.

Justin chuckled. "We'll need to work on that." He winked at Wills and walked off towards a group of jugglers warming up on the lawn.

Cuthbert and the two Johns walked up to Lizzy and Wills.

"Do we have a deal?" Cuthbert got right to the point.

"What, no foreplay?" Wills said. He made a face and looked at Lizzy. "You sure do bring out the vulgar in me, Pet."

"Sorry," Lizzy replied.

Wills chuckled. "Very well, Cuthbert. She missed that one measure in her solo and she lacks confidence. But she continued to play, even after that mistake, so that suggests she has had some formal experience. Under normal circumstances, we would not accept her into our troupe without at least a couple more years of formal study elsewhere, but..." He glanced down at Lizzy. "Under these circumstances, I believe we can make an exception." He looked up at Justin, who talking to one of the jugglers in the circle as she passed pins back and forth amongst the three other people in perfect precision.

"Besides, I believe you charmed my husband with that song of yours, Pet—he's always been partial to silly songs. I've found over the years that I just can't say no to that man." He smiled and glanced at Cuthbert. "Please give my regards to Baron Red, and inform him that I expect all favors are now fulfilled." He looked down at Lizzy again.

"Congratulations, Apprentice Pet. May you break a leg."

"Oh, thank god," Cuthbert muttered. He turned to John. "I need a drink. First round's on me."

After Lizzy changed out of her gown and put on more comfortable clothes, she spent the afternoon and evening with Cuthbert and the two Johns.

"Enjoy your last day of freedom," Wills had told her. "I'll expect you for breakfast tomorrow and to help break down camp afterwards. The chatelaine of our troupe is Sweet Bess of Ipswich—you'll find her at the great hall helping out the feastocrat. Bug her at the beginning of court to help you find some crash space until we get you a tent. Don't wait too long, though—she's the wife of the Miller and the Reeve tonight, and curtain's up right after court."

The party from Caradoc walked the streets, admiring the celebration that was going on around them. There were street performers on every major artery: sword-swallowers and fire-eaters, jugglers of various objects, and musicians. Lizzy noticed that all the performers had bowls in front of their acts, and every so often someone would throw in a lumpy coin.

"How does money work here?" Lizzy asked.

"It's like what fairs and carnivals used to be like before the demons came," Cuthbert explained. "People purchase coins from troll—that's the entrance booth—and use them at the event. The town mints the event coins just for the occasion, so they're useless anywhere else; this encourages folks to spend all their coins. Then the townsfolk divy up whatever troll got."

"Huh," Lizzy said. "But is there a common currency, like amongst the kingdoms?"

"In the larger baronies, like Barony of the Brandywine, they're starting to establish a standard currency, but most places are still on the barter system. Here's the troll booth now."

They stopped at a small booth by the back gate. Cuthbert undid one of his pouches and pulled out two articulated wooden horses, each about six inches tall. He showed the woman at troll how the neck and each joint of the legs moved, and that they held their positions so the animals could stand. The lady at troll was impressed—Lizzy was, too.

"I like how the joints are so smoothly flush with the legs," the woman said with a slight Irish lilt as she manipulated the legs into different poses. "You can barely see the pegs. I may keep these for my granddaughter. How much were you thinking of?"

"Fifteen each."

"Oouch. Well," she said, examining them again. "Cathy's birthday is next week, so I'd better get them. Deal." She handed Cuthbert thirty coins. Cuthbert handed one to Lizzy.

"They're rather crude," Lizzy observed. "They're more like lumps. And there's pits and holes in them."

"But they're are uniform," John replied, holding up another one. "They are all of the same mold—crude and bumpy is hard to forge. By the time someone figures out how to replicate it, the event is over. C'mon, I think I saw a meat pie and ale booth down this street."

Around sunset there was a feast under the main tent, which Cuthbert paid for. She noticed there was a long table on the stage, and the several people eating at it were dressed in expensive-looking garb.

"Who are they?" Lizzy asked John; Cuthbert's mouth was full of squab and was engaged in a conversation to a man on his left about brewer's yeast.

John squinted up at the stage. "I don't know everyone, but the couple in the middle are the Crown Prince and Princess of the North Kingdom. See the crowns?"

Lizzy squinted herself. "Sort of. Not very big, are they?"

"I think the current king and queen here step down next month. Then those two will get the royal crowns, and whoever won Crown Tournament will get their crowns."

Lizzy looked at the man sitting to the prince's right. "The guy in the black and red has a larger crown than the prince has. Why isn't he in the center?"

John chuckled. "That's Baron Heaven's Gate—you don't say the 'of,' he founded the barony—and that's his baronial coronet. Remember how you can tell a prince's crown from a baron's coronet?"

"A baron's coronet has six points. Most princes' crowns have four points, though that isn't a hard rule."

"Excellent." John leaned back and took a sip of beer. He smiled as he watched Little John tear into a turkey leg.

"Are you going to be OK, Pet?" he asked as he glanced back at her. "Not that I'd know what to do with you if you didn't stay here, but this doesn't seem like the best of fits."

Not that I'd know what to do with you... Wrapped up in his dead wife, he really wouldn't. Which was a shame, because John was an attractive, nice guy, in a Non-Stop SCAdian Information Faucet kind of way...

Lizzy shrugged. "I'm not looking for family. I'm just looking to survive until I figure out what I really want to do—this will suit for now. I just hope I can earn my keep here—I'm out of my league musicwise."

John smirked. "You don't even know the half of it. Wait until you see them do an entire show."

Court was next, and Lizzy found it to be a little boring. The baron held court first, and there were several flowery speeches about the new wall and announcements about upcoming weddings and events. When they started handing out local awards, Lizzy slipped away and headed towards the kitchen. She walked through the doors and saw that the closest person was a lanky woman washing dishes in a stand-alone sink. She decided to ask her first about Sweet Bess.

"Hi. I'm looking for Lady Sweet Bess?"

The woman turned around. "Yes? Oh, you're the girl who auditioned today. I almost didn't recognize you without that dress. I'm Sweet Bess."

"Hi," Lizzy said again as she approached her. "I'm Pet. Master Wills told me to find you and ask for crash space."

The woman sighed. "Well, first off, congratulations: this is a fun troupe to be in, even though it can be exhausing. As for crash space..." Sweet Bess straightened up and seemed to be thinking for a moment. "I suppose you could bunk with Ella until we get you a tent. She won't mind, especially since we're more than halfway through the season."

"You don't travel around all year?"

"Heavens, no. We take a long break during the winter—not enough work to make it worthwhile. Besides, how do you think we eat? Performing gets us the nice-to-haves, but it couldn't support us."

"Oh."

Sweet Bess dried her hands on a worn dish towel. "Sandra, I've got to go now," she called over her shoulder. Instantly, about three woman crowded around her, thanking her for her time and offering hugs.

"Boring trip home!" Lizzy heard one of them say.

"See you at A&S!"

After a minute or two, Sweet Bess waved her final farewells and motioned for Lizzy to follow her out to the great hall. They walked around the back of the crowd—the princess was on stage now, talking to a woman kneeling before her—and went outside. It was very quiet.

"Everyone either went home or is at court," Bess explained. "The troupe is getting ready—we start as soon as court is over and everyone gets settled in. Have you seen us before?"

Lizzy shook her head. "I'm new to this area."

"Well, I hope you like our show. It's one of our old standards, but everyone always likes it." They arrived at the large tent, which was glowing with torchlight. Lizzy and Sweet Bess stepped in.

There were about five people putting the final touches on some forest scenery that decorated the round stage. Another ten people were climbing into horse costumes, designed so it looked like the actors were saddled and riding astride mounts. Wills was running around in a flurry, calling to one person to adjust the one of the overhead lights one moment, talking quietly to someone else and pointing off-stage a second later, picking up some tufts of hair off the stage seconds after that and cursing that the goddamn horses were falling apart. He saw Sweet Bess and Lizzy out of the corner of his eye and whirled to face them.

"There you are, Bess! Do get ready—Pet, please help her. That one costume is always a pain in the ass." He shot out his hand and caught a teenager by the elbow as he was hurrying across the stage. "Do me a favor and see where they are at court ..."

Sweet Bess took Lizzy by the arm and pulled her to a large curtained-off area off to the side of the stage. She quickly stripped off her day garb and took a velvet-looking purple gown down from a small wardrobe. It was gaudy and revealing, but Lizzy supposed that was the point.

"I just need help with the headdress," Sweet Bess said from inside the dress as she climbed into it. A second later, her head emerged at the top. "And doing up the back. There's a zipper."

"Not period," Lizzy observed as she zipped up the costume.

"Period enough," Sweet Bess replied, frowning. "Oh, god, you're not a seam checker, are you?"

"A what?"

"Never mind—I'll explain later." She looked around. "Where's the make-up table?" she yelled.

"Over here," someone said near the back of the tent.

"C'mon," she said, dragging Lizzy along.

About ten minutes later, Lizzy heard Wills yell, "The house is open! Places, everyone!" By then, Sweet Bess had finished applying a heavy coat of make-up while Lizzy had pinned her tall, cumbersome headdress to the top of her head. Sweet Bess shook her head a bit.

"Good—it's stable. Thank you." She glanced out at the rows of bleachers around the stage where the crowd was assembling. "Why don't you have a seat? You probably won't get to see many shows from the audience after tonight."

"OK," Lizzy said. She looked around for Cuthbert and the two Johns, but she didn't see them. She eventually sat in the middle of one of the third rows, surrounded by hordes of people.

As it turned out, the show was selections from *The Canterbury Tales*. Lizzy vaguely remembered reading the book in high school, but she didn't remember any of it. It didn't matter: though the actors spoke in Old English, their performances made it easy to understand what was going on. Their actions were exaggerated and heavy on the slapstick, which seemed perfect for a late-night show after a very long court. The audience laughed and clapped when it was appropriate, and individuals from the bleachers heckled the stage when a character was about to do something foolish or sneaky. These comments sometimes earned the person an obscene gesture from the actor, which made the crowd laugh even more. Overall, it was the best time Lizzy had in years.

As the play ended and the Star-Crossed Travelling Players received their standing ovation, Lizzy felt light-headed. She was so lucky to have this opportunity—she hoped it was as great as it seemed to be.

Chapter Four

Diablo's Keep
The Barony of Winter's Gate
June 10th
10:32 a.m.

"*What?*"

Lizzy looked at Sweet Bess in disbelief. They hadn't even finished breaking camp that first morning, and already she was getting shitty news...

"Them's the rules, Pet." Sweet Bess smirked at Lizzy's distress. "All new players start with a two-month stint working days with Dr. Goldberg. You'll still be getting lessons from Master Paul and starting your improv training during your free time. It's so you don't get too overwhelmed, being new and all. Helps you adjust."

Lizzy sighed. On the ship, nonrates arriving from basic training went straight to work on the mess deck for the same reason. FNGs were often worse than useless—being in the galley kept them from fucking up stuff too badly until they got their bearings. Realizing that she was being reduced back to *bootius campus* status didn't sit too well with her, especially after being in charge of so much at Ruth and the laboratory.

"What will I be doing?" she asked as they started towards Dr. Goldberg's trailer.

"From what I understand, you'll keep the place clean, help with dental procedures, take care of his horses, that kind of thing. When we're on the road and you're not actually driving he'll show you how to make compounds and medicines. He has an apprentice, Murray, so it shouldn't be too hard."

Dr. Goldberg was a thin man in his fifties. He had a kind, smiling face and gave off a heavy *Mr. Rogers' Neighborhood* vibe. He took Lizzy's hand and shook it warmly.

"It's so good to have you here," Dr. Goldberg said. "The Lord is so wonderful with his blessings!" He then took a breath and broke out into song, jiggling around in a little dance.

"Oh, the Lord is good to me...and so I thank the Lord! I thank him for the things I need, the sun and the rain and the apple seed! The Lord is good to me!"

Oh...wow...

Lizzy had just finished helping Murray harness the team of horses when she heard someone call her SCAdian name. She turned around and smiled.

"Hey, Little John!"

Little John ran up and stopped short of bowling her over. John and Cuthbert followed soon afterwards.

"Did you see the play yesterday night?" Little John asked. "Dad said I was too young, that it was too raunchy. Was it?"

"Yeah," Lizzy agreed, "In a couple of years, Little John. Hey Master Cuthbert, Sir John."

"Pet," Cuthbert answered. He looked at the horses. "They sure don't waste time, do they?"

"As it turns out, I'm working for Dr. Goldberg for the first two months, anyway. It's not as fun as performing all day, but I suppose I have to pay my dues."

Cuthbert and John nodded.

"We're headed back to Caradoc," John said. "Take care of yourself, and we'll see you either at Paradiso or next year at Odin's Challenge."

Lizzy raised an eyebrow at him as she hugged Little John. Or, the closest thing Little John would tolerate—he *was* eleven years old.

"They're a festival and a tournament," Cuthbert explained. He held out his hand; Lizzy shook it. Sir John took her hand as well, but bowed over it instead. "Pet."

"Sir John," she replied as he released her hand. "Master Cuthbert, Little John, thank you for everything." She smiled. "Boring trip home."

The three of them grinned at that.

"You, too," Cuthbert said. Then they turned around and left her by the horses, disappearing into the crowd.

"Now, the first thing we need to do," Master Paul told Lizzy at her first lesson, "is do a complete diagnostic. You can play, sure, but I'll be putting you through your paces for the first couple of days. I think you might do well for flash acts."

"Flash acts?"

"Acts done on the fly—maybe for filler, or if something goes wrong and we need to stall, that sort of thing. Did you do a lot of sing-alongs with kids?"

Lizzy grew menancholy. "Yes, for almost four years, and adult sing-alongs a couple of years before that."

"OK," Paul said. "By the way, one of the things you'll find out about us is that we'll try not to ask a lot questions about your past. For instance, I really would like to know more about where you did your sing-alongs, but I won't ask, and neither will anyone else, except for maybe Wills or Justin. We've gotten several people here under...unusual circumstances...and Wills encourages folks to keep their secrets until they're ready to share. OK?"

"Yes, Master Paul."

"Good!" he strummed a series of chords and picked a few bars of a happy tune. "Let's get started."

Within a week, Lizzy had settled into a routine: an hour of sword and shield training with Sir Malcolm before breakfast, followed by a full day of working for Dr. Goldberg with a lunch break, an one-hour guitar lesson with Master Paul, dinner, improv games and short performance work when they didn't have an all-hands evening show, bed. Repeat until Sunday. Sleep all day Sunday. Start again Monday. She barely saw her roommate, who was a tumbler and an actress and mostly lived with her boyfriend, François.

Being with Dr. Goldberg, she could see the current of the group from the outside—how chaotic and everchanging it seemed at first. It became clear after a day or two, though, that it wasn't. Because the members of the troupe had been with each other for so long, they were natually coordinated with one another. A Player, at any given moment, just knew when it was time to get props ready, when to meet members for teasers, who was mess cook for which meal. After her two months, Lizzy knew she would be expected to jump in and know their dance; she hoped she was coordinated enough by then not to screw up their rhythm.

The troupe could spend from one day to one week in a town. Wills had a map of the Known World in his trailer with the full route of where they were going, the autocrat there, how much they were getting paid, and other useful information. He had synchronized the dates so there was a minimum of travel time. Days off, except for a Sunday here or there, were non-existant.

"Not even holidays?" Lizzy asked Murray after a week. He was in his late teens to early twenties with a deep scar down his right cheek. He always seemed slightly annoyed when talking to people, but he didn't seem like a complete asshole.

"Nope," Murray replied, cleaning the cable on one of the pedal-driven drills. "They work straight through until the off-season, and then you'll be so bored you won't know what to do with yourself. You'll see."

As it turned out, working for Dr. Goldberg and Murray wasn't too bad. There were the mandatory morning devotions—he had about twenty years-worth of *The Upper Room* in a storage chest in his office—and he tended to sing hymns while he worked. But he was open-minded enough to accept the co-managers' orientation, and he never tried to convert Lizzy, even when she admitted she was an agnostic at best.

Several members of the troupe would show up for his morning prayers and would often seek out Sunday services when they were in a town. Lizzy asked Murray about it one day about two weeks after she had arrived as they were hard at work field day-ing the trailer.

"That's nothing," Murray replied. "Wait until we get to some of the border towns—those people are scary. The demons sure did a number on them: church every day...sometimes twice a day... Wills and Justin and the other gays have to really be careful or they'll get lynched—has anyone told you about Wills' rescue projects?"

If there's one thing a nonrate is good for, it's gossip. Lizzy smiled to herself and settled in for the story. "Nope."

"I only got here a little more than two years ago—Wills was booking venues by then. But in the beginning, Wills and the troupe would travel from town to town, basically giving a show and hoping for compensation later. While they were travelling, sometimes they'd find someone beat-up and left for dead by the side of the road. Sometimes it was robbers or ex-Infected, but a lot of times they were homosexuals, or sometimes Wiccans or pagans. Or, at least that's what the assholes claimed they were as they were beating the shit out of them." He paused to move some bottles from a top shelf to dust underneath.

"Motherfucker..." Lizzy breathed. She watched her language around Dr. Goldberg, but Murray didn't care what she said.

Murray shrugged. "Folks gotta have a dog to kick, especially when times are hard—that's something my grandpa used to say a lot. You'll meet most of those guys when we get back to Shangri-La."

"Sorry?"

Murray turned around to look at her. "Home. Where the troupe lives."

"Oh," Lizzy said, feeling foolish. "I never heard the name before."

"Yeah," Murry continued, "A lot of the folks recovered, some even moved on, but a lot of them were beat up pretty bad and decided to stay. They work the farms and fields for the troupe while they travel. There's even one guy that got his tongue cut out—he does the bookkeeping."

"Shit! What the hell did he do?"

"Wills probably knows, but no one else knows the story. Why *would* anyone get their tongue cut out?"

"Either because they said the wrong thing," Lizzy reasoned, "or to keep them quiet, I guess."

"That's what I figure, too. " Murray turned back around and went back to dusting shelves.

The Hamlet of Antioch, WY

Lizzy was taking her turn on the pedal-driven drill—she figured her legs would look awesome by the end of her two months—when Sweet Bess popped her head through the trailer door.

"Dr. Goldberg? Oh, I'm sorry, I didn't realize you were with a patient."

"It's OK, Bess," Dr. Goldberg said, his eyes crinkling above his mask with pleasure. "What is it?"

"Justin would like to see Pet at your earliest convenience, and he would like to see you after dinner—we're doing *The Life and Times of Jesus* tonight, and was hoping you could be Nicodemus again."

"Oh, I'd love to!" Dr. Goldberg beamed. "I can't tell you what a thrill it is to be on stage for these roles! Please tell Wills I'd be happy to. I'll send Pet by after we're done with this patient, maybe thirty minutes?" He turned back around and began to drill again.

"Great!" Bess turned to Lizzy. "Wills is at the main stage. Maybe you'll be able to hear Lord Hammerthrow Two-Axe." She grinned.

"Who?" Lizzy asked, a little out of breath. *This cavity must be a doozy...*

"Hammerthrow is an old-school SCAdian. Every so often, he tracks down Wills with his sons and plays metal songs—thrash metal, heavy metal, he's done it all. He *really* wants to have some of 'his' music at his baronial festival this coming September, but with just acoustical instruments it usually sounds just *awful.* But he keeps trying, and Wills always listens."

"OK," Lizzy said, panting. "I'll be there as soon as I can."

Dr. Goldberg stopped drilling about ten minutes later, and then Lizzy helped him finish filling the tooth. As soon as he said she could go, Lizzy jogged out of the trailer and headed down the hill to the town below.

The hamlet of Antioch was a last-minute addition to the schedule. Nestled in-between two SCA towns that were already scheduled, they struck a bargain with Wills that, for a reduced rate, they would host a break-in of the *Jesus* production for their Saint Francis of Assisi Festival and the Blessing of the Animals. Lizzy slowly worked her way through the herds of sheep and goats and other livestock that were currently overrunning the village streets and soon saw the square where the stage was set.

About ten yards out, even over the almost-deafening bleets and snorts of the animals, Lizzy could hear screeching violins and the thumping of a drum set. By the time she reached the boards, she saw that she had arrived in the middle of Hammerthrow Two-Axe's set. Wills, Paul, and about six other members of the troupe were sitting in chairs next to the stage as farm animals swarmed all around them.

Hammerthrow and his sons were oblivious to everything except their music. They all had stringy long hair, complete arm sleeves of tattoos, and wore various combinations of armor and leather. They also were beating, strumming, and blowing their instruments as loud as they could: whether they were trying to rock out or just be heard over the din was hard to tell. Lizzy honestly couldn't recognize the song they were playing. Finally, they made the motions of a grand finish, and all five men slid across the stage on their knees towards their small audience.

"Ow," mouthed the son on Hammerthrow's immediate left, who had the misfortune of wearing shorts on the raw wooden stage.

Wills made sure the men were done performing before glancing around at the other members of the audience, and then he addressed Hammerthrow.

"I think you were at a disadvantage, Lord Hammerthrow, having to perform with all of these distractions," he half-yelled. "Yet, I'm not sure Megadeth is the right fit for an acoustic-only interpretation. But, I think your getting closer, my lord! Let me know when you have another idea!"

Hammerthrow and his sons looked disappointed, but they recovered quickly.

"That's OK, Master Wills, we'll be back! Thanks!" He and his sons nodded to each other and walked off the stage. Wills and the players stood up.

"Let's get the hell back to my trailer!" Wills shouted as he pushed a small pig away with his leg; it was chewing on the laces of his boot. "Miss Pet, good to see you. Follow me!" The group steered through the tide of livestock and soon walked through the village gate, where the herds thinned out quite a bit and a person could see the ground beneath his feet.

"I'm not sure if they did this for all the free fertilizer that's currently piling up on their streets, or they didn't think it through," Wills commented, "but Antioch is going to stink for weeks after this."

"Does anyone know what song Hammerthrow was playing?" Justin asked.

"He said something about 'Last Rites?'" a percussionist named Daniel offered. "He said the intro part was by Bach, which is why he thought it might work."

"Hmm," was all Wills said. The other players swapped stories about Hammerthrow's previous attempts that season, including selections from Anthrax and Metal Church.

"Why not Metallica?" Lizzy asked. "They did the *S&M* album."

"We did that last year," Justin explained. "A whole suite of their songs. They wanted something different this year, but so far no other metal bands have been as...versitile." Justin frowned. "But, as long as they come to us to perform—and they do—we will always listen. Hammerthrow was one of the first barons to actually pay us for a performance, so we try to accommodate him. I just hope we find something that works soon."

Lizzy stopped in her tracks; the group stepped around her. "He's a baron? So why did Master Wills call him 'Lord Hammerthrow'?"

"His true SCAdian name is Marco Raúl Cande Félix de Lengua de un Gato, Baron Hispania Baetica. Lord Hammerthrow Two-Axe is his stage name."

"Oh." Lizzy wasn't sure which was stranger: that a SCAdian baron had a SCAdian rock star persona, or that everyone just accepted this without a thought.

They arrived a minute later at Wills' trailer, where Sweet Bess was brushing and watering Wills' horses. Sweet Bess looked up and smiled at the group.

"I hate to tell you all this, but I could smell you coming. You all might want to wash off your shoes before tonight."

The group, almost in unison, looked down at their shoes. There was a collective groan.

"All right," Wills said, "enough of this. Pet, fetch a pail of water, please? Sweetheart, is everything ready for tonight?"

"Yes," Justin replied as Lizzy walked towards Sweet Bess, who was holding up an empty pail. "We'll put up the scenery this afternoon. Curtain is a hour after the blessing service, so everyone has time to pen up their animals and come back."

Lizzy filled the pail with water and placed it in the center of the group. They all started taking off their shoes and boots and used palmfuls of water to rub off the manure. Mumbled curses could be heard as they worked.

"Good." Wills said, as he used a long finger to dig in between the treads of his boots. "Pet, report to the stage with a guitar when the service begins. You've been here a good month now; it's time we started working you in."

Lizzy nodded as she flicked a more solid piece of dung onto the ground with her hand. "Flash act?"

"More like an opener," Wills replied. "We'll need you to run a selection of Christian songs and hymns while the audience comes in. It's a sight act—they'll be so loud, they probably won't be able to hear anything you're playing—but it's good practice. Paul has a fake book you can use. You'll probably be up there about twenty minutes. Think you can do that?"

"Yes, Master Wills."

"Good," Wills replied, as he wiped his hands on the grass and pulled his boots back on. "Did Jonah say he would perform tonight?"

"Yes, Master Wills."

"Excellent—he actually suits Nicodemus quite well. Bring him with you."

"Yes, sir." She finished cleaning off her sneakers and slipped them back on.

Wills wasn't kidding that no one would notice her playing—she was strictly background music to the people that night as they chatted and laughed and found seats. She could have stood the whole time playing scales, and no one would have been the wiser. If she were to be honest with herself, it was a little disappointing—this was her first performance with the troupe, and the audience was cold.

Finally, Bill whispered to her to play her last song—the curtain was about to go up. Deciding the hell with it, Lizzy started playing and singing "Beautiful Scandalous Night" by The Choir, which Lizzy had never heard of until a couple of years prior when there was a conference at Headquarters for chaplains and musicians. She was drawn to it immediately, maybe because it wasn't overly preachy, and it was very popular during Sunday services at Ruth. By the time she finished the song, she realized that the audience had quieted down and was listening to her; they clapped when the song was over. She bowed and made her way off-stage.

"Well," Bill said as she approached. "You got their attention. Don't be surprised if their music director tracks you down and has you transcribe it."

"It is pretty," Lizzy agreed, grinning.

Slowly, very slowly, Lizzy was incorporated into the troupe that season. She continued the sight act as the mostly-ignored guitar player, but towards the end she found the courage to start interacting with the audience and engaging them in some sing-along activities. She learned a ton of songs that summer—mostly songs from the Medieval period, but also some folk music and all of the known verses to the SCAdian "Happy Birthday" song.

For each SCA event and festival they performed, the bill was pretty much the same: the musicians and street performers would canvas the event during the day, staging impromptu performances and sometimes running workshops. The main act would be scheduled in the evening, usually after feast and court but sometimes during feast. They had a repertoire of plays based on works from the Medieval and Rennessaince periods, such as *The Canterbury Tales*, *The Song of Rowland*, and *La Morte d'Arthur*, but they also could perform *Camelot* and an interesting stage rendition of *Monty Python and the Holy Grail*. It was well known within the troupe, however, that Wills itched to expand and try new things.

"We'll always do SCAdian towns," Wills explained to her one evening during dinner, "but there's so much more to theater than just what's in the SCAdian timeframe. Besides, folks will get tired of the same old stuff eventually, and we'll need to be flexible as other troupes come up."

"Like who?" Lizzy asked.

"Well, there's King's Men—their circuit is mostly the West Kingdom and the Badlands. They're a mud show compared to us, though I admit the last time I saw them was two years ago; they've probably made some improvements since then.

"Then there's Raven Moonwitch—I knew her for years before the demons came—her group is strictly folk and filk music. We'll probably run into her before long.

"And, of course, there're lots of mundane companies out there: the New Globe, the Broadway Spotlight Company, Carpe Diem. I'm just waiting for someone to rig up a way to show movies again, and then we'll really have to hustle." Wills paused to take a sip of lager.

"What do you want to do?" Lizzy asked.

Wills grinned. "Whatever is out there. If we can find it, we can do it. If there's one thing I *don't* miss about life before Infusion, it's paying royalties. As to what we're *going* to do—we'll start working on that during the off-season at Brigadoon."

"Brigadoon?"

"Home—where we reside when we're not travelling."

"But...Murray said it was called Shangri-La."

"Brigadoon, Shangri-La, Nysa, Avalon—it has many names. Since only me and my people live there, we've never seen a reason to give it a permanent name. Besides, we like our home to have a little mystique."

"Unless Kevin Costner shows up with letters," a juggler and actor named Gunther quipped. "Then we'll probably have to give it a name that sticks."

"Oh," Sweet Bess sighed. "I haven't thought of him in a while. He was scrumptous in *The Untouchables*."

"Remember *Dances with Wolves*?" François asked. "I must have seen that movie twenty times..."

"Hey, wasn't Graham Greene in that movie? Who saw *Maverick*?" a third person asked.

Wills gave Lizzy a sour look. "See what I mean?"

The Edge of Cornwall
Barony of the Brandywine
September 8th
3:28 p.m.

The final event of the official season was Paradiso in the Barony of the Brandywine.

"If it wasn't for the fact that Isabella pays us three times our standard rate," Wills grumbled as they travelled towards Cornwall, the baronial seat, "and that *everyone's* going to be there, I'd rather skip this one. That whole business with El Hajj...everyone's still wary about that." He sighed. "But after it's over, we can wash the stink off ourselves and head back to Asgard, where we have an entire winter to forget we were ever there."

"Good grief," Lizzy said. "Is it really that bad?"

"No," Wills admitted. "It's actually the closest to civilization you'll ever see. It's clean, the people are all employed and well-fed, and I understand they have enough steady money now to start an actual college that will house an academic library. It'll be the first one I've heard of since Infusion.

"Quite exciting," he finished flatly. "But it's like serving a filet mignon on a shit-covered toilet seat."

They arrived the afternoon before the Opening Processional. Bill and Paul had left a couple of days ahead of them for land grab, and Wills and Justin were both pleased with their results.

"Right in the corner pocket, between Raven and Audra Mae," Wills observed. "Well done! We won't have to be so concerened about folks wandering into our camp, and we only have to have one or two camp moms at a time."

Lizzy glanced at Paul, confused.

"Camp moms are folks that stay behind to watch the camp during big events," Paul explained. "For the most part the performers are fine, it's the civilians we'll have to watch out for, especially the kids."

They had a rather small space to work with, but considering all the people that had to squeeze into the site—hundreds, from what Lizzy could see—it was understandable. Justin was afraid that troupe members might have to pair or even triple up and share tents during the festival, but after some sketching in the dirt and some rearranging of tents they managed to get everything inside the markers with some manuvering room.

After a quick, late dinner, Lizzy and some other members of the troupe took a look around. There were more people here than Lizzy had seen in years, and the view was spectacular. People were not just walking or sitting around, but they were practicing their acts, juggling balls, and giving impromptu performances around the beginnings of campfires. She saw several belly dancers accompanied by drums and woodwind instruments, a fire-eater wowing a crowd of kids, and guitar players harmonizing on camp chairs. It was an artist's paradise.

"Isn't this great?" Paul asked Lizzy as he saw the look on her face. "As much as Wills complains about coming here, it's times like this that makes it worth the trip."

Lizzy nodded in agreement. "This must cost a fortune to run."

"Sure," Paul agreed, "but this is the biggest event in the kingdom, if not in the Known World. This is just the performer's campsite: there are two other ones to the north and to the east of Cornwall for travelling guests. There's a fee for all those sites, of course, and then folks will have to buy food, pay for shows, there's games of chance and a huge midway—all sorts of things. Believe me, the barony will turn a profit."

Later that night, it was hard to get to sleep. Between the excitement of seeing the festival open tomorrow and the noise from the neighboring camps, Lizzy couldn't help but toss and turn in her rack. She had gotten used to the peace and quiet of the country night—the clamor of this temporary city-outside-of-a-city would take some getting used to.

Lizzy too soon awoke to the sound of bagpipes droning somewhere in the distance. Fuzzy-headed, she pulled on some clothes and stumbled out into the camp. Several members of the troupe were already up and eating their breakfast.

"Good morning, lazybones," Murray called from inside the screen door of Dr. Goldberg's trailer. "You stop working for us, and suddenly you're sleepin' all day!"

Lizzy smirked and flashed him the bird. "I couldn't sleep with all that racket last night." She walked up to the screen door. "How come you're so chipper?"

He reached over to his left, and then held up a used set of foam earplugs.

She gasped. "Are there any more?"

Murray frowned seemed to think for a moment. "I'll look for you. If we don't have a spare pair here, I know we have a ton at home."

Well, that doesn't help me now, does it? she thought.

"That's OK, Murray," she said instead. "If you find some, great. If not, don't worry about it. Where's Doc this morning?"

"He's at a friend's house in town. He'll arrange for a place for us to set up the trailer, and then we'll be there for pretty much the entire festival. You won't see us much—there's at least a couple of permanent dentists here, but they aren't as good as Doc. People wait for him, unless they just can't take the pain. I don't know what folks are going to do when he isn't here anymore."

Lizzy paused. "Why wouldn't he be here anymore? Is he going somewhere?"

Murray gave her a funny look. "You don't know?"

"Know what?"

"Shit." He opened the screen door. "I thought he told you. You'd better come in."

Lizzy stepped inside. "What the fuck is going on? Is something wrong with Doc?"

Murray sighed. "I thought you knew, and it's not for me to tell you, but I don't want you to bug Doc about it, so here it is: about three months before Infusion, Doc was diagnosed with cancer. They started him on all sorts of drugs and chemo and stuff like that—the works. He was making some progress, and then the demons came. Obviously, Doc had to stop everything. He's been waiting to die ever since."

"Shit." Lizzy didn't know what else to say.

"But, you've seen him—he's fine! He says he feels good, he's not in pain, so he just takes his blood pressure every morning when he wakes up and just goes from day to day. Wills eventually convinced him to get an apprentice—that's why I'm here. I'm going to take over the practice when Doc—well, when Doc can't do it anymore."

"I'm sorry, Murray."

He blinked a few times. "Me, too. He's a really strange dude, but he's really nice to work for." Murray pulled his mouth into a thin line.

"Thanks for telling me," Lizzy said. "I won't say anything."

He nodded. "I'll look for those earplugs today, before we go."

"OK, I'll catch you later." Taking the hint, Lizzy left the trailer and went to find some breakfast.

She was shovelling some barley and beans into her mouth before the morning roster when she saw Wills and Justin approach her. She quickly swallowed her food, placed her bowl on the ground, and stood up. She made her best curtsey. Justin smiled.

"Better!" he said. "You've been practicing."

"Almost every night, after my opening act. Were you coming to see me, Master Wills, Lord Justin?"

"Yes," Wills replied. "For the processional this morning, I would like you to ride next to Justin, as his bodyguard."

Lizzy looked at Wills, then to Justin, and then back to Wills. "I'm a five foot, four inch-tall female."

"Yes," Wills acknowledged.

"You are both several inches taller than me, and you each outweigh me by at least fifty pounds."

"True."

"I can barely take care of myself."

"I doubt that," Wills replied. "But it's just for show, Pet—it's more like a color guard, really. Though, believe me, if something untoward happens, Justin can take care of himself." He smiled at Justin.

On cue, Justin straightened his gambeson and puffed out his chest; his face was quite fearsome.

Lizzy smiled. "Very scary. What would you like me to do?" she asked.

"See Raul for your costume after morning roster—the processional will start a little before noon, so there's time to alter your outfit as needed. I think the black and gold will suit you." He looked at Justin. "What do you think, dear?"

"I think so," Justin agreed. "Also, ask Raul to spray paint your basket hilt to match."

The Opening Processional was a sight and sound to behold. It began with a conglomeration of several pipe and drum bands kicking off the parade, followed by a hodgepodge of dancing groups and musical ensembles, with several peers of the realm and their entourages mixed in between. The streets were packed not only with SCAdians, but also mundanes—a lot of mundanes.

"What's with the mundanes?!" Lizzy yelled to Paul; they were still waiting their turn to join the procession, but even at the start gate the noise was off the charts.

"They think this is a Ren Faire!" Paul hollered back. "SCAdian barter, mundane barter—all spends the same!"

Finally, they were given the green light to merge into the pageantry. Raul had done a quick altering job on her new costume just a couple of hours before, and Lizzy was surprised at how well it fit. The outfit consisted of pants and a shirt that were made of a black satiny material and a black gambeson with gold trim and buttons. She had swapped out her sneakers for some black period boots that Sweet Bess managed to find last month at a local event. They were a bit big, but she was riding Trigger, so at least she didn't have to worry about her feet blistering for now.

Being on a horse for the parade was also a surprise: there were only six horses in the troupe, and they were always used to pull the wagons on road trips; no one ever rode them. But being a member of the color guard had its privileges, apparently, because she was leading the troupe on horseback along with Wills, Justin, Dr. Goldberg, Bill, and Ella, who was wearing an identical costume to Lizzy's. The rest of the troupe didn't seem to mind, however: they were having too much fun interacting with the crowd and throwing flower petals.

The main grandstand was located in the center of the town square. The VIP reviewers were standing on a raised platform about ten feet from the ground, arranged so that they could see everything and everyone could see them. Lizzy noticed that Baron Duke Red and Baroness Mistress Elspeth were there on the outskirts of the cluster, smiling and watching the parade. The king and queen of the Middle Kingdom, guessing by the height of and number of points on their crowns, was in the center of the group. Lizzy's attention, however, was caught by the two women that stood to the right of the king.

The woman to his immediate right was a beautiful lady of medium height, garbed in an orange gown that accentuated her fair skin and dark brown hair. The gown was encrusted with jewels and pearls that dazzled the eye, and the cut of the dress accentuated the woman's narrow hourglass figure. She wore a gold filagreed coronet with six points—it was obvious that this was Baroness Isabella. She smiled continuously with perfect white teeth, and waved to the members of the procession as they passed.

The woman next to her was more heavy-set compared to Isabella, but not obese—Raul would call her *Rubenesque.* She wore a magnificent white gown with dark red embroidery and seed pearl accents. Around her throat she wore a white Elizabethan ruff so wide it tilted her chin upwards; she had no choice but to constantly look down her nose at the crowd. Her dark hair had been scraped back from her face into a bun, and her severe widow's peak was even more pronounced against the glowing white paint that covered her head and neck. Her mouth was a tiny bow of red, a stark contrast against the white. Her eyes were nearly imperceptible except for the sharp emerald green of her irises.

It wasn't just an outfit: it was an entire, incredible presentation. As Lizzy looked at her, admiring the artistry and the beauty of the woman's ensemble, their eyes suddenly met.

In that one glance, Lizzy recognized that this was Christina. She had a half-fearful, half-crazed look in her gaze, like a person long trapped in a cage. She was standing ramrod-straight and still, her hands carefully crossed in front of her, outwardly showing no emotion and not reacting to the crowd, projecting a regal, aloof approach. Yet Lizzy saw through that in an instant— one look into the woman's eyes, and she saw that beneath that mask was an oppressed soul straining against the intangible bars that confined her.

Help me, Christina seemed to silently plead as their eyes momentarily locked. But Lizzy could do nothing except give her a sympathetic nod and then turn away. She felt sorry for the girl, but she was powerless to assist her. If she thought praying for her could do any good, she would have.

But instead she rode on, her mood now subdued, and she thought of the tenuousness of her own life. The parallels between the Isabella and Christina situation, and what could have been between between her and Abby, did not escape her. She knew to celebrate the freedom that she now enjoyed, and she understood that it was not guaranteed.

Right now, at this moment, she would move about freely. But at which moment from now would they find her, and *she* became the one contained?

The days at Paradiso were packed with not only the usual performances and workshops, but also competitions. There were act-offs, dance-offs, and musical duels, both scheduled and spontaneous. Bill was especially busy: he was judged the baroness' grand violin champion the year before, so he was constantly being challenged around campfires and street stages. It was all in good fun—there was no monetary compensation to being a champion, just bragging rights—but yet it was a title that all the performers strove for. Though *The Canturbury Tales* was well-received by the audience of the acting competition, the Star-Crossed Travelling Players were knocked out in the first round. For the rest of the festival, Wills muttered about needing new material.

When she wasn't assisting with the Players' performances or helping out in other ways, Lizzy was at the Children's Tent. Wills had scheduled her for three performances there, though he hadn't bothered to tell her about them until an hour before her first set.

"I forgot, Pet!" Wills exclaimed when Lizzy protested. "I have a lot going on here, you know. You'll be fine—just get out there and knock 'em dead." He turned on his heel and walked towards his trailer before she could say another word.

As it turned out, she did just fine. Raul and his apprentice Sasha threw together a hybrid jester/peasant costume for her earlier in the season for children's activities at events, but those audiences were miniscule compared to the full pavillion of kids that greeted her on that first day. There were kids of all ages, from toddlers to pre-teens, who were mostly dropped off at the tent so their parents could have some fun. Between the crying young ones and the bored older ones it was a tough crowd, but when she was introduced she dug in her heels, forced a smile on her face, and started to play.

Some songs bombed, but most of them were received well, especially the ones she had learned while counseling at summer camp all those years ago. Still, she was glad when her set was over and she could leave the squirming mob for the next poor bastard, who she saw was a magician. She sat on a bench behind the stage to catch her breath and relax for a moment before heading back to the campsite. As she sat there, a young boy with a guitar approached her.

"Hi," he said.

"Hi."

"You know what I liked about your show?"

"No."

"You didn't treat us all like babies. Some women who do these shows actually talk baby talk and sing nursery rhymes. You didn't."

"Thanks," Lizzy said. "Do you see a lot of these shows?"

"I go to pick up songs and tips—I want to be a guitar player when I grow up and travel around. There was a song you played about 'dem bones gonna rise again.' Could you teach it to me?"

Lizzy smiled at that. She was often approached by civilians to teach them a song she performed. "Sure. Do you know chords?"

She strummed the opening sequence slowly. The boy mimicked her perfectly. After a few minutes, Lizzy stopped.

"I really have to get back to the campsite—I have to be camp mom this afternoon. Do you want to come along? Would your parents mind? We could work on the song more while I wait for someone to need something."

The boy's eyes grew large. "What troupe are you with?"

"Star-Crossed Travelling Players. Heard of us?"

"Sure—I don't think I've ever seen you perform, but I've heard of you. My mom won't care, as long as I'm home for dinner prep at the inn." He paused. "Hey, do you want to come for dinner? My family runs the Coach and Four in Hamilton, which is right next door to Cornwall—it's not far from here, about a ten minute walk."

Lizzy stood up. "Let's see what's going on at the site, and I'll see if they need me tonight. C'mon." If the kid got in trouble with his mother for walking off with a strange woman to a troupe campsite, she figured that was his problem, not hers. The offer of dinner was nice, though—after a quick lesson, most people just said thank you and wandered away. She started to walk, and then stopped to look at the boy, who was probably about twelve or thirteen. "I'm sorry—what's your name?"

"Robert Bruce."

"Like the Scottish king?"

"Yup."

It turned out to be a quiet afternoon, so Lizzy and Robert Bruce swapped songs almost without interruption. The troupe was performing *Holy Grail* that night for the after-hours stage show, so she was able to go to Hamilton for a while. The boy had to leave before she could, but he gave her detailed instructions on how to get to the Coach and Four Inn.

Within fifteen minutes of walking through Cornwall and out past the gate, she arrived at a large building with a barrel attached to the side. The building was brightly lit with torch and candlelight, and it was packed with patrons eating dinner at roughly-hewn tables and benches. Lizzy stepped through the door. A buxom woman in a peasant blouse and a long skirt approached her.

"How many?" she asked.

"Actually, Robert Bruce invited me here." She paused, hoping that her arrival wasn't a surprise.

The woman smiled. "Oh, hello! He said you might be here tonight. You taught him some songs?"

"A couple."

"I figure when a performer takes the time to work with my nephew, there should be at least a good meal as payment." She held out her hand for Lizzy to shake. "Ellen Wrightson, his aunt. I co-own the Coach and Four. Come in."

She led Lizzy to a back room where her nephew and a slightly older girl were sitting around a table. He had his guitar, and the girl had a tin whistle.

"Hi!" Robert Bruce exclaimed. He pointed to the girl. "This is my cousin, Eugenia."

Lizzy raised her eyebrows as she waved. "I'm Pet. Is that your real name or your SCAdian name?" She now knew of one good thing that had come out of the fall of civilization: this girl would have been beaten up on a pre-Infusion playground on a daily basis with a name like "Eugenia."

Eugenia sighed. "Right now, it's both; it's period, so it passes. I've already told Mom that I'm changing it when I get my AoA." She brightened. "I was thinking about something cool, like 'Dame Boudicca Wrightson'—something like that."

"Very impressive," Lizzy replied, smiling to herself.

"It's chicken stew tonight, Pet." The boy jumped off his chair. "Let me get you a bowl."

After Lizzy ate she, Robert Bruce, Eugenia played some more. The cousins were both pretty good already—by the time Robert Bruce was eighteen, they could probably both perform professionally with a group. When Lizzy told them this, they both beamed. Around the time Lizzy was thinking that Garth Brooks' song "The Dance" would sound very pretty on the tin whistle, Ellen poked her head through the doorway.

"It's about 9:00 p.m.," she said. "When do you need to head back?"

"Now, thanks," Lizzy replied, standing. She waved at Robert Bruce and Eugenia, smiling. "Thanks for the jam, guys. It was fun."

"Thank you!" they replied in unison.

"You won't see me again during Paradiso," Robert Bruce told her. "Today was my day off, and I need to work for the rest of the festival. Will you be at Odin's challenge next spring?"

"I should be. Maybe I'll see you? You, too, Eugenia?"

They both nodded.

She held out her hand to Ellen, who shook it. "Thanks again for dinner."

"You're welcome!" Ellen said, smiling. "Come back again anytime."

Bill was the baroness' grand violin champion again that year. He was presented with an olive wreath during the closing ceremonies along with the other champions. A new company, The Chamberlain's Men, received the actor's crown.

"Unbelievable," Wills grumbled to the troupe as they broke down camp. "If I would have known that kabuki theater was all it would take to win the accolade, you all would have been in whiteface!" He paused to cinch down a strap. "It wasn't even that good a performance, it was just...not done before. I'm not even sure if it's period."

Justin smiled as he rubbed Wills' shoulder. "We'll stun 'em next year," he assured him. "We have all winter to work on it."

It was a long, several-day trip back to the place the Players called home. It was high up in the mountains, nestled between two gigantic crags where rich, dark loam had been deposited during a long-gone glacial age. The land stretched for miles, still scarred with the furrows of crops recently harvested. As the convoy travelled towards the center of the basin, two men approached on horseback carrying rifles at the ready. They smiled when they saw Wills and Justin at the head of the caravan.

"Hail and well met!" one of them called.

"Hail and well met!" Justin replied. "Carl, Scott! It's so good to see you." The group and the two men met in the center of the road. The men spoke with the co-managers quietly for a few minutes, and then Justin gave the signal for the convoy to start up again. The two men lead the way.

The Players' compound contained several metal buildings of various sizes. There was a large open area in the center of the compound where about fifty men and women were gathered, all appearing happy to see the troupe return. Several members of the troupe, including Paul and Bill, ran up and hugged various members of the receiving party. As Lizzy watched the joyous reunions, she detected vanilla and sandalwood in the wind.

"What happened on the road stays on the road, Miss Pet," Wills told her as he walked up; there was a slight warning in his voice. Lizzy looked over her shoulder at him and gave him a wry smile.

"I understand, Master Wills—it's none of my business. Though, I have to say that I didn't know this many people in the troupe were married. Or," she corrected herself, "married to people here." She turned back around to watch the crowd slowly disperse. "I really don't give a shit. I just hope no one brought back any surprises—I understand husbands and wives get angry when they start peeing fire."

Wills watched her for a moment, as if deciding upon something, and then he shrugged. "So far, so good. Considering the breadth and depth of your secrets, I suppose, I shouldn't be worried about you keeping theirs."

Lizzy shook her head. "Where I come from what happens in port stays in port...and let's just leave it at that."

During the first two months at Fiddler's Green, there were plenty of chores to do: canning the harvest, drying the last of the herbs, racking wine, casking beer. But as Yuletide approached the preparations for winter dwindled, and Lizzy found herself with little to do. There was still a fighter practice for a couple of hours each Wednesday, and Paul gave lessons on Tuesdays and Thursdays, but Lizzy missed the excitement and the freshness of the open road. She even started attending Dr. Goldberg's daily devotionals, just to have something new to listen to every day.

"See? I told you so," Murray said with a smirk that first morning she arrived at the trailer.

"Fuck off," she replied. "What's the Bible passage today?"

The worst part of the peace and quiet, however, was that it gave her ample time to be homesick. She missed Mary and the kids, and Joe and Anna at Ruth; she missed Bea, Mike, and Jessica at the lab. She wondered how they were, what they were doing—and if they ever thought of her. She desperately wished she could send them word that she was alive and well.

Hell, she even missed Erin. Sometimes she found herself staring into space during odd times of the day, reliving that pool party again, remembering how it felt to disintergrate someone alive. She wondered how much pain Erin herself was in, especially during those last moments. It was always a struggle to snap out of those spells, and afterwards it was a day or two or three before she could sleep well again.

They had given her a small shelter of her own, which was fortunate: sometimes when she woke up, she found herself on the floor next to her bed with a new bruise on her hip or arm. She suspected that she sometimes yelled in her sleep—she knew she cried; she would wake up drenched in tears—but either she wasn't loud enough for people to notice, or they were too polite to mention it.

Finally, during the coldest time of the season, Justin and Wills called the troupe to a meeting. They were all crowded in their living room, which was completely coated with scripts, papers, and sheet music. As Justin spoke, Lizzy pondered over the Library of Congress story Cuthbert had told her.

"I hope everyone is well rested," he began. "It's time again for our annual shopping expedition. As usual, everyone please give me their shopping lists before we leave. Pet, you'll need materials for a suit of armor, and we'll have to find a plastic armor box for you somewhere. We should also be on the lookout for a trumpet for you, so you get your embouchure back."

Lizzy only nodded in reply. *What the fuck is he talking about?*

"We'll stop by Riverton first," Wills continued, "and then whatever we can't find there we'll go to Lander. We'll do the lottery again this year, though Pet's going for sure this time." He looked at her directly. "Any objection?"

She blinked. "No?"

"Good," he replied, grinning at her. "I'll let everyone know who's going by week's end. In the meantime, let's start talking about next season..."

Three hours later, when the meeting finally broke up, Lizzy found Paul in Wills' kitchen, brewing water for tea.

"Hi, Master Paul. How's it going?"

"Good," he smiled. "Jen and I are finally used to each other again. It's always a transition, but it's always worth it. You?"

"Bored, but good." Lizzy liked Paul for several reasons, including the fact that he stayed married on the road. "Could you tell me about the shopping expedition? This afternoon was the first I had heard of it."

Paul blinked. "No one told you?"

"No."

"Oh." He looked a little baffled, as if he didn't know where to start. "Well, most of the time we can do fine with the resources we have, but sometimes we need pre-Infusion stuff, so we loot an abandoned town."

"No one's moved back?" Lizzy found that hard to believe.

"Some towns are occupied by local folk—people that were here before Infusion—but others are left empty on purpose, so people can take what they need. Folks are hired out by the kingdoms and swapped out regularly to keep intruders out. The abandoned areas are assigned to specific kingdoms, so any one area isn't overpicked. Wills is from the North Kingdom originally, so our territories are what used to be Fremont and Carbon counties in Wyoming. People tend to notice if you get greedy, so folks are conservative in what they take. Besides, it's quite a-ways from here, so you really have to want something to go and get it.

"As far as living in old towns...the buildings aren't in as good a shape as you might think. Modern houses really weren't designed to be used without power or heat, and the water and sewage systems don't work. Most SCAdians I know, at least, prefer the houses they built.

"But, you'll see all this when you get there." He paused to pour hot water into mugs.

As she watched him make tea, Lizzy thought about the homes and buildings she had seen in the Known World. They were almost always made of thick walls of adobe or stone with plenty of ventilation, and they all had at least one cooking hearth. She supposed they would be better for surviving the elements than wooden-frame constructions—less chance of fire damage, too. Then she realized Paul had said something to her.

"I'm sorry, Master Paul, I didn't hear you."

"Would you like to stay for the officer meeting? You wouldn't be able to contribute, of course, but you might be interested in how decisions are made around here. The meetings can get quite lively."

She hadn't had a "quite lively" experience in a long time. "Yes, I'd love to. Thank you."

Commune Matthew
Location Classified
Six Years after Infusion

Miller the Tree Trunk

I've been cast down into the pit of vipers; I am the guardian of the unclean and the unholy. I betrayed my country and my creed: I'm living what I deserve.

I wonder what happened to her.

I took my oath a week after I left high school. I wouldn't say I graduated, more like they decided I could have a diploma since I stayed 'till the end. From my hometown deep in the heart of the South I was transported and baptized into the Marine Corps, and I served with my brothers and sisters in every corner of God's earth. Before Infusion I walked through deserts, swam in swamps, and even ran through gunfire for my love of the Corps and my country. For eight years I rose in rank; I looked after those under my care. Then the demons came.

I was TAD in South Carolina when the first call came in. We hadn't even finished watching the breaking report on the TV when we were mobilized and shipped off to Biloxi. We were given physicals there and tested for Sensing. As it turned out, I can Sense the hellborn very well: I puked all over the nurse that shoved that demon-Infected ear in my face. They even did it again to make sure I vomited because it was demon-flesh, not because it was an ear.

Like I'd puke over an ear—I saw worse than that for breakfast at boot camp. I see worse than that every day here.

I was assigned to a mobile attachment at first, infiltrating abandoned cities and towns to scrounge for supplies. The Infused were pretty much dead by then, but there were other things that could kill you just as easily. Fires would spontaneously start—maybe a boiler would explode in a house, who knows—but entire neighborhoods would be in flames in a heartbeat, and it wasn't like there were fire departments—we had to run and hope we didn't get cornered. We knew more than once the terror a deer must feel trying to outrace a wildfire.

Once, for about two weeks, we were sent to an old nuclear power plant to give the permanent party some R&R. When the world was Infused, the rods in the power plants had to be secured so there wasn't a meltdown. Too bad for everyone that it can take up to six years for the rods to become stable enough to bury for good, so all the plants have to be manned and the rods cooled until they settled down. Those men we relieved actually had it pretty good at that plant, but they told us they were getting stir-crazy and needed a break. Not sure where they sent them, and no one said a word when they got back, but we really enjoyed just hanging out, looking at dials in a one-in-forever watch rotation and cleaning out their food stores. Now that I think about it, maybe that was our vacation, too. Maybe vacation is relative to what kind of work you're used to.

I guess after a while they decided that my company had been in the weeds long enough. We were disbanded, and I was assigned to the military police at Headquarters, District Tango for a scheduled four-year tour. If it wasn't for the demon-Infected materials there it would have been a great post, but I was constantly sick to my stomach. They had meds that helped a little, but I lost over thirty pounds in the two years I was stationed there—just didn't feel like eating. It was still better than running for our lives in unnamed streets, though, hoping we didn't run out of road.

I was on guard duty at the front gate the day Townsend and her OINC approached. She had puked in the bushes before she got to our guard shack, and she commented that I looked sick. Honestly, I didn't think much about her or anyone coming in that day: it was unusual to have a conference between the quarterly meetings, but it happened sometimes. Then that pool party got started the next evening, and all hell broke loose.

I was there: they had asked several permanent party members to attend to fill out the numbers. I don't like to swim much, and I had the mids, but I volunteered to DJ—I did that sometimes. It was a mostly white crowd, so I kept the music cracker-lite: The Beach Boys for the officers, some Chemical Brothers as people got buzzed, and Britney Spears to get folks to dance. During one of the officer songs—I recognized it from somewhere, but I didn't really know it—two females come running into the pool room with knives and start cutting people up. They were hot with demons—I almost lost my dinner when they came into the room—and I was unarmed and caught off-guard. Then I saw those metal doors slam down, and I knew we were done. We were all getting possessed, we all were going to die, and someone wanted this to happen.

I was watching the attack and trying to figure out my options when the pool began to boil. I mean, it wasn't actually boiling, but it was bubbling and churning—it was holy water. A whole damn pool of holy water—I had never seen anything like it. I mean, I had seen videos of people making it, but sweet Jesus...

I looked around the perimeter of the pool, and there was that Townsend female in coastie-blue BDUs, arm-deep in the water, and a dazed civilian woman standing next to her. Townsend had her eyes closed, concentrating, and seemed to be mouthing words—maybe a prayer? Whatever she was doing, those Infected people were being exorcised, and people were helping them out of the pool. I ran over to help, and that's when I noticed that there was one person still possessed in the pool—and she wasn't getting better. In fact, she was turning black, like she was burning to death.

Then, just like that, the boiling stopped, and everyone saw that the female in the pool was dead. A few seconds later she just crumbled apart, like ashes. As soon as that happened the metal doors came up, and tons of soldiers came in to secure the area. I found out later that the female in the pool was Townsend's OINC, Petty Officer Erin Phillips. No one else was killed, but of course there were some bad burns from the holy water.

They told me to sleep in because I stayed to help clean up, and they rescheduled me for the 1200 – 1600 watch the next day. Even as I relieved the watch I still felt stunned, like I had gotten kicked in the head. They had trapped us like rats, we were fixin' to die, and I still didn't know how to do with that. The guards that I relieved passed on that there was an investigation going on, and that no one was leaving the base until further notice; that was fine with me.

An hour later the sirens went off, and Townsend ran up to me, asking to leave. She told me they wouldn't stop with killing her OINC, that we were all in danger. I believed her; I still do. I let her go, told the other watchstander that I'd take the blame, and waited for the hammer to come down.

And come down it did: a captain's mast, a loss in rank, and a transfer to the Military Police Attachment at Commune Matthew by the end of the week. I accepted everything they gave me without complaint.

I knew I was going to a prison, though no one calls it that out loud. I was a stone when I first saw those walls topped with rows and rows of barbed wire as we went over that final horizon. I had sinned against my country and my code, and I earned my descent into hell. And so I remain to wait for the end of Infusion, which is the Tribulation, and the Final Judgment.

I'm told that it really isn't too bad here. The old-timers say the first few years were filled with riots, gang rapes, and the worst of the unspeakable. The guards would wake every morning and look to see who was killed during the night and left in the courtyard. Everyone lived in fear, wondering when they would be jumped and if they would survive. When someone screwed up in another commune, they were shipped here with no hope of return.

Then, about a year before I arrived, a new OINC was assigned to Commune Matthew. The day LT Douglas McClellon arrived at the commune he assembled the men together for an all-hands meeting. During this meeting, which was taped and I saw later during my orientation, he explained that he believed that the problems at Matthew were caused by what he called a "lack of purpose." He understood why all of the men were angry: they had nothing to do, nothing to live for.

"I think it's a crying shame," LT McClellon said on the video, "that we have some of the finest soldiers and sailors and airmen in the military stationed here, and they give you no purposeful work. Hell, they don't even ask you to help repopulate the species. I wish I could do something about that, but it's not in my power. To my knowledge, they have no plans for you, and you exist at the discretion of the government to ensure the continuation of the human race, and are to remain in reserve until further notice.

"But today, I am going to give you a purpose. I am going to give you a reason to live and to be the outstanding soldiers and sailors and airmen that I know you are. Today, you and I are going to share a secret. I would like the following personnel to come forward."

I watched the video as, one by one, he called the leaders of the five main gangs to come forward and stand before him. Once they were secured, LT McClellon dismissed the rest of the group. When the company of men started to protest, he raised his arms and shouted, "They will be safe, men! I am going to address them separately, and they will be back among you, unharmed, within the hour. You have my word." He turned and walked back towards the main building, the five men following him with their armed escorts. They disappeared inside.

There was a moment of black on the video, followed by some jumping around as the camera was turned back on and focused on the door. When I saw those five gang leaders come out of the main building, it was clear that they were different men. They had gone into that building with swaggers and winks, knowing that they were the rulers of their territories and the commune itself. Coming out, they looked like they were about to shit themselves. The commune men watching them come out were all off-camera, but I heard them gasp as the gang leaders saluted LT McClellon, each and every one of them, as they left the building. No one had saluted anyone in Matthew...but they have since that day. Now, if it has stars or bars, it gets saluted every time.

The gangs still rule here, but there is peace between them. The men are still bored and miserable, but they accept their lot. Suicides went up for a while after that day, but they eventually settled out. If folks are on the down-low, it's mostly mutual.

Three times in six years, Commune Matthew had bugged out of its location after a Red Blossom call, and each time it eventually returned to this exact same place. I don't know much about communes, but I'm pretty sure that's unusual—most of the members from other communes said that was unusual, too. There had been rumors of something located under the sand for years, but no one had known anything for sure—not until that day.

The night after I arrived here, I saw what those men saw. I cannot speak of what lies beneath us, not to anyone; not even to myself. I accept that I guard the unclean men of the commune from themselves, and I also guard the unholy, both the living and the dead. I've been wearing my humanity like a coat, quiet-like, as long as I dare here, but since that day it itches me. Everyone around me is freezing to death, but no one wears theirs. Seems to me it's time to take mine off, too: I can't wear it quietly much longer. Maybe freezing to death like that ain't that bad—no one seems to mind it.

I wasn't here before LT McClellon arrived, so I don't know how much "better" it is; I only know how much better I had it before I let Townsend go. Disgruntled is also relative to what kind of work you're used to, it turns out.

I know this, though: if I ever see Townsend again, I'll correct the mistake I made that day. When I do pray, in the darkest of night, I pray for this: that the Lord Jesus gives me my chance. If He grants it to me, God help me, I will do right.

Act Two

Chapter Five

Lizzy could see her breath rise up into the air as she helped set up for the first official event of the year. After the countless times she had done it last season, putting up tents was now a snap. When Lizzy was assigned to the advance—which was almost always—she usually managed to put up about three tents an hour. When the last tent was raised and staked, Lizzy found Master Paul to see what he wanted her to do. He waved when he saw her.

"OK, Pet, see you Saturday night for the performance."

"Huh?"

Paul looked confused. "You're from Vagabond Haven, right?"

"Yes."

"You don't know about the charter?"

She shook her head.

"It's in our charter that when we perform an event, and someone in the troupe is from that jurisdiction, we're supposed to release them until the final performance. Didn't anyone tell you?"

"No. I guess I thought people would just volunteer to be...nice?"

"Does that sound like something Wills would just allow: volunteering to be *nice?*"

"No," Pet sighed. "OK, I'll check in with Baron Duke Red—he'll probably have me mucking out the barn the whole time."

An hour later, she arrived at Red's house; it looked exactly as she remembered it. She knocked on the door, and Red himself answered. He looked surprised to see her.

"Oh, yeah, the charter," he said. "You're still with Wills?"

"Yes, Your Excellency."

He chuckled. "I really didn't think you'd last this long. So, are you here to report to me?"

"Yes, Your Excellency. Where would you like me to report?"

"Nowhere around here." He stared into the distance. "I know. Go to Cornwall and find John and Cuthbert at Isabella's place. Tell them I told you that you're to assist them throughout the event. Be their gofer, whatever." He stepped back inside the house.

"Stay out of trouble." He closed the door in her face.

Lizzy stared at the wood grain of the door. "Very well, Your Excellency, thank you. How do I get to Cornwall?" She sighed and started back to camp.

Fortunately for her, Justin was camp mom that morning. Unfortunately, he was running around the camp, looking frazzled. She called out to him to get his attention.

"Lord Justin, how do I get to Cornwall?"

He stopped and turned to face her, looking dazed. "Huh? Oh... you can't walk there, Pet. You'll have to arrange transportation." He started to leave.

"I'm sorry, my lord," she said, walking after him. "But I have no idea how to do that. Would you help me, please? Baron Duke Red wants me to go there."

He stopped again and started searching through his pockets. "Umm...go to the main gate and ask the AOD who's going to Cornwall today." He pulled out a handful of comp coins and gave them to her. "Use these to barter with. I'm having a situation right now, Pet, I'm sorry, but good luck!" He waved in her general direction as he took off towards his trailer.

She managed to hitch a ride on a donkey-drawn wagon for only four comp coins—she still had six left for food and maybe to get back, she supposed. By wagon, it took about forty-five minutes to get to the west gate of Cornwall. From there, she walked to the center of the city, where Isabella's mansion sat.

And, it was a mansion in every sense of the word. It was the first building she had seen in the Known World that looked as if it was entirely of wood construction with slate roofs and elaborate wood trim. It probably had at least ten bedrooms, and the lack of outhouses around the perimeter suggested that it was plumbed.

There was a small guard shack at the beginning of the path to the front door. Lizzy bobbed a curtsey to the guard inside.

"I'm Petunia of Vagabond Haven. I have been sent by His Excellency, Baron Duke Karl the Red von Worms, to seek out Master Cuthbert of Lewes and Sir John the Younger. He said they would be here."

The guard nodded. "They're here. Writ, please." He held out his hand.

She extracted her Writ and handed it to the guard. Wills had added a paragraph below Red's in peerese, vouching for her and assuring the reader that she may be dangerous, but that she was also was a fine, upstanding citizen who helped old ladies across the street. He read it, and then handed it back to her with a smirk.

"This way, Miss Pendragon," he said. He led her down the manicured path to the front entrance and opened the door for her. She stepped inside the front foyer, which was large and painted beige with white trim. Cuthbert and John were sitting on a bench along the wall. They stood as she approached.

"Master Cuthbert, Sir John," she said as she did her best curtsey. "I am here at His Excellency's request to assist you as needed."

Cuthbert grinned. "Red told you to get lost, didn't he?" he asked as he shook her hand. "That curtsey's much improved."

"I've been getting a lot of practice, thanks."

John took her hand and bowed over it. "How's it been going?"

"Pretty well. I got through my initial apprenticeship just fine, and I'm pretty much integrated into the troupe now. It's fun." She smiled. "Just exhausting until winter, and then you're bored out of your mind." She looked around the entry hall; they were the only ones there. "So...what are we doing?"

"We're waiting for an audience with His Lordship Driscoll Baili," Cuthbert said, "to finalize the purchase of some fresh produce for feast. We've been here for...how long now, John?"

"Two hours, now? Maybe three?"

"Yeah, and our appointment was for start of business. I hate dealing with Isabella's people." He gestured to a bench adjacent to theirs. "Might as well have a seat—we'll probably be here a while longer. You can keep us company while we grow old together."

They discussed the upcoming Star-Crossed schedule, gossip

from the barony, and Little John, who at that moment was working on his Algebra I coursework if he knew what was good for him.

It was about another hour before Baili finally entered the hall. He was a younger man, perhaps in his late twenties, and he was downright chipper. Cuthbert, John, and Lizzy stood as he approached.

"Greetings, all!" he said, beaming at the men. "John, Cuthbert, good to see you as always." He stopped short and gave Lizzy the once-over. He frowned at the dust covering her clothing; his eyes narrowed at her breeches. "And you are?"

"Petunia of Vagabond Haven, Your Lordship." She curtseyed. "I am with the Star-Crossed Travelling Players, and I am here at the behest of His Excellency Baron Duke Karl von Worms to serve my peers." She was very proud of herself; she hoped she was getting the hang of SCAdianese.

"Ah, very well. Please stay here while Cuthbert and John and I complete our transaction. My lords?" The three men disappeared into another room.

Lizzy sat back down and waited. She wished she had brought some scripts to read or something. A couple of people came and went from the entry hall, but no one that sparked any interest. She considered that this was probably was exactly what a servant's life was like in medieval times—hurry up and wait—except she would probably would have had no teeth and would have gotten knocked around every so often.

Finally, the three men came back into the room. There was the usual shaking of hands and the passing around of "my lords," and then Baili went down the hall and away from view. Cuthbert paused to make sure His Lordship was truly gone before he turned to Lizzy.

"I'm sorry that guy was such a prick," he said. "He's a very efficient manager, but he has the people skills of a piranha, especially with those who aren't peers. I have to say, though, that was quite the turn of phrase with him. Well done."

"Thanks," she replied. "I've been hanging out with Master Wills and Lord Justin—it rubs off after a while."

"So," Cuthbert looked at his companions. "Where shall we get lunch?"

John shrugged. Lizzy said, "There's a pretty good inn in Hamilton called the Coach and Four. Ever been?"

Both men shook their heads.

"It's pretty good fare, and it's right at the Cornwall border."

"OK," John replied.

"Let's go," Cuthbert said as they left the mansion and merged onto the street. Lizzy looked around.

"Didn't you bring horses?"

"No," John said. "There's a walking path between Hamilton and Caradoc—it only takes about twenty minutes. How did you get here?"

"Wagon."

"Oh, no—the main road makes a wide arc that more than doubles the travel time. We always talk about fixing it, but it's kind of what we were given, so that's what we use. We'll take the path on the way back."

"No, *you'll* take the path on the way back," Cuthbert interrupted. "I have to go with the driver to show him where to drop off the produce. It's a good idea, though, to show Pet the path, in case we do need her to do some gofer-ing, though I can't imagine why she would."

"OK," John replied.

Great, Lizzy thought sullenly. At least the conversation flowed when Cuthbert was around. Twenty minutes alone with John would probably turn into a pop quiz on heraldry, or a hearty discussion about the different makes and models of royal crowns...

The Coach and Four Inn was busy but not packed. Ellen Wrightson was seating people at the front door.

"Hi!" She smiled when she saw Lizzy. "It's Pet, right?"

"Yes, my lady," Lizzy replied, surprised. "Good memory!"

"It helps when you're in the hospitality industry to be good with names." She looked at the two men. "Are they musicians, too?"

"No, this is Sir John the Younger and Master Cuthbert of Lewes, both of Vagabond Haven," Lizzy said as the men bowed. "This is Ellen Wrightson, owner of the Coach and Four."

"Are you still with the Players?" Ellen asked her.

"Yes—I'm fulfilling my baronial obligation to serve during Odin's Challenge. We're here for lunch."

"No problem—right this way." She led them to a table with

four stocky chairs. "We're serving turkey pie and turnips, with a pale ale."

"Sounds good," Cuthbert replied as he and John sat down; Lizzy remained standing.

"Ellen, may I speak to you at the bar, please?" she asked.

"Sure." They both walked to the bar. "What's up?"

"I have six comp coins for the main performance Saturday night, but no money. Can that in any way, shape, or form buy me lunch?"

"I think we might be able to arrange something. What's playing?"

"*Doctor Faustus* by Christopher Marlowe."

"Hey, Eugenia and Robert Bruce would like that—they haven't seen it. I haven't, either. Are you in it?"

"No. I'm an understudy; I'm not ready for prime time yet."

"Six passes, did you say?"

Lizzy nodded.

"We'll ask my brother-in-law, Max, and maybe a friend of Eugenia's to come along, as well. Tell you what: one comp coin, one meal; we'll start a tab for you here. Between Odin's Challenge and Paradiso, we'll be squared up in no time. If you want extra, we can arrange for more music lessons or something. Sound good?"

"Yes, thank you," Lizzy said with a smile. "Road food gets old after a while, and I like Eugenia and Robert Bruce."

"You know," Ellen said with an amused grin. "Melinda may have something to say to you on Saturday. After you left, he told her that you took him to the troupe camp for the afternoon, and now he wants to be a travelling musician—it's all he ever talks about."

"Do you think she would like me to try and talk him out of it?"

"Probably, but I think he'll drop the idea eventually." She looked towards the front door. "Customers." She took a scrap of paper and a pencil from underneath the bar, wrote herself a note about the promised additional five meals, and then gave it to Lizzy. She gave Ellen the coins.

"This will be fun—see you Saturday!" Ellen called as she went to seat her next guests.

Cuthbert left Lizzy and John after lunch, and the two of them started walking through Hamilton towards the back gate. John didn't say anything; he looked preoccupied about something. She was fine with that.

The back gate emptied out into a meadow with some scraggly woods behind it. John started walking towards them, and Lizzy had to hustle to stay with him. When they entered the woods, John took a careful look around to make sure they were alone, and then looked at Lizzy.

"I have some questions for you," he said. He really looked agitated now.

"OK." It was plain that heraldry was not on John's agenda, but she couldn't guess what was.

He started walking again, but this time purposely slowed down so Lizzy could match his stride. "You said that you were at an all-female commune with the government."

Well. She wasn't expecting this. "Yes."

"What happened to the married couples—those with children already?"

"There are family communes—they're named after saints. Single-sex communes are named after books of the Bible."

"How many family communes are there?"

"I'm not sure—I know some of their names from meetings at my headquarters, but there's a lot I don't know." *Where is this going?*

He visibly swallowed; he was walking fast again. "Do you think the medical care was as good there as at your facility?"

"Probably." She stopped—she was tired of chasing after him.

"Look, I'll tell you anything you want to know," she called after him, "but can we please sit down? What is this about?"

He stopped, but he didn't turn around to look at her. He stood there for a minute, and then walked over to a boulder that was half-buried next to the path. He sat down. She walked over and sat on a smaller rock next to it. He glanced around again before speaking, and then concentrated his gaze on the path.

"My wife was pregnant when Infusion hit," he began. "We had just found out. At the time, I was a reservist with the Air National Guard. We were mobilized, and for the first two days we just hung out at the base, waiting for orders. Finally, our CO called us in and told us that we were evacuating. Families would be taken to one location, single members to another."

"Yeah, that sounds familiar." Lizzy remembered Patton Air Force Base, and the warehouse full of telephones they used to locate family or friends. Mary, a friend from high school, was the only one who answered her phone.

"But, our CO told us that it was our choice—he wasn't going to order someone to go if they didn't want to. He said that the government was about to fall, anyway, so he figured that what his command said wouldn't matter much before long." He paused.

"Regina hated the military. I was in before I met her, and she made it clear that she expected me to get out at the end of my last enlistment." He smiled bitterly. "I had two months to go."

That sounds familiar, too... She was supposed to be on terminal leave when Infusion occurred, but they had extended her time in service so she would finish her last patrol.

"So I went home. When the demon mobs came across Ohio's borders, we went to Baron Red's house. When they got too close for comfort there, we came here. She died a few months later in childbirth." He paused again, long enough that Lizzy wondered if that was the end of it. But John spoke again.

"There are roads we don't use, we don't go anywhere near them, because it's understood that those are the government's roads. Sometimes, though, you'll see an unfamiliar vehicle going past, using our highways—I'm guessing it's them. When I see those vehicles, I wonder how it would have been if I had insisted that we went with the military, even though Regina would have hated it. It's obvious that the government has more resources than we do, but how much better was anyone's guess.

"Then you told me about your commune, and how much better the facilities are there." He took a deep breath. "I don't think I made the right choice. I should have made her go."

Lizzy nodded. They sat in silence for a few moments while she considered her answer. It was her turn to look around to make sure no one was listening.

"There are a lot of problems at the family communes," she began. She glanced over at John. He was watching her with glistening, bloodshot eyes; there was a haunted look about him.

"Commands vary, of course," she continued, looking away, "but it's pretty much like living on a military base: all the families live in close neighborhoods, the kids attend the same schools, that kind of thing. They regularly take the military members on work assignments—I'm not sure to do what, exactly—but they can be gone for weeks at a time, so it's like going on patrol or TAD somewhere." She looked over at John again. He was still listening, still watching her.

"For those couples that enjoyed the military life to begin with," she continued, "they seem to do fairly well. For families, though, that were already having marital problems, or the spouse wasn't too hot on the military lifestyle to begin with, it can get pretty awful. Living in an isolated commune with nowhere to go tends to exacerbate issues, puts families in pressure cookers. If couples want to separate—and there were a lot that did, especially in the beginning—it's a very difficult process, because there really isn't anywhere else to go.

"I don't know why Regina didn't like the military life—as a married member, I wasn't a big fan, either, towards the end. But if she had gone to the communes, I don't think there was anything there that would have changed her mind, and she probably would have been miserable—you and Little John, too." She paused.

"For what it's worth, I'm sorry about your wife," she finished. She and John sat in silence for a few moments, not looking at each other.

"Thank you," he finally said, looking at the trees. "She didn't like the...unpredictability...of the military. I'd be shipped off somewhere, and sometimes she didn't know where I was, and that would drive her crazy, especially with Johnny being so young." He stood up; Lizzy stood up, too. They started walking again, but at a much slower pace than before, almost ambling. "She would tell me that she had her fill of being a single mother, and that Johnny deserved a father."

"Little John's not your biological son, then?" she asked gently.

"No...his biological father was a piece of shit—he was totally out of the picture by the time I arrived. Johnny's my son in every way that matters. He thinks that way, too." He looked at Lizzy for her reaction.

"You guys look very good together," she said, smiling.

He gave her a shadow of a smile in return. "He and I have been through a lot together. He's been very good for me, especially after Regina died.

"So," he asked in a calmer voice, "you were married?"

My turn, I guess, she thought. "Yes, for about a year. His name was Brydan, and he was in the Coast Guard, too. He was stationed in Virginia; I was in Rhode Island."

"Ouch," he replied. "Alternating patrols?"

"Of course—maybe three weeks ashore overlap at a time. We would bank leave."

"What happened to him?"

Her heart grew heavy in her chest, as it always did when she thought about the days immediately after Infusion. "I never found out. I was underway at the time, and I was told on our way back up to Patton that he had disappeared during his 72's—he had just finished his last patrol. His next duty station was ashore; I was supposed to get out. Since I never heard anything else about him, I've accepted that he died during Infusion."

"I'm sorry," he said. To Lizzy's surprise, he *did* look empathetic—it wasn't just lip service. Maybe this guy was more than just a walking SCA encyclopedia after all.

"Thanks." She saw the woods clearing ahead. "So, what's next?"

He thought for a moment as they walked. "The squires are working on repairing armor and weapons for tomorrow's tournament by now. Would you like to help?"

"Sure."

She ended up staying at the tournament fields for the next three days, only returning to the troupe camp to catch a meal and sleep. Seeing medieval combat like this was new to Lizzy: there were combat tournaments at many of the events she attended last season, but she was always too busy with the troupe to sit and watch them. There were a lot of heavy-weapons fighters in attendance at this event, as well as several fencers and SCAdians who threw knives and other sharp objects. She was told that most events also had equestrian competitions, but Odin's Challenge was too early in the season—a lot of people were using their horses for spring planting.

The kick-off of Odin's Challenge was fun to watch. The king and queen of the New Middle Kingdom were there, dressed in elaborate Viking attire, with Baron Red and Mistress Elspeth attending them. The opening ceremony began with a grand procession around the fighting fields, with subjects bowing or curtseying as they walked past. The king then called all of his subjects to his dais in front of the heavy-list field, where he gave a short talk about defending the realm and the honor and glory that can be acquired in battle. The queen gave a brief prayer for the safety of the fighters, which everyone at least bowed their heads to, and then the marshals took their respective places and began the first rounds of tournament.

Lizzy was also impressed by the rounds of salutes that each fighter made at the beginning of their bouts. Before each confrontation, the marshals instructed the fighters to first salute the king and queen, and then salute their opponent. For the very first round of an event, the marshal also instructed the fighters to salute "the one who inspires your deeds this day." She was a fan of military ceremony and custom, and this was a nice civilian equivalent. Plus, it was sweet to see the inspiring younger women giggle and blush.

She was very busy during the tournament. She rarely saw John and almost never saw Cuthbert; Little John waved a couple of times as he passed by with his group of friends. She helped fix equipment and carried water for the fighters, but she mostly assisted the Mistress of the Lists, a quiet woman named Baroness Morgan of Aquitaine.

"I'm a court baroness," she explained when John introduced them and Lizzy looked confused. Morgan looked at John. "She doesn't know?"

"She's new," John explained. He turned to Lizzy. "She was granted her title before Infusion, so Baroness Morgan is allowed to keep it. Kings and queens are forbidden to make them now."

Overall it was a very nice experience, except for the half-hour or so Friday evening when Tex plopped down next to her at the water station and started talking her ear off about Beretta-this and M4-that. Finally, when she had enough, she turned to him and smiled.

"So, Tex. Have you asked Eloise out yet?"

He froze completely, staring at her while he turned five shades of red. He sputtered something about needing to go and left.

On Saturday afternoon she was relaxing on the ground, watching some pick-up fights, when John approached her water station. He was still in his armor, but he had removed his helmet—his hair was soaked with sweat and was sticking out in all directions. She had noticed early in the tournament that SCAdian armor was like a military uniform—guys just seemed to look naturally good in both of them. John looked...especially good in his armor.

Damn shame. She stood up and took his water mug from him to fill it.

"Thanks," he said. He took a few swallows of water before he spoke again. "Have you fought yet?"

"No."

"Why not?"

"I'm not that interested. Besides, I suck."

"What?" He grinned as he tilted his cup back again. "Caradoc fighters don't suck."

She shrugged and smiled a little. "This one does. Sir Malcolm has never come right out and said that I'm the worst fighter he's ever seen, but I'm sure I'm up there."

He gave her his mug to fill again. "Are you authorized?"

"Sure—I had a quick-and-dirty done at Barnswallow..." Too late, she realized her mistake. She closed her eyes. *Damn it. Unwanted activity in three, two, one...*

"Please go get your gear and your authorization card," he told her. "I want to see how well you fight."

No, Sir John, I'd rather not, she thought to herself. *I've been working my ass off for three days. Go fuck yourself.*

"Yes, sir," she replied. She handed the refilled mug back to John and walked to her camp. Twenty minutes later she returned, pulling her wheeled tote behind her. He had removed his gloves and was sitting on a hay bale, waiting for her. She handed him her card, and then unhooked the box lid and began unpacking her armor.

"Nice armor box!" John said, handing her back her card. "Where did you get it?"

"At the store," she replied. She threw her card in the box.

He paused as he watched her pull on her H-harness. It was a new design that she was experimenting with, giving support to her weight belt so all the weight of her leg armor didn't hang around her middle. "Which store?"

She gave him a pointed look as she threaded her belt through her harness; the legs were already attached. Then she remembered her gorget; she stopped to put that on first.

His eyes widened. "They let you go on a shopping expedition?"

She gave him a wry smile. "Is it that so hard to believe?" She buckled her belt around her waist, and then reached over and pulled out her armor for her right arm. She had made it one piece, from shoulder to forearm.

"Those trips can be very dangerous."

"As crazy as it sounds, considering I'm with a bunch of actors I'm probably the most qualified," she said as she buckled her right arm. "For one thing, I've actually fired a 9mm before." She had the armor for her left arm placed where she wanted it, but she was having trouble with the straps. She sighed in frustration. "I'm sorry, Sir John, would you give me a hand, please?"

"Sure." He walked over to her and started cinching the arm straps. He had to crouch down a little to see what he was doing while she ignored the butterflies in her stomach. She *really* needed to find someone else to have a secret crush on...

"Yeah, I guess in the Coast Guard, you did a lot of law enforcement, huh?" he asked.

"The boat did. I stayed in the hole...the engine room," she clarified. He straightened up, and Lizzy moved her arm around. "Thanks." She put on her chestpiece and tightened the straps around her torso. She put on her helmet, cinched it tight, and then put on her gauntlets. The last pieces of equipment were her shield and her rattan sword; the sword had been presented to her the day she qualified, and was only to be used for the heavy list. If the sword had lain in her armor box for the rest of her days, she would have been OK with that.

John called to a woman who was talking to Morgan. "Hey, Sally, come marshal for us, please?" He finished putting his armor back together. They both picked up their swords and shields and got into their fighting stances.

"Salute your opponent!" Sally instructed. "Lay-on!"

"You know, you didn't *suck*," John said a couple of hours later as they disassembled their gear. "You would be a lot better if you practiced."

"And, if you put monkeys in a roomful of typewriters and wait long enough, you get *Hamlet*," Lizzy replied with an oversweet smile.

That earned her a dry chuckle. "Either you went to the best high school ever, or you've had some college in the military, I'm thinking."

"Before the military, I got my BA in psychology from a college you've never heard of. Couldn't find a job, enlisted as an OCS candidate, they never picked me up, end of story." She fumbled out of her chestplate. "You?"

"I was a high school English teacher," he said as he changed into a dry shirt, "twelfth grade. In one of my undergrad practicum courses, the professor mentioned the SCA. I went to a local fighter practice, got hooked."

Well... she thought, *a high school teacher. That explains the whole spontaneous lecturing-and-questioning thing...*

John looked at the sky—it almost sundown. Squires were running around the paths, lighting torches. He turned back to Lizzy.

"I'm warning you now, I'll be asking you to spar with me or someone from the barony whenever you're in the area, so it'd be in your best interest to practice—at least a little."

"Yes, sir." She finished stuffing her armor in its box and closed the lid. She wanted take the time to clean off her gear, but she would be expected to at least help with the show prep tonight, if not also open. She promised herself she'd do it later.

"Are you guys coming to the show?" she asked.

John shook his head. "Not this time. *Doctor Faustus* is still a bit out of Johnny's league. I volunteered us to help clean up after feast."

"OK, maybe next time." She almost stuck out her hand for him to shake, but then she remembered herself and curtseyed instead. "Nice seeing you again, Sir John. Please tell Cuthbert and Little John I said hello."

He took her hand and bowed over it. "You bet. Thank you for all your help with the tournament."

"My pleasure. See you around." She turned her armor box in a circle and started walking towards the bright lights of the main tent.

Max

The play was good, and it deserved the hearty rounds of applause it received at its end. As the first house torches were lit, Robert Bruce disappeared into the crowd.

"I'm going to find Pet!" he managed to call out before he vanished.

"Great," Melinda said, irritated. "It's already more than an hour past his bedtime, and now he could be out all night." She turned to her brother-in-law. "Max, would you please find Robert Bruce and get him home, please? I have to go home and prop my feet up for a minute—my ankles are starting to swell. Ellen and I still have some prep for tomorrow—we'll be up for a while."

"Shall I stop at home and bring some mead?"

She smiled. "Oh, that would be great! Thank you!"

"Certainly," he replied. He watched his two sisters-in-law and Eugenia start walking towards Hamilton, and then he started maneuvering against the crowd towards the main stage. At one point, as he paused to scan the departing crowd, he felt a tickle on his jaw. He turned and saw Nell standing there, a flower in her hand. She had used the flower to get his attention.

"Hi," she said, stepping closer to him until her breasts were almost touching his arm. "Haven't seen you in a couple of days. You haven't forgotten about me already?" She looked very confident that he hadn't.

And, she was right about that. "No," he replied, smiling at the memory of their last encounter. "I've been very busy getting the hives ready for spring."

"Need help?" she asked, trailing her fingers down his forearm. "I'm very good with my hands, y'know."

"Oh, yes," he replied, shifting his weight. "I remember, and I will take you up on that offer later.

"*But*...right now I need to find Robert Bruce. Have you seen him?"

Nell pouted in disappointment that the game was over, but she answered the question. "No, but I saw a bunch of people by the fountain. You might try there." She pointed towards the

123

opposite end of the tent.

"Thanks." Max flashed Nell the grin he knew endeared him to all women. He also bent down and kissed Nell's neck. "I'll catch up with you later."

After Nell sauntered away, Max searched the crowd for his nephew and any other women he knew that might have seen him with Nell. While he was sure that Maria and Naomi knew he didn't date exclusively, he still tried to keep all of his girlfriends happy. After a minute, he concluded that he saw no one he was searching for and kept walking. When he was about a hundred feet from the fountain, Robert Bruce appeared out of thin air.

"Hi, Uncle Max!" he yelled. "I found Pet! Come with me!" He ran back towards the fountain; Max jogged behind him to keep up. When they reached the fountain, he heard Robert Bruce say, "This is Pet, Uncle Max!" He looked in that general direction and saw a woman sitting on the fountain's edge.

He recognized her—she was the musician that played the guitar before *Doctor Faustus*. She mostly played background music as people took their seats, but then towards the end she had led them in a couple of songs. He took a moment to look at her again before he introduced himself.

She wasn't beautiful—her long hair was non-descript, and her chin was a little too big for her face. He thought she might be a little older than he was...maybe five years or so?

Not that any of that mattered, though, because she had brown-green eyes that were the perfect shape, and they glowed in the torchlight. When he saw her smile at Robert Bruce, his heart skipped a beat. On stage she wore a loose-fitting overdress, but now she was sitting with her guitar by her side, wearing a pair of brown suede pants, a white shirt, and a green jerkin, and they fit in such a way that Max could see every curve of her body. He realized all at once that he was in trouble. He waved as he approached them.

As she saw him move towards her, he noted a subtle change in her expression, as if there was something about him that she didn't like. The glow in her eyes diminished, and she became guarded. She stood, extending her hand.

"I'm Pet," she said, smiling politely.

"Max," he replied, taking her hand. She had a firm grasp, like a man's, and she looked him in the eye as they shook hands. After a moment, she released his hand and sat back down.

For the first time in a long time, Max wasn't quite sure what to say. "So... are you coming over for drinks?"

Pet raised an eyebrow as her mouth curved a little. "I guess it depends—where is it?"

"Over at Melinda's house. Ellen and Eugenia will probably be there, too."

Pet turned to Robert Bruce. "Is that OK with you?"

"Yeah, sure! Eugenia and I have been practicing some things, maybe we could play some. When will you be there?"

"I can be there in about an hour." She turned towards Max. "Will that be too late for you?"

Max shook his head. "Melinda and Ellen are prepping, so we'll all be up a while. Robert Bruce may be in bed by then, though."

The boy scowled. "I'll try to stay up. See you in an hour, Pet! Let's go, Uncle Max."

Max gave Pet his signature grin. "We'll see you back at the house. It's right next door to the Coach and Four."

"OK, see you then." She turned, picked up her guitar, and started walking towards the troupe camp as Max allowed Robert Bruce to lead the way back to Hamilton.

Max was a little bewildered as he followed his nephew. For the first time since his crush on his sixth grade teacher, a woman that he found attractive had absolutely no interest in him whatsoever—the grin hadn't worked on her. He felt...challenged by that.

But, he had heard all about her visit last season, and that she had a running tab at the Coach and Four, so he knew she would be by from time to time. He also got the feeling that this might a woman of quality—something that was lacking in the other women he'd been with lately. He could bide his time—he would just have to win her over slowly.

When Max and Robert Bruce got back to Melinda's house, she and Ellen and Eugenia were already kneading dough for the morning's breakfast rolls. He gave them each a kiss on the cheek hello.

"So, did you see Pet?" Melinda asked her son.

"Sure did! She said she would stop in."

Melinda glared at him. "You invited her without asking me? We are *not* prepared for guests—we're up to our elbows in dough!"

"I invited her," Max interrupted with a grin. He looked at

Ellen. "You didn't tell me she was pretty."

"Robert Bruce told you she was pretty," Melinda reminded him. "And the house is still a wreck. What will she think?"

"That we're a working household, and I'm sure she's seen worse." Max helped himself to a dipperful of water. "It'll be fine. I'm going to get the mead, I'll be back soon."

"Do you still have that blueberry mead?" Ellen asked, smiling at him. "That would make a good first impression."

"I may have a bottle left—I'll check. See you in a few."

It was a quick trip to his house—it was just three structures down. As he approached his front door, though, he thought he saw a figure huddled in the doorway. He was concerned until he saw the outline of a skirt and the color of the flower that the person was carrying in her hand.

"Is *now* the time?" he heard Nell ask.

He paused to think. Well...he was a little jittery. Maybe this was just the thing to calm him down, to get his mind focused for the night ahead...

The Village of Caradoc
Barony of Vagabond Haven
Two Weeks after Odin's Challenge V
5:15 p.m.

Eloise

Oh, no... She closed her eyes. She knew he was sweet on her, but she never thought he'd actually *ask*...

"Tex," she began carefully, looking around the courtyard, "I'm sorry, but...I just don't think of you that way. It's very sweet, but..."

"It's OK," he interrupted quickly, holding a hand up to silence her. "I understand. Forget it—forget I said anything." He leapt up from the porch swing, turned on his boot heel, and almost ran towards the front gate.

Chapter Six

Lizzy

Lizzy was returning from a water run when she got the word that there was an all-troupe meeting that afternoon in the theater tent.

"Are Wills and Justin back from their secret mission?" she asked Sasha, who was sent to deliver the message to everyone.

"Late last night—they slept in this morning, and now I guess we'll see what the big deal is."

I hope so, Lizzy thought—it was weird not having Justin and Wills around. Bill and Raul did a good-enough job running things while they were gone, but it wasn't complicated—they just had to oversee a jump from Bad Ischl to Chikuzen and set up for their Baronial Birthday event.

Later, she was sitting next to Murray in the theater tent with the rest of the troupe when Wills and Justin came in from stage left.

She noticed something right away: Wills had shaved his beard and mustache at some point, because there was now only a few days' worth of stubble on his face. She waited for their news.

"Thank you all for coming!" Wills was even more exuberant on the stage than usual, if that was possible. "We'll get right to the point: we are booked for a two-week engagement, plus one week prep, at the Jersey Lily Resort next May!"

There was a good deal of gasping and happy chatter from the troupe. Lizzy turned to Murray.

"What the hell is the Jersey Lily Resort?" she muttered.

"Hell if I know," he replied.

Lizzy looked over at Dr. Goldberg, who was sitting on the other side of Murray. He was sitting ramrod straight and looked as though he had sucked on a lemon. Lizzy got Murray's attention and nodded towards Dr. Goldberg. Murray looked at the dentist, and then turned back to her and silently agreed.

He knows, and we'll ask him later.

"This is a mundane gig, of course," Wills continued when the commotion had died down, "and we'll be having several meetings to get a roster together and design costumes. In the meantime, I'm sure I don't have to tell anyone that we'll need fishnet—lots and lots of fishnet!"

Lizzy raised an eyebrow while the company laughed. *Well, that's a hint...*

After the meeting, Lizzy walked with Dr. Goldberg and Murray back to his trailer. When they all got inside, Dr. Goldberg sighed and went to the sink for a drink of water.

"You're wanting to ask me about the Jersey Lily Resort?" Dr. Goldberg asked them.

"Yes, sir," Murray replied.

He sighed again. "Let's all sit down, and I'll tell you what I know."

Dr. Goldberg sat at his desk while Murray sat on a stool and Lizzy sat on his foot locker, crossing her ankles in front of her. He took a sip of water before he began to speak.

"It was started about four years ago as a house of ill repute for a higher-class crowd." He paused. "Since then, it's had several patrons and sponsors, so it's become a large vacation destination for anyone that can pay, though I hear they still offer...services." He made a face, took another sip of water, and then looked at his apprentice.

"Sorry, Murray, but we won't be going with them; I just can't see me there. I'll make arrangements for us to set up somewhere else, and we'll catch up when it's over."

"That's fine, Doc." Murray nodded in agreement.

Lizzy wasn't sure if she liked the sound of it. "Is it that bad?"

"Oh, no—I've heard of a lot of married people going there and having a nice time. They have a lot of modern conveniences that we just don't have here, like plumbed hot showers."

"*Really!?*" She couldn't believe it—when was the last time she had an actual hot shower with water pressure and not a trickle out of a camp shower bag? "What else?"

"Electric lights in some rooms, and a full dining room with dancing after dinner. And shows, of course. During the day they have a lot of activities, too."

Now Murray looked as though he had eaten something sour. "Couldn't we stay long enough to take a shower, and *then* skip town?"

Dr. Goldberg chuckled at that. "We have some time to plan out where we're going—I'll see if we can get similar accommodations."

Crown Tournament
Petersburg
Barony of Wettin
July 15th

"Well hello, Pet!"

Lizzy heard the cheery voice of Dr. Goldberg behind her. She turned away from the backdrop she was painting and stood.

"Hi, Doc!" She smiled at him—she almost never saw him anymore, except when he had a bit part or at a meal.

"I was wondering if you would do a favor for me." He held up a large cloth sack. "The chirurgeon in town wanted me to make these analgesics for him. He's already paid, but I just don't have time to deliver them, and Murray needs to help me with some root canals. Would you be willing to take them to him?"

"Sure!" She took the sack. "I'll just check with Master Paul or Lord Justin."

"I saw Justin on my way here—he's already said OK, and he told me where to find you." He smiled. "Thank you, Pet. The chirurgeon's name is Wulfric, and here's how you find him..."

Sure enough, Wulfric's office was exactly where Dr. Goldberg said it would be. It was dark inside, but the door was opened, so she walked in. Three men and a woman were sitting in what Lizzy assumed was the waiting room. She recognized one of the men immediately.

"Hi, Sir John," she said. *Stupid heart flip.* "How's it going?"

John looked up from his chair and smiled, but it was obvious he was in pain. "Hi, Pet. Nice to see you." He was holding his right arm close to his body.

"That isn't dislocated, is it?" She looked around the room. "Is Wulfric here?"

"No, it's not dislocated—I just have a bad muscle spasm in my shoulder. And, no, Wulfric isn't here—he had an emergency on the field, so he told us all to stay put. Unfortunately, I'm supposed to be on the field in a while for a bout, and don't think he's going to be back in time. I don't want to forfeit."

"Hmm." She considered the situation; she supposed she had the time. "Are you sure that's all that's wrong—a spasm?"

"Yeah—it does this every so often." He winced.

"I can probably help with that," she said. "I've been trained. Why don't we find a patch of grass somewhere, and we'll give it a go?"

"Really?" He looked hopeful and dubious at the same time.

"Really. I'll tell you all about it, but let's go—I have some time, but not all day."

John stood and followed her out of the office; Lizzy was still carrying the sack. She felt bad for the other people in the office—she hoped Wulfric was back soon.

"So," she asked, looking around the bustling street, "where to go?"

"Probably back to the Caradoc tent—there should be plenty of room there."

"OK—I have no idea where that is. You lead."

She followed John down the main street, which eventually emptied out onto the fighting field. For once, there were more spectators than fighters on the field, though there were some pick-up matches going on the sidelines. The large crowds were scattered around, watching about a dozen bouts.

"Wow," she said, matching John's pace so she was walking next to him. He was walking slower than usual, still holding his arm. "How far along are you?"

"If I win this round, I go on to the quarterfinals."

"Wow," she said again. "I didn't know you wanted to be king."

John smiled at that. "I don't. I won't get past the quarterfinals, even with a good shoulder, but I still like to compete."

"Glory and all that?" she teased.

"Something like that."

Lizzy could see the Caradoc coat of arms painted on a tent just ahead of them. The two sides facing the field were opened, and Lizzy could see a couple of fighters milling around inside. It was a big enough tent that John could lay down inside without getting in anyone's way. The fighters grunted acknowledgements to John as he stepped in. They pretty much ignored her.

"Are there any field blankets around?" Lizzy asked John.

"There should be some behind Red's chair." He nodded to a large wooden chair in the back of the tent. Lizzy walked behind the chair and pulled out two wool blankets. She spread them out next to a tent pole, well out of the way of foot traffic.

"Can you get that shirt off by yourself, or do you need help?" she asked him.

"Nah, I can get it," he said, wiggling his left arm through his sleeve. She watched him struggle for a minute, and then she stepped forward to assist him in getting the tunic up and over his head and off the hurt arm. When his shirt was removed he paused for a second, and then turned to ease himself onto the blankets. He sighed in relief as the weight of his arm was taken off his shoulder.

Lizzy cracked her knuckles and considered how to proceed. She wished she had some oil or something, but she could work without it. She knelt down beside John.

"OK," she said, exhaling. "I'm first going to examine your back, give it a once over. Please let me know if anything hurts."

John grunted.

She realized within the first few seconds of placing her hands on him that she needed to start talking, because otherwise she was going to start overthinking the fact that she was massaging the naked torso of a man she found fairly attractive—no matter how much she wished she didn't. At that moment, she needed to concentrate; she'd ponder on how much she enjoyed the experience later.

For the next half-hour, she addressed the muscle spasm in his shoulder, as well as some secondary issues down his right arm and across his lower back. As she worked, she told him stories about life at the commune, but in a cryptic enough way that a casual listener could not glean too much information about her origins. She told him about "Doc" back where she came from, and how she had insisted that certain people be trained in deep tissue massage to help ease the symptoms of pregnancy.

"It really seemed to help, too," she said as she worked her thumb into a particularly hard knot of muscle, "especially with edema and lower back pain. I'd be surprised if folks *didn't* do it around here, it's so low tech."

John gave a grunt; it seemed all he was capable of doing as she worked. In Lizzy's experience, that meant she was doing a good job. As she kneaded and pushed, fighters came into the tent and left, but no one seemed to pay them any attention. Finally she straightened herself up, her vertebrate popping.

"OK, just lay there for a minute, and then get up slowly." She got to her feet and maneuvered herself into a nearby chair to rest for a moment.

John rotated his shoulder a little before he stood up. He looked at her and grinned, moving his arm around.

"That's better!" he declared. He tried a full arc of motion and winced, but just a little.

"Yeah," she said, noting his discomfort. "Don't push it too hard, but you should be able to finish the tournament." She reached down and picked up her sack of medicine before she got to her feet.

"I wish I could watch you fight, but I should have been back by now. Good luck!" She waved at him as she left the tent.

4:20 p.m.

She was painting the finishing touches on some leaves when Wills tromped up onto the stage.

"Your stick-jock is here." Wills sounded annoyed. "He wants to do some sparring."

Lizzy felt her jaw drop open. She couldn't believe it.

Well, that just serves me right. You're fucking welcome, Sir John...

"He's not *my* stick-jock," she retorted. "And who do I work for, anyway? Couldn't you tell him I was busy...Master Wills?" She threw in the "Master Wills" as an afterthought—she realized mid-stream she was on the verge of insubordinate.

The honorific did not placate him. His eyes narrowed. "No, Miss Pet, I could not tell him you were busy. He's the seneschal of your home barony, and if he wants to see you, that's his prerogative. You're here because I was obligated to fulfill a bargain with Baron Red—at *his* discretion. He can yank you out of here at any time, and there's nothing I can do about it." He paused, waiting for her response.

"Yes, Master Wills. I apologize, Master Wills," she said as calmly as she could, seething underneath. "Where is Sir John, please?"

"He's out behind my trailer—I told him you'd be there within fifteen minutes. Don't waste his time." With that, he stomped off the stage and into the prompt tent.

4:30 p.m.

John

Maybe fifteen minutes after Wills left him, John saw Pet in the distance, towing her armor box. As she came nearer, he could see she was furious. Probably at him.

Well, that was too damn bad. Her survival someday could rely on the proper execution of snaps and moves, and she needed to be at least adequate at them.

Sure enough, when she arrived and set down her armor box, her expression was about as friendly as a lightning storm. She bobbed a curtsey.

"Sir John," she greeted flatly. "How's the shoulder?" She turned and started opening her armor box before he could answer.

Wow... "It's a little sore, but I managed to fight through to the quarterfinals. I was defeated by Duke Mattheson of Berkenshire; he eventually won Crown."

"Vivat. Noble victory." She was putting on her armor in angry pulls and jerks. He felt like he should at least ask what was troubling her. At the very least, if this temper tantrum was about him coming to the camp to spar, he could address it.

133

He sighed. Regina had gotten this way sometimes, too, and he always felt like he was walking on eggshells around her when that happened. She was not Regina, though. And, somehow, he was a little comforted by that thought: maybe Pet was more reasonable.

"You seem angry," he began, adapting a familiar script. "Would you like to talk about it?"

"No, thank you."

So much for that idea...

But she wasn't finished talking. "It's not about you, OK?" She paused, her arm hanging in midair. Then she continued to buckle her arm. "OK, it's a little about you, Sir John, but it's nothing you did, really."

"OK," he said. He waited. A few moments later, she spoke again.

"Master Wills reminded me that my presence here is at Baron Red's discretion—that I could be called back at any time." She looked at him, holding her chestplate in her hand. "And I would just have to be OK with that." She pulled the armor over her head.

John couldn't help but be amused by this, because he had standing orders from Red to keep Pet out of the boundaries of Caradoc whenever humanly possible. Of course, she didn't know that. Still...

"Would that be so bad?" he asked her.

"I don't know. I just know I enjoy being with the troupe, travelling around." She pulled on her gauntlets. "With all due respect, Sir John, I'd just like to get this done, please. I'm supposed to help with the concert tonight."

He was not offended. "Certainly."

Throughout their early bouts, John noted that she was sloppier than she was at Odin's Challenge, though he couldn't tell if it was due to a lack of practice, her anger, or if it was just a bad day. Consistently, though, she was hitting a little too hard. Finally, he had to call her on it.

"Dial it down, Pet." he told her. "You could hurt someone, hitting like that."

Looking at her face past her helmet grill, he could see that she was dismayed. In a tournament there were severe penalties for hitting too hard, considering there were no hospitals and a severe-enough head injury could be life-threatening. A fighter could even have his card pulled permanently, if not also criminally charged.

"I'm sorry," she said. "I didn't aggravate anything, did I?"

"No." He raised his sword and shield. "Fight!"

After about an hour or so of steady improvement, John figured that she had enough.

"I think we're done for the day, Pet. Stand down."

She nodded as she began disassembling her gear. When everything was back in her armor box, she turned to him, her hands on her hips. She looked uncomfortable.

"I think..." she paused, looking down at the ground and then back up at him. "I think sometimes I just get tired of not having a say, is all."

He could appreciate that. He sidled up to her and gave her a quick side hug, not unlike ones he sometimes gave Little John. "If it helps, I understand that Baron Red has no plans for you to return to Caradoc to live anytime soon, even after your two years are up. I think he figures that you are doing the best possible service for your barony by being here with the troupe." He was pleased at how diplomatically he put that.

It worked. Pet looked up at him and smiled slightly. "Thank you. I'm sorry I was such a jerk earlier."

"I understand." He suddenly felt a twinge in his shoulder. Maybe sparring wasn't such a good idea...

Pet looked at him with concern—she had noticed his grimace. "The shoulder?"

"Yeah."

She looked around and sighed. "Sit down, and I'll take a look at it before you go."

He sat down on her armor box, and then he felt her fingers along his back, gently pressing down. As before, he simply closed his eyes and enjoyed her ministrations.

God, her hands were magic. Working on all of those pregnant women had made her an excellent masseuse. She was very professional about her work—nothing sensual or teasing—but she just seemed to know where to apply pressure and when to move on to another area. How long had it been since a woman had touched him like this?

Then, as she was massaging a muscle group in his neck, he had a realization.

He liked this.

He could *really* get used to this.

And, when he considered another woman touching him like this other than his wife, he didn't feel guilty anymore, just... interested.

It was as if a weight had been lifted from his chest, and he could breathe again for the first time in years. It was a wonderful feeling, and he was suddenly overwhelmed by all of the possibilities.

So...where to go from here?

He thought about all the women who had made passes at him or had asked him out over the years. Being the seneschal of Vagabond Haven, he did a lot of travelling, so there was almost always a woman somewhere asking him to dance at an event, or offering him her favor, or asking him for tea after a meeting...

Say...there was the chatelaine up at New Swampkeype—Rowan. She was always asking him back to her house for tea. Maybe he would take her up on that, he was due in for a visit...

His thoughts were interrupted by Pet sweeping her hands down his shoulder and back—that meant she was done.

"How's that?" she asked.

He rotated his arm.

"Never better," he replied, grinning. "Thank you."

He felt as though he could take on the world. *Oh, let the games begin!*

Paradiso Festival
The City of Cornwall
Barony of the Brandywine
September 3rd
10:15 a.m.

Lizzy

Once the troupe was settled inside their camp markers, they started the word-of-mouth that the Star-Crossed Travelling

Players were looking for extra musicians, specifically brass and woodwinds, for a three-week gig at the Jersey Lily Resort during the last three weeks in May.

"We should get some interest," Justin had told the troupe. "The crops will be well into their growing period by then, so there's a break in the hard labor, and the amenities are good at the resort. Make it clear that they won't get paid, though—they should think of it as a working vacation."

Lizzy hadn't been involved in the planning process of the Jersey Lily gig so far. She practiced her trumpet more frequently to get her chops in better working order, and she was told that she was to help audition any brass people that responded to Wills' solicitation. On the first rainy morning, Paul knocked on her tent post.

"We've got a trumpet player," he told her. "He says he knows you. Can you be at the theater tent in fifteen with some sheet music?"

"Sure." She had no idea who it could be—no one ever mentioned playing the trumpet that she could recall.

As it turned out, it was Max Wrightson. He waved to her from the stage of the small theater tent they borrowed as she came in.

"Hi!" he called to her.

She waved back she as walked up to the front row; Wills, Justin, and Paul were already seated. She sat down next to Paul.

"Very well, my lord," Wills said to Max. "Let's start with some scales. Concert B flat to start, please."

For the next few minutes, Max performed every scale asked of him to perfection. Lizzy was impressed.

"Not bad," Wills told him. He gestured for Lizzy to go up on stage. "Pet will give you some music to sight read."

Max grinned at her as she approached his chair. She smiled back as she leafed through her stack of music until she found Chet Baker's "It's You or No One." She placed it on his stand.

"Ever play it?" she asked.

He looked at the title and the first few bars. "It looks familiar, but I've never played it before."

"OK." She took a couple steps back and sat down on the stage, crossing her legs in front of her.

Max took a few moments to look at the music, and then started to play. It was rough, but very recognizable.

"What did you prepare?" Wills asked him when the song was over.

"Bach, First Suite for the Solo Cello, the Prelude," he replied. He fished his sheet music from behind hers and arranged it on the stand. He twitched his fingers on his trumpet keys, raised the mouthpiece to his lips, and began to play.

Holy shit... He was good. No—he was *great*; he must have at least studied at a university, if not played professionally at some point. When he was finished the piece, the men in the front row whispered amongst themselves for a few moments, and then Paul gestured for her to come down and join them. When she arrived, he asked for her opinion.

"What can I say? He's fantastic." The men nodded.

"Is he better than you?" Wills asked her.

She gave him a wide smile; she had to be honest. "Yes, he might be."

Wills twitched his mouth in amusement as he glanced up at Max. "Well...he doesn't have to know that. You do seem to know each other—do you think he'll fit in, short-term?"

"I think so—he's from Hamilton; I know his family. I don't get 'asshole' vibe from him—he should be OK for three weeks."

"Excellent!" Wills said in his stage voice. He stood up and addressed Max. "You've got the job. Have you had lunch yet, my lord?"

"No, Master Plantagenet."

"Please, it's Master Wills. And you shall join us."

"Thank you, Master Wills." He stood and bowed to the men.

"Miss Pet will show you where to stow your gear and where to wash up. Gentlemen?" The three men stopped to put on their jackets, and then walked out of the tent and into the rain. She walked back up onto the stage and watched Max shuffle out the sheet music on the stand.

"You never mentioned you played," she said as he handed her back her music. "That was amazing."

He smiled as he reached down to get his case off the stage. "Thanks—it feels good to get a gig again. I play in local groups to keep my chops up, but this'll be the most professional engagement I've done since Infusion." He secured his trumpet in its case and stood up. "Where are we going?" he asked, tucking his sheet music under his arm. They started walking towards the exit.

"Probably the closest, safest place is my tent—too many people walking around here. Then we'll head over to the cook tent." She and Max looked out into the rain, which was now a hard downpour, and then simultaneously at their sheet music. Lizzy pointed where they were going and started to count.

"One...two...three!"

They both bolted out of the tent and ran through the mud towards her tent. By the time they were inside her tent, their shoes and pants were soaked through with water and muck. Lizzy groaned as she looked at her sneakers.

"Great," she muttered. Fortunately, her sheet music was damp but salvageable. She looked around to verify that her rack was the driest place in the tent, and then turned to Max.

"Go ahead and put your stuff on the cot for now. I hope it stops raining before you leave."

"Me, too," he replied. He set his case and his music on her camp bed. "Ready to go?" he asked as he turned around.

She gestured towards the tent opening, and then they started towards the cook tent, the rain dripping from their clothes and faces. After so many years of living outdoors, she sometimes remembered with amusement how skittish she was before Infusion about getting wet, always grabbing umbrellas and seeking shelter at the first hint of a rain shower. Now during the warmth of summer she didn't care anymore, only changing clothes when she reached her final destination—it just seemed easier that way.

"So...where did you learn to play like that?" she asked Max through the steady pour.

"I've played the trumpet since I was a kid, though I wasn't serious about it until high school when I realized I wanted to be a professional musician. I practiced constantly, and when I graduated I struck out on my own, waiting tables and doing odd jobs until I got regular work. I was doing pretty well, playing in jazz bands and shows, until Infusion. Then I moved out here."

"College or a music school wasn't an option?"

"Nah—I never did well in school, and my parents wanted me to go into the family business, like my two older brothers—Ellen and Melinda's husbands. I think they were waiting for me to give up music, but I never did." He paused.

"It was a good thing, too… I guess…for me, because they all went to work one morning and never came home. My parents and my brothers—never heard from any of them. I had a late-night gig and had slept in that day, so I was there to pack up my sisters-in-law and their kids and get them out of there. We stumbled onto Hamilton, been here ever since."

"I'm sorry," Lizzy said quietly. They were at the door of the cook tent.

He shrugged as he stepped inside, not saying anything. He pressed his hands down through his hair and shook some of the water from his clothes; Lizzy did the same. They both quickly rinsed their hands with a canteen of water that was hanging on a tent peg and dried them on a hanging towel.

"So, you weren't SCAdian before you came here?" she asked as she pointed towards the serving line. They walked to the food tables, where there was a bean and barley casserole with ham hock, some sort of potato dish, water for drinking, and…bread pudding.

"Wow!" she exclaimed, forgetting her question for the moment. "This is a treat!" She scooped some of the pudding into her bowl along with helpings of the other fare.

"You don't have dessert much?" Max asked, amused, taking a large spoonful for himself.

She smiled in anticipation; she was actually drooling a little. "Sweet Bess makes the best bread pudding in the Known World. She only makes it every so often, though." They both looked around, and Max gestured towards the end of a bench that had room. As they settled in across from each other, Lizzy had to focus on eating her lunch first and not the pudding.

"So…not SCAdian?" she reminded him.

Max shook his head; he swallowed his bite of casserole before speaking. "We had never even heard of the SCA before we found this place. But they seemed to know what they were doing, and we all got jobs at the hydroponics fields pretty quickly, so we put down roots. You?"

Lizzy took a sip of water before she lied. "I knew a woman named Eloise from my hometown in Ohio. She invited me to come and stay at Baron Red's during the demon mobs, and then I followed them here. Then, this opportunity came for me to join

Master Wills' troupe, and I jumped on it." They both ate in silence for a few minutes.

"Are you an actual AoA lord?" she asked after she finished her potatoes.

"Sure—it's pretty easy in the Barony of the Brandywine. You wait two years, you fill out your application, you find peers from each of the orders to sign off for you, and then you give it to one of the heralds with your application fee. I got mine in the mail maybe...three weeks later? Lord Maximillian Wrightson—that's me."

"The *mail?*" Lizzy had never heard of such a thing. She had seen plenty of AoA ceremonies when they papered the house for court. They were mostly given anymore to sons and daughters between 18 and 20 years of age that had proven themselves worthy, or a half of a couple that wished to wed and one of them wasn't already a lord or lady. The ceremony itself was simple, but it was always seemed to be a fairly big deal to people—until now. "Could you *have* a ceremony?"

"Sure, but that's extra. I didn't care one way or the other, but it's good for the business, for dealing with vendors, that kind of thing."

"Oh," she replied, scooping up the last of her casserole.

"You haven't gotten yours yet?" Max asked her, taking his first bite of his bread pudding. Before she could answer, he made a *mmmph!* sound and smiled with obvious pleasure.

"Wow!" he said through his mouthful of bread pudding. "This *is* incredible! I need to get the recipe!"

"Good luck with that," she said, taking a sip of water to cleanse her palate before she partook of the ecstasy herself, "Her recipes are her closest secrets."

He took another bite, challenge flashing in his eyes. "We'll see about that."

"To answer your question: no, no AoA yet." She pushed her spoon through the crust of her dessert and secured a small portion. "Maybe after my apprenticeship, but I'm not in a hurry." She placed the spoon in her mouth, closed her eyes, and simply allowed the flavors to burst over her tongue. Sweet Bess was a *goddess...*

When she opened her eyes and looked at Max, he had the same expression on his face that he had the night they met at the

141

fountain, which was a look of attraction. This time, though, as he watched the unadulterated pleasure bloom on her face, it was attraction turned up to 11...and it smoldered.

Lizzy felt herself blush as she chuckled and smiled back at him. "Sorry," she said through her grin, "I really like this stuff."

He leaned forward and placed his chin in his hand, like he was watching a show. He was obviously amused at her reaction.

"Don't mind me," he said with a grin. "Please continue."

She rolled her eyes at that and quickly finished her dish, though she couldn't stop smiling for the rest of the meal. It was nice to be flirted with, even if was completely superficial. Player-types were a dime a dozen in the military, and she had his number the second she had laid eyes on him. He would be good for a lay, or even for fun evenings out, but that would be the end of it. He would flit from girl to girl until he knocked one of them up, and even then he may keep right on flitting.

Though, Townsend, he can only break your heart if you give it to him. He was attractive enough arm candy—maybe she could use some meaningless fun. When her bowl was empty, she wiped her mouth on her napkin and stood. He stood up, too.

"Rain's stopped," she said, looking out the door of the tent. She looked back at Max. "Shall we get your stuff, and I'll tell you what I know about the Jersey Lily details? Then I can see if I can go back to the Coach and Four for a while."

"Sounds good," Max replied, smiling at her. "This is going to be a lot of fun."

"The resort trip...or this afternoon?" Lizzy asked with smolder of her own.

He paused as he raised his eyebrows, and then a slow, wicked smile appeared. "Yes."

Max

He dropped Pet off at the Coach and Four before the dinner rush—she could catch a meal with one of her comps—and she told him that she would meet him at Melinda's house later. In the meantime, he needed to talk to Reggie at the mill about his new gig in May and start the ginger mead at his house.

142

By the time he was done with his errands, it was well after dark. Reggie told him to remind him after the New Year, but that it shouldn't be a problem to take the time off. The ginger mead, now in its primary fermentation stage, was bubbling happily in its buckets. After he changed into a pair of jeans and a pullover shirt that he knew was particularly flattering, he grabbed a bottle of chicha and headed over to his sister-in-law's house. He didn't bother to knock, but just let himself in.

To his surprise, both Ellen and Melinda were sitting around the fire with Pet and his niece and nephew, finishing off the porter they had served with the evening meal at the inn. Pet and Robert Bruce were sitting across from each other beside the flagstone, a guitar on each of their laps. Eugenia was also sitting on the floor, leaning back against a lounge chair, her tin whistle in her hand while she listened to the guitar players harmonizing together.

"Hi guys," he said to the group. "You're done prep already?"

"Hi yourself! Pet was a big help," Ellen told him, smiling and nodding towards their guest. "What did you bring us?"

"Chicha." He smiled at Pet, who stopped picking a tune long enough to smile at him and wave hello, the firelight glinting off her hair.

This is a nice scene to come home to, he thought. Max walked over to the kitchen counter and fit his bottle into the lever-operated bottle opener. "Have you ever had chicha before, Pet?"

"I don't think so," she called back. "What is it?"

He poured two glasses and walked back to the great room. "It's a kind of corn beer; it's mostly from South America. It's technically period, but the die-hards would argue that the Europeans didn't know about it until after 1500. We still serve it." He handed Pet a glass. She looked hesitantly at the yellow, opaque liquid, and then took a sip.

"It's good!" she said with pleasure, flashing him a grin. "Thank you." Pet took another sip, and then set it next to her by the fire. "What did your supervisor say?"

He took a swallow of his drink. It wasn't the best batch of chicha he had ever made, but it had a nice flavor to it. "He didn't see a problem."

He ignored the dark looks his sisters-in-law exchanged with each other. As long as he had enough beer and mead prepared before he left to last while he was gone, he honestly didn't see why they should have a problem with it. It wasn't like he was running off and *joining* Star-Crossed, for Christ's sake.

Though...wouldn't *that* be nice? Being with musicians again, seeing new places... He noticed Ellen was looking at him expectantly.

"Sorry—I didn't hear you." He flashed his patented charm grin.

She gave him a look. "I said, before I forget to tell you, the mill tax is due tomorrow."

He sighed. "OK, I'll take care of it." He glanced over at Pet, who had stopped playing and looked thoughtful.

"I never considered that anyone paid taxes," she said, scrunching her mouth slightly. "Everyone always pays us." She looked over at Ellen and Melinda. "Are they very high?"

The women exchanged a glance.

"They're reasonable," Melinda admitted, "considering the services we get: sanitation, piped water, that kind of thing. They went up a bit when they broke ground for the university last year, but once it opens that should stabilize things for a while."

Pet frowned. "Is everyone...OK with Baroness Isabella?" She glanced around the room. "Cornwall *is* the nicest place I've ever seen in the Known World, but she's always seemed a little..." She paused. "All that stuff with El Hajj..."

"Yeah," Ellen interjected quickly. "That was some bad business, but I don't think anyone was..." She paused. "Surprised by what happened, exactly...how it was handled..."

"Show her the book," Max suggested, interrupting her.

The air in the room grew heavy and silent.

"The book?" Pet asked.

Robert Bruce sighed. "She wrote a book—every household received a free copy. I'll get it," he said as he set aside his guitar. He rose and went to the stairwell. Taking the steps two at a time, the rest of the group heard the boy thump around upstairs for several moments, and then heard him clomp back down the steps. He was carrying a rather large, thin hardback volume with a cream-colored cover. He handed it to Pet. She stared at it.

"*The Story of Baroness Isabella de Castilla*," she read aloud. "A children's book?" She opened it and began to read.

"*In the Barony of the Brandywine, we always have plenty to eat. All of the people have places to live. Everyone works hard to make the barony great. But it wasn't always that way..."* She turned the page and gasped.

"What the fu—hell?" she breathed as she looked up, glancing at Robert Bruce before addressing the adults. "Who the hell is this written for—you can't show a little kid this!"

"Keep going," Max prodded, understanding her discomfort, because they all felt the same way when they first saw the book. Eugenia got a hold of the book soon after it was published, and she had nightmares for weeks after seeing that first sketched illustration of Infusion. He couldn't look at it himself without shivering a little—especially since that one man in the corner ripping the guts out of a still-screaming baby looked a lot like his dad...

"The demons came," Pet continued, *"and a lot of people died. But Baroness Isabella, who was living in the great state of Texas, knew just what to do."* She looked up again. "Seriously?"

He smiled wanly at her. It felt good to have an outsider verify that, no, it wasn't just you: this *was* really fucked up. "Keep reading."

She sighed. "OK, but I'm ready to puke, and I'm not even on page four yet." She glanced back down and turned the page.

"Baroness Isabella and her niece, Christina, got into a car and began to drive. They both trusted in the Lord to guide them to safety, like Moses and the Israelites did in the desert." Pet looked at the corresponding illustration. "Well, they certainly look pious." She read on as the story chronicled some of the trials and tribulations that occurred during their trip. Finally, after a lot of faith in divine intervention...

"The Baroness and Christina's car broke down right in front of Baron Rothbert's house!"

"Actually," Max said with a grin, "they broke down a mile from town and walked the rest of the way here—artistic license."

"Isabella and Rothbert fell in love and got married. They were very happy, and the barony grew and thrived under their rule. The End." She looked at the drawing of the couple. "Were they?"

"I think Baron Rothbert was," Ellen commented. "I think Isabella was just glad to fall into favorable circumstances: nice house, political position, all that."

Pet continued to study the drawing of the couple. "How did he die?"

"Bad spinach," Max replied. "A lot of people got sick after the water got contaminated, and a few died. Rumor was that Rothbert wasn't in good shape to begin with—high blood pressure or something."

"Wow," Pet said as she closed the book. "So, she was elected after the baron passed away?"

"Well, the elections were held right after that, and I think folks were still reeling," Melinda said. "It turned out OK, though. She kept all of Rothbert's people right where they were, so it really was like nothing had happened—business as usual."

"Until El Hajj," Eugenia said softly. "Would the baron have allowed all that to happen?"

No one answered at first.

"Hard to say," Max finally said. "Technically, the nephew should have been tried in our baronial court—I don't think that would have changed. Maybe Rothbert would have been a lot more reasonable, though—he always seemed like a fair man." He looked at his sisters-in-law, who nodded in agreement.

Max saw that Pet noticed Robert Bruce yawning, immediately followed by Eugenia. She smiled at them both.

"I should probably go," she announced to the group as she uncurled herself and stood up. She stretched and arched her back, which from Max's perspective was quite sensual, her body in silhouette against the firelight.

"Would you like me to walk you back to camp?" Max asked, his voice huskier than he meant it to sound. Pet glanced at him and grinned—it seemed she had picked up on the tenor in his voice.

"No, thanks," she said, reaching for her guitar. "I'm sure you all have an early day tomorrow." She clapped her hand on Robert Bruce's shoulder, smiled at Eugenia, and waved at Melinda and Ellen, who smiled and waved in return. She did allow Max to walk her to the door.

"Will I see you again, during the festival?" she asked him.

"Probably not—I won't be around much. I have to oversee the deliveries of extra food for the tourists, things like that."

"OK. So, if I don't see you during Odin's Challenge, I guess I'll see you in May," she said to him with a shy but alluring smile as they paused in the doorway.

He reached up and caught a stray lock of her hair that had fallen near her eye and tucked it back behind her ear; even that small amount of contact felt delicious. "I'm looking forward to it," he replied, smiling in return. "Be safe."

"You, too." She turned and stepped out into the night.

After Pet left, Ellen and Eugenia went back to their house, and Robert Bruce went to bed. Max and Melinda stayed up a bit longer, sipping one more glass of chicha and staring at the fire.

"I like Pet," Melinda said after a while as she took a sip of beer.

"I like her, too," Max replied, feeling the hairs rise on the back of his neck. When Melinda mentioned a girl to him, it was almost always an uncomfortable conversation.

She set her glass down on the flagstone. "Max," she said with some hesitation, "maybe you should leave her alone."

Excuse me? "What's that supposed to mean?"

His sister-in-law sighed. "I saw the way you two were looking at each other. I'm not trying to tell you how to run your life, but...how many girlfriends do you need?"

As many as I can have? Why did the conversation always have to go this way? "She's an adult, Melinda, and I think she likes me, too—I'm not going to dissuade her. Besides, how often do I see her—twice a year?"

"You're about to see her for three full weeks," she pointed out. She huffed out an exasperated snort. "Time restraints don't seem to matter with you; they always succumb to your charms. I just don't see where this is going, do you?"

He measured his words carefully as he drained the rest of his corn beer. "It could turn out that she's the one, and she comes back and moves here with us. You'd like the third set of hands, I think."

He thought about that for a moment. He supposed anything was possible, but a woman he permanently bunked with would have to allow more flexibility in their relationship than he thought Pet would be willing to do.

Melinda studied him evenly, and then he watched the corner of her mouth tug upwards as she finished her glass, too. "OK, I'll drop it for now. We just want you to be happy."

147

"I am," he protested gently. "And, life just got better because I'm able to play in a professional ensemble again—thank you, by the way."

She nodded in acknowledgement as she got to her feet. "You're welcome. Ellen and I know how much you miss your music—I'm reminded of that every time Robert Bruce plays." She walked over to the kitchen and placed her glass in the sink.

"Good night," she said as she walked past the fireplace and up the stairs. It was understood that he would lock up when he chose to leave—old night-owl habits die hard.

But, that night was not a night to exercise old habits—he was tired. He checked to make sure the fire was burning down safely before he set his own glass in the sink and left the house.

He considered Pet again as he walked towards his own home. He wanted her, sure—there was an understated but deep passion within her that would translate well into every debauched thing that he wanted to do with her. She would be *a lot* of fun.

Though what he *really* desired, truth be told, was Pet's life. He knew that his sisters-in-law were scared that, instead of him pulling her into their world of consumer hospitality and business, she would draw him into hers. He also considered that it wouldn't take much convincing on her part to do that.

But...he couldn't leave his family in the lurch—he was vital to their operation. Max was a grown-up with grown-up responsibilities, and until such time that he could follow his dreams again, he would make do with what he had...and he would take what he could get.

Paradiso Festival
The City of Cornwall
Barony of the Brandywine
September 10th
11:12 a.m.

<u>John</u>

John had finished currying Socks and was adding fresh hay

to his manger when he heard one of his old squire brothers, Aitor, calling his name.

"Look at you, covered in road dust!" he grinned, giving John the once-over before shaking his hand. "Just get back?"

"Yeah—renewing the trade agreement with Ghent." He looked around. "Where is everybody?"

"Last day of Paradiso," Aitor replied. "The face-offs were particularly brutal this year, so folks are watching the final competitions. Going over?"

"I have to report to Red first, but...yeah, I'll probably stop over." Wasn't he supposed to do something there with someone, anyway? Something to do with dancing...

"He's over there now, at Isabella's."

"Good to know—I'll clean up and head there, thanks! Are you going?"

"You bet—I was the AOD yesterday, so I missed the theater semi-finals. I'll be going over with Tami to see who wins."

John only knew a couple of theater companies by name. "Do you know how Star-Crossed or the Chamberlain's Men did this year?"

"Not sure. I think they both might have made it into the semi-finals this time, though."

Oh, wait... John suddenly remembered. If he got back in time from Ghent, he promised Alexia of Bristol that he would find her camp and take her to a dancing workshop. He wondered if there were any left on the schedule.

"Maybe I'll see you there," John said as he waved and walked towards his house. At the very least he could find Alexia, apologize, and then see what he could do to make amends— maybe an offer of dinner back at his house would do the trick. Little John was staying with Kit until tomorrow morning, so he'd have the house to himself.

Two hours later, he was wandering aimlessly through the performer's campsites. Alexia was nowhere to be found at Bristol's camp, but he left a message with the camp mom that he'd be back later. In the meantime, he wasn't sure what to do with himself.

What was Pet doing? Not that he wanted to spar—he didn't have any of his gear, and he was too tired for that, anyway.

149

Rather, he had realized a couple of days after Crown that he had acted like an over-entitled jerk towards her. She really did him a favor, fixing his shoulder so he could fight, and he barely said thank you; at the very least he wanted to offer his gratitude properly. Eventually, he saw the company's flags and mural-covered tents in a corner lot. He stopped a young woman and asked if she knew where Pet was.

"She's in her tent, sick," the woman replied. "It's over there, the one covered in Wild Things."

He went up to the small canvas tent and circled around it. Sure enough, it was decorated with the characters from the book *Where the Wild Things Are*, with Max in his boat sailing in and out of weeks and almost over a year and the creatures in the middle of a wild rumpus. Three of the monsters weren't familiar, though—maybe it was supposed to be Grendel, his mother, and the dragon from *Beowulf*, dancing along with the others? He'd have to ask her about it. He went back around to the tent opening and knocked on a tent post.

"Come in," she called hoarsely from inside. He pulled back the tent flap and stepped through. The windows were opened and tied back, so there was enough light coming in that he could look around. There were two foot lockers, a folding chair, a guitar case, another rectangular case—maybe for another instrument?—and a Pet-shaped lump lying on a camp cot under a blanket.

"You can tie the flap open, let more light in," he heard her say. "Who's there?"

"It's Sir John." He tied back the canvas door and walked to the cot. "I heard you weren't well."

She just didn't look unwell—she looked *awful*. Even in the dim light of the tent he could see her face was pale with dark circles under her eyes. Her hair was braided, the plait lying limp on the pillow next to her head. He sat on the chair next to her bed and took her wrist, checking her pulse; it was strong. He also pressed the back of his hand to her cheek and forehead. She was warm, but not overly so.

"No fever," he reported.

"There was one, but Doc Goldberg gave me something." She looked at him with mild amusement. "It's nice to see you, Sir John. Are you apprenticing chirurgeon now?"

"No," he said with a smile. "But, I have a lot of experience with tending sudden illnesses in the middle of the night. How long have you been ill?"

"Two days now—it's been making the rounds." She propped herself on an elbow and reached towards the tent wall. John saw that there was a crate tucked between the cot and the wall with an oil lamp, a pitcher, and a cup filled with water. She picked the cup off the makeshift table and took a sip. He noticed as the light hit the black sweatshirt she was wearing that it was slightly crusty. "One of my old company commanders told us once that when you're seasick, the first three days you think you're going to die, and after the third day you wish you would. It's been like that so far." She took another swallow of water before setting the cup down and settling her head back on her pillow, giving him her full attention. "I'm surprised to see you here."

"I was trying to catch up with a friend for dinner, but she wasn't on-site." He took a quick survey of the tent. There were no decorations, nothing more contained within the walls than what was absolutely necessary; it was very military. He also supposed it would get old quickly, taking down and putting up a multitude of mementos at every stop.

"That's too bad." She closed her eyes as she swallowed. "Please don't let me keep you. I don't want you to get sick."

"I have a few minutes, unless you'd rather be left alone."

"No—I'm bored out of my mind. I'd appreciate a few minutes of company, thank you. How have you been?"

"I just got back from Ghent. They manage to grow blackberries and strawberries better than we do, so we trade tubers with them every year."

She nodded. "We always perform at their Strawberry Festival in July. It's a nice town."

"Have you ever met their baron, de Lengua de un Gato?"

She suddenly laughed out loud, and then abruptly stopped as she erupted in a brief fit of coughing.

"Lord Hammerthrow Two-Axe?" she finally managed to say, grinning through wet eyes. "Sure—he commissions us to play metal at their baronial birthday every year with his family. This year we've been working on a suite of Blue Öyster Cult, which isn't too bad."

"Really?" He *loved* BÖC. He had a few of their earlier albums on an external hard drive, which meant he'd probably never hear them again. "What songs?" He held his breath. "'(Don't Fear) The

Reaper?'"

"Of course—with plenty of cowbell." She paused and looked at him hesitantly. "Because the only prescription..." She trailed off, seeing if he knew the punchline.

It felt like coming home. "Is more cowbell!" They grinned at each other, and then she exhaled in relief.

"*Nobody* remembers that SNL skit!" she told him with disbelief. "Except for Lord Hammerthrow and his sons." Her expression turned a little melancholy. "I miss Christopher Walken. He was the shit in *The Prophesy*."

"Yeah, he was," John agreed. "He was good in *Biloxi Blues*, too." There was a mutual, respectful moment of silence. Then his curiosity got the best of him. "What other BÖC songs are you playing?"

They talked about a lot of things, including the upcoming repertoire for the Baronial Birthday event, other bands they mutually liked, some favorite movies, and the Player's upcoming gig at the Jersey Lily Resort.

"The Jersey Lily?" he asked, surprised. "Isn't that a mundane cathouse?"

"Yeah, but they have very generous sponsors, apparently. It really *is* a resort-type place now, I'm told, just with some pay-to-play amenities."

He thought about the logistics of performing in an upscale whorehouse. Then he abstractly considered how Pet *was* a fairly attractive female.

Well, when she doesn't look like death warmed over, anyway... "What kind of costumes are you wearing?"

She smirked, her eyes filled with levity. "Raul and Sasha are just starting to design the costumes. He was talking about a combination of burlesque and steampunk with a lot of fishnet—should be interesting." She suddenly strained a little and slowly sat up.

"Well, I have to go to the head," she said, pulling away her blanket, "and you said you had to meet a lady friend." She smiled at him warmly. "Thank you." She eased her legs onto the tent floor and carefully stood up.

Showing a woman's legs in public wasn't period in the genteel sense, but there were times in the barony when women wore shorts. Baronial meetings, for example, or working at the co-op—

it happened a lot, actually. But John hadn't really paid much attention to women's anatomy until about six weeks ago, so he wasn't mentally prepared for the presentation that was Petunia of Vagabond Haven's legs walking unsteadily away from him towards a foot locker on the opposite end of the tent. They were long for her size, shapely, and muscular—perfect, if he dared to admit it to himself. The show only got better when she crouched down to open the locker and rummage inside, the gym shorts she was wearing creeping up another inch or two. He imagined those legs clad in fishnet tights and black high heels, and he smiled in approval.

"When'd you tell her you'd be back?" Pet asked him as she pulled out a pair of sweatpants.

Sweatpants? How long had they been talking? He realized all at once that it was well into evening, and the air was rapidly getting cooler. He looked around at the thin walls of the tent and made a snap decision.

"You should come home with me," he said in his best authoritative voice. "It's going to be cold tonight, and at least my house has a roof and walls, and it's warm."

The left corner of her mouth turned upwards as she eased herself to a sitting position on the foot locker and began to pull on her sweatpants.

"Thank you," she said as she worked, "but I can't in good conscious ruin your date night.

"*And,*" she interrupted quickly before he could object that it wasn't *exactly* a date, "I have a kid from the Coach and Four delivering a meal any minute now, and Murray left another dose of whatever Doc gave me earlier. If it gets too cold, I can sleep in Doc's trailer—sick people do that all the time around here." She got to her feet and tightened the drawstring on her pants. "But, really, it's a generous offer—thank you."

Show's over, he thought with some wistfulness as she tied a firm knot in the cord. But, hey, that *was* a show...

"All right," he said begrudgingly as he rose from the chair and stretched himself out. He could force the issue, but it was clear she had everything planned out with the least amount of assistance and fuss from anyone.

And...he *did* have another engagement he had promised to keep. As he walked towards the tent opening, he remembered what had brought him there in the first place.

"Hey, Pet?"

She had just lit the oil lamp next to her bed; she turned around, still kneeling on the cot. "Yes?"

"I almost forgot." He walked back towards her as she twisted herself around and sat on the edge of the cot, facing him. John crouched down next to her and looked into her eyes.

"I never thanked you properly for helping me out with my shoulder at Crown. I really appreciated it." He took her hand and kissed it. "Thank you."

She was obviously pleased with his thanks: he watched with some satisfaction as Pet smiled and blushed. "You're welcome."

He released her hand as they both got to their feet.

"I really have to go," she said, walking him to the tent flap. "Good luck tonight."

"Thanks," he replied, though he wasn't nearly as enthusiastic about dinner with Alexia as he was earlier. He thought about offering to stay a little while longer, but Pet needed to rest— Paradiso was over, and they'd be tearing down tomorrow. "What will they do with you if you're still sick tomorrow?"

"I'm already feeling well enough to manage my own tent. After that, I can ride in the back of one of the wagons if I need to." As they stepped outside, he could still see a little of her face with the light from the oil lamp from her tent and the torches that lined the path. "Thanks again for the visit."

"Feel better," he said, taking her hand and bowing over it. "I'll see you in the spring."

"You bet—safe trip home." She gently pulled her hand away and walked away towards the main courtyard.

You, too, he thought as he went the opposite direction towards Bristol's camp. About halfway there, he realized that he forgot to ask Pet about her tent murals.

Oh, well—always next year.

Chapter Seven

Branford

It was well after nightfall when I heard a tapping at my door. I put down the book I'd been reading—a very interesting novel about a Native American man possessed by the soul of General Custer—and went to see who could want my company this late at night. It could have been Jason looking for a chess game, or Katie just coming to chat—I'm the only person here who will allow her to ramble on to her satisfaction because I shall never be able to verbally interrupt her. Unless, of course, I grunted at her, but that just seems rude.

When she visits, I usually just sit and nod in approximate places while thinking about past lovers, or what Sweet Bess' bread pudding could taste like—I'll never know—or dreams deferred. Since the attack, I have discovered a new appreciation of the writers from the Harlem Renaissance: Sweet Bess and Jason have standing orders to pick up copies of works by Hughes, Cullen, or Zora Neale Hurston when they're out and about. African American poets and authors from the 1920's and 1930's are not really in the purview of SCAdians or militia towns, but sometimes I get lucky. I haven't muddled through all the ways a dream can be deferred yet, in case you were wondering, but I'm certain it's only a matter of time.

To my surprise, Wills was at my doorstep. He would sometimes come over in the evenings for a personal visit, but he always came with Justin. In fact, the only time I ever had a solitary visit from my benefactor was in the beginning, when members of the community would come and take turns nursing me back to health. I believe I went through the entire roster of members at least three times before I could manage on my own.

I just stood for a moment at the door, admiring his form and features. He was glorious when he and Gunther had picked me up, broken and barely alive, and carefully set me into his own wagon more than four years ago. Since then, he's just gotten better looking with age. I could see him being like Sean Connery someday: one of those timeless faces that could still make the public swoon even when his body betrayed him and he was sitting in his wheelchair or pushing his walker.

But, alas...I gestured for him to come inside, but not before offering my hand for him to shake. He took it in his usual, firm grasp, his long fingers folding over my twisted ones.

"Good evening, Branford," he said. "Is it too late for a visit?"

I shook my head.

After releasing my hand, Wills stepped across my threshold and into my home. As usual, Wills walked into my house like he owned the place—and, well, I suppose he did—and looked around. I kept it Spartan and tidy, but it also had homey touches, too, like the braided rug Katie gave me last Christmas and the curtains made by Jen, Paul's wife. The fire in the hearth was warm and gave the only light in the room, but it was more than enough to read by. He nodded in approval, I believe, and then turned to face me once more.

"How are you, my friend?" he asked.

I gestured to my table, where four chairs were clustered around. We each pulled back a chair, the legs scraping along the stone floor, and sat down upon them. I reached for my slate and chalk, adjusted my fingers around the nub, and wrote, *"I'm well, thank you."*

It only took a glance for him to read it. Because the bones in my right hand never healed correctly—hammers tended to cause that—my writing looked a lot like chicken scratches, but Wills never had a problem reading my handwriting: I always guessed it was because he had to read the hurried notes he made in the margins of his scripts when he directed. I had a slate and chalk for home and a manual typewriter in my office for business conversations. The typewriter was slower, because I could only use two or three fingers at a time, but then no one had to ask me to rewrite what I was saying at work.

"I'm glad to hear it," he said, smiling. "I know it's late, and I don't wish to burden you, but I need your help."

I made a face at him as I wrote, "*You're never a burden, Wills. What can I do for you?*"

He leaned back in his chair, and for the first time since I had known the man he looked uncomfortable. "This is not going to be an easy conversation for you at first, but please humor me."

I nodded, not having the foggiest idea what he wanted to talk to me about. I told him my story; he knew my secrets—well, all but one or two. What else could there be?

"It's election year and, from what I hear, Zane is the clear winner."

I pursed my lips as I closed my eyes for a moment and focused on remaining calm. So, Harrison Zane's eternal god hadn't seen fit to smite him for his evil yet. In fact, he was going to be rewarded for his secret transgressions yet again, it seemed— figures. I opened my eyes, looked at Wills, and shrugged as if to say, *c'est la vie.*

"We are going to perform at his re-election party," he informed me. "I just got word today that we won the bid."

I stared at him; this must have been some sort of sick joke. I told him as much.

"No joke," he said, though he paused for a second and rumpled his mouth in thought. "Strike that: it is a joke, but not on you. It will be on him."

"*I don't understand.*" What was he playing at?

He took my hand and squeezed it. It had been a long time since someone had done that, just held my hand in friendship—or in any other way, for that matter.

"That has to be my secret for now." He released my fingers, and they immediately grew cold from the absence of his touch.

"At the moment, I need some information," he told me. He leaned back and studied my face, giving me that signature look of his. I wonder if anyone else had figured out his tell when he was about to read a person. He had an extraordinary talent for it, and there were stories about how his abilities had gotten the troupe out of many a scrape. "When you told me about the blowout between you and Zane, you mentioned that he broke several things. I need a list, please."

I gave him a puzzled look, but I placed the chalk nub on the board and began to write. Before I was the mayor of McCaffrey's Pass, before Infusion, I was an art dealer and collector, and I had brought several of my favorite pieces with me when I relocated there a few years before the world fell. When I originally acquired my art, it was valuable. When Zane and his thugs shattered and tore and broke my collection, it was very possible that it included the final remaining examples of certain artists' works, and therefore it was priceless. As much as I grieve for my loss of my tongue, I've wept and mourned for my lost collection a thousand times more.

As I wrote my list, the only sound in the room was the tapping of my chalk against the slate. At one point, Wills stood up and walked over to stand behind me and read over my shoulder; I focused on my list. Then I sensed his body leaning a little into mine, and saw his finger point to an object about halfway down the slate.

"This," he said. He leaned over to the side of me and looked at my face. "Tell me more about that piece."

I erased the list and wrote what he had asked for as he went back to his chair and sat down. It was by no means the most valuable piece—actually, I remembered it was more an impulse buy, because it was striking—but it apparently suited Wills mysterious purposes. I remembered vividly the look of malicious glee on Zane's face when he had smashed that particular piece on the floor. I hoped he choked on its dust afterwards when it was swept away so he and his family could comfortably move into my home. When I was finished writing, I gave him the slate to review. I watched his vibrant blue eyes dart to and fro as he translated my scribbling. Then he looked up at me and smiled.

"This will do." His grin widened. "Do you think you could make a sketch of some sort? I need to know what it looked like."

I gave him a dubious look. I took the slate out of his hands, erased it completely, and wrote, "*Not until I know your plan. You need the troupe. When you tell them, I will be there.*"

He was not happy with my response, I could tell, but he seemed to accept it. "Very well—I have a little planning to do still, but the troupe will be told by next week. I'll be sure that you are in attendance." When he stood up, the chair legs screeched in protest.

"Justin and I were hoping to see you at game night tonight."

At the mention of his husband's name he broke the spell, the manipulative son of a bitch. I knew what he had been doing, of course, but I was a willing participant in his apt performance. I shrugged in response to his comment.

"I think the others would have liked to see you, too." He looked around the room again.

"You know," he said, looking back into my face, "this is not your crypt. You are not dead. You're like a turned-about spirit, that only are seen in the shadows during the day, and you seclude yourself in this makeshift tomb at night. Please tell me what I can do to help you come out into the living world."

I shook my head. If I had known him before the attack, we would have shared a mutual love for the spoken word. As I communicated to people verbally, which I did almost every waking moment as an art broker and later in public service, my words were at my command. They flowed, harmonized, danced into a construct of meaning and context that was every bit as powerful as a stage soliloquy, or as moving as a violin's song, and they could seduce... Oh, how I used my words to take what I wanted, and all gave to me freely—including Zane, for a while.

But now, that was all over. I breathed, I ate, I worked, and I slept. I dreamt of dreams deferred. I contributed to the community that sheltered me by doing Wills' financial legers, and I never turned away the visitor or two who came to my door. But the chasm left by the loss of my own art was too vast to mingle in groups, especially with improvisers as talented as the Players. I would attend Wills' meeting, but every laugh, every sentence, every nuance and turn of phrase would torture me, because I had been magnificent, too, and none of them would ever know it.

Wills frowned at my answer, but did not push me. Instead, he held out his hand. I shook it.

"I will be making a dangerous proposal at the meeting," he told me. He released my hand, and I accompanied him to the door. "You will probably object, because you do not wish to drudge up the past, or you fear for their safety, but all I would ask is that you hear me out." He opened the door, and then looked at me. "Will you do that?"

I nodded. I would have pointed out that I was in no condition to object to anything, not only physically but also in principal, since my existence relied on his good graces, but that option had been relieved of me long ago.

He smiled at me, but there was little joy in it. "I'll see you tomorrow."

I smiled back and waved as he left my home and disappeared into the night. It was only after I had closed my door that I allowed my face to fall.

Damn Wills—what the hell was he up to? Didn't I make it clear to him how dangerous Zane was? Wasn't the fact that I almost died with *my tongue cut out* enough of a deterrent to stay hell and gone from that place? I couldn't guess what he was planning, but I was fairly certain that he was going to get himself and any fool that went with him killed.

I cursed my lack of speech. Maybe I could have talked him out of it when I had my faculties, but no mere letter of flat, stationary language was going to persuade that man. I could only collapse back into my chair by the fire, weaponless and impotent to stop whatever was to come.

Fiddler's Green
October 6th
3:00 p.m.

<u>Lizzy</u>

Word was spread after lunch that there would be a special meeting immediately after the dinner hour for the entire community at the horse paddock. Lizzy was asked to help Carl and Scott clean up the area and set up the torches and warming fires—Justin had warned them that the meeting may last past nightfall. Justin and Wills' house could hold the troupe, but it was too small to hold everyone.

"This hasn't happened in a while," Scott observed as they topped off tiki torches with fluid.

"No," Carl agreed. "Not since Lauren got here, when they had to arrange her care, God rest her."

Lizzy kept quiet while she carefully screwed on lids. Unfamiliar names flew around her all the time at Avalon, and about a third of them were followed by "rest in peace," "God rest his soul," or some such sentiment. This must have been quite the hopping place when picking up injured and dying people along the road was almost the norm.

On cue, immediately following the dinner hour, folks started to seep out of houses and public areas and flowed towards the farming area. Lizzy watched them arrive as she sat on the paddock fence. It was a cold evening, and everyone's faces were distorted by the steam of their exhalations as they entered the corral. No one seemed overly concerned about the meeting, but was content to wait and see what Justin and Wills wanted to talk about.

Once everyone seemed to be present, the two leaders stood on wooden crates so everyone could see their faces. Lizzy spun around the wooden fence crosspiece that she was sitting on so she faced the proper direction. Wills spoke first.

"Thank you, one and all, for coming tonight. This meeting will be in two parts: I have a general announcement for the community, and then there will be a second meeting for the troupe members and their spouses at our house."

A slight murmur of surprise stirred within the crowd. Troupe meetings and rehearsals were common; a troupe meeting with spouses in attendance had never happened before, at least not since Lizzy arrived. Not because troupe meetings were a big secret, but there just wasn't much of a point of them being there. It would be like taking your spouse to work and having them sit in your cubicle all day, not doing anything.

"For all of you," Wills shouted over the crowd. "We have booked a special gig during the second week of November this year—we shall be doing something very different. The town of McCaffrey's Pass is having their mayoral election, and they have requested a short week of festivities. I offered several workshops for the youth of the community and a small production on Tuesday night of their choosing, and they have accepted. Considering this is not on our usual off-season roster, I wanted to give everyone ample time to rearrange their schedules and make arrangements. Those who are going shall be leaving November 2nd, and we should be back by the 16th. More details will be available when I know who is coming with.

"That's really all for now." Wills glanced at Justin, who shrugged in agreement. "Thank you!"

That was a lot to do about nothing, Lizzy thought as the crowd dispersed and she climbed down off the fence. Early November wasn't a make-or-break time of year to gather or process the harvest, though folks might have to double up on shifts a bit to get the casking, canning, and woodcutting done. What was surprising was that they had the outdoor meeting at all—it was completely lacking in meaningful information. Why not just post something, or spread the word? She wondered what was in store at Justin and Wills' house.

By the time she arrived there were no more chairs available, so Lizzy sat on the floor, her back against a piece of the sofa. From there, she had a good view of the two chairs by the fireplace in the great room; the two co-managers always sat on them when they ran their meetings. She chatted with Ella and François—who both managed to get the sofa—about the harvest, what was left to be done, and if they thought Shangri-La would have enough to barter with this winter. Eventually, Justin and Wills came in from the kitchen. Nothing seemed out of the ordinary as they took their seats and called the meeting to order.

"Sorry to be so dramatic, folks," Justin began. "But considering this is such a new direction for us, and the circumstances are a bit unusual, we had to do it this way. Let's get to it: who here has heard of Augusto Boal?"

Silence ensued.

"Right," he sighed as he glanced at Wills; he took a breath. "Boal was a Brazilian actor, director, and writer who believed that theater was a tool that could be used for the common good of the people. He believed that traditional theater—with performers separated from the audience by the fourth wall—was in itself oppressive. Rather, he promoted theater with active audience participation to work out problems, address social issues, even create legislation; he called this movement the Theater of the Oppressed.

"The problem-solving piece, which he called Forum Theater, is what we are doing with the youth of the town, along with some social awareness and team building activities. We'll be working with them, at first, to re-enact problems and issues the kids might have to improvise some possible solutions through acting, and then we will present one of our own, which will be performed for the parents and the public that Friday evening in a grand finale. It should be quite the crowd-pleaser, because the issue will involve how parents and children can communicate better with each other."

OK, Lizzy thought—she never realized Justin was so tree-huggy. This was a new direction for the troupe, sure, but she still didn't see the justification for tonight's build-up. Then Wills addressed the group.

"This is the dangerous part," he said, looking around the room. "Branford, our bookkeeper, was the mayor of McCaffrey's Pass before his arrival here at Brigadoon. The current and future mayor was his protégée, and the man who ultimately betrayed him. He is the reason Branford is here."

A hue and cry, mostly from the spouses, swept through the room. Wills and Justin let the disruption linger for a minute while they spoke amongst themselves, and then Justin called for order.

"We will be asking for volunteers," he told them when the group had calmed down, "but not tonight. We want everyone to think about it for a day or two before making a decision. But, before you do make a choice, we'd like you to consider some things." He turned to his husband and gestured for him to continue. Wills stood up.

"We've lived a pretty good life here," he began. "We want for nothing, not just because we work hard, but because we have had opportunities to succeed. I have always been so proud of you all that you have been willing to share our largesse with the people we have rescued, and have welcomed them into our community when they've wished to stay.

"But the elements that brought them here—traumatized, battered, and cast aside—are still out there. Just because we don't stumble upon the victims of these elements anymore doesn't mean they aren't happening every day. Even as I speak to you right now, people are suffering and dying under persecution, and you know it." He paused to let that sink in for a moment.

"Justin and I believe that we have a moral obligation to improve the world around us, for all of us, and I believe you all do, as well. Boal's movement was very successful before Infusion; this new world needs it more than ever." He noticed Raul had his hand raised; he pointed at him. "Yes?"

"Why this place?" Raul asked. "We all know what happened to Branford. We shouldn't be anywhere near that town."

"That something like that happened in McCaffrey's Pass is *exactly* why we should go there," Wills replied. "Besides, Forum Theater can be rather subtle in execution. They won't suspect

163

what's coming, they won't know what hit them, but the results will be well known, believe me.

"There will also be an added meaning to the performance, something that will only be known to the mayor." Wills grinned an ugly, reptilian smile. "But, that's just for fun."

"The message of the first performance piece," Justin cut in, "to work out differences amicably between those in authority and those who are not, reflects those prior events. There will also be a visual cue that should resonate with the bastard. It's not justice," he said as he and Wills shared a look, "but it's a reckoning. For that moment, he will be reminded of what he did, and through our actions he will see that, if the townspeople knew about Branford, they would not approve."

"And, he'll have no choice but to eat that," Wills finished.

No one said anything for a few long moments; it was a lot to take in. Finally, Wills broke the silence.

"Please let us know within the next three days if you're in—we need at least five Players to pull this off, Justin and I included. Zane requested *The Iliad*, specifically the triumph of Achilles...*the asshole.*" He growled out that last sentiment; Lizzy didn't know *The Iliad* well enough to know why the mayor's choice was so objectionable.

"This gig is above and beyond your regular duties," he acknowledged, "so know that there will be no retribution or ill will towards those who decline—we recognize that you all have done more than your share.

"You all have a lot to discuss—you're dismissed." At that, Wills took Justin's hand, and they both retired to the kitchen as the group dispersed, the troupe and the spouses muttering amongst themselves. Lizzy didn't say a word to anyone, but followed the crowd outside to go to her shelter to contemplate the men's words.

A day later, she returned to the managers' house. She heard piano music coming from inside, and she recognized it as the piece from the Tom and Jerry cartoon when Tom gave a formal piano concert; she smiled at the memory. She visualized the cartoon in her mind as she knocked on the door. The music stopped just before the place when Jerry would have slammed the piano lid on Tom's fingers. There was the sound of approaching footsteps, and then Justin swung open the door. He looked more than a little surprised to see her.

"Come in, Pet, please." He gestured her inside. When they were both seated in his great room, Justin asked, "Are you here about the McCaffrey's Pass job?"

"Yes, Lord Justin," she replied. "I'm here to volunteer."

He heaved a slightly exasperated sigh. "We can suspend the formalities—Justin is fine. To be honest, I don't like the title, anyway. I put up with it because Wills is SCAdian, but in private...please call me Justin, OK?"

"Sure."

"Thank you." He leaned back a little and relaxed. "So, why do you want to go with us?"

She leaned back herself before she gave her answer. "Wills was right—oppression is everywhere. I'm not sure if I believe that this Forum Theater is going to do what you say it's going to do, but you two seem to believe it will, so that's good enough for me.

"Plus, I admit that I feel like I haven't done my share here—I wasn't here when you were taking in the refugees. Maybe this is my way of doing my part."

"Maybe this isn't your fight in the first place," Justin countered. "You're just here on a layover, Pet. You have no obligation here except as an apprentice."

Ouch. That hurt, and made her a little irritated. "The only thing necessary for the triumph of evil is that good men do nothing; Edmund Burke said that.

"And," she pressed on, "do you really think I'm just going to sit around here and do nothing while you and Master Wills and whoever else is crazy enough to sign on runs into harm's way? I don't know much about the situation, but I'll be damned if I'm going to quietly stay home; screw you."

Justin looked mildly entertained at her rant, like she was an angry, yapping Chihuahua. "How do *you* know about Edmund Burke?"

"I wasn't hatched fully grown in the Coast Guard," she said, rolling her eyes. "My parents had that quote on a plaque in the living room—it stuck." Then she stopped herself short.

Damn it—she had mentioned the Guard. Apparently, Wills wasn't the only one in their household that could extract information. She looked at Justin's face and, yes, he looked pleased with himself—he knew he had gotten her to admit something. She drew her mouth into a thin line and continued like it hadn't happened. "And, I have two summers-worth of experience in facilitating youth in cooperative group activities and low ropes. Is that worth something to you?"

He raised his eyebrows slightly. "Possibly," he admitted. "Do you remember any of it?"

"Bring me five beanbags, and I'll have a lively round of group juggling going in ten minutes or less. Make me three platforms and give me a six foot board, and I'll have a group working together to cross the river of toxic peanut butter, no worries."

"Huh," he replied. He just looked at her for a few moments, and then called back over his shoulder. "Sweetheart? Could you come out here, please?"

Wills came into the room a few moments later, dazed; it looked as though he had been wholly concentrating on something in his study. He saw Lizzy and blinked, then looked at Justin.

"You want to take her with us?" he asked doubtfully.

Wow. She had no idea they thought so little of her. This was turning into a depressing afternoon...

"She said she'd be damned if she would allow us to leave without her," Justin explained, smiling. "And, our little Coastguardsman here knows CGAs and low ropes."

That snapped Wills out of his stupor. He grinned at Justin, and then looked at Lizzy.

"*Was* she in the Coast Guard?" He turned back to Justin. "Well done, my love!"

Lizzy just scowled at them.

"Oh, Miss Pet, relax—it's just that you share so little information about yourself, though it does add mystique to your charm and effervescent personality." His grinned widened for a moment as he made his comment, and then he sobered. "Seriously, you understand the risks here?"

She nodded.

He studied her for a moment. "No, I don't think you do." He sat down next to Justin. "By the time they were done with Branford his tongue had been cut out, his fingers and hands were beaten into mush with hammers, and he sustained several body blows; it's a miracle he didn't rupture something. The *only* reason he survived was that he kept his back teeth clenched down on the bloody stump in his mouth until we could get to him and cauterize the bleeding. We are about to tweak the nose of the person who did all that, and he doesn't even *know* us, so I'm pretty sure we'll just get a quick hanging or shot in the head if it goes badly. So, are you sure you want in on this?"

She looked Wills in the eyes as she offered him the hint of a smile. "Do you want to live forever?"

He looked at her blankly, his brows furrowed. "Who doesn't?"

She closed her eyes for a moment and sighed. She supposed that meant he had never heard of Chesty Puller, nor had seen *Conan the Barbarian* or *Starship Troopers*; did he live under a rock in New York? "Never mind, Master Wills. Yes, I think I know something about being in danger, and I accept whatever comes. Put me in, coach, I'll make you proud."

He studied her for a couple more seconds. "OK, you're in," he replied. He turned to Justin. "Add her to the list—it looks like we're officially going now."

"Who else?" she asked.

"Me, Justin, you, Gunther, and Malcolm at the moment—we might get one or two more later, it's only been a day."

"How does Branford feel about all this?"

Wills and Justin exchanged a glance.

"He...doesn't like it," Justin admitted.

"He thinks it's a waste of time," Wills added. "But, it's not up to him."

"Has anyone asked him about the other people involved—Zane's accomplices?"

"We have names," Justin replied. "We know who to look out for."

Lizzy paused before asking her next question; it was technically against their unwritten rules to ask, but it was important. "Do you know why the attack was personal?"

Both men's eyes widened slightly at the question; that was all. But it was enough.

Yes, they do.

"What do you mean?" Justin asked calmly.

Lizzy twitched her mouth in annoyance. She looked at Wills. "Request permission to speak freely, Master Wills?"

He smiled, obviously tickled by her turn of military phrase. "Granted."

"A person doesn't get their tongue cut out and their fingers destroyed because they're queer. They get lynched, they get shot, they get strung up on fences, they get beaten in general, but not like this."

Wills face grew stormy. "You think you know a lot about it, Miss Pet."

"I don't *know*, but it's just logical." Actually, she *did* know something about it—Olin the Crazy Psycho-Bitch at Ruth gunned for lesbians at the commune before she was stopped. In her case, it appeared she mostly strangled her victims and left them in the desert to mummify. Lizzy would never know whether Olin really was homophobic, or she jonesed after the thrill of killing and it was a convenient excuse. But, either way, no one here had to know about that.

"It's like you said," she continued, "they could have just shot Branford in the head and have been done with it, but they didn't. Either whoever did it didn't have the stomach for murdering outright, or they wanted him to suffer in a very specific way. Which was it?"

Wills looked at her for a moment, then at Justin, and then sighed. "I'm not at liberty to say. If you really want to know, ask Branford yourself, but we will not betray a confidence, spoken or implied. He is always at home in the evenings; my only request is that you don't badger him if he refuses to share."

Lizzy nodded. "Understood—what's next?"

"I'm almost done with *The Iliad*," Wills said, "and then we'll start rehearsals, probably next week. The performance selection will be short—about thirty minutes. Then, you and the others will get a crash course in Forum Theater, which will take us to the 2nd and our departure."

"Mundane clothes or garb?"

Wills raised his eyebrows and seemed to consider the question. "Not sure yet—I'll have to think about that one, but probably mundane."

"OK. Is there anything you wanted to ask me?"

Justin's smile at the question was slow and easy. "Sure, but you'd never tell."

Lizzy waited until a full week later before approaching Branford's door. By then, the list of players had been finalized and announced—Ella and François joined up at the last minute—and she figured he knew she was going. She knocked on the doorframe and waited. When Branford opened the door, he looked at her vacantly.

"Hi," she said, smiling. "We met briefly when I arrived last year, but we've never really had a conversation. My name is Pet; I'm Master Paul's apprentice."

Branford nodded, and then stepped aside so she could enter. His great room didn't contain many things, but there was a table and chairs, a comfy-looking chair by the hearth, and a bookcase full of books along the far wall. Branford gestured for her to sit at the table. He took the chair opposite her and grabbed a slate and a piece of chalk from the table. He scribbled something, and then handed the slate for her to read.

"You are going to McCaffrey's Pass."

"Yes," she replied. He took the slate back and wrote something else underneath before handing it back.

"Can you read my writing OK?"

"I'm left-handed and stereotypical—my own handwriting is atrocious, so I can read other people's handwriting just fine, usually. If I can't read something, I'll let you know. Do you know why I'm here?"

"Wills told me you would be asking about my attack."

"Yes. I thought it might be an attack against you personally, and not against a gay man, *per se*. Maybe it won't make a difference in how we behave at McCaffrey's Pass, but...maybe it would be helpful."

Branford paused, and then stood up, scraping his chair against the stone floor. He walked to the bookcase and extracted a few sheets of paper from a thick book on the top shelf. He walked back across the floor and handed them to Lizzy. There were three pages in all, double-sided with single-spaced, typed lines. She leaned back and began to read by the hearth's light. Branford sat back down and waited. It only took a few minutes for her to read his statement, and then she looked up at him.

"Did his wife know that he felt this way?" she asked him. Even with the scars on his face he was an attractive man—she could see how anyone could be smitten.

He shook his head.

She stared back down at the paper, and then back up at him. "*You* did, though, well before this happened." she inferred quietly, looking into his face.

He paused for a moment, but then nodded.

She turned pink when she considered the next question but, the way she saw it, the answer was the difference between them having to hustle out of town and having to run for their lives. "Did the two of you get physical in any way? Did you do anything that he would be ashamed of now?"

He scowled as he wrote his reply on the slate.

"*No—he was married, and my subordinate.*"

"OK," she said, holding her hands up in an acquiescing gesture. "So it was exactly as it says here: he made a pass, you refused, and he went apeshit. It also didn't help that he wanted to be the mayor, the sooner the better?"

He nodded.

She leaned forward, smiling in understanding. "But, you did string him along. You just never thought he'd ever offer himself that way."

He made a complicated gesture that said, *yeah, you got me.*

"And, there was nothing shady, right? No money laundering or bribes..." She rolled her eyes and then glared at him. "Oh, please, spare me the hurt look, Branford, you *were* a politician. So, nothing like that?"

He shook his head, smiling slightly at her rebuff.

"OK," she said, handing him back his paperwork. "What you described is not worth murdering strangers over. They might not give us a good reference for doing this for other towns, but they shouldn't rack up a body count." She stood up and extended her hand. "Thank you."

He stood and shook it. Before she turned to go, he raised a twisted finger and walked over to the bookshelf. He took a slim volume from the second shelf, walked back to her, and placed it in her hand. She looked at the cover.

"Chess?"

He nodded.

She looked at the instructional manual skeptically. "I suck at chess but, sure, I'll read it when we get back."

He walked over to the table and wrote on his slate. She joined him and looked over his shoulder.

"You're better at chess than you think."

She smiled at him. "There's the charmer."

It took about five days to make the trip to McCaffrey's Pass. Three of the nights were spent in towns along the way, either staying at inns or community camp sites, but the last two were out in the open under one tent, the seven of them stacked almost like cordwood in their own individual sleeping bags. Of course, being all smushed together in the same tent meant once or twice the two couples in the group took an extra-long time "gathering firewood," which mostly consisted of the twigs in their hair and clothing that everyone else politely ignored.

It amused Lizzy to consider that, even just a year ago, this sleeping arrangement would have made her exceedingly uncomfortable to the point that she would have slept outside. But theater and improvisation training had taught her to be comfortable in her own skin, and to be comfortable right next to the skin of others. Her final acclimation was a couple of months ago at Paradiso, when she and Jason had to come up with and perform a fifteen-second interpretation of the "Victoria's Secret Recipe" sexual position for an after-hours improv game. They were fully clothed, of course, but she was pretty sure she had no inhibitions, or maybe even dignity, left after that.

They arrived at McCaffrey's Pass a little before dusk, and the electric street lights were already on and shining brightly. This had been an established town well before Infusion, and no one had become Infected. Everything had remained untouched, including the local wastewater facility, their tiny hydro-powered electrical plant, and their ultra-conservative, orthodox values. For the citizens of this small town, life just continued on pretty much the same way as it always had, though now they had a twelve-year waiting list to move into their community, the cars all sat around gathering dust, and the electrified fences surrounding the town were actively guarded. One of the sentries approached them as they passed by the town's "Welcome!" sign and stopped at the main checkpoint.

"Can I help you?" he asked Wills.

Wills reached in his jeans pocket—they had decided on mundane clothing—and pulled out a folded sheet of paper. He opened it up and handed it to the guard.

"We're here for the election celebration," he explained. "We were told to report to Dylan Forrester?"

"Sure," the guard replied as he looked at the document and then handed it back to Wills. "You can keep your wagons here; no one will bother them. This way." He looked over at another guard. "I'm taking these guys to the city hall; I'll be back."

They walked down the main street, which was paved in brick and bordered on either side by concrete sidewalks. The downtown area was right out of a Norman Rockwell painting, and it was bustling with after-dinner activity: people sitting and talking on porches and stoops, kids playing last-minute games, and customers in teahouses playing darts. She didn't see any pubs or bars anywhere, so Lizzy concluded it must have been a dry town; Brydan had told her about those from when he lived in Texas.

In the center of the town, there was a building faced with marble and surrounded by Ionic columns. The guard led them up the marble steps and through a large rotating door made of glass with brass accents. The inside of the building was beautiful, with high-vaulted ceilings and floor-length maroon curtains. The crystal chandeliers above them were brightly lit, as were the wall sconces and the table lamp at the reception desk—all glittering and beaming cool, unwavering electric light. It was a little weird for her, not having seen electrical lights for a while, but it wasn't disconcerting—she had been to the laboratory and headquarters on a regular basis before she ran away, both of which had all the modern conveniences and were fully powered.

Her companions, on the other hand, seemed to be having a more surreal experience. All of them were looking around the interior of the building in star-struck wonder, their eyes wide, including Justin and Wills. She supposed after more than seven years it must have been like going back in time, except that would usually mean *less* technology, not *more*, which would make it all the more disconcerting. The guard directed them to the elevator.

172

"Mr. Forrester is on the second floor, 203. Can you make your way from here?"

Wills stared at the two buttons on the wall as if he had never seen their like before. "Yes...thank you, sir." He reached out a tenuous hand and pushed the "up" button. It lit up, and the hum of machinery could be heard as the elevator descended to the ground floor.

When the doors opened, the seven of them squeezed themselves into the compartment. Lizzy noted that the guard just shook his head as he walked away, and the doors closed behind them. There was a collective gasp from the group as the elevator lurched and then slowly made its ascent.

No one said anything for moments as they listened to the motors perform their functions. Gunther finally quipped, "I keep expecting Rod Serling to step out in his suit and to hear creepy music, don't you?"

They all laughed nervously except Lizzy, who rode the service elevator quite often at the lab. She noticed that Wills was watching her and her lack of reaction, but then the elevator *dinged*, and she turned away as the doors opened and she quickly stepped off. She looked at a placard on the wall as everyone else piled out. "Room 203 is this way," she said, pointing left.

They all made their way down the hall until they found Forrester's office. The door was wide open, and light poured out from the doorway. Wills made a motion for the group to stay put, and then he walked to the door and knocked on it.

"Mr. Forrester?" he asked into the room. There was a mumble of a reply, and Wills disappeared inside.

As they waited, Malcolm looked around and commented, "I had forgotten how clean electric light was."

"No fire watches," François observed. "And it's so *warm* in here!"

"I can tell already that it'll be hard to leave," Ella added with a longing look.

Lizzy silently agreed. It *was* nice to be in a building and be warmed just by the ambient air, rather than have to wear layers of clothing or huddle by a fire. She never really thought about it at Ruth, since it seemed that she was *always* in the Courtesy Tent on canary watch freezing or roasting her ass off. She'd bitched about it, sure, but it just came with the job—she had expected a certain level of hardship when she had joined the military.

These people, on the other hand, were civilian survivors of a demon apocalypse, and while she was sure they were grateful to be alive, they hadn't signed up for what they got. A minute later, Wills stepped back into the hallway.

"They've graciously offered to have us stay at a church that is next door to the community center where we'll be performing and running our workshops. They have a foldaway bed for each of us—men in one room, women in the other." He smiled at that. "Their restrooms have showers, and there are volunteers that will be feeding us our meals. I'm told that, if we hurry, we can catch some late dinner."

At the possibility of a dinner that was not stale road food, the group declined to take the elevator but instead hustled down the cascading marble steps and almost ran to the church, which was just down the main street from the town hall.

As they hurried up the steps, Wills told them in a low voice, "Remember: we say grace, no swearing, they don't play cards, and praise Jesus!"

"Amen," said Gunther as he opened the door for the group.

For the next two days, the group prepped the stage at the community center and rehearsed. They were open rehearsals, and there was a constant trickle of people coming in and out to watch them work. They were always respectfully quiet, even the large groups of children and youth that were ushered in by teachers to show them an *Actual Travelling Theater Troupe!* The only interruption was from the older elementary kids, who were especially impressed at how they used red scarves to represent blood pouring out of their chests.

"*EWWWWWW!*"

The once and future mayor did not come to see them practice, which was fine with everyone concerned. Forrester did attend their dress rehearsal Tuesday afternoon while the polls were opened. He seemed very interested in the performance and in the troupe in general.

"I've always enjoyed the theater," he told them. "My family would take us to Shakespeare in the Park and musicals at the community theater. This play is a little...bloody, but it's very compelling!"

"It's what Mayor Zane requested," Wills replied dryly. "I suppose we could change some things, but it would be very last minute..."

"No, it's fine," Forrester interrupted. "We could use a taste of a different culture once in a while—modern civilization originated with the Greeks, after all."

"Quite," Wills agreed, giving Forrester a friendly smile. He glanced over at the group. "I'm pleased, and I think we're ready. That's all until the polls close—dismissed!" He turned his full attention back to Forrester as the rest of them left the stage.

Malcolm waited until they were changed into their street clothes and outside the auditorium before muttering, "The *Greeks* were the first civilization? Never mind the Chinese, the Egyptians..."

"Does it matter?" Justin interrupted, sounding annoyed. "Big picture here, Malcolm. Let's just get through this week, and you can mail your Op-Ed on the way out of town, OK?" He pushed opened the door to the men's room a little too hard and disappeared inside. Ella and the rest of the men stared at the closed door in surprise for a moment, and then made their way downstairs to the kitchen area.

Lizzy sat on a bench in the lobby of the community center and opened her script. When Justin came out of the restroom she rose, walked over to him, and gave him a look of concern as she took his hand. She squeezed it, just once, and then let it drop with a slight smile.

He nodded in response, just once, with a sad smile of his own. He glanced at the auditorium door before they walked downstairs to see what was for dinner, neither of them speaking a word.

The results were in by 9:00 p.m., and Mayor Harrison Zane was pronounced the winner by an overwhelming margin. When the house opened Lizzy played her guitar as usual, supplying background music for the entering townspeople. She noticed that there were a lot of people wearing buttons with the opponent's name, but there seemed to be no hard feelings—everyone was talking amicably, regardless of affiliation. She considered leading them in a song or two, but then decided against it—her heart just wasn't in it. Besides, Zane wanted to make his victory speech before the performance, and she *certainly* wouldn't want to delay anyone that pleasure.

Zane was not what she expected. He was actually short in stature and a little frumpy, though eloquent enough as he spoke of his political platform and complimented his opponent on a good race. Then he and his wife and three kids exited stage left, a prayer was given by a local minister, and the curtain rose.

When Lizzy saw that Wills and Justin had brought a packed-tight box of red scarves the size of a microwave oven, she didn't really think they'd need so many; she was mistaken. The particular scenes in *The Iliad* that Zane had chosen were an absolute bloodfest, and by the end of the performance a sea of red satin thickly covered the stage. Wills had directed them to leave the scarves where they lay, even when Hector was dragged behind Achilles' chariot, and the effect was powerful as the scarves bloomed and erupted in the actors' wake. There were even moments when an actor would accidently slip on a scarf, but they were instructed beforehand to recover and continue on.

The scarves might have been trite if it were not for the talent of the performers themselves, especially with Wills playing Achilles. It was the first time she had seen him formally perform on the stage, and the disdain and ferocity he brought to the role secured the play's gravity. The reaction of the crowd was mixed at times—it *was* a very violent play—but the applause at the end was loud and hearty. The mayor seemed especially pleased, a wide grin brightening his face as he clapped his approval from his boxed seat.

After the stage had been cleared and the costumes put away, Lizzy and Gunther found a quiet picnic table out back and pulled out cigars. The mayor's election committee had passed them out to all the males in the auditorium, including the men in the troupe. Neither Malcolm nor Justin wanted theirs, so Lizzy was happy to take them. Gunther had even managed to borrow a lighter from one of the cooks at the community center. There were no cedar sticks to properly light the cigars, but travelling actors couldn't expect to have it all.

"I find it interesting," she said to Gunther as she took a draw, "that you can't have a beer or play games of chance, but you're more than welcome to rot your lungs out."

Gunther chuckled as a fine halo of smoke diffused around his head. "I can't believe they just *gave* us these, either. They're so expensive back home."

"Yeah," she agreed. "This is my first one since before Infusion." Lizzy thought about the last cigar she had smoked. She had been on the ship, a week from home...

"There you are!" Wills' bright voice resonated throughout the square. "The two I've been looking for." He was dressed in a dark business suit and tie to attend the after-election party at the mayor's house. When he saw what they were doing, he stopped several feet in front of them. "You smoke, Pet?"

"Old habit," she replied. She patted the side pocket of her field jacket, an old army surplus coat she found at a merchant's symposium. "Got the Victory Dance right here, for when we're out of town." She gestured at him with her cigar. "You look nice, boss."

He reached behind his head and scratched the back of his neck. "Thanks. I have to make an appearance—I shouldn't be long. I did want to make sure you two were comfortable about the activities you were running tomorrow."

Gunther nodded as he exhaled, smoke streaming out his pursed mouth in a rush. "I am."

"I'm good," she added.

Wills nodded. He stood there for several seconds, watching them smoke and looking a little lost, like he knew he had a line to say but just couldn't remember it. Finally, Lizzy carefully set down her cigar on the picnic table and walked over to him.

"I'd like to go with you, boss," she said, smiling at him. "Would that be all right?"

He gave her a confused look, but deep underneath his mask she saw a suggestion of relief. "Do you have something suitable?"

She turned around. "Hey, Gunther, cut the cherry for me and hold on to the stub, please? I'll smoke the rest tomorrow."

"You bet!"

"Thanks—good night!" They exchanged waves, and then she turned back around to Wills.

"I'm sure Ella has something suitably girly," she told him as they started to walk towards the church. "Isn't she around?"

"She and François disappeared right after the curtain dropped. I just hope they're not doing something that will run us out of town," Wills said with a scowl. "I'm not sure how I would get them out of something like that."

"They're not stupid," she assured him. "They're probably just out for a walk or something, or they're at a teahouse."

"They'd better be." They walked up the steps of the church annex; Wills stopped at the door.

"It's probably best I wait out here," he said. "If you can't find something to wear, please let me know immediately."

"Of course—if I can find something, I'll be out in less than fifteen minutes."

He gave her a sardonic look. "A woman never takes just fifteen minutes to do anything."

She just smiled at him and went into the church.

Wills

He leaned against the black iron handrail of the church steps and waited, shivering a little in the cold November air. The suit was woolen, but it was a colder night than he had expected—he really should have packed his formal coat, as well.

Christ, he desperately wanted to be able to take Justin to this shitstorm nightmare of a party, just for support, but he didn't trust himself in social situations in towns like these. They only needed one asshole to make a suggestion, the gossip would spread like wildfire, and then the whole group would be in danger.

It had only been two days, but already he missed the daily intimacy he and Justin shared. Not just the sex—though he missed that, too—but the way they completed each other's thoughts in conversations, how they supported each other professionally and personally, and even the brief hugs or caresses they gave each other at just the right moments. Wills constantly had to stop himself from conferring with Justin on details about the play, and also about everything else. His husband was granted only equal treatment and input amongst the group, which wasn't very much. The work they were doing here was important, but the personal toll was undeniably high.

Suddenly the church door opened, and Pet stepped out in a solid mauve dress that was accented with folds of fabric cascading down the front and along the hem, tan hose, and black, strappy shoes with two-inch heels—all items he had seen on Ella several times before. The dress was a little tight in the shoulders and a little too long for her frame, but it would do for the occasion. Pet had taken a gold chain from her Athena costume and wore it as a belt—it actually looked pretty good that way. What was most extraordinary, however, was that she no longer smelled of tobacco smoke, her hair was slightly damp but presentable, and it couldn't have been more than fifteen or twenty minutes since she went into the church. She looked at him pensively.

"Is this OK?"

He smiled at her. It was easy to see that being in that outfit under these circumstances was well beyond her comfort level. He was touched that she was willing to do this, anyway. "Yes. Where's your coat?"

"It reeked of cigar smoke; I'll be fi—oh, don't do that!" she protested as he took off his suit jacket and placed it around her shoulders. She took a breath and looked as if she was going to argue, but then exhaled in a sigh of acquiescence and pushed her arms through the sleeves.

"Smile and say thank you," she said, no doubt quoting her mother or some other long-lost relative as she gave him a resigned smile. "Thank you." Pet linked her arm around his and placed her hand on his forearm. "Let's go before you freeze to death."

He *was* cold, but as they began to walk it became less noticeable. "You really were out in fifteen, twenty minutes. I'm impressed."

She smiled; a glint of triumph and humor twinkled in her eye. "You've never been on a ship when they've granted liberty."

The walk to the mayor's house was a short one. It was fairly large house, perhaps four bedrooms, and it probably had all the extra rooms that dwellings of the well-to-do had: a den, a home office, a dining room, maybe a sitting room. When they arrived at the front door, Pet quickly took off his jacket and gave it back to him. As he was putting it back on, she knocked on the door. As they waited for a response, they could hear strains of chamber music coming from the rear of the house. An older man in a suit—a butler, perhaps—opened the door. He narrowed his eyes at them, though not unkindly.

"Good evening sir, ma'am. You must be from the travelling company?" he guessed.

179

"Yes, good evening. I'm William Plantagenet, and this is Petunia. Mr. Forrester insisted we drop by to pay our respects."

"Of course; please come in." He stepped aside so they could enter the foyer. "No coat, miss?"

"No—I forgot it."

"This way—I'll show you where Mr. Forrester is." He led them down a short hallway that was lined with entryways. Two of them had doors and were most likely closets, but the other two were open arches that led to small, intimate rooms where small groups of people were talking and laughing. The house had the feeling of being full of people, and there was an audible undercurrent of conversation in the air that seemed to come from everywhere. The hallway opened into what looked like the main living room. Dylan Forrester saw them come into the room and immediately strode over to greet them.

"Welcome, Mr. Plantagenet!" he exclaimed, shaking Wills' hand. He turned to Pet. "Good evening! I'm Dylan Forrester, Mayor Zane's Chief of Staff."

"I'm Petunia; I'm pleased to meet you." She shook his offered hand.

"Weren't you Athena in the play?" Forrester asked.

She smiled, looking pleased that he had noticed. "Yes, and many numerous soldiers that met their untimely deaths. Did you enjoy the performance, Mr. Forrester?"

"Please call me Dylan."

Wills raised an eyebrow at that. *He didn't ask me to call him Dylan...*

"It was quite unique!" Forrester continued, addressing both of them. "It would have been awkward if we had lost the election, considering the subject matter, but the mayor was confident in his success." He looked around the room. "Would you like to meet him?"

"Of course!" Wills replied enthusiastically, his stomach clenching. "It would be a pleasure."

"He might be in the library—come with me." He gestured towards the other side of the room as he took Pet's arm and tucked it under his.

"So, how long have you been with the Travelling Players?" he asked Pet as they walked.

Not particularly interested in their social banter—Pet could take care of herself—Wills took note of their surroundings. He didn't blame Forrester for seeking an inhalation of fresh air by breathing in the novelty of his guitar player: she was new, she was attractive, and she would be safely gone in three days.

It was exactly the type of party he expecting: a boring one. The music was well-played, but it was not suitable for dancing—he wondered if that was even allowed here. There was no alcohol, so the excessive joviality and indulgences that made for the very best parties were nonexistent. People were chatting in small groups of four or five, reminiscing about the past, telling war stories about the election campaign, recycling conventional jokes—probably the same things they did at every gathering.

This event exemplified why Wills had chosen the lifestyle he enjoyed, leading the troupe and never stagnating: he always wanted to know what was on the next horizon. These people, on the other hand, had died long ago, and they didn't even know it. They were *alive*, safe within their electric fence and their vacuum-sealed time capsule, but as far as Wills was concerned they weren't really *living*.

Zane was in the library with his wife, sitting on a love seat and holding court. Forrester kept a hold of Pet's arm as they approached, but did glance back to make sure Wills was still with them.

"Mr. Mayor, this is William Plantagenet and Petunia, both of the Star-Crossed Travelling Players. This is Mayor Harrison Zane and his wife, Iris."

Zane and his wife stood and handshakes were exchanged all around. It took everything Wills had to take Zane's hand without flinching and smile without malice. He noticed that Pet had tucked away her usual animation, her face smooth and placid but not unfriendly.

"I hope you enjoyed the performance tonight, Mr. Mayor," Wills said with all due politeness.

"Oh, yes!" Zane replied. "You were an excellent Achilles, and you were Athena, weren't you? You didn't have much to say, but what you said was good."

Pet glanced at Wills with an amused smirk, her true personality revealed just for an instant—*Hear that, boss?*— before she answered him. "I'm still new to the troupe—this was actually my first performance; I'm glad that wasn't obvious."

"Not at all." Zane addressed Wills again. "The fake blood was especially good—I doubt folks around here have ever seen anything like it, have they, dear?"

"No, I doubt it." Iris was looking at Wills with blatant, unadulterated interest. He inwardly groaned.

Jesus, woman, could you be a little less obvious? Wills thought with repulsion. All he would need now was for the damned *mayor's wife* to start getting ideas...

Then he felt Pet's arm curl around his arm again, but this time she added the subtle motion of stroking her hand casually up to his bicep and then back down to rest on his forearm.

"We saw your children at the performance, Mrs. Zane," Pet said brightly as she smiled up at Wills, and then back at Iris. "Will they be participating in the workshops tomorrow?"

Well played, Miss Pet. He placed his hand over hers and squeezed it, trying to make it look like an absentminded gesture as he waited for Iris' response. She got the message and returned to her assigned role as the dutiful, happy politician's wife.

"Of course—we were very pleased when your bid included team-building exercises with the children. Harrison and I are always interested in promoting cooperation."

"Absolutely," Zane chimed in.

"If only everyone was as forward-thinking as you two," Wills remarked. Zane and his wife beamed at the back-handed compliment.

Wills and Pet were eventually allowed to make a graceful exit, but only after Zane and his wife introduced them to every fucking person in the house. Wills had never intended to stay that long, but Zane apparently liked the actor couple and wanted to show them off. Everyone they met asked polite, obvious questions, made the usual inquiries when they found out they were actors, like if they had ever been to Hollywood or had been in any movies that they would know, and were superficially pleasant. Somewhere along the line, Forrester had dropped away; Wills supposed that Pet's unspoken claim on him had suited her purposes, as well.

There was one interesting event during the evening, however, that came right at the end. They had been introduced to an elderly gentleman with a cane who was a foreman at the power plant, and his first question to Pet was if she had been in the military.

Her pleasure at his observation was obvious. "Coast Guard—you, sir?"

"Puddle pirate? Sorry to hear it. I was in the Navy, retired."

"Paint it grey, underway. Paint it white, overnight," she quipped in reply. They both chuckled and sat down in chairs next to each other. Wills sat, too, though both of them seemed to forget he or anyone else was there. Zane and his wife lingered for a moment but eventually wandered away, thank god. He made it a point to shrug and smile at them both in a silent apology— *She does this—what's a man to do?*—before they moved on.

"What was your rate?" the foreman asked her.

"Damage Controlman, which for us was a combination of DC and Hull Technician. You?"

The older man raised his eyes in surprise. Apparently, this was not a rate a woman usually chose. "Boatswain's Mate." He grinned and seemed to be waiting for a very specific response. He got it when she groaned in feigned disgust.

"Well, nobody's perfect," she said. They then started speaking in a strange language that Wills could only half-follow—something about ship designations and operational missions. He didn't feel slighted, but entertained himself by sitting back and watching her as she conversed with the military veteran.

For the first time since he had met her, she seemed totally relaxed. Her pipeline of information flowed uninhibited as she asked where he was stationed and if he was a shellback, whatever that was. When she was entirely absorbed in a conversation, he noticed, she used her hands for emphasis. At one point he studied the older man and saw active engagement mixed with longing—for his glory days or for Wills' apprentice, it was hard to tell; maybe a little of both. Then, as she was telling him about something called OBAs, and he looked shocked that they were still in use on some Coast Guard ships when she was in, she suddenly blinked and looked over at Wills.

"Oh," she said sheepishly. "Sorry, boss." She stood up.

"No, it's OK," she told the older man as he struggled to get to his feet. She gave him a warm smile. "We have to go; we have an early day tomorrow. We're here until Friday morning at the community center. Come by after dinner if you can Wednesday or

Thursday, we'll swap sea stories. Can I get you anything before we go?"

"No," the man replied. "Thank you." He gave her a grateful look. He shook hands with Pet, and then with Wills. Then she excused herself to go ask where a bathroom was.

"That woman is something," the foreman told Wills under his breath as they both watched her leave. "Makes me wish I was twenty years younger. Are you together?"

Wills nodded; it was literally true.

"I hope you appreciate her."

"I do," Wills assured him.

Or, at least, I might be starting to...

Wills gave Pet his jacket to wear during the walk home. She didn't even try to protest this time, just smiled and said thank you again. As they walked, he thought back to Forrester.

"Dylan Forrester seemed to like you," Wills said neutrally.

She gave him a sideways look. "I was just hoping I wouldn't have to give one for the team," she said. Her face hardened over into a cold mask of revulsion for a moment, but then she sighed and quickly relaxed again. "I'm almost glad Zane's wife looked at you like you were dessert...it got rid of both of them." She looked up at him. "I hope that caress wasn't too uncomfortable—it was just for show."

"I know," he said. He pondered on what she had just said for several steps.

"I hope you know that I wouldn't expect you to sleep with anyone you didn't want to, just for our sakes," he told her. "In fact, I don't think I'd like you to do that at all."

She smiled grimly as she took his arm and looked towards the church in the distance. "The most important thing about the job is to get us all out of here alive. If screwing some horny, hypocritical asshole would guarantee that somehow, you bet your ass I'd do it."

Well... If he had any lingering contemplations that she reciprocated Forrester's feelings, that statement certainly stopped them. It also testified to her loyalty to the group, which he supposed he had known about on some level but had never consciously considered before.

184

"How did that man know you were in the military?" he asked, changing the subject. "You didn't seem that surprised."

She openly smiled at that. "Sometimes you guess wrong, but most military folks can just tell when someone's served and it stuck—when it's gotten in their bones, there's just something about them that's innate. It's about how a person presents themselves." She looked up at him pointedly.

He grunted in response. There were many levels to what she was saying, and they were all relevant.

They arrived at the church, and he held the door open for her. She shrugged herself out of his jacket and handed it back to him.

"Thanks for letting me come with you," she said with a friendly expression.

"You're welcome—thank *you*."

"See you tomorrow." She waved as she turned and went down to the women's sleeping area, the heels of her shoes *clack*ing with each step.

Justin was still awake in his cot when Wills came into the room. The other men were fast asleep nearby, at least two of them lightly snoring.

"How'd it go?" he asked in a stage whisper, raising himself on one elbow. Wills could see his face and bare chest in the glow of the hallway light; he suppressed an almost violent urge to go to him.

"Better than expected," he admitted quietly as he looked away. He busied himself by peeling off his jacket and loosening his tie. "Pet went with me."

There was a pause. "Really?"

He nodded as he rummaged in his knapsack for his bedclothes. "She did well—she can be quite charming when she wants to be." They stopped their conversation for a few minutes as he stripped off his suit, put it away, and then pulled on his bedclothes. He lay down on his cot and pulled the blanket over himself, easing his head down onto the pillow. He sighed in relief—the evening was *finally* over.

"In fact," he admitted, looking at Justin, "it only went as smoothly as it did because she was there. One of the women was...overly interested...and Pet implied, in a non-threatening but very clear way, that I was spoken for."

Justin nodded, but said nothing.

"There's more, but I'll tell you about it later. I'll see you in the morning." They exchanged benign smiles, but their gazes were hot. Then they both rolled away in opposite directions, and each man did his best to get some sleep.

Lizzy

The next morning, Wills only stopped for breakfast long enough to grab a bagel with some soft cheese and swallow down a mug of tea before he ran out to meet with the youth coordinator for the workshops. Lizzy honestly didn't know how he had so much energy all of the time—she was seriously dragging ass, even after two cups of high-octane tea. She was just grateful that Ella understood about Lizzy borrowing her clothes the previous night.

"How was it?" Ella asked as they were getting dressed.

"About what you'd expect," Lizzy replied with a shrug. "A lot of talking, the instrumental group was pretty good for background music."

"Did Wills get hit on?"

Lizzy gave her a speaking glance.

"Yeah—that happens," Ella acknowledged.

After they were finished eating, the group went next door to the community center. Wills was waiting in the lobby with several pieces of paper in his hand. After he greeted the group, he handed one to each of them.

"Lucille," he explained, "the youth coordinator, allowed the kids to sign themselves up into their chosen groups."

"So we have clique-y groups of friends and at least one group of outcasts," Justin surmised.

"You got that right. Lucille informed me that there are two jock groups, a nice girl group, a mean girl group, a nerd group, and a misfit group. The nerd group and the misfit group are mixed gender. I put which group you have on the top of everyone's list, along with where you'll do your activities. The mayor's kids are in the two jock groups."

Lizzy looked at her paper: she had the nerd group on the front lawn. She supposed it could have been a lot worse.

"Do you want to keep them this way, or do you want to mix them up?" Malcolm asked.

"We'll leave them for now, and then for the final performance we'll have an all-hands workshop, get the groups interacting with each other. I'll be roaming around, helping as needed. Anyone have any questions?" He paused; no one did. "OK, they'll be here fairly soon. Remember to open with prayer. Good luck."

When they were training at Fiddler's Green, Justin had shown them several activities that he had used in the past to warm up groups and facilitate collaboration, mostly from Boal's work. Then he suggested that, for their first time, they concentrate on the activities they felt comfortable running.

"Later, when you get better at this, you can pick and choose games to fit groups," he explained. "This time, just know that the activities you use might fall flat, and that's OK—you can debrief, ask them what went wrong. Your groups will learn more from failure than success, anyway."

For Lizzy, the first round of games would be from her camp days: cooperative group activities and low ropes; she would use theater-based games the following day. She built a portable spider web of wood and bungee cords back at Avalon for one of the activities that doubled as abstract scenery for the play. She asked Malcolm to give her a hand, and they hauled it outside from the auditorium. Her group was standing there, waiting for her. They looked at the prop with interest.

"Thanks," she told him. She made sure her bag of stuff was still on the lawn and then turned to her new group. She introduced herself and told them they'd be doing some activities with her.

"Did you all want to be here, or were you told to be here?" Lizzy asked the group. A tall, gangly boy wearing a red plaid shirt spoke up.

"We get out of class to do this," he explained. "Were you in the play last night?"

"Yeah, I was Athena and a lot of dead soldiers. Were you all there?" She saw a chorus of nods. "What did you think?"

Silent shrugs were their only reply.

"Fair enough," she said, not offended: shrugs were often teenspeak for, *it didn't suck.* "Let's get started. Everyone get into a circle." Once they were formed up, she reached into her bag and pulled out a small beanbag. She squeezed herself into the circle.

"The first game is called 'group juggling.' I'm going to pass the bag to you," she threw the bag to a girl with long blonde hair, "and I'd you to tell me your name, and your favorite type of *baked-good* cookie."

There were still snickers. She didn't clarify that once with a group of particularly worldly teenagers, and she received some very interesting responses. Her camp director was not pleased with her that day.

"I'm Geo," the girl replied. Then she frowned. "Do you mean cookies now, or cookies before?"

Lizzy pondered that for a moment. "That's an interesting question. I guess whichever—'favorite' is still 'favorite,' even though you can't make it now."

Geo nodded. "Chocolate chip, then."

"Yeah," Lizzy agreed. The trade routes to the cocoa bean-producing countries dried up when the demons came, not to mention access to real sugar. Even when she would go to meetings at Headquarters there was never anything with real chocolate in it, just artificial crap. "OK, Geo, pass the bag to someone else and remember who you pass it to."

Geo passed the bag across the circle to another girl. This one wore a lot of makeup, especially around her eyes.

"I'm Emma, and I liked gingersnaps."

"Hi, Emma. Now remember who gave you the bag, and remember who you pass the bag to."

They continued in this way until she met Josh, Andrew, Caroline, Monty, and Mac. Not one of them said a cookie that could be made in present day—she supposed there were a few points to that. She told Mac to pass the bag back to her.

"OK, let's see if we've got it. From the top, slowly." They did have it, first try.

"Good!" she praised. "Shall we give two bags a shot?"

By the time the exercise was finished, they were up to seven bags, and the kids were actively engaged in the process. Lizzy was pleased, and she told them so.

"Ready for the next activity?" she asked. The group collectively nodded.

For the next few hours, she led them through the games she remembered. While they were pretending to stand on their 8' X 8' magic carpet, trying to figure out how to turn it over to read the landing instructions while hovering 100 feet in the air, Wills walked by. He watched the group bicker and contort for a minute before turning to her.

"They're talking," he observed. "That's a good start."

"They're a pretty tight group already," she replied. "Monty is the leader of the group—the tall one in the red plaid. I think they hang out a lot, maybe already do projects outside of school together. How's the rest of the troupe doing?"

Wills smiled slightly. "Surprisingly, the nice girl group is having the most trouble—they're *too* nice. They all just agree with whoever makes the first suggestion, and then they want to move on. There was some resistance from the one jock group and the mean girl group at first, but they're settling in." He looked over at the spider web apparatus. "Have you used that yet?"

"Not yet—after they're finished landing the magic carpet, I think they'll be ready." She glanced up at the town clock. "After lunch."

"Have you ever had a group drop someone?"

"Not on purpose, though I always worked with campers who had only met a day or two before the activity—they wouldn't have a motive to drop someone." She gestured to the nerd group. "These guys won't. Other groups...?" She shrugged. "I guess the answer is, if you think that might happen you don't do this activity. Not every time will be a win."

He nodded. They were interrupted by a loud cheer—the group had worked out, through some acrobatics and climbing on top of each other, how to solve their problem.

"That's my cue," she said, grinning. "Anything else?"

"No, though I'll be by later to see this in action." He waved a hand at the spider web.

There were a lot of things Lizzy wasn't going to miss about McCaffrey's Pass—constantly looking over her shoulder and watching what she said, for examples—but one thing she *was* going to miss was hot food that didn't always taste like smoke. Sometimes it was appropriate and even wanted, like with steak or roasted peppers, but fettuccini alfredo just didn't go with "open hearth" flavor. After two helpings, she went back out and met her group; they were already waiting for her.

"You weren't at lunch," she said to the nerds. "You're all welcome to join us, you know."

189

"We know," Monty replied, tucking his hand in his jeans pocket. "We've been working on a project at my house, so we all ate there."

"OK." Lizzy kept her tone neutral. She *was* curious about their project, but she figured that when they wanted to disclose, they would. "I figured you guys were already working together—you're just punching through these activities."

They all smirked at her in smug, adolescent satisfaction.

"OK, here's your big moment." She reached into her bag and pulled out several red scarves from the play and a bell on a string and then walked the group over to the spider web. She stopped when saw Wills come out of the community center and approach them.

"Hi, boss." She gestured towards him while she addressed the group. "This is Wills; he's our director. He was also Achilles in the play."

While all the nerds seemed to appreciate her master's physical beauty, only four sets of eyes warmed with a dreamy, star-struck quality. The fourth individual recovered a split-second later, but she saw the look.

Huh.

Wills waved at the teenagers. If he noticed, he didn't indicate it. "I've been watching your group—you all work well together. Do you hang out together a lot?"

There were various nods.

"Right now, we're rebuilding the Internet," Geo volunteered with a smile.

Both facilitators raised an eyebrow.

"It's true," Caroline said, nodding. "We're starting with our own version of a social platform first, and then we'll start inputting data and information and create a viable search engine." She smiled shyly at Wills.

Monty glared at Caroline, and then at Lizzy. "Weren't we doing something with that web thing, Pet?" he grumbled, pointing at the prop.

"Yes," replied Lizzy with a grin, though she might have enjoyed watching at least one more minute of teenage fawning and angst. "Let's get started."

The group was gelled enough that she could make the rules as challenging as possible. She attached a small bell to the top of the two posts and the cords—if any of them touched the web it would ring, and they would have to start over. When they passed someone through a portion of the web that hole would "close," as indicated by the red scarf covering the opening. She didn't even give them a large hole as a freebie. She told them the typical story about the flesh-eating spider that lived in the web, that they had to get everyone to the other side without disturbing the arachnid, and then let them go to work.

Wills and Lizzy stood aside as the group began to talk amongst themselves, gesturing and interrupting each other. On their first attempt they managed to get Emma through an opening to the other side, but then she was unable to support Mac as he was passed through. Monty and the others were surprisingly quick as they caught Mac and then eased him down to the ground, the bell above him chiming with every motion. More discussion followed as Emma went back to rejoin the group.

"This isn't easy," she heard Wills mumble.

"No, it's not," she agreed, "but I didn't make it easy. I wanted to challenge them." They watched in silence for another minute.

"Let me know how it turns out." He gave her a brief clap on the shoulder and went towards Ella's group.

Lizzy had to hand it to them—they never gave up, and they never asked her for advice. They all got eaten as least once— usually twice—before they were successful. By the time Geo had twisted herself through a lower hole and somehow defied gravity as the others pulled her through, the nice girl group and one of the jock groups were watching, their activities done for the day. All three groups cheered and clapped as Geo was set down on the far side with her group, completing the activity. Lizzy was very proud of the nerds, and she told them she hoped they were proud of themselves. They all nodded, beaming. She spent a few minutes going over what they did, figuring out what was successful and what wasn't, and asked if this was how they worked when they did their programming projects.

"Not exactly," Monty said thoughtfully. "We usually just follow Mac's lead, since he's the best programmer."

"Hey—I always ask for ideas!" Mac protested.

"And when we're playing Holy Lands, we all talk to each other," Josh offered.

"Holy Lands?" Lizzy asked.

"It's a d-20, pencil-and-paper Christian role-playing game—it's the only RPG we're allowed to play," Josh explained. "D&D and Call of Cthulhu freaked out our parents *before* the demons came. Now..." He shook his head.

"Yeah," Caroline agreed in a whisper.

Lizzy nodded, though she only understood about half of what was said—too geek for her. She decided to wrap things up.

"OK, guys, great job today!" she said brightly. "Tomorrow morning we'll be doing some warm-up theater exercises, and then all the groups are going to be working with Wills in the afternoon. See you then."

When the nerds all left in a herd towards the community center, three of the jocks approached her. Pointing a thumb at the web, one of them asked, "Can we try that?"

"Let me check with the boss. If there's time tomorrow, I don't see why not," she replied. "I'll let you know in the morning."

Iris

"Y'know, they might not let us, anyway."

"Why not? We could do it over lunch or something."

"Let's just figure they will. Who should go over first?"

"Dude, if you were here at four like you were *supposed* to be, you'd know!"

Iris had been listening to bits and pieces of this conversation all evening. Boys had been slowly gathering at the house since that afternoon, and whenever one or two new classmates would go into the den the discussion would begin all over again, always with the fear that they wouldn't be able to do this "spider web" activity in the first place—whatever that was. She had brought in enough sandwiches to feed an army at dinnertime, which was met with a chorus of "Thanks, Mrs. Zane!" but no further volunteering of information. As usual, she was merely the food-dispensing furniture. Iris decided that the only way she would find out what they were talking about was to go there herself around noon tomorrow.

Being the mayor's wife earned her a certain level of deference, and her visit to the community center was no different. As soon as...

Petunia? Was that her name? saw her approach, she smiled and waved for her to come over. Iris saw her sons with a group of eight other boys, standing in front of a prop from the play. The other children that volunteered to participate in the workshops were standing and sitting around them, watching and cheering them on. The web divided her sons' group almost in half, and all of them were engaged in a heated conversation. Petunia offered Iris her hand as she came up to stand beside her.

"Mrs. Mayor," she said pleasantly as they clasped hands. "It's good to see you again!" The woman gestured to a man standing next to her. "This is Malcolm—he's another facilitator."

"A pleasure," the man told her as they shook hands. "Did you come by to see your boys?"

"I heard a lot about this contraption last night—they were strategizing for hours at our house."

Malcolm nodded and Petunia's mouth twitched in amusement, but neither one of them said anything. The three of them watched three boys on one side of the prop pick up the center of the basketball team and slowly maneuver him through one of the spaces. The five boys on the other side grabbed his feet as soon as they came through, and they successfully carried him through the web. Petunia walked over and placed a red scarf over the hole they had used. Iris noticed the bell above the prop.

"Have they rung the bell yet?"

"No, not yet," Malcolm replied, "but they chose their first person well. It will be the last person that will make or break this."

"Someone should go find Wills," Petunia said to Malcolm as she returned. "He'd want to know Ms. Zane is here. Shall I?"

"No—this is your activity, Pet. I'll go. Mrs. Zane..." He bowed slightly and walked towards the community center.

The two women watched in silence as the teenagers continued through the activity. Only a minute or two later Malcolm returned with Wills, looking as amazing as before. The director waved at Petunia and flashed a toothsome grin.

How could they possibly be a couple? Not that Petunia was unattractive, but she was not nearly in the same class as this man. She just couldn't see it...

"Mrs. Zane!" Wills looked happy to see her, for he knew his role, as well. "What a pleasure to have you join us!" He took her hand with both of his for a moment, and then gestured to the apparatus. "Some of your sons are in the group, aren't they?"

"Yes, my two oldest," she replied in her politician voice to hide her annoyance. There were times she didn't want to be reminded she was old enough and dowdy enough to have three teenage boys—this was one of them. Sometimes, she wanted to be flirted with and pursued and made to feel beautiful. She had stopped expecting this from her own husband a long, long time ago, and both his position in government and the isolation of the town made it impossible to seek fulfillment elsewhere. But, she could dream...especially about this sinfully handsome man that should have been alive during the golden age of film.

In fact...she could visualize her and William Plantagenet in a cinema feature, him leading her onto the dance floor at a dinner club, a seductive rendezvous later...

Before Iris could indulge in any further fantasies, however, she saw Wills and Petunia exchange a playful but meaningful look. Petunia actually *blushed* and grinned at him before turning back to the group.

Lucky bitch... She reluctantly went back to being the mere mother/wife and focused on rediscovering her interest in her surroundings. To be honest, it wasn't that hard—since Harrison had checked out of the marriage, her main focus of love and attention had been on her children. She liked to think her devotion would result in three good, strong men someday.

The team only had two members left to cross—she noticed that her children had already crossed over. She watched one of the remaining boys get a boost from the other teenager, and her two sons grabbed the lifted boy and carefully threaded him through the grid.

"What happens if they can't finish?" she asked the facilitators.

"I explained to them that this was an exhibition," Petunia said. She glanced at the town clock. "They only have about ten minutes left, anyway. I promised them I would leave construction plans with Lucille if they wanted to build their own and try it to their heart's content. They said they understood."

The final teenager, Cliff Bowman, was animatedly talking to the rest of the group across the web. Then he slowly crouched down and stood on his hands with his feet in the air. He carefully walked on his hands and eased his feet and legs through a larger hole. The tallest boy on the other side grabbed Cliff's feet and started to lift him diagonally until he was almost off the ground. Her middle son came over and reached through the net to grab Cliff's pelvis, and then Cliff bent backwards at the waist, allowing his arms to come up and his body to curve in an almost unnatural arc.

"Wow," she heard Petunia mumble.

The rest of the trick went perfectly. The boys synchronized their pulling up Cliff with him adjusting the angle of his body until he was free and clear of the web. The cheering was long and loud as Cliff was set on the ground; high-fives were shared all around. The facilitators also joined in the applause.

"Cliff is a gymnast," Iris explained to Wills over their clapping. "He had wanted to compete in the Olympics someday."

Wills nodded, a sad expression on his face. "I guess it doesn't hurt to keep practicing, just in case." They watched Petunia walk over to the group and huddle the boys together.

"She'll just debrief a little, ask how they made the decisions they did, that sort of thing." Wills told her. "They did very well— your boys, too."

She beamed at her sons, who were listening to something Petunia was saying. "They're used to working together as a team with all their sports, but I don't think they're used to this level of problem solving."

"This is nothing," Wills replied. "This afternoon we're going to have all the kids participate in some Forum Theater exercises— that should really get them thinking." He paused, and then he really looked at her. "Would you like to stay and watch?"

Iris studied his face, looking for evidence of guile or deception—she had years of experience discerning that. At the party, his almost-undetectable, but definitely insincere flattery was evident to her, from the slightly-forced smile on his face to the manner in which he shook hands. Today, however, she found nothing deceitful in his manner, only curiosity in what she had to say.

He is not asking the mayor's wife, she realized, studying his face. *He's asking* me.

When was the last time someone wanted her opinion—wanted *Iris'* opinion? She couldn't even remember.

"Yes, Mr. Plantagenet," she replied, smiling at him. "I would like that."

Wills started off the afternoon session by immediately getting down to business.

"So, you've all seen me lurking around," he began. "My name is Wills, and I'm the director of the Star-Crossed Travelling Players. But this afternoon, you will all be your own directors and your own writers. What we're about to do is something called Forum Theater, which is a way for us to act out problems and situations and change events to see if we can come up with better ways to interact with one another." He walked to the edge of the stage and took a sheet of paper from Justin's hand, who was sitting with Lizzy and Malcolm by the edge of the curtain. Wills turned back to the audience.

"This afternoon, because you will be interacting and suggesting, you shall all be more than spectators, you shall be *spect-actors*. I'm going to play the role of the Joker."

"I don't see a jingly hat," Lizzy heard Monty mutter to Josh in a half-whisper from the front row. Wills heard, too.

"No, no jingly hat," Wills acknowledged with a grin. "I'm not here to mock or entertain, but to moderate the action, keep your thoughts flowing, and to make sure that the actions portrayed on the stage are realistic.

"So," he shook the paper slightly in his hand as he looked at the crowd, "here is a list of issues that some of you submitted—all free game." He looked over at Ella, Gunther, and François, who were congregated around a table in the center of the stage. "Which one are we doing first, just as a demonstration?"

"The one about hunting," François replied.

"OK." Wills read the paper for a few moments, and then back up to the teenagers. "So, it says that someone here had a problem with getting their parents to let them go out hunting with their friends. Is that something folks have to do a lot?"

Almost all the heads in the group nodded.

"There's a forest not far from here," a jock called out. "There are a lot of deer and rabbits out there, and it helps to go out and shoot some."

"So, why wouldn't parents let someone hunt? It sounds like it's pretty necessary."

A nice girl raised her hand; Wills pointed to her. "Usual stuff—it's too dangerous, or sometimes we get too close to the wall and the guards think we're trying to get in. Actually," she glanced at a girl sitting next to her, "there was that one time that kid Danny got shot and died, not long after the wall went up. I didn't know him, but he got too close to the wall—it was an accident. After that, we have to be really careful."

"So, getting too close to the wall with a rifle in your hand and getting caught would mean your parents would find out?"

The audience collectively nodded.

"Grounded for months, at least?"

They nodded again.

Wills looked at the trio at the table. "What do you think, Players? Is that enough to go on?"

Ella and the two men exchanged looks, and then nodded.

"Just give us a moment, boss," Ella said as they formed a huddle around the table. The students talked amongst themselves as the actors conversed, but then quickly quieted down again when the huddle broke up and the actors began grabbing materials and taking their places.

There were only a few props: a table and two chairs, a small table with a vase, a dishcloth, and a couple of plates. Ella donned an apron and picked up the dishcloth and a plate, pretending to dry it. François sat at the table and stared into space, waiting for the play to begin. After a moment, Gunther walked onto the stage, exhibiting adolescent swagger. Ella and François turned to look at him.

"Hi Mom, Dad," Gunther said.

They both acknowledged him.

"Brandon and a couple of the guys are going hunting this weekend. Can I go with them?"

Ella looked up from her plate, frowning. "I don't think so, Jeff."

"Why not?!"

"You know very well why not! You know very well what happened six months ago."

Gunther stared at her. "That was *six months* ago! I was grounded for two months; I did what you wanted me to do! Why are you still punishing me?"

François cleared his throat. "Now, Jeff, your mother and I are just trying to keep you out of trouble..."

"I *know* what I'm doing!" Gunther interrupted. "I learned my lesson! No, I shouldn't have gotten so close to the fence. I *know* I almost got shot, but I won't do it again, please!" Gunther's voice was now pleading. "All my friends are going—it's not fair!"

"You have proven to us in the past that you aren't responsible!" Ella yelled, throwing the dishcloth onto the table. "The answer is no, and that's final!"

Gunther exploded, his face seething with rage. "*You lied to me! I'm tired of being told what to do!*" He picked up the vase and threw it on the floor; it shattered into a million pieces.

"I'm out of here!" he screamed. He stormed off the stage while Ella and François looked on in anger and dismay.

There was a long, silent pause, and then the room erupted into nervous clapping. Wills came back out as Lizzy walked over with a dustpan and hand broom to sweep up the pieces of vase.

"What did you think?" Wills asked the crowd.

Geo raised her hand. "He's *so* grounded for life—especially since he broke that vase."

There was a rumble of agreement from the other teenagers as Wills and Justin looked across the stage at each other and smiled.

"So, what am I hearing about the vase?" Wills asked.

"That was their property," an outcast called out. "More than getting him in more trouble, it wasn't his. It could have been an antique or something, something irreplaceable."

"It was a dickweed thing to do," a jock agreed. "Though, I can see why he was so mad—he *got* punished already. It wasn't right for the parents to just shut him down—especially since it sounded like they knew that he *really* wanted to hang out with his friends."

"If he was asking, does that mean that they told him he could go hunting again sometime?" Geo asked Wills. "They didn't just tell him 'no' forever?"

He shrugged. "Does it matter?"

"Yeah, it does!" a mean girl replied after a moment. "If they were just teasing him along, making him feel that he would be able to go hunting when they had no intention of letting him, then they were really being jerks! Didn't they think he would ask?"

Though the situation on stage wasn't a completely perfect parallel, Lizzy had to smile sadly at that last statement—it did speak directly about Branford and his onus in his own downfall. He had freely admitted that he had led Zane on, making insinuated promises that he had no intention of keeping. What the former mayor hadn't expected was that Zane would want to collect on what Branford was offering, or that it would end so badly.

"So, how could the situation be addressed differently?" Wills finally asked after a few more minutes of discussion about the injustice of the situation.

There was a long silence as the group all seemed to pause in thought. Lizzy glanced over at Iris Zane, who sat in the back of the auditorium, observing. It looked as though she was thinking about the disagreement, too.

Finally, a different mean girl said, "I want Jeff to ask the parents if they were *ever* going to let him go hunting."

"Sure," Wills agreed. "Do you want Gunther to do it, or are you going to?"

The mean girl stared at Gunther for a moment, and then looked at the girl sitting next to her. The other girl gave her a shrug and a look of consent.

"OK," the mean girl agreed as she stood up.

Wills gifted her with his most charming grin, the one usually reserved for barons and revenue collectors. Giggling and applause erupted throughout the crowd as she made her way down to the stage. "What's your name?"

"Camie."

"All right, Camie, let's take it from the top," he maneuvered the girl to where Gunther had been standing. "And, action!"

Camie walked up to Ella and François, who were staged exactly as they had been before. "Hi Mom, Dad."

They both smiled at her and said hi.

"I wanted to go hunting this weekend. Can I go, please?"

Ella looked up from her plate, just as before. "I don't think so."

"Why not?" Camie asked in a much calmer tone than Gunther had used.

"Because of what happened six months ago." Ella's voice was softer, too.

"But, I was just supposed to be grounded for two months, and that was six months ago," Camie pointed out. "Does this mean I'm still grounded?"

"No," Ella replied. "You know full well your privileges were reinstated after your two months were up."

Camie looked confused. "So...that should mean I can go hunting, right?"

Ella sighed and exchanged a glance with François before answering. "We just don't think it's a good idea, honey."

"But why not?!"

"Because you almost got killed!"

Camie frowned at her answer, her face turning red. The girl turned to Wills and pointed a finger at Ella. "She's being unreasonable!"

Lizzy noticed Ella smirking; her roommate did enjoy playing the bitch parts.

Wills gave the girl a sympathetic smile as the audience snickered at her distress. "You're doing great, Camie. Maybe we can get some help." He turned to the group. "Anyone got any suggestions?"

There was a pause, and then Josh raised his hand. "Ask them if there is anything you could do to ease their minds."

Camie considered this, nodded, and then turned back to Ella. "Is there any way we could work something out, that would make you feel better about the situation?"

Ella thought about it for a moment, then turned and smiled at François. "How about if your dad went with you?"

François gave Camie an over-friendly grin as a united teenage groan of sympathy echoed throughout the auditorium.

"So, no, I'm never going hunting again." Camie sighed when the noise died down. There was a rumble of collective chuckling, including from the Players on the stage.

"Your mom is tough," Wills acknowledged. "Do you want to keep going, or should someone else take a shot at it?"

"No, I'm good, thanks." The girl waved at Ella and François as she took her seat. The audience applauded her effort.

A jock raised his hand. "Maybe if the mom said what she was afraid of? Maybe then they could reach an agreement?"

Wills waved him down to the stage, grinning at the energy in the room and the subtle execution of invisible hooks that dug into each and every teenager, captivating them into his theatrical process.

That night, the auditorium was swarming with people—almost exactly the same crowd that had been at the performance that prior Tuesday evening. The house lights were flicked on and off promptly at seven o' clock, and the audience took their seats and settled down. Wills came out, dressed in his dark suit and tie, with the other members of the troupe following after him. They formed a semi-circle behind the director as he spoke. The kids were already sitting on bleachers at the rear of the stage.

"Good evening and thank you for coming!" Wills began. "Before we get started, on behalf of the Star-Crossed Travelling Players, I would like to take this opportunity to thank you all for your kindness and hospitality this week—we've felt right at home. I would also like to thank Mayor Harrison Zane and his staff, Lucille Johnson of the community center, and the men and women of the Grace Baptist Church who have fed us and have met all of our needs." He paused as the members of the troupe led the audience in a round of applause.

"Tonight, the youth that have been working with us these past few days will demonstrate Forum Theater. For those who are unfamiliar with the process, please allow me to take a few minutes to explain.

"Forum Theater allows people, who we call spect-actors, to problem-solve and debate about a presented situation, either by acting out their possible solution within the situation itself or by offering a suggestion that one of the actors will play out. My role tonight will be as the Joker, a facilitator who is not to suggest or solve any problems, but to keep the ideas flowing and to keep everyone honest—Superman cannot swoop in and save the day." This got a chuckle from the audience.

"The first play will be a before-and-after presentation—the members of the troupe will first show you the situation as it was presented to the spect-actors, and then the spect-actors will demonstrate the possible outcomes that they came up with— Players?" He gestured to his people, and they broke their semi-circle to take their places or to leave the stage. Lizzy would not be acting tonight. Rather, she was to watch for trouble.

Ella, François, and Gunther performed the original first scene for the audience. Sure enough, when Gunther's character described his close call at the fence, Lizzy heard more than a few gasps and saw several nods in the mostly-parental audience. The kids were right—this scenario *was* a real fear in this town.

Then Gunther spoke his final lines—*"You lied to me! I'm tired of being told what to do!"*—and threw the last vase down onto the floor, the clay exploding to tiny bits upon impact.

Lizzy kept her head pointed in Ella's direction as Gunther left the stage, but adjusted her peripheral vision so she could see the mayor's expression. He was only about twenty feet away, sitting by the aisle with his wife in the center section.

It was safe to say that he was profoundly affected by the scene. At first, he looked completely shocked, his face pale and his eyes unfocused, almost as if he was having a flashback. After a few moments, however, his color returned and increased until he was bright red, and he was no longer paying attention to the stage; he seemed too lost in his own thoughts. He watched Wills with an eerie detachment as the Joker came out to address the crowd, and he completely ignored Malcolm as he quickly swept up the mess and set another vase on the table.

Lizzy watched as Wills asked for the volunteer spect-actors to come down and show the audience the alternatives that they had thought of, telling their parents that the point was not to come up with a solution, but to create meaningful dialogue. It was obvious that Zane wasn't listening to a word Wills said, but just glared at him with a mixture of fear and bewilderment and anger: *Could they know? How could they know?*

Lizzy fingers twitched for a pommel that wasn't there. They carried no weapons, and now she wondered if that had been wise. Even though they would have been clearly outmanned and outgunned, she preferred dying well in a fight rather than passively submitting. But to die well, one would have to show a respectable measure of resistance, and there would be none of that here—they would merely be surrounded at gunpoint and escorted to their demise. Lizzy watched as Camie took Gunther's position, and she waited.

Then, as the actors and the spect-actor began the scene over again, Iris Zane leaned over and began to speak to her husband in low tones, pointing at the stage. When she saw that her husband was neither paying attention to her nor the performance, she placed her hand on his arm. His head jerked in surprise at her touch, and he spun to face her.

She saw the look on his face and appeared to ask a question, looking concerned.

Zane shook his head and waved his hand as he made a short reply.

After a moment, Iris recovered and continued to talk to Harrison, smiling and gesturing at the teenagers, no doubt explaining what she had seen that afternoon. When one of their sons took the stage, the mayor blinked and began to watch the action before him.

After a few moments his face smoothed over and, while his eyes were still wary, he seemed to relax a little. His body language suggested that, while he had just been reminded of something unpleasant, he had pushed it to the back of his mind to concentrate on what was before him.

When the youth had completed their first play and the audience applauded, the mayor glanced around and noted the very pleased expressions and the looks of pride that their children were so wise. For the rest of the evening he looked uncomfortable, but was no longer on the alert or looking to kill somebody.

Fucking Wills, Lizzy thought, *he was right.* Everything was as he said it would be: Zane didn't know what was coming, but the results were now well-known. It would be foolish beyond reason for the mayor to actually consider that the Players knew of his transgressions—and really, what *were* the odds?—but he was reminded of them tonight.

And the thought, the consideration that someone, somewhere, *could* know, and that his constituents would not have approved, would niggle in his mind for a long time to come. Lizzy watched, in the middle of that auditorium full of people, as the mayor choked down all of that knowledge.

It wasn't justice—but it *was* a reckoning.

And as long as they lived through the night and managed to get out in the morning, it would be sweet, indeed.

Lizzy figured that, if there was going to be a posse, there would have been one by now. She had been sitting in a grove of trees, watching the front gate, since the Players left after breakfast. They would make camp after about four hours of walking and then wait for her to arrive. If she was not back by nightfall, or she was not smoking her Victory Dance as she walked to meet them, they would make all haste and run for the Known World. Justin wanted to join her, but she wouldn't hear of it—what purpose would it serve? She stood up to make her way through the trees and soon found the main road.

As she walked away from town, she fingered the Zippo lighter the retired Navy man had given her Thursday night after an evening of sitting around the community center and telling each other stories about their patrols. He had mentioned he was the only sailor in that town, so she was glad she could spend some time with him, reminiscing.

"Keep a hold of that director boyfriend of yours," he had advised her before he left. "He seems like good people."

"I will," she had promised, hoping that she could. Even with the inherent dangers, if the troupe kept having adventures like this one, she wanted to stay forever. *This* was a life worth living.

About an hour into her walk, she heard rapid hoofbeats fast approaching from behind her.

*Shit and fuck me...*so much for a smooth getaway. She stopped by the side of the road and waited for her fate—she'd stall them as long as she could.

Then she realized that it only sounded like one horse, and that did not a posse make. Fear was swiftly replaced by curiosity, especially when she saw that it was a lone male rider in the distance, and then that it was Mac from the nerd group. When he saw her, he slowed his horse considerably and trotted towards her. He looked around.

"Where's everyone else?" he asked her, stopping the horse so he could climb down.

"They're up ahead—I had to wrap up some business before I left."

"Oh." He paused. "Would you like a ride to catch up?"

"Nah. Thanks, though—I'd get teased the whole way home." *And, I don't want to freak them out...* "But, I wouldn't mind some company for a bit. Did we forget something?" They started walking, Mac leading his horse by the reins.

"I told them you did," he admitted. "They gave me a pass to give your property back to you."

"They didn't ask what it was?"

"My dad is the police lieutenant for the town, and I'm an Eagle Scout—they trust me."

"I see." They walked together for a full minute in silence. "So, why are you here?" she asked gently.

He paused again and twisted his mouth, like he wasn't sure he wanted to say his thought aloud. Then, he did. "What's it like where you come from?"

Lizzy considered her answer for several steps. "No electricity to speak of save for special occasions, some running water, outhouses for all, and cooperative farming. Oh, and everything tastes like smoke. It's like camping for eternity."

He considered her response. "Are there different types of people there?"

"It depends on where you are. In the militia towns, like tends to gravitate towards like, I hear. Where I'm from, you could say they appreciate diversity. Race, gender, religious affiliation or lack thereof, sexual orientation—all accepted." She smiled gently at him.

His eyes widened for a moment; he offered nothing further. He didn't have to.

She stopped in the middle of the road and gave Mac an assessing glance. "If an adult were to find us, they would travel down this road," she gestured with her head, "until he found people who dressed like soldiers and cowboys. Then an adult would go south until he found people dressed in medieval garb— those would be the SCAdians."

Mac looked skeptical. "Medieval clothing—seriously?"

"I know," she said, rolling her eyes, "but, yeah, it's just their way. They are...a diverse people."

He looked down at the ground, and then back up at her. "Thank you."

She smiled at him. "Thank you for returning whatever it was—we appreciate it." She offered her hand.

"You're welcome," Mac replied, shaking her hand. "Are you sure you don't want me to walk the rest of the way with you?"

"No, thanks." She watched him take a couple of steps back and swing himself back up into the saddle. "Take care."

He smiled slightly. "You, too."

When Mac was out of her sight Lizzy lit her cigar, turned, and then continued her journey. A long time later, she saw a collection of colors way, way down the road, and what looked like wagons. By the time she arrived, however, there were only the wagons and Malcolm, whittling a stick.

"Where did everybody go?" she asked.

Malcolm looked at her dryly. "When they saw you smoking in the distance, everyone suddenly decided that they needed to go gather firewood."

She smiled. *Well...they would, wouldn't they?*

"OK." She sat down on a rock along the road to rest. "What about Gunther?"

Malcolm held up his hands in a gesture of uncertainty. "He *may* have gone to get firewood, though he *did* go in Ella and François' general direction..." His voice drifted off.

"Oh," she sputtered. She scrambled back on her feet, trying to shake her head clear of the sudden, unwanted images. "Wow, just...point me in a safe direction, and I'll really go and get firewood."

He pointed down the road with his knife, and Lizzy made sure to make some distance before she veered into the woods. Folks were free to be consenting adults, but some things were just best not seen.

Abby

"*What*?! You can't be serious, Abigail!"

"I want th-them, Donald."

"I know you are frustrated with your progress, Abby, but you *are* getting better..."

"Hobbling around lik' an old crone with a whalker isn't good enough! I have the clear-rhence to go to the top of the list, and I wan' them *all*! Eith-her you get your people t' do it, OR I'LL GET SH-OMEONE WHO WHILL!"

On the Road to Montréal
The Barony of the Three Trees
February 28th
2:19 p.m.

John

"I don't get it," John complained as he and Cuthbert rode down the trail. "All of these women, and I just don't seem to jive with any of them."

And over the past few months, there had been a lot of casual contacts with women: dances, socials, quiet cups of tea. But no one caught his interest for long.

"Maybe you're bad in bed?" Cuthbert suggested.

John gave him a look. "None of them have gotten that far. I'm not interested in a quick lay."

Cuthbert shrugged. "Dating is hard. Why do you think I've stayed with Jane all these years?"

"Because she's the only woman in the Known World that will

put up with your shit?" John asked with a smile.

"Exactly!"

They rode in silence for a while. The whole time Cuthbert had a look on his face, like there was a question on the tip of his tongue that he was just dying to ask. John finally decided to let him off the hook.

"What, Ben? You look like you're about to explode."

"OK!" Cuthbert grinned from ear to ear. "What about Pet?"

Huh? "What about her?"

Cuthbert looked at him like he was an idiot. "What about asking *her* out? What about that half-hour back massage she gave you at Crown?"

How the hell...

"You weren't even there." John observed.

"Didn't have to be—everyone was talking about it at Crown."

"*What?* I had a back spasm!"

"With your shirt off?" Cuthbert clarified with a sly grin.

"Oh, for crying out loud!" John felt himself turning red. "That's how you *get* a therapeutic massage! You don't all gossip like a bunch of old women when a chirurgeon asks me to take my shirt off!"

"Pet isn't a chirurgeon." Cuthbert pointed out.

"Whatever. No one seemed to think it was weird at the time—no one said anything! No one even noticed."

"Oh, Crown Tournament noticed." It appeared Cuthbert was having the time of his life with this conversation. "Either they didn't want to interrupt a pretty woman giving you a massage, or they were just too stunned to speak."

This dialogue was going beyond ridiculous. John decided to answer the original question now, and ponder on how absolutely nosy SCAdians could be later. "For one thing, Red doesn't want her around."

"OK—she doesn't live in Caradoc. What else?"

"Propinquity."

"You're speaking Latin again, John. Quit it."

"It means that she isn't close by. Besides, she told me she likes to be with the troupe and travel around."

Hearing that, Cuthbert spread his arms wide and made exaggerated gestures at the fauna.

"What do you think we're doing now?!" Cuthbert exclaimed. "Take...her...with...you! Hell, I like Pet—we could spread out latrine duty. Little John doesn't seem to have a problem with her, either."

"No..." John's brain was starting to hurt. "I guess I never thought of her that way." He was now more than glad he hadn't told Cuthbert about seeing Pet in her tent or inviting her back to his house during Paradiso—he *really* would have taken that the wrong way. "I've never thought of her as a wife."

"*Wife?*" Now Cuthbert was *really* looking at him like he was an idiot. "Setting the standards a little high, aren't you, pal?"

"No—what's the point of dating if you're not looking for a permanent relationship?"

"That's fine, but you haven't been doing that." Cuthbert paused for a moment. "You've been taking ladies' favors, asking women to dance, whatever, but I haven't seen any serious courting coming from you. You've been like...a rooster in a henhouse or something.

"Don't get me wrong, I'm not complaining—I'm actually very relieved about that. For a while there, I wondered if you *had* a dick."

John knew it was out of character for him, but gave Cuthbert a sideways look and smiled. "Why are you thinking about my dick?"

His friend's eyebrows shot up, and then he played along and gave John a shy smile. "Well, you *are* a handsome man..."

"Ugh." He couldn't do it; Cuthbert just wasn't his type.

"Stop trying to distract me; it won't work," his friend warned, abandoning the scene. "So, you've been a social butterfly all over the Known World, but when I suggest that you treat Pet the same way, you talk about permanent commitments. What's up with that?"

At that, John's mind went completely, totally blank. It was as if Cuthbert was talking in a different language.

"I don't know," he finally said.

Cuthbert rolled his eyes. "All I'm saying is, she's about the same age as you, and she's pretty. She's surprisingly patient when you get all Dr. Scholastic on her, and that's saying something. She makes you laugh; I've seen it.

"I'm not telling you to marry the woman...but maybe she's

worth trying out for size?"

John didn't answer him.

They rode in silence for a long while after that. He had a lot of thinking to do.

Captain/7 D.J. Lewis

"Donna?"

D.J. looked up. "Yes?"

"Please come with me."

D.J. hauled herself out of the chair in the waiting room and followed the office assistant through the main doorway into a maze of white walls and tan doors. The assistant made a few various turns until she reached a door that had "Dr. Tonya Whitaker, Psy.D." on a black plaque attached to the front. The assistant motioned Captain Lewis into the office.

For a doctor's office, it was quite small: there was only enough room for a tiny bookcase, a desk with a rolling leather chair behind it, and two standard chairs facing the desk. Almost every conceivable vertical space, including the carpeted floor, was filled with paperwork and file folders. D.J. hoped that the doctor was one of those types that had a messy office, but knew where everything was.

How does anyone clean in here? she wondered as she sat in one of the standard chairs to wait. Though, at least the doctor had an office—D.J. worked out of a modified hybrid van that was lined with shelves filled with her case files and other paperwork. Her clients called it the Theravan or the Shrinkmobile. As a mobile therapist it was convenient, but it got tiresome sometimes—especially when her leg began to hurt from too much time on the road. But, she was doing good work out there, and had been since Infusion.

210

Or, she thought she was doing good work. The Coopers shook her world a bit, and she needed to get her bearings.

A couple of minutes later, a tall, middle-aged woman with reddish-blonde hair hustled through the door. She looked a little weary, but she gave D.J. a huge grin.

"Hi! I hope you didn't wait long—I just got out of a meeting." She shut the door and carefully walked the narrow path of carpet around her desk to her chair. She rummaged a few seconds through a pile in front of her until she pulled out a thick manila file folder—it was D.J.'s file. D.J. was always amazed that, for all of the government's bouts of inefficiency, they always managed to have her file at the closest base, just in case.

"So," Dr. Whitaker began as she sat down and opened D.J.'s file. She began to scan through. "This is the first time we've met, Captain Lewis?"

"Yes, I believe so. Please call me D.J."

"What's the 'J' stand for?"

"Joanne."

"All right, D.J." She read some more. "And you asked to see someone now? Because it looks like your quarterly debriefing is scheduled for next month at Uniform."

"I had...something disturbing happen at Family Commune Augustine two days ago, and I need to process it out."

Dr. Whitaker looked up. "OK...are you all right to go through the standard review, or should we dive right in?"

"No, no...do what you need to do, I'm fine right now."

"OK." Dr. Whitaker read down the first page, and then stopped. She read the page again.

D.J. smiled. Everyone always stopped at that exact place.

Dr. Whitaker gave her an once-over. "You were Infected for a week."

D.J. nodded. "Well, about five days, when Patton was taken over, three weeks after Infusion. If I had been Infected a full week, I probably would have died."

Dr. Whitaker nodded and read on. "How's the leg?"

D.J. lifted her pant leg and knocked on her prosthesis. Her knuckles made a *tink, tink* sound on the aluminum. "Still instant street cred."

"Infusion Gangrene?"

"Yup. They were as gentle as possible with the exorcising—taser first, they said, some slicing, and then they finally had to blast buck shot into the leg. *That* one I felt, and damn, did it hurt." D.J. still got tears in the back of her eyes sometimes remembering that sequence of events, going from feeling that wave of Infected people slamming into her one second, and then waking up while being held down, screaming in agony the very next...

"They did their best, but the leg had to go. I also needed an emergency hysterectomy and some work done to my rectum. I was...torn up pretty bad."

Dr. Whitaker looked her in the eyes. "I'm sorry."

D.J. tried to smile. "It was a long time ago, and it was awful, but I got a lot of good help to help me move on. I'm just glad that the leg and the plumbing were the only things that had to go—I saw some people working with some pretty gruesome problems at the physical therapy clinic. My work also helps."

Dr. Whitaker nodded. "Any problems with the leg now?"

"Nah, not for a while. I hear that they just got done developing new prostheses, though, that respond to mental commands."

"Yeah, I heard about that, too. Are you on the list?"

"Yeah, but it's going to be a couple of years, they tell me. Higher-ups are slated to get them first; counselors have to wait."

Dr. Whitaker nodded again. "What are you on right now? Your records say that you're on...Chtahpropailine and Transproansil."

"I was, but they took me off Transproansil and started me on this stuff." D.J. opened her knapsack and fished around until she found the larger bottle. She pulled it out and handed it to Dr. Whitaker. The psychologist read the bottle and smiled.

"Yeah, I can't pronounce it, either. We've just been calling it 'D-ance.'" She carefully wrote out the unspoken, multi-syllable word into D.J.'s chart. "How's it working for you?"

"So far, so good. My insulin resistance seems to be diminishing a little, and my white blood count went down within a week, though they still don't like it."

"The records don't mention dialysis. You don't need it?"

"Not so far." D.J. found a spot of wood on Dr. Whitaker's desk and knocked on it. "The Chtahpropailine helps with that a lot."

"Good." Dr. Whitaker leafed through her file for a couple more minutes without further comment. Finally, she closed the jacket and looked at D.J. "So...what do you need to process out?"

D.J. inhaled, and then exhaled. "Have you been briefed on the rise of infant Infected?"

Dr. Whitaker's eyebrows shot up. "What?"

D.J. grimaced, and then took another deep breath; she hated telling this story to the uninformed. "Over the past few months, several babies have died from what looked like failure to thrive. It happens, but two months ago a baby was born to a Level Four Sensor, and she reported that four days ago, last Monday, she went to get her son after a nap and her baby didn't seem right, that he was...different. I was assigned to the case, and we brought in a Level Two from Commune Albert, and he confirmed that the baby was Infected.

"There were plenty of cases during Infusion of Infected babies, but they all died within hours. These babies..." D.J. stopped and shuttered a little.

"The COs from three communes authorized their personnel to dig up their most recent FTT cases the next day, and the tissue samples from those autopsies revealed that the infants were Infected for up to four months before they died.

These babies lived possessed for *months*, Doc. The oldest one—her name was Jenny Storm—was six months old when she died, and she apparently had been Infected for twelve weeks, at least.

"But for me, what screwed me up was telling these parents that the babies they loved and cared for were possessed, and that they didn't even know it. Can you appreciate what a mind-fuck that is?"

Dr. Whitaker leaned back in her chair. She was still taking all this in, D.J. could tell. "No, I can't imagine. What is it like?"

D.J. shook her head. "I suppose in some ways, it's like a typical death of a baby, which is horrible in itself. But these parents told me—*insisted*—that these babies acted like all the other babies: they cried when they needed something, they were able to be soothed, they played like babies. They even demonstrated secure attachment, and yet...they weren't human children. They thought they were theirs, but they were... changelings."

"Changelings?" asked Dr. Whitaker, furrowing her brow. "Wasn't that an old Angelina Jolie movie?"

"Yes, something like that. The term is from old folklore. Parents of intellectually-challenged kids or babies that failed to thrive or had other abnormalities would claim that fairies or other supernatural beings had stolen their child and replaced it with a deformed child. That's all I really remember about it, but it does seem to fit, doesn't it?"

"I don't know," Dr. Whitaker replied. "They started out OK and then got Infected, it seems. Would it be like being diagnosed with a terminal illness?"

D.J. thought about this for a moment. "It would be more like giving aid and comfort to the enemy. It's a sick, cruel joke, and right now my biggest problem is my own countertransference. I don't know how to talk this one through with the parents, especially the current case."

"The two-month-old?"

"Yes—Charlie Cooper; he's still acting like a typical two-month-old. He hasn't shown any signs of deterioration yet, but the parents don't know what to do. They love their son, but...it isn't their son anymore, is it?" D.J. felt herself starting to cry.

"I mean, what's the right thing to do here? Do they go through the motions of caring for it until it dies? Do they authorize trying to exorcize it—cut *his* leg off, too? Just put it down? Elie was nursing, but...she just couldn't bear to do that after the diagnosis, so their bottle-feeding now, which Charlie doesn't like. When I left, they had decided to take care of it for now. But the clock is ticking, and if we are going to try something for Charlie, it has to be soon—the sooner the better."

Dr. Whitaker leaned forward. "Why is this your decision? Isn't it up to the COs to come up with a protocol?"

D.J. frowned. "Yes—they're initial conclusion is to euthanize. However, until a final decision is made—and you know how long *that* could take— there's some flexibility to this particular situation. They are willing to let the Coopers call this one. The Coopers..." She paused to take a breath. "The Coopers want to take care of this child until it dies and not do anything, and I'm having a hard time dealing with that."

"Someone saved you," Dr. Whitaker pointed out. "It sounds like a lot of people worked very hard to exorcize you, to save you.

From what you're telling me, no one is talking about saving the boy Charlie, the one trapped inside."

"*Exactly!*" D.J. started to sob again. "Why the hell don't they fight for him?"

Dr. Whitaker sat quietly for several minutes, allowing D.J. to weep, only moving from her seat to offer D.J. a handkerchief. When it appeared that D.J. was winding down, Dr. Whitaker asked, "Do you realize that you referred to Charlie Cooper as 'Charlie' and 'it' simultaneously?"

D.J. looked up, puzzled. "No, I guess I didn't."

"What do you think that means?"

D.J. paused for a full minute, considering this. "I suppose I'm confused about what Charlie is, and if they are going to allow him to stay Infected, then it isn't Charlie anymore. They're taking care of a shell."

"This is very complex," Dr. Whitaker acknowledged. "Do you believe Charlie is still in there?"

D.J. gave her a wobbly smile. "Of course I do. I was in my body the whole time I was Infected; I just don't remember any of it." She paused.

"It's true," D.J. continued, "Charlie doesn't realize any of this. When the body does die, he'll just be released." She sat for a few minutes, and she could feel her calm beginning to return. Then she lost it again as the same reoccurring thought sprang into her mind.

"I hate that the Coopers are giving up." D.J. said. "I think they are being irresponsible. They should fight for their son, save him, whatever it takes."

"You help families make decisions every day that you don't agree with, I'm sure," Dr. Whitaker replied. "What makes this so different?"

"Because...even with my leg and all of the medical issues, I'd rather be alive. And it's frustrating that Charlie wasn't old enough for us to know what *he* would want."

"Does the family know about what happened to you?"

"Yes—I told them the whole story. I even told them that I was grateful when I was released, even with all that came later, but it didn't change their minds. You know what they told me?"

Dr. Whitaker shook her head.

"That all life is precious," she replied, "and it's God's will... GHAHH!" D.J. suddenly threw her hands in the air. "I mean... what the...what the *fuck*?"

"You're angry," Dr. Whitaker observed.

"Damn right I am! There just is no good response for *divine providence*," D.J. said with a sneer.

"Nope," Dr. Whitaker agreed. "This is what they want, it seems."

D.J. sat in silence. "I couldn't do it."

"Couldn't do what?"

"Raise the baby, knowing it was possessed."

Dr. Whitaker paused. "What do you think about their decision?"

D.J. thought. "It's brave, in a twisted way. I mean, watching this baby diminish and finally fail would be hard to watch."

Dr. Whitaker nodded.

"And," she continued, "I know, I know it's their choice, and I believe they are doing it out of true love. And I know they realize that, without intervention, Charlie is gone—they have no illusions about that."

"So...where does that leave you, in all of this?" Dr. Whitaker asked.

D.J. scowled at her. "Sucking it up and supporting the Coopers, like a professional."

Dr. Whitaker looked into her eyes for a long moment. "What are you really afraid of, D.J.? What is this really about?"

To answer that question, D.J. finally allowed herself to say what was in her core—what she couldn't say to anyone before this moment, because she just realized it herself.

"What if the child lives?" she whispered. "Maybe not this one, but what if a demon *doesn't* die? What does that mean... for *us*?"

Act Three

Chapter Eight

<u>John</u>

He was flat on his stomach, lying on field blankets in the middle of the woods between Caradoc and Hamilton. It was quiet and peaceful, and there was a beautiful woman straddling his hips, gently massaging his shoulders. She wasn't wearing a dress, but soft suede breeches—he could feel their texture and the weight of her legs across his naked back. It had to be Pet—no one else made him feel like this.

"I've tried, you know," he told her, "to date other women."

He could almost feel her smile at that. As she bent down to rub his neck, her long hair tickled his shoulder. He groaned at the sensation—it was light, and teasing, and so exquisite.

"It's good that you're dating," she told him, continuing to massage his neck as she gently rolled her hips against him. "You deserve to love, and for someone to love you." He could feel her playfully nip at the base of his neck.

"Flip over," she instructed. "I need to reach all of you."

She lifted her hips and gave him the space he needed to rotate around. When he was solidly on his back, she settled back down on top of him, groin to groin. She was wearing one of those white tunics she often wore, except this time she wasn't wearing a jerkin, or even a bra—he could see her nipples clearly through the shirt. Impulsively, he reached up and took her breasts in his hands and started caressing them. She arched her back and closed her eyes, moaning softly as she allowed him to touch her as he wanted to. Then, she opened her eyes and looked at him. Her eyes were the

218

most beautiful combination of brown and green...

"When was the last time a woman touched you like this?" she asked him. Before he could answer, she leaned over him and took his mouth with hers.

She kissed him passionately, dipping her tongue to meet his, and he responded immediately, reaching up to cradle her head in his hands, threading his fingers through her hair, adjusting the angle of her mouth to deepen the kiss. Her hands were all over him, touching him, her hips grinding against his. She broke off the kiss and began nuzzling his ear.

God...he almost came right then. How did she know that would drive him crazy, being licked right...there...

"Do you want me, John?" she whispered into his ear.

Was she kidding? "Hell, yes...please..." he managed to say.

Suddenly, though she was still wearing all of her clothes and his pants were still on, he felt himself pushing inside her. She was wet, so ready for him, and it felt incredible. He put his hands on her hips to brace her up against him, to guide himself inside until she was totally stretched and filled with him; she was panting with need. Then they both started to move, gaining a steady, almost frantic rhythm together. He tried to hold on, to make it good for her, but just watching her move and writhe on top of him, close to coming herself, he just exploded. His entire body was racked with tremors, and the release was transcendent—he couldn't feel anything else but her, and him throbbing inside her, for a long, long time.

Finally, finally, he felt himself coming back down to earth, aftershocks still pulsing occasionally throughout his body. Pet was lying limp on top of him. He gathered her up and kissed her, taking his time about it, savoring it. She convulsed every so often—she must have orgasmed, too. Good.

When she finally broke off his kiss and looked up at him, he saw that her eyes were wet with tears; his were, too. She looked satisfied and happy.

"Any other inhibitions I can help you with?" she asked with a smile. She leaned over and bit his ear, right at the sweet spot she had found before.

He tried to answer, but then he convulsed, and he could feel himself getting hard again, still sheathed within her. "Later," he croaked.

She chuckled at that before kissing his mouth, her tongue sweeping inside to mingle with his.

"Remember what we did here," she said when she finally broke off her kiss. She looked deep into his eyes. "I'm yours for the taking...fight for me."

"I only want you." He reached up to kiss her, to start thrusting again...

And then he woke up.

He bolted straight up in his bed, bewildered and out of sorts. His sheets were tangled up in his legs, and his pillows were on the floor. He was still rock hard, and he was still shivering with orgasmic aftershocks from time to time, but he wasn't sticky. It must have been a dry orgasm—weird.

Weirder still... He fell back onto the bed, remembering the dream he just had. He could remember all of it, down to the last detail. It was the most erotic experience he had known in his life...and it was because it had been with her.

It had always *been* her, he realized now. She made him so uncomfortable when they first met and spent that week on the road together. She had opened up a lot of old wounds, but yet by the end of the trip he couldn't find a reason not to like her.

Then, he talked to her about Regina that afternoon in the woods, finally admitting to someone aloud his guilt and sorrow, and she had been so accepting about that. He had begun to heal that day.

The massage at Crown—was he really so stupid to think anyone else could make him feel like that? He would make her spar with him, even though she grumbled, because it was the only viable excuse he had to see her. He liked being with her—he enjoyed her company.

Looking back, he supposed that spontaneous invitation for Pet to stay at his house during Paradiso was some sort of unconscious suggestion of his desires, though she was far too ill for them to do anything that night except talk.

That morning, though, his unconscious libido had gone past suggesting and made it very clear that what he *really* wanted to do with her was to fuck her until the end of time.

God, that was unbelievable. He had just had amazing sex with Pet...well, in his head, but still...and he wanted nothing more than to do it again—but with the real Pet this time.

Oh...maybe she could wear her fishnet stockings and black high heels? He pondered over that for a moment...

But, wait, wait...*shit.* The real Pet didn't know any of this. *That* would have to change...

His thoughts were interrupted by a knock on the front door.

The Village of Caradoc
The Barony of Vagabond Haven
Odin's Challenge VI: Day 1
9:00 a.m.

<u>Lizzy</u>

Just like last year, Pet walked up to the baron's house on the first morning of Odin's Challenge and knocked on the door. Just like last year, Red answered it.

"Oh, hi," he said, smirking at her through his mustache. "Staying out of trouble?"

"Yes, Your Excellency."

He stood in the doorway and stared into space for few moments. "You did a good job at the fighting fields last year—I think we'll just keep you there."

"Yes, Your Excellency. Should I go there now?"

He stared into space again. "Yeah—that'd probably be best. Swing by John's house first, though—he was out late last night, and he may need a wake-up call."

"Yes, Your Excell..."

Red closed the door in her face, just like last year. And she didn't know where John lived.

Maybe this will become a tradition... she thought as she walked away. *The Annual Closing-the-Door-in-Pet's-Face Kickoff, followed by her Wandering-Aimlessly-through-the-Middle-Kingdom 5K Walk. We could sell tickets...*

She made her way down to the fighting fields and asked a random fighter where John lived. About five minutes later, she found a house with his coat of arms on the doorframe. She knocked on the door.

It took a minute, but the door finally opened and John peered outside. He looked a little raw—he was still in his bedclothes, and it was probable that she woke him up. He squinted at her, looking confused.

"Pet?"

"Hi, Sir John," she greeted, curtseying. "I apologize—Baron Duke Red asked me to come and make sure you were up."

"Oh." He stood there, blinking at her. "That's OK, what time is it?"

"Mid-morning."

"Oh," he said again. The knight shook his head a little as if he was trying to clear it. "I'm sorry, come in." He stepped back into the house, gesturing for her to enter; Lizzy followed him inside.

The first floor was one big room, like other houses she had visited, with a tiny kitchen tucked in the back. The main room was clean and tidy, with an overstuffed sofa and loveseat in the center of the room, facing a fireplace. A bookcase overflowing with books sat adjacent to the kitchen entrance.

"Please sit down—I'm going to get dressed." He went through the staircase entryway and up to the second floor.

Lizzy suddenly felt very tired. She had travelled with the advance, and they were up very early this morning setting up the camp. The main room had a warm, comfortable feeling to it, like a bed when it's been slept in for a good, long while. She sat down on the couch and nestled herself into a corner—it was the right amount of squishy. She leaned back and closed her eyes, only meaning to rest for a moment.

But then, she suddenly registered that she heard sounds coming from the kitchen, and she could smell and hear meat cooking. She awoke with a start and headed to the back of the room.

John was dressed and cracking eggs into a bowl. Bacon was frying in the hearth in a large skillet suspended over hot coals.

"Hi," he said, smiling at her. "Are you hungry?"

"Sure—thank you. Can I help?"

"Nah, I got this." He walked over to the hearth to flip the bacon over.

"Where's Little John?" She paused to listen if she could hear anyone else in the house.

When John straightened up and turned back towards the

222

eggs, he had a strange, almost confused look on his face.

"By now? He's with his girlfriend, I'm guessing." He got a fork from a basket and began beating the eggs.

Lizzy couldn't help but smile. "You don't like her?"

"I like her fine. Her name is Cynthia, and she's about his age. I just can't believe he's interested in girls now." He put the fork down and checked the bacon again. "He's growing up."

"They do that," Lizzy agreed, nodding.

He reached up and grabbed a plate from the shelf, and then used his fork to transfer the meat onto the plate. "Be grateful that you didn't have teenagers where you came from, Pet. They are a bumpy ride."

"Oh, we did have one," Lizzy replied. "His name was Joe. He's the nephew of the chaplain, and he was my assistant."

John smiled at her again. "Was he a hormonal mess, too?"

"No." Lizzy frowned a little. "Or, if he was, he didn't show it. He was the most serious young man you'll ever meet. He wasn't depressed, exactly, but I'd say he was stoic. He had a...a bad time of it before the soldiers found him after Infusion." She sat quietly for a minute, thinking about being nine years old and having to hide under your dead mother so you weren't eaten by Infected mobs. The thought still made her shiver. But then she thought of Joe in the present day, and she smiled again.

"He was a hard worker, though, and he had this dry sense of humor that he liked to zing you with. When I left, I asked that he take over my job." She remembered her conversation with Stagger Lee. "I hope they followed through." She had to believe he was working at the lab now, because Joe at a gang-raping male commune was too horrible to consider.

By then, the eggs had been poured into the skillet, so John had his back to her as he stirred them. "Sounds like a good kid," he observed.

"He's the best." Lizzy grinned at the thought of Joe, and of his character. "All the women in the commune looked out for him, but I think Anna and I were the closest to mothers that he had." She chuckled. "That's a scary thought."

"Eh, I don't think so." He turned and looked into her eyes. "You've always seemed very responsible to me." John turned back around to attend to the eggs.

Wow...that was a nice compliment, Lizzy thought. *He's smiling a lot, too. Maybe he's gotten laid recently.* She was a little horrified at the thought, but there were very few things that would make a man smile like that...

"I guess," she responded as he scooped eggs onto another plate. She confirmed her suspicions as she looked at his face: yes, he was downright glowing.

Oh, that's just great, she concluded. *Even the Monk of Vagabond Haven is finally getting a piece. I wonder if it's anyone I know or have heard of...*

"So, what's on the agenda today?" she asked, changing the subject. All this talk of Joe and her thoughts about the lack of a sex life was making her a little sad and frustrated.

He divided the eggs and bacon between the two plates. "What did Red say he wanted you to do?"

"Fighting field, which is fine with me." She paused and looked at the plates. "I'll never eat that much, Sir John, please take more for yourself."

"Thanks." He pushed more eggs and bacon onto his plate. "Cornbread?"

"Thanks."

They sat and ate breakfast with some tea, swapping stories and making observations. He did manage to coax a few Joe stories out of her, and he told her about some of his adventures on the road with Little John.

While they were talking, Lizzy couldn't help but compare the closed-off, silently suffering man she had met almost two years ago with the man sitting next to her that morning. This current version of John smiled easily, and he shared his opinions and feelings rather than hiding behind impersonal facts and quizzes. He talked *with* her, rather than *to* her, and he acted like he could sit and converse with her all day. There was also a shift in the power dynamic between them—he seemed to be considering her as an equal that morning, rather than...well, whatever she had been.

Could we be...friends? When had that happened? Maybe it was at Paradiso? She really wished there was some sort of formal memo system for this kind of thing, though she wasn't complaining about it—she liked being with him, too.

Too much, actually—their fingers brushed often as she helped him wash and dry the dishes after breakfast was over, and she felt a tingling jolt go through her each and every time. When the last dish was put away, he surprised her by taking her hand and pressing his lips to the backs of her fingers.

"Thank you for your help," he said pleasantly as he smiled into her eyes. "Ready to go?"

She knew it was insane for her heart to be racing in her chest—*this is afterglow from someone else, Townsend, he doesn't really mean it like that*—but it was beyond her control. She smiled at him and wanted to quip that, if she got a kiss on the hand for doing the dishes, what could she get for cleaning the house, but she refrained.

"You bet," she replied instead. She grabbed an end of his armor box as they walked out the door and made their way to the lists.

The next three days were pretty much like last year. Baroness Morgan kept her busy, and there were hundreds of gallons of water to fetch and rivets to hammer. In fact, the only way it was different from last Odin's Challenge was that Cuthbert and John each made it a point to stop by every day to see her and chat, often pitching in to help with whatever she was doing. All in all, though, it was the same until Saturday afternoon, when Master Paul arrived at her water station. She was very surprised to see him—members of the troupe never came to the lists unless they were seeking out someone for Wills.

"Hi, Pet." He looked out of breath and troubled.

She stood and gave a slight bow. "Hi, Master Paul. What's wrong?"

"We have a problem. Sweet Bess has come down with a bad cold and laryngitis—we need you to play Katherina tonight."

She was stunned. "But...what about Ella?"

"She's not feeling well, either. You're up."

"Oh, shit! But...but..." Her mind began to race; she took a deep breath and exhaled. *Suck it up and deal...* "Yes, Master Paul. But I don't think Sweet Bess' dress or Ella's will fit me."

"That's OK—Raul tells me your stage dress is almost ready. He wants you to come now for alterations."

"What about the charter?"

"Considering we need you for the lead role for the performance tonight, I don't think Baron Red would mind, but if you feel you need to tell someone, let's go. I told them you'd be back immediately."

The first person she ran into that would care if she wasn't there was Cuthbert.

"There's an emergency back at the troupe camp, Master Cuthbert. May I return with Master Paul, please?"

"Sure! I'll let John and Red know. I hope it's nothing serious."

"I have to fill in for the lead tonight," Lizzy said with a shaky sigh.

Cuthbert's eyes softened, and he smiled at her. "First time?"

"Yeah."

He clapped her on the shoulder. "You'll be great. Go break a leg, I'll see you later." He walked off towards Red's tent.

The dress Raul had designed for her was two-piece. The floor-length dress itself was of a black silken material with a wide belt of woven gold; its long sleeves were tapered to her wrist. The accompanying dark green velvety jacket was much more elaborate, with gold embroidery that matched its lining and pearls and tiny rhinestones scattered throughout. The jacket hung below her hips, and it brought out the green in her eyes. When she put on the ensemble for the first time and looked in the mirror, her eyes grew moist—even ill-fitting, it was obvious that the outfit was designed to accent her shape and features. She told Raul as much, and he looked pleased that she had noticed. However...

"Isn't the cut in the front a little low?" she asked, a bit apologetically.

"For period? Sure. But for the stage..." he grinned mischievously. "The sooner you realize that Shakespeare's plays, for the most part, have a deep, pulsing channel of sex and sensuality running through them, the better off you'll be."

About three hours later, there was a knock on the post. "Is everyone decent?"

Lizzy's first thought was a crude joke, but then she decided to play it straight. "Sure, Gunther, come on in."

Gunther stuck his head through the door. "There's probably going to be a light turnout for court tonight. Master Wills wants us to paper the house; court's in an hour."

Raul looked up from his sewing machine. "We can't go to that! There's no way I'm going to be done by then—curtain's up right after court. If Wills wants me to do miracles, he needs to leave me the hell alone."

Gunther paused. "So...no?"

"No."

"OK..." Gunther's head disappeared.

"Besides," Raul continued to say aloud after Gunther had left, "I have no interest in attending court. Boring as hell."

Lizzy smiled in agreement—another bullet dodged. As Raul was pinning up her dress earlier, she realized that John had never managed to ask her to spar. And since she was going to be on stage all evening, and they were packing up in the morning, chances were he wouldn't have the opportunity.

The thought made her want to do a jig. It made her smile, just thinking about it.

It was almost worth the sensation of her stomach using a pickaxe to climb up into her throat. *Damn*, she was nervous.

Finally her dress was on, her hair was done, and the matching hat was attached. Raul even offered to apply her makeup for her when her hands were shaking too badly for her to do it herself. He had just finished applying the last of her lip pigment when Justin came into the tent, dressed in his Byzantine court garb. He stopped in his tracks when he saw her.

"Wow," he said in amazement. He blinked a couple of times before he spoke again. "You're being called into court, Pet."

Her stomach suddenly stopped its assent and just free-fell to the bottom of her hips. "What?"

He grinned as he reached down and pulled her up from the chair by both hands. "C'mon." Justin led her out of the tent, tucked her arm into his, and walked her down the path to the pavilion where court was being held.

"What's this about!?" Lizzy hissed.

"No idea," he replied.

It was clear, though, that he knew full well what it was about, and he was enjoying not telling her. She was glad she had kept dinner light—she was now in danger of losing it.

"I can't go to court like this!" she protested. "This dress is the definition of *strumpet*."

"You look beautiful," he assured her. They arrived at the pavilion, and he led her inside.

The torches were lit, and all of the seats were filled. She saw everyone she expected to see: citizens of the barony, other SCAdians, members of her troupe. What she wasn't expecting to see, however, was Wills, John, and Red kneeling in front of the king, all of them watching the entrance as she came in. She even saw Dr. Goldberg and Murray sitting in two aisle seats, dressed in loaner garb.

An onslaught of emotions charged through her as she realized what this had to be. Justin continued to accompany her down the aisle as she her face flushed hot from a strange combination of flattery and embarrassment. At the moment, it was mostly embarrassment.

SCAdians and their damned love of surprises...

"My two years aren't up, Justin," she whispered out of the corner of her mouth.

Justin shrugged slightly and smirked. "Close enough."

"You all have to sleep...sometime."

He chuckled silently at that. "Enjoy it, Pet." He kissed her cheek and released her arm as she walked the rest of the way to the dais and knelt before the king. She had seen enough of these done from the troupe papering the house to know how the ceremony went. The king smiled down at her, and then turned to Red.

"Is this the lady who wishes to serve our Society?" he asked Red in a stage voice.

Red stood. "Yes, Your Majesty," he replied, also projecting his words.

The king nodded. "Very well; you have our leave to proceed." Red knelt back down, and Cuthbert began the preamble.

"Since the very beginnings of our esteemed Society, its strength and stability lay in these virtues of its people: creativity, service, and chivalry. For, if any of these are lacking, the Society would fall. These virtues are witnessed in all SCAdians, but the Orders of Chivalry, the Pelican, and the Laurel have always been tasked with supporting the Society by their efforts and with their dedication to preserve the Society from Extinction.

"Then, dark shadows swept across the land." There was always a respectful pause at that point. Cuthbert waited five whole seconds before continuing.

"This new age brings difficult challenges to our World, so the Orders, in their wisdom, requested a special title for those who would also serve the Society and hold its virtues dear. Less than a peer, but more than a citizen, a person who is a Lord or Lady in our current Society embraces the ideals of each of these orders, and swears to dedicate their life to serve, that one day they may become a peer in their own right.

"Is there a member of the Order of Chivalry here who will speak for her?"

Lizzy looked over at John, who rose to address the king. She wasn't sure from which timeframe his garb was patterned, but even for court garb it was on the eclectic side. He wore a gathered white shirt with a wide band of cream material and gold brocade along the top. The neckline of the garment hung well below his neck to his clavicles, exhibiting just a hint of his chest underneath. The doublet covering the shirt was cream with black stripes along the edges and down the forearms, and he wore a tan cape-looking thing with a braided cord that went across his chest. The hosen was cream and black on opposing sides to match the doublet, and his head was covered by a floppy hat of cream and black with large tassels. She wasn't quite sure what to make of it—maybe it was one of those outfits that a person could to grow to like over time. He cleared his throat before he spoke.

"Your Majesty, she is authorized for heavy combat and has demonstrated, in both word and deed, her dedication to the Society and the defense of our lands. She is welcome in our ranks as a guardian of the Barony of Vagabond Haven." He glanced over at Lizzy and gave her a small smile.

She returned it with a smile of her own before he knelt back down. This was all scripted out for the most part, but it was still nice to hear the words applied to you.

"Thank you, Sir John the Younger," Cuthbert announced. "Is there a member of the Order of the Pelican here who will speak for her?"

Wills rose. He was in a completely black outfit of hosen, a shirt, and a doublet, accented by a white, pointed lace collar and a tan hat. Being Wills, he wore it to perfection.

"Your Majesty, I shall speak as a member of both the Order of the Pelican and the Order of the Laurel. She has demonstrated proficiency in many of the performing arts, including theater and music. Further, she has served the Star-Crossed Travelling Players and the Society with honor and humility, and has proven worthy to be a Lady of the realm."

"Thank you, Master Plantagenet." Wills knelt back down. The king turned to Red.

"We accept the testimony of these Peers, Baron Duke von Worms, and you have our leave to administer the Oath of Homage."

Red stood up. "Thank you, Your Majesty." He maneuvered around until he was standing in front of her. But instead of addressing her, he turned back around to the king.

"If it be pleasing Your Majesties," he said. "There is one more order of business before I can administer the Oath of Homage."

Lizzy tried to ignore the view of Red's rather corpulent ass two feet from her face as her blood ran cold.

This is not in the script.

"Oh?" said the king, smiling. "And what business have you before us, Baron Duke von Worms?"

Red took a few steps to the side so she could see their interactions clearly. In fact, if she didn't know better, it looked like a deliberate staging of a scene, with proper form and placement so the audience had the best view of the action.

Oh, god, what the hell is this?!

"It is the business of her name," Red replied. "It is unsuitable for a Lady of the realm."

The king looked confused. "What's wrong with her name?"

If I hear one fucking thing about a hamster I'm going to kill them, Lizzy thought, feeling ill again. *I'm going to kill them all...*

"She is currently named after an animal that was the beloved companion of a member of our household. However, now perhaps she deserves a name of her own, considering the circumstances."

Lizzy silently sighed in relief.

The king stroked his chin in thought. "Perhaps." He turned to the queen, who was also his wife. "Shall we name her?"

The queen seemed to consider this. "Well, we would need more information." She turned to Wills. "Master Plantagenet?"

Wills stood and bowed. "At your service, Your Majesty."

"What singular quality does this lady possess, that we may consider when choosing her name?"

Wills looked over at Lizzy. "She's stubborn, Your Majesty."

Lizzy made a face at him while the troupe chortled.

"Am not," she grumbled under her breath. The only person

who heard her was the king, who gave a sudden bark of laughter.

"Very well, Master Plantagenet," the queen said. As Wills knelt back down, she looked over to his left. "Sir John?"

John got to his feet and bowed. "At your service, Your Majesty."

The queen seemed to be enjoying this dialogue. "And you, Sir John? What quality do you think this woman portrays above all others?"

John gave Lizzy a sideways glance as he seemed to consider his answer, and then told the queen, "She's formidable, Your Majesty."

Huh. She was pleased by his answer, but she wasn't sure why he picked that word. He regularly...OK, *always*...kicked her ass whenever they sparred. He looked very satisfied with his response, though, as the queen acknowledged him and he knelt back down. She had to remember to ask him about that later.

"Baron Duke von Worms?" The queen's attention was now directed at Red. "What quality do you offer to us?"

He looked down at Lizzy, meeting her eyes for a long moment, and then he smirked.

"She's resilient, Your Majesty."

Call it nostalgia or just utter shock, but that this crusty old Senior Chief had just publicly acknowledged that she was actually worth a shit made her teary. In her experience this was high praise, indeed, and she was genuinely touched by his choice. She quickly dabbed her eyes on her sleeve so her makeup wouldn't run as the queen turned to her husband.

"So, the lady is stubborn, formidable, and resilient." She paused as if she was in thought. "That sounds...solid, like a boulder, don't you think?"

The king grinned, almost gleeful. "We're naming her Boulder?"

That got a laugh from the crowd. Lizzy truly hoped that wasn't the final answer, or she would have to consider some sort of homicide again.

"We have it," the queen announced. She walked over to the edge of the dais and looked down at Lizzy.

"We name you Petya of Vagabond Haven: Petya, the feminine of Peter, meaning 'rock.'"

Hey, that's not so bad. She could even keep her SCAdian nickname and not have to remember yet *another* alias. Perhaps she also would have preferred something like "Dame Boudicca", but it would do.

She smiled at the king and queen. "Thank you, Your Majesties."

They both smiled back at her. Then the queen returned to her throne, and the king got back to the usual script as he instructed Red to administer the Oath of Homage. Red returned to his original position and held out his hands to Lizzy. "Are you prepared to take the Oath?"

Lizzy placed her hands in his. The only other oath she had ever taken was to serve her country, and she was about to take this oath as seriously as she took the other one. She still didn't feel like she belonged there, but these people were worth defending. "Yes, Your Excellency."

Cuthbert walked to the edge of the dais. "To your Baron and to those of the Society assembled, repeat after me:

I swear my service to the Society
and to the Barony of Vagabond Haven.
I do to You, my Baron, homage,
and to You and the Society shall be faithful and true,
and faith to You shall bear for the tenements I hold of you,
saving the faith I owe to Our Sovereign Lord the King,
until the Baron departs,
or death take me,
or the World end."

After she repeated the oath, Red placed a cord around her neck with a pendant of the Barony's coat of arms.

"So all will know in whose service you are beholden."

He then retrieved a small scroll and handed it to her.

"So the Known World knows you are a Lady." It was her AoA, which was mostly blank: she'd have to design and register her coat of arms later. She tucked it in her belt.

Red bent down and kissed her cheek. His mustache was bristly against her face.

"So you remember the oath you swore this day."

Lizzy breathed a sigh of relief. Men always got slapped across the face at that part; she'd seen women go either way.

"Thank you, Your Excellency," she said quietly, smiling at him. She got a smirk in return before he turned around and ascended back up the dais.

"Arise, Lady Petya of Vagabond Haven," the king commanded.

She got to her feet and curtseyed low. "Thank you, Your Majesty." Wills and John stood and bowed, as well. She turned to make her departure, but John appeared at her side and offered his hand in a courtly manner, chest-level with a slight bow. She grinned at him as she took it and allowed him to escort her back down the aisle, Wills and Justin following close behind.

"For Lady Petya of Vagabond Haven," she heard Cuthbert call out, "our newest SCAdian!"

"Vivat! Vivat! Vivat!" the crowd cheered, followed by a round of applause.

Once outside in the cooler air Lizzy leaned forward, bracing her free hand against her leg—John was still holding onto the other one. She looked up at him and grinned.

"That was *so* cool!" Now that it was over, she was completely electrified with joy. "Thank you for the romantic finish; that was a nice touch."

She thought he might have looked confused for a moment, but then he smiled. "You're welcome, my lady."

She straightened up and gave his hand a gentle squeeze as she gave him an once-over. Yes, the garb looked better over time. In fact, he was so handsome, just standing there...

"And, thank you for speaking for me," she said. "Good words."

He raised her hand to his mouth and kissed it, lingering just a little. "True words," he replied, looking into her eyes for emphasis.

Lizzy suddenly recognized this: they were having a moment, she was sure of it. They were standing together outside the court pavilion, holding hands and smiling at each other. If they were in a movie he would kiss her, or make some sort of statement, *something...*

But...no. He looked over at Master Wills and offered him Lizzy's hand.

"Wills, I leave her to you."

C'mon, John, you said you've been to the movies! Goddamn it. She repressed a frustrated sigh.

Wills stepped forward and took her hand from John. "Thank you." He gave Lizzy's hand a friendly press before he released it.

"Will you be attending our performance?"

"Johnny and I wouldn't miss it." He smiled again at Lizzy. "It's Petya's first public performance, isn't it?"

"As lead? Yes, it is!" Wills replied.

Lizzy whirled around; disappointment forgotten. *Wait...what?*

"But, this was a trick..." she spluttered at Wills. "I saw Sweet Bess in the hall, she looked fine!"

"Oh, no, Miss Pet, I would never deny you your audience!" He took her shoulders with both hands and started steering her towards the theater tent. He looked back at John. "See you at the show, John!"

John waved and walked back into the pavilion.

Lizzy glared at Wills as they started walking towards the main tent. "Haven't I had enough excitement for one night?" Her stomach was knotting up again.

Wills smiled at her. "You'll be fine—you've done very well in rehearsal, and I think you're ready." His smile broadened.

"Besides, looking back," he told her, "between receiving your AoA and giving your first public performance in a lead role, you'll remember this as one of the greatest nights of your life! And," he said with a grin at Justin, "what's the point of taking apprentices if you can't humiliate them from time to time?"

Lizzy was not amused—not a bit.

"I should throw up on you," was the only thing she could think to say.

Cuthbert

After court, Cuthbert found John outside the pavilion. He grinned and clapped him on the shoulder.

"Are you going to the play?" he asked.

"Yup—I'm meeting Johnny there." They started off together towards the theater tent.

"So," Cuthbert began, dying of curiosity. "That was quite the thing at Pet's AoA."

John smiled but said nothing.

Oh, no, Cuthbert thought, *you're not getting out of it that easily...*

"Did you *mean* to announce to the entire Known World that you are officially off the market with that escort down the aisle?" he pressed.

John looked thoughtful. "Until she gives me a reason to think otherwise, I think I might be."

Wow! Cuthbert never thought he would see this day, not in a million years. He felt a warm satisfaction that his friend had finally found a woman that he really liked. "So, is she quitting the troupe? Moving back here?"

"She doesn't know yet, I guess," John replied, frowning. "She thought the escort was for dramatic effect."

Cuthbert felt his eyebrows shoot up—hadn't she been to court before?

For that matter...hasn't John? He felt his warm satisfaction disintegrate into acrid disbelief.

"OK...so you told *the World* that you were interested in her...but didn't tell *her*?" *Wow.* In all the years that he had known John, he had never known him do anything so careless.

"C'mon," Cuthbert said, grabbing John's doublet and pulling him around to a side alley—this was really confusing, and he wanted to get to the bottom of it. When they were both some distance away from the crush, he let go of him.

"That was jumping the gun, don't you think?" Cuthbert asked, trying his level best not to bite his friend's head off. "Implying to everyone that you two are dating, when you're not? These really aren't medieval times, John—she does have a say."

John didn't say anything at first. He just stood there, staring at the wall in thought.

"I thought," his friend finally admitted, frowning, "that she would get the hint. I mean, we've been getting on so well all event. The way she smiles at me...how could I feel this way, but she doesn't?" He paused, looking a little...nervous...at that possibility.

"I guess...*shit*," he continued, sighing as he ran a hand through his hair, "I got carried away. I kind of had a... revelation...the other morning that I wanted to be with her, and I guess I wasn't thinking straight." He looked at Cuthbert. "Did I just make an ass of myself?"

"You may have," Cuthbert replied slowly, thinking of the countless times he had made an ass of himself with Jane, "but then, you're kinda due..."

Hey, wait a minute... Cuthbert was suddenly having his own kind of revelation. *This is great!* He brightened up, and he felt a grin spreading from ear to ear.

"In fact," he added, "I can't remember when you've potentially screwed up more! Sir John the Younger, the careful, all-considering seneschal of Vagabond Haven, took an emotional risk tonight, and damn the consequences! You *really* must like her to do something so totally stupid." He whacked John on the arm.

John glared at him—and he looked a little ill. "Glad to oblige. When I finally ask her out and she shatters my pride, I'll be sure to appreciate that experience, too."

"She won't." Cuthbert was pretty sure of that—he had noticed the chemistry between the two of them from the beginning. "Just grovel." They started walking towards the theater tent again. "So, when are you going to tell her?"

"Dumb move aside, I have been working all event on her seeing me as John, and not as Sir John or Dr. Scholastic." John smirked a little at that, and then looked serious again. "I'm willing to bide my time. I've already decided not to fight in Crown this year, so I can spend more time with her while she's there.

"Besides, I didn't want to say anything tonight—she was already a wreck, and a formal declaration from me before her first performance would have been the worst timing ever." He paused. "When I do suggest my intentions—to her face—I don't want it to be a surprise to her, and I want no distractions. I want to take her somewhere quiet." He paused again as his eyes glazed over a little. "Somewhere private..."

John flushed and said nothing more.

Cuthbert grinned to himself. He figured that his friend was imagining what he might do with the new Lady Petya of Vagabond Haven in a quiet and private place. It must have been one hell of a "revelation" John had that morning—Cuthbert had never seen him so out of sorts.

How absolutely marvelous. He couldn't wait to tell Jane.

John

Damn Ben—he *had* to talk about Petya on the way to the play, and that got John thinking of the two of them alone together, and now his imagination was in overdrive. He finally had to give up and go to a privy to adjust himself before he met Little John and found seats. He hoped the production was good enough to distract him, because otherwise it was going to be a long, long night.

He was very familiar with *The Taming of the Shrew*—they had studied it every year in his classroom as part of a unit on the treatment of women throughout literature. This particular play was famous for its misogynistic overtones and its message that women should submit to their husbands. Modern performances, however, tended to reinterpret those passages or treat the play as a farce, so he wasn't surprised that their Katherina was portrayed as a somewhat willing participant in her trials and an unspoken equal at the end.

Petya, as it turned out, made a respectable Kate. It was obvious that she was nervous during her first few lines, but then she relaxed and played the role well. He figured Wills wouldn't have allowed her on the stage if she couldn't make a good show of it, but he was still relieved. He really had to concentrate, though, on *not* looking at how form-fitting the dress was...or how it was cut in the front...or how the coat followed the swells of her...

Goddamn it! This was *not* going well...

Star-Crossed had a reputation of inserting elements of slapstick and improvisation in their performances, and this was no different. The induction of the play, of course, lent itself to physical humor, but there were other scenes that got downright raunchy, especially amongst Bianca's suitors. Petya played it straight most of the time, but there were two occasions when she went off-script.

The first time was during a scene when Petya "slapped" the man playing Petruchio, but there was no sound, just the motion of his face whipping around. She looked genuinely confused for an instant—this was a stagehand's mistake, obviously—but she recovered and turned to the audience, raising one finger in the air as if to say, *just a moment.* Petya then vigorously shook out her hand as if to fix it, flexed her fingers, gave a covert glance off-stage, and then let her hand fly again.

Crack! Laughter and a round of applause followed.

The other time was during a romantic scene towards the end, when Petruchio was holding Kate—her back to his front, both facing the audience—and he told her to kiss him. Sure enough, she leaned back against him and kissed him full on the mouth.

"Whoa," he heard Little John say.

But then, the actor playing Petruchio reached up with his left hand and cupped her breast, copping a feel while they continued the kiss.

"*Whoa!*" his son exclaimed. The rest of the audience reacted with a start, as well. John said nothing, but he felt a strong stab of jealousy and anger as he waited to see what Petya would do.

Petya grinned against the actor's mouth and chuckled, breaking off the kiss. She then calmly reached over with her left hand, pinched his sleeve between her thumb and forefinger, pulled his hand off her breast, and then let it drop. The crowd laughed in approval as the actors continued with the scene.

Good, John thought—he didn't have to kill the guy. And yet, in that moment, he wanted nothing more than to *be* that guy. He wondered if they were seeing each other.

He wondered if that made a difference.

Soon the play was over, and her hometown crowd was very warm and generous in their applause. John was so proud of her— he couldn't think of too many people that would be able to go through the stressors she had that night and yet conquer it all with such grace and aplomb.

Actually, he thought as he clapped through the last curtain call, she had shown her tenacity since the day they met: running from the government to come to a strange place for refuge, going where she was told to go, and accomplishing any task that was given to her. She did it all with a spirit of service. Petya accepted everything...and she flourished.

Then, all the facts just came together into one blinding conclusion.

He admired her; he enjoyed just being in her presence; he wanted her so damn much, it drove him to distraction; he couldn't wait to see her again.

He was in love with her.

Yes—he was very much, with all of his heart, looking forward to Crown.

Chapter Nine

The Village of Sunshine Pass
Barony of Nocturne
May 7th
1:38 p.m.

Lizzy

One afternoon, about a week before the Jersey Lily Resort gig, Raul asked her to come over to his tent for a fitting. When she arrived, he showed her an interesting ensemble that involved a dark crimson corset with lightly boned supports, a tie-on black and crimson skirt with a slight bustle, and black fishnet tights. It was finished off with black flats.

"Was I right, that you wouldn't wear stilettoes?" Raul asked her. "I've never seen you in heels, not ever."

"You're right—I won't wear anything that I can't run in. Thank you," she replied.

He nodded, though it was obvious he was hoping for stilettoes. "Let's try it on."

She took the outfit and slipped behind a sheet that was hung next to a tent wall for privacy. "This is more conservative than I thought it'd be," she called. "I was expecting pasties."

Raul sniggered. "That was my first design, actually, but Wills shot it down. High-class place, you know."

After a few minutes, Lizzy stepped out from the curtain. Raul gave her an appraising look.

"Well, that'll do," he commented. "The bustle does a nice job of accentuating your figure; Sasha was right about that." He reached over and picked up a small black cap from his desk that was covered in black sequins with a fountain of black and crimson feathers cascading off the top and down its back. He secured it to

239

her hair with bobby pins and turned her around to face the mirror.

When she looked in the mirror, she barely recognized herself. She never thought she could pull off strapless—not with her over-large shoulders—but the slight padding in the bust and the fluffiness of the crinoline in the skirt balanced out her dimensions, giving her a classic hourglass figure and the appearance that she was ready to commit any multitude of transgressions. It was empowering in a way, like one day discovering that you had a chainsaw in your toolbox when you had made do with a hand saw for years.

This is *going to be fun*, she thought to herself. She couldn't wait for Max to see this.

After her fitting, she stopped in to see Murray. He was sitting at the lab counter in the office trailer, making Dr. Goldberg's favorite local anesthetic by lamplight. He nodded in greeting as she sat down next to him.

"Hey," she said. "I just tried out my costume for the Jersey Lily."

Murray smirked as he handed her a pair of safety glasses. "How revealing is it?"

"Worse than my stage dress, but I probably wouldn't get arrested wearing it." She paused as she placed the glasses on her nose and adjusted them. "So, where are you going while we're at the resort?"

"A monastery," he replied with pursed lips as he poured a particularly foul-smelling chemical into a beaker. "Dr. Goldberg thinks it will do us good to reflect and meditate as you guys party your asses off at the resort."

"Good lord." Three weeks of reflection and meditation sounded like absolute hell to her. "Would you like a crash course in the trumpet? It's not too late..."

"Nah, it'll be all right," he assured her as he added another liquid to the beaker. "They have hot water, home-cooked meals, and a full library of books, a lot of them fiction *and*, Doc said, comic books and graphic novels. They want to maintain the literary culture, any and all of it, so they have a huge warehouse-full that anyone can borrow from—you just can't remove a book from the property. They're giving us full access in exchange for dental procedures."

"Huh." That sounded pretty good, actually. "So...how's Doc these days?"

Murray shrugged as he mixed a pink powder into the liquid. "I think he's losing weight, but he seems to be doing OK."

They both sat in silence as he stirred the solution and they watched the powder dissolve.

"Hey, Murray?"

"Yeah?"

"Are you happy here?"

Murray turned and looked at her through his safety goggles, surprised. "Um, sure. Why do you ask?"

She shrugged. "You kinda keep to yourself; it's hard to tell."

The powder had dissolved by then, so Murray reached up to grab some screw-lid containers from the shelf above the counter, lids from a drawer beneath it. When he had finished arranging them on the counter, he pointed to his face. "See this?"

She nodded. The jagged scar that ran down his cheek was hard to miss.

"I got this before Infusion. I was in a gang in Phoenix, and I got caught up in a fight one night." He lifted his shirt, and Lizzy saw another scar that ran from his lowest right rib down across his stomach and disappeared below his waistband on his left side.

"Shit," she breathed.

"I got disemboweled—guts hanging out, all of it; I was in the hospital for weeks. When I got out, I got sent to Wyoming to a group foster home in Rock Springs under some new program. When Infusion hit, we never saw demon activity at all—they passed us right by. Maybe we were too small a town or somethin'. It still sucked to be there, but we were safe." He got a funnel from a drawer and started pouring the finished mixture into jars.

"So, one day Doc comes by the home with Wills and Justin, and he tells them he's looking for someone to apprentice for him in dentistry; he picked me. To this day, I don't know why. I've even asked him a couple of times, and he just says that the Lord told him to." He finished emptying the beaker and started screwing on lids.

"My life is full of random bullshit, Pet. I should have died that day in Phoenix, but I didn't. It just so happened that I got sent to Wyoming, where I'd be safe. Doc happened to pick me to apprentice for him, so here I am. I always feel like I shouldn't be

241

here, like I don't have the right." He screwed on the last lid and looked at the row of full jars he had just made.

"I don't have much in common with you guys, either. I don't play an instrument, I can't act. I could barely read and write when I got here. Just...a different life story, y'know?

"Plus..." He took a breath. "No offense, but the demon mobs lasted, what, a month or two at the most? For most folks it was over in a week, one way or the other? Then there was some hard living, sure, but now they're living good." His voice became tinged with anger.

"I lived in an absolute shithole, the worst you can imagine, since I was born, me and my family and my neighbors, where you didn't know when you were going to get jumped, didn't know when you were going to get shot by a stray bullet—hell, kids used to die from an abscessed tooth, for Christ's sake. There were days when I was just surprised I lived through the day." His voice rose as he continued to stare at the jars on the counter.

"None of them gave a *shit* when that happened to us, but now I'm supposed to give a shit when it happens to *them*?" He shook his head. "Just can't do it; just can't listen to them. I know they didn't ask for it, but neither did I." He picked up two jars, exhaling sharply. He stood there for a moment, looking a little regretful, like he had said too much.

"But, being here is better than dead any day," he acknowledged. "Help me put these away?"

She picked up two jars. "You bet." She followed him down the short hallway to the supply closet. "I'm sorry, man. I didn't know."

Murray shrugged as he balanced the jars in one arm and opened a screened-in cabinet door with the other.

She couldn't think of anything else to say; an awkward silence filled the room.

Finally, when he had carefully placed the jars on the shelf, he turned around and asked her a question. "Are *you* happy here? You seem to be."

She considered his question for a moment. "I think I might be. I feel like an outsider still, even after the AoA, but maybe at the end of my apprenticeship I'll feel differently." She gave him a look of worry. "I just wish this life suited you better."

"It does," he replied, gesturing for them to get more jars. They walked back to the front of the trailer. "I really shouldn't bitch.

I'm learning a trade, and Doc's great to me, even with all the hymns and stuff." He smiled as he picked up two more jars, leaving Lizzy the last two. "And, I get three weeks to read comic books. Could be worse."

"Sure," Lizzy replied, picking up her containers. She thought about what it might have been like, growing up in Murray's neighborhood, wondering if you were going to die *that* day, or maybe the next one?

Then, her thoughts transposed to the image of charred flesh in a swimming pool, and of being ordered to burn people to death again, and again, and again.

"Yeah," she said, her mouth watering with sudden nausea, "it really could be."

May 13th
8:24 a.m.

They broke down the stage tent and packed up the camp in record time the following Sunday morning. The troupe was happy and chittering with excitement as they made their way past the easternmost border of the Known World and into the unclaimed territory that stood between SCAdian lands and the resort.

As they passed over the creek that officially marked the boundary, Gunther and Malcolm reached underneath the seat of their small Conestoga wagon and pulled out bolt-action rifles, loaded and ready just in case. No one was expecting trouble—bandits liked to target smaller convoys than theirs—but it was worth having the firearms out, even in case they came across some game along the way.

Around noontime they came to a four-way intersection, and Lizzy saw Dr. Goldberg and Murray split away from the group and take the north road. The two men waved at the group before turning away and spurring their horse-drawn wagon towards the monastery.

Godspeed and good luck, she wished in their direction. She happened to know that Murray carried his own pistol, and that he was a crack shot—he came by that from years of practice. As long as someone didn't get the jump on them, they should be fine—it was only another hour's ride to their destination.

Finally, when the sun was low on the horizon, they saw a large white building starting to come into view ahead of them. It was four stories tall, and each roofed surface glinted in the dying sunlight. As they got closer, they could see people milling around outside, and that the roofs were actually covered with black solar panels. The architecture was modeled after classical Roman design with a large glass dome in the center, columns along the front, and tall arched entrances behind the columns and along the sides. It seemed very, very new. They circled around the driveway surrounding the main building and stopped by the rear entryway. The grounds just seemed to span out in all directions, dotted with smaller white buildings, stone paths, and gardens that had no end in sight.

Men, women, and couples of all types were walking around in various forms of dress, from casual mundane to formal clothing to peplos that matched the décor to leather gear. Most of the men and women who wore costumes were also wearing lilies, either in their hair if they were women or somewhere on their clothing if they were men, like on a lapel. The men on staff who wore...not much...had clearly-displayed lily tattoos on their arm or side.

The entire troupe was in awe of the grounds, Lizzy included. She hadn't even noticed Wills and Justin enter the building until she saw them come out with an attractive woman dressed in full Roman noblewoman regalia, including a gold and purple palla that accented her lustrous nutmeg skin tone and her carefully piled-up ebony hair. Her makeup and jewelry were expertly applied. She was as tall as Wills, and she also exuded his regal demeanor in similar measure. She stood at the edge of the portico and waited.

"Gather around, everyone!" Wills raised his arms and beckoned them to come to the steps in front of the woman. "This is Madame Serena—she is the owner and proprietor of the Jersey Lily Resort. She has asked to go over the rules of the house with you personally." He turned to Serena and made his best courtly bow. "By your leave, my lady."

Serena favored Wills with a slight smile and a nod of her head, and then turned to the troupe.

"Welcome," she began in a rich contralto voice, "I've found it best to address our rules before our new performers even enter the building, so that there are no misunderstandings and everyone begins their experience on the correct foot. I shall be going over the rules again with the rest of your company when they arrive."

Max had arranged for the supplemental musicians to meet at the Coach and Four Inn that evening in Hamilton—they would arrive at the Jersey Lily the following afternoon. Wills and Justin had requested this, so the Players could get their bearings and begin to blend into the existing staff before adding new, unfamiliar people.

"Here at the Jersey Lily Resort, there are guests, escorts, performers, concierge, and support. If we are doing our jobs correctly, you will not notice the support employees at all unless you are specifically looking for them. They are the gardeners, the housekeeping crew, and the maintenance staff. They all wear tan jumpsuits, and they keep a low profile. I would ask that you do not address them except when absolutely necessary. Rather, please report any problems or concerns to the concierge, who are either at the front desk or tending bar. They have nametags to identify them." She paused to make sure everyone was listening to her, and then continued.

"You and the wait staff are all considered performers. Please feel free to mingle with the other performers and the guests, but please do not solicit or accept solicitations from the guests themselves—that is why we have escorts. What the performers do amongst themselves here is their business," she gave them a pointed look, "as long as the guests are not disturbed in any way."

"Escorts are easily identified by the lily somewhere on their person. You are allowed to solicit them, but understand that you *will* be compensating them for their time, just as a guest would. If you don't intend to pay them for their services, do not engage them—time is money here." Serena looked over at Justin and Wills and grinned broadly, her demeanor changing from stern schoolmarm to beneficial sovereign in a single moment. She made a stunning monarch.

"We are *very* happy to have you all here," she said first addressing Wills and Justin, and then the rest of the troupe. "We work very hard to make this an enjoyable place, and it is my wish that you enjoy your stay here as you entertain us. Again, if you have any questions or concerns, please see the concierge." She nodded at the co-managers of the troupe again, and then walked back into the building. As Serena retired, Lizzy resisted the urge to curtsey.

By the time the supplemental musicians had arrived the next day, the hard work had been done: the wagons were unpacked, the luggage and costumes distributed to everyone's rooms, and they had set up their initial practice area in one of the side buildings. Lizzy was by herself, arranging music stands in front of chairs, when she saw the front door open and Max walk in. He saw her immediately and grinned.

"Hi!" he said as he stopped next to a tangle of chairs and stands. He was wearing his costume: a pair of dark tan pants and a cream-colored button-down shirt, with light brown suspenders that held up his pants by dark brown buttons and crisscrossed over his back. With his medium build, narrow waist, and slightly built ass, he looked absolutely delectable in his farm-boy-gone-to-sin costume.

He knew it, too: he tugged on his sleeve as he turned around to give her the full view. "What do you think? There's a bowler hat, too, but I left it in my room."

Something unexpected happened to her at that first glance at him—something wicked and irresistible and almost primal that made her want to push him down to the floor and have her way with him *that second.* They were alone, those suspenders were just *begging* to be removed like a ribbon off of a gift, and it was Max Wrightson, the embodied promise of sex with no consequences.

Are pheromones being pumped into the air somehow? The Players hadn't even been at the Jersey Lily a day, and yet the hedonism of the place had been immediately affecting, the permission to cast caution to the winds as real as the quiet, deep breaths she now took to try and control herself.

Or, maybe she had just reached her breaking point and finally needed to get laid already. She started walking towards him.

Or maybe, Townsend, she considered with the part of her brain that still functioned, was it that no matter what she said or did, Max had already thrown down the gauntlet, and he had made it clear that anything she offered would be accepted? The power in that knowledge, that she could not fail, was intoxicating, freeing.

When she fully recognized that fact, though, she felt her impulsivity and horniness retreat as quickly as they had sprung. He wasn't going anywhere for a while, she *could* take her time, and it would be a lot more fun that way—at least for her. She calmed herself.

"You look very handsome," she managed to reply lightly, making her way down to greet him. "How was the trip?"

He looked puzzled for a second, having watched her face change from a bit startled to predator-aggressive to friendly, but he quickly recovered.

"Uneventful—being poor musicians, I guess it looked like there was nothing worth stealing from us." When they finally met at the edge of the second row, he leaned over and gave her a platonic kiss on the cheek in greeting. "They're serving dinner— did you know that?"

Great, no one comes to get me except the new guy—thanks a lot, comrades! "No—have you eaten yet?"

"Thought I'd find you first." He offered his arm. "Shall we?"

Jason, at least, had a guilty look on his face as Lizzy and Max sat down at his table.

"Sorry, Pet," he said with a grimace when she glared at him. "I figured you were busy."

"It's OK," she sighed as she picked up her fork. "New place and all. Jason, this is Max Wrightson, one of the new trumpet players. Max, Jason, one of our best improvisers and actors." The men awkwardly reached across their plates and shook hands. "Jason felt me up during my debut performance of *The Taming of the Shrew* back in March."

Jason nearly spewed his food out of his mouth; he did smile convivially, though. "*This* is how you're starting our conversation?"

Max said nothing, but looked at Jason with something resembling esteem as he ate a forkful of pork loin.

"Well, it always comes up in conversation eventually these days, so I thought I'd mention it first." She took a bite of her green beans. As she was chewing, she noticed something glittery out of the corner of her eye. She turned to see what it was.

Stunning was the first thought that came to her mind as she gazed upon the woman. She was tall, full-busted, and was formally dressed in a red sequined evening gown with long white gloves and bejeweled red heels. Her long white-blonde hair was carefully sculpted; her makeup subtle except for her ultra-long black lashes and crimson lipstick. She walked into the room like she owned the place and looked around expectantly.

"I don't see a lily," Lizzy muttered. "She can't be an escort—though she should be."

"She's hot," Jason acknowledged. He turned to Max. "What do you think?"

The musician looked at the stranger critically. "Something's not right..."

"Everything looks right to me," Lizzy countered. The woman's gaze stopped when she saw Lizzy's puzzled face from across the room, and then the blonde confection grinned with perfect white teeth and winked at her.

OK... Lizzy was even more confused. The woman began to sashay towards the table.

"You don't recognize her?" Jason asked.

Lizzy shook her head, unable to take her eyes off her. She went through her mind, trying to place the woman, but she came up empty.

"Well, she apparently knows *you*—good luck!" Jason said with amusement. "This ought to be good."

The woman stopped in front of the empty seat next to Lizzy, paused, and then looked at Jason, her blue eyes issuing him a silent command. Jason immediately stood up and pulled out the chair.

"Sorry," he murmured as the lady gracefully glided down into the offered seat. She nodded to him as he pushed her chair in and then dismissed him with a wave of her hand. She turned and directed her full attention at Lizzy, her eyes dazzling and full of humor.

"I couldn't help but notice that you were stunned by my beauty, Miss Pet," the woman said in a sultry voice. "Would you like to buy me a drink?"

Oh. My. God.

Pet did look stunned, almost bewildered as she muttered softly, "Now, you see...that just isn't fair."

The stranger—Max wasn't altogether convinced it was a woman—gave Pet a teasing look. "What isn't fair?"

Pet blinked, and then seemed to recover as she smiled back, bewitching Max at least, if not the stranger and Jason and anyone else in a mile-wide blast radius.

"That I've never had the pleasure of an introduction," she purred. She took the alleged woman's hand and kissed the gloved fingers. "I'm Lady Petya of Vagabond Haven."

Oh—she must have finally gotten her AoA.

And...she's kissing someone's hand?

"Lady Petya." The mysterious person seemed flattered. "You may call me Mistress Guinevere."

Pet lowered his hand back down onto the table—Max could now see the slightest bit of stubble on the stranger's cheeks when the light was right—and ran a fingertip down the inside of the elbow-length glove. The drag queen's eyes widened slightly.

"I would love to buy you a drink," Pet said, looking at the stranger through her lashes as she stroked his forearm. "But my mostly magnanimous, but sometimes stingy boss won't give us our own money, I'm afraid."

Guinevere leaned forward, showing ample cleavage. "What if I were to tell you that your *always* magnanimous boss arranged in the contract for each of the Players and the support musicians to get one free drink at the bar each night?"

"Then I would ask," Pet answered softly, her lips turned up in a suggestive grin, "what you would like to drink?"

"Anything schnapps, my darling, preferably apple."

"I'll be right back." Pet bowed to the blonde bombshell in drag and made her way to the bar.

The drag queen leaned back and addressed Jason over his shoulder. "I don't know why you don't ask her out."

"That's easy," Jason replied before taking a sip of water. His tone was matter-of-fact, but his eyes stayed on Pet as she leaned across the bar to talk to the bartender. "When I kiss her on stage, I'm not playing a scene; she is."

The stranger made a moue with his ruby-colored lips. "Hmmm..." He turned to Max. "And, you—you're one of the new trumpet players...Max Wrightson?" He held out a gloved hand.

Oh, what the hell. When in Rome... He took the gloved hand and kissed it. "Yes, Mistress Guinevere. Have we met before?"

"Oh, yes—at your audition." Guinevere turned back around as Pet returned to the table. The Player looked dejected as she sat back down in her chair and set a small glass of green liquid in front of the drag queen.

"I'm afraid you have led me astray, Mistress, and you have broken my heart." Pet pointed towards the main door of the dining hall. "You have a husband."

Max turned and saw Lord Justin Maplewood dressed in a tuxedo, looking around the hall.

Mistress Guinevere *tsked*. "Husbands can be *so* inconvenient," he muttered. The stranger stood up and waved. "My love! Over here!"

Justin saw Guinevere and smiled broadly, waving in return. He started towards the table.

Oh. So if Mistress Guinevere is Justin's husband... He watched as the director of the Players kissed Justin passionately on the mouth.

Wow, Max was now *so* glad he had played along. *That*...was close.

"Making friends already?" Justin asked Guinevere. He looked at Pet. "I'm Lancesalot, Guinevere's musical and otherwise life companion." They shook hands as a slow grin spread across Pet's face.

"Oh, that's just brilliant!" she exclaimed. "What brings you to the Jersey Lily Resort, Mistress Guinevere and Sir Lancesalot?"

"No," Lancesalot corrected, "no title—I'm not a stick-jock. Or, not that kind." Everyone at the table smiled; theirs was one of the few tables in the room that would appreciate the full joke.

"We're here to perform our cabaret show," Guinevere told her. "We are on our way to a command performance at Madame Serena's home for some of her more intimate friends. It will also be an opportunity to get the kinks out."

Max allowed himself the slightest of smirks as he took a sip of water.

"Thank you for the drink, Miss Pet. Good night, all!" Guinevere waved to the table as he and Justin walked towards the exit.

Pet gave Jason a sardonic look. "You could have told me."

"And miss all that fun?" he asked, his smile full of mischief.

"Fun for *you*," she clarified.

Max watched them bicker as he pondered over everything he had seen so far tonight. She wasn't encouraging a good-looking guy like Jason at all, according to him, but then she was more than willing to flirt with her gay married director in drag? He was *sure* she was about to jump his bones when he first walked into the practice room, and then she suddenly stopped herself.

So, that meant she was either a cock-tease, more flexible than even *he* was about whom she'd invite into her bed, or she was insecure.

Or...yes? He supposed he had three weeks to puzzle that out.

Practice Building 1
The Jersey Lily Resort
May 7th
9:03 a.m.

Lizzy

Justin and Wills managed to find a former college-level music professor with conducting experience, and Dr. Hanks was a good choice. He was serious about the music, but had a light hand with the musicians themselves. After warm-ups and tune-ups, he gathered the group around him in a circle.

"For the first hour," he told the ensemble in his thick Bronx accent, "I want you to fight amongst yourselves for chairs. Get it out of your systems! Ask for opinions, flip coins, see what the escorts think, whatever, but we have a lot of work to do, and we don't have the time for formal challenges. Once everyone's settled, we'll start with the first set of dinner music—and I want it error-free!"

The four trumpet players looked at each other. Lizzy didn't even have to think about it: she maneuvered around to the last chair in the trumpet section and sat down. The remaining three trumpet players just looked at her.

"You're not going to challenge anyone?" Rob asked, a young man from Raven Moonwitch's group.

"Nope," she replied. "I was at all of your auditions, and you are all better than I am. Besides, I've already been practicing the fourth part of all the music, and I don't have the time to practice solos and complicated riffs. You guys have fun."

The rest of the trumpet players enlisted the xylophonist to judge their interpretations of solo from Louis Armstrong's "Wild Man Blues." It was clear that Rob was third chair, but first chair was a dead heat between Max and a mundane musician named Jake who had been visiting the "Paradiso Renaissance Faire" and had heard about the auditions.

"Flip a coin?" Jake asked.

"No way," Max replied, looking around. "Let's get another opinion." After several split decisions, Dr. Hanks finally had to settle the issue.

"Divide the parts," he finally exclaimed, "and the solos! It's not the New York Philharmonic; it's a background music gig at a resort." He clomped away.

"Who sits where?" Jake asked Max.

"Oh, I'll sit second chair," he said, taking his seat. He pointed at Lizzy. "It's closer to her." He leaned back in his chair and grinned at her.

"Well, for all that," she said, looking him in the eyes, "why not take third chair?"

He gave her an assessing look. "Too tempting—I'd never pay attention."

Very cheesy...and not true. It was his pride, even in this small matter, that kept him there. *Flattering enough he took second chair, I suppose.*

There were a lot of good moments during the preparation week. Musical direction under Dr. Hanks was unlike anything she had ever experienced in high school. For one thing, every morning began with backrubs in a large circle.

"Always needs to be in a circle!" the conductor called out on the first morning as he massaged the shoulders of a saxophonist, a clarinet player kneading his. "We had backrubs when I was in my university choir as an undergrad, and because I was on the end of the row I always got screwed! Never again!"

He was also very free with his language and allegories. He was never directly insulting—it was implied that neither the situation nor the musicians were worth the energy his full wrath—but his made his displeasure clear when he wanted to.

"Too much embellishment, Mr. Wrightson!" he called out once after one of Max's solos. "People, this isn't a porn film—good vanilla sex is all the circumstances require, if you know what I mean! Meaning, yes, feeling, yes, fucking, yes, but no swinging from the chandelier! Let's try it again!"

She also had pleasant dinners with Max every evening, always at a table full of Players, supplemental musicians, or even performers from other companies. He had a natural talent for engagement and inclusion, which she was sure came in handy as a businessman. It was always interesting to learn about the other musicians, whose backgrounds and ideas were as varied as the instruments they played. Other than the practice room and the dining room, however, the musicians didn't have time see much of the resort that week, or to see the current acts.

"You're not guests, people!" Dr. Hanks announced one afternoon when he overheard some wisps of grumbling about their full rehearsal schedule. "You're performers! I don't know about you, but this is the best working vacation *I've* ever had, and we'll only be invited back if we do this well! Work your asses off now, and you can enjoy free time between gigs for the next two weeks!"

And, it *was* a great working vacation. The performers had to share a room with another person—Lizzy shared hers with Sweet Bess—but each room had its own bathroom with a plumbed shower *with a bathtub* and the resort provided *laundry service!* Lizzy was amazed the first time she left a pile of dirty clothes on her bed in the morning and came back to freshly washed and folded pants and shirts in the afternoon. There was even room service, but that was extra and therefore unavailable to musicians with sometimes stingy bosses.

Then suddenly it was Sunday afternoon, and it was showtime—they were dismissed early from their final practice to change into their costumes and get ready. Lizzy took an extra-long hot shower and took her time putting on her outfit and applying her makeup. She was a little dismayed that the fishnet tights didn't camouflage the through-and-through bullet hole scar that she acquired just before leaving Commune Ruth, but if the light was dim enough perhaps no one would notice. She knew the Players had seen it—she caught them all looking at it at one point or another—but in Player tradition no one ever asked about it. She slipped on her flats and her fingerless fishnet gloves, grabbed her trumpet case, and then walked out the door to go to the dining room.

The main dining room was located below the glass dome in the center of the building. It was a huge open area, with the orchestra area located in the front, dining tables and the bar in the back, and a hardwood dance floor in the center. There were alcoves along all the walls that contained intimate eating areas, including a few triclinia and some recesses that were darkened by heavy curtains on either side of their openings.

Several musicians were already tuning each other and warming up, and she saw Dr. Hanks talking to Justin. It was good to see the co-manager—she hadn't seen the non-ensemble Players much at all that week. Dr. Hanks seemed to be very excited about his costume, pointing out to Justin the aviator goggles on his black top hat and the way the long black tails of his gentleman's coat and his tan poofy aviator pants hid some of his more paunchy flaws. The intricately tied dark green cravat above his multi-button vest and the knee-high spats were especially nice touches.

Raul and Sasha do work their magic. Lizzy didn't know when the two of them found the time to design and make all of these costumes. She was so distracted, being pleased that Dr. Hanks was so pleased, that she almost ran straight into Max, who was standing straight and as rigid as a statue staring at her, delectably wrapped in his suspenders and the aforementioned black bowler hat, his trumpet slack in his hand.

Oh, right, she remembered, seeing the hungry look in his eyes. *I'm wearing the chainsaw outfit tonight.* She looked up into his face and smiled. "Hi."

"You look…" He looked at her legs and visibly swallowed. "Oh, I should have taken third chair."

"Oh, well," she replied brightly. She walked past him and took her seat next to Rob, who was in a more wild-west-type outfit with a black vest and pants and a white billowy shirt. "Hey, Rob, how ya doin'?"

He gave her an assessing glance. "Better now?"

She grinned as she unsnapped her instrument case. "Good answer."

A couple of hours later the last of the audience's applause died away, closing out their first set. Dr. Hanks looked very pleased.

"Not bad!" he said to the ensemble from his podium, loosening his cravat as he spoke. "We had some guests dancing at the end there, and everyone seemed to enjoy our repertoire. That's all, people! See you tomorrow for the noon rehearsal."

Lizzy cleaned out her trumpet and put it away. When she looked up after securing her case, she saw that Max had moved over and was sitting in third chair, quietly admiring her. She felt herself turning pink under his gaze.

"Going to dinner?" she asked him, getting to her feet.

"Sure." He rose from his chair, as well. He reached over and took her case from her hand, and then offered her his arm. "Let's go."

After she was finished with her dinner, she stood up to go change—Bill and Paul were opening their show tomorrow night, and they wanted her at their final rehearsal in the practice room. She felt a hand on her shoulder.

"Care to dance?" It was the first evening they didn't have a rehearsal, and the band on-stage was playing selections from Glenn Miller.

"Sorry—gotta get back to work," she said, flashing Max a glance of apology. "Paul and Bill are expecting me."

He kept his hand on her shoulder and reached for one of hers with the other one. He smelled like the resort's soap and valve oil, which wasn't a bad combination. "One dance."

She heard the clarinets play the opening strains of "Moonlight Serenade," one of her favorite songs.

What the hell. "OK." She took his hand and allowed him to lead her onto the dance floor. They found an empty space among the sea of couples, and she felt his arm curl around her waist and pull her close. As they moved together in silence for several measures, listening to the music, she could feel his fingers casually running along the boning in her corset along her back.

"Maybe you could come back later tonight?" he whispered, his breath silky and warm against her ear.

"I could try," she replied softly, fingering his suspenders. "Will I have you to myself?"

He stiffened ever so slightly in her arms. Max pulled back a little so he could look into her face; his was impassive.

"Relax," she told him gently. "It was an informational question. You're not getting any action from me this gig, so you might as well take advantage."

"What's that supposed to mean?" He actually sounded a little insulted.

She made it a point to keep her tone genial. "It means, you've arrived at your own personal version of heaven at the Jersey Lily Resort, and I totally appreciate that you'd want to sample the candy, specifically that pretty little violinist and at least two of the female wait staff."

He looked genuinely surprised, even shocked. "I thought I was being discreet," he muttered flatly.

He had been discreet, actually. Unfortunately for him, as tight-lipped as the Players were about themselves and each other, they were horrendous gossips when it came to outsiders. He hadn't stood a chance.

"You don't have to be," she suggested, lightly stroking the nape of his neck. "Of all the places on earth, why *would* you choose this place to behave yourself—seriously? If I was having sex with you I might be pissed off, but I like to know the men I sleep with a little better before I fuck them."

"OK." Now he looked confused. "So...you've been having dinner with me every night and you're..." Max cleared his throat, "...driving me crazy, doing that back-of-the-neck thing because...?"

"I'm getting to know you better," Lizzy said, slipping the fingers of her other hand underneath a tan strap and trailing them down his back, following below the suspender until it ended at the top of his trousers. "I find you attractive," she continued, resting her hand just below his waist, easing herself in closer so their faces were only a couple of inches apart.

"I'm enjoying our time together," she murmured as she looked into his eyes, "a lot."

He leaned in and kissed her, a supple, gentle press of his mouth against hers. "Me, too." He still looked confused, but he also looked relieved.

She smiled at him as she heard the conclusion of the song and the other dancers begin to applaud.

"That's good," giving him a quick kiss in return and pulling away. "Thank you for the dance—see you tomorrow!" she said, gifting him with her sunniest smile before she walked off the dance floor. She didn't look back.

Providence, WY
*May 21*th
12:00 p.m.

Zaki

They weren't SCAdian anymore, but Zaki didn't know what to call themselves. *Militiamen* didn't seem to fit, either.

What was ironic about their situation was that El Hajj had been the purest SCAdian group in the Middle Kingdom, perhaps in the Known World. Mundanes who took refuge in SCAdian lands and adopted their ways rarely ever wanted to travel around with a nomadic tribe. The majority of El Hajj was made of two pre-Infusion households that had merged when they realized how confining the Known World had become even after only two years. People were expected to live in permanent dwellings, work assigned schedules, give away a cut of their business profits— what was next, paying sales tax? Buying permits to carry weapons?

Charge association fees, like they were living in fucking condos?

So the two households and a few other families became El Hajj, the finest and most respected traders in the Known World, but not of it. Their specialties were transporting people in style and carrying breakable items, such as wine bottles or blown glass tributes to royalty, and they answered to no one except perhaps the kings. They treated the land with respect, they were paid well for their services, and they enjoyed a fine heritage, with some members three or even four generations SCAdian. His uncle, Maalik, was a noble man and a fair businessperson. The tribe thrived.

Then Zaki met Christina.

He should have known better than to see her—her aunt Isabella, that playacting whore, hated the tribe for their freedom and their autonomy. To the baroness, El Hajj symbolized everything that was wrong with SCAdians and was the complete inverse of what she wished to accomplish in her own barony. She thought herself a religious prophet—that was well known—and yet she strove to make the Known World the corrupt and eroded shell that the United States was before Infusion cleansed the earth.

That the demons were mankind's ultimate salvation was not a popular belief, but Zaki believed it. There were plenty of instances where nature had rid herself of millions of people through famine or disease—this just could be the latest round, right?

Christina was just...so vulnerable, so fragile. She was attracted to his strength and confidence as strongly as he was enticed by her devotion to him—she made him feel like a man, like someone who could take care of her. They had both lost their virginities together earlier that summer, in a deserted clearing not far from Hamilton. After three clumsy tries of him coming inside her easily but her not going anywhere, they had both watched the waterfall for a while before he awkwardly fingered her off. They decided to try again at Paradiso, in a barn that was never used during festival time.

The entire World knew what happened next. He could never forget running for his life, her juices still smeared on his flaccid cock and the cold wind on his bare ass as he sped naked back to their campsite. At least a hundred SCAdians and mundanes who had been attending the festival had seen him and his tear-streaked face. Even more than being discovered by Isabella fucking Christina, *that* had shamed him.

The first two years after that incident were the worst. Maalik had insisted that they were still SCAdians, and that they could just pick up trade in another kingdom. But that bitch slut made sure that no SCAdian barony would offer legitimate trade, so El Hajj was forced to eat the crumbs no one wanted. They started transporting vats of shit, barrels of discarded chemicals, even half-spoiled goods that stunk for miles in the summer heat. The tribe lived, but they were a shadow of what they had been. They were scorned in public by mundanes in SCAdian clothing, forced off campsites, and even had rotten fruit and rocks thrown at them. He understood now the plight of the Romany, the Jews, and the oppressed. Hate and prejudice had begun again in this new World—to them.

Then, a cleansing of another sort began in the tribe. His Uncle Maalik became ill, and as his health faltered, his father Rohan's power rose within the tribe. Rohan began to negotiate deals with the nearby militia towns, and they were now transporting alcohol, weapons, and even narcotics. Zaki was amazed at how powerful some of the drugs were that they were carrying, made of things he had never heard of.

"It's never disgraceful to feed your family," his father told him. "We transport goods, we don't ask questions, and we take care of our own."

After a year under Rohan's *de facto* leadership, El Hajj became notable again, but not exactly respected. They thrived again, but they were more cautious now—meaner, too, though Zaki thought through no fault of their own. They also might have even been doing a public service in some cases: there were entire villages full of people that relied on their daily fixes just to get through the day, happily trading everything they had for an oblivious existence.

Sometimes, though, the tribe would return a community like that and notice that it seemed empty and too quiet. El Hajj wouldn't look too closely then, but would silently move on.

He had last seen his uncle the night before he died. He had wasted away from some sort of cancer, everyone had thought, and Zaki hadn't even recognized the flesh-covered skeleton that lay on the pallet in his grandmother's tent. Maalik didn't talk, he didn't move—he just breathed in with these horrible, rattling gasps, and then made thin exhalations. It was a blessing when he finally passed. Zaki never wanted to grow old, never wanted to die like that—he swore he'd put a bullet in his own head or overdose first.

They had recently begun a partnership with the Patriot's Defense Force, a militia group from up north rumored to have ties to the former US military. Zaki had heard stories of the group overwhelming rivals with *way* superior firepower, including automatic weapons and rocket-propelled grenades. Rohan had assigned Zaki to be their liaison, which surprised him at first. After the Paradiso incident, his father was cool and stand-offish towards his son, blaming him—and rightly so—for everything that had happened to the tribe. Rohan had recognized his look of puzzlement.

"You've done everything I've asked since I've led the tribe, and you've never complained," Rohan explained. "You even married Fidelma without me having to formally ask you to. I'd like you to be a part of our new era—I have big plans for us."

It felt so good to have his father's love again, and he would not let him down.

The tribe's first official meeting with the Patriot's Defense Force had been in a saloon in the half-deserted town of Providence. When he met the Force's representative, he asked how El Hajj could be of service.

"The usual," the man replied, a scrawny, slight scarecrow named Pete. "We need some things transported, mostly non-perishable items."

Non-perishable items always meant drugs or weapons. "That's fine."

Pete took a sip of moonshine, grimaced, and then leaned back in his chair.

"Though," he said casually, "there's something special that you may be able to help us with."

"What is it?"

"Part of how we make our living is to sell crops to the former US military," he began. He looked at Zaki's face for his reaction.

There was nothing there—Zaki didn't give a shit.

"But recently," Pete continued, "they've been asking for goods during the winter months, offering double their payment if we can deliver. We've been trying to set up hydroponic gardens to accommodate them, but... it's trickier than we had thought. It only takes one thing, and then the whole crop is ruined." His chair creaked as he leaned forward, meeting Zaki's eyes.

"We understand that you may know a way to help us with our problem." He took another sip from his shot glass.

Zaki's eyes burned with excitement. "I might." He now understood why his father had given him this task. "What did you have in mind?"

Dining Room
The Jersey Lily Resort
May 22nd
7:39 p.m.

Lizzy

"Do you have anything planned this evening?" Lizzy asked Max over dessert.

"No." He took a sip of his tea. "What's going on?"

"The Mistress Guinevere and Lancesalot Cabaret Show opens tonight. I was hoping you would take me."

He grinned. "You want me to take you to a drag show?"

She leaned over and gently traced the curve of his ear with her fingers. "I'd like you to take me to a show—it just so happens to be a drag show."

"OK," he said in between a couple of shallow breaths, "whatever the lady wants."

"Now we're talking," she said pleasantly. "Thank you."

Lizzy was absolutely, totally shocked at how good Mistress Guinevere's show was. With Wills singing and Justin on the piano, they made an incredible performance team. Gwen, as Justin's Lancesalot called her during the act, kept her patter light but, somehow, she seemed to connect with every person in the audience, making them feel at home. She didn't move around much at all, but was able to change the mood in the room with just a turn of her head, or the tilt of her chin, or even simply

261

sliiiding her leg up and over as she sat on a stool, crossing it over her knee. And, *god*, could she sing.

Lancesalot was her perfect complement as her piano accompanist. He was dashing in a tuxedo, gave her patter affirmations when it needed them, and made the air crackle around them just by looking at her. They were an attractive couple, and they shared their love for life and for each other freely with their audience. They received a standing ovation at the end of their show, with *two* encores.

The Moonstruck Performing Company came out next with a small band and started playing a jazz set. Lizzy stayed at her table with Max and Gunther, stirring the remains of her drink and occasionally listening as the two men swapped brewing recipes and debated about the best ways to keep their equipment sterile. Just about the time she was ready to stand up and turn in, however, she saw Wills striding up to their table as fast as his heels would allow him. She made no mistake that this was Wills in drag, and not Mistress Guinevere, because his Gwen persona would never look this scared. Lizzy and the two men stood up.

"What's wrong?" she asked Wills as he reached over and grabbed her hand. He was still wearing his elbow-length cream gloves to match the sequined floor-length gown.

"Dance with me, Pet!" He dragged her over to the dance floor. "Can you bump and grind?" He took a breath and exhaled, put his hands on her hips, and started to gyrate to the beat of the snare and the hi-hat.

"Sure, though it's been several years—Brydan didn't like to dance." She put her arms around his neck, tilted her pelvis up, and started to move with him. When he saw that she was willing to go with whatever was happening, he visibly relaxed.

"So, what's wrong?" she asked him after a couple of measures.

"If you look over by the bar, there's a table with a man and four women; the women are all escorts."

Lizzy glanced over. "OK."

"He...misunderstood what a drag show was. He thinks I'm a woman, and he made it clear that he wouldn't take no for an answer."

Oh, really? After she smashed a liquor bottle over his head he'd take no for an answer. "Where's Justin?"

"Changing clothes—it's been so long since I've played a straight venue, I forgot to take the necessary precautions." He looked into her face and sighed. "He wasn't violent, just persistent. Put your claws back in, Miss Pet; we're playing a scene right now."

She took a deep breath and exhaled as she stroked Wills' fake breasts and ran her hands down his sides before sliding them up his back and around his neck again. She made her best seductive smile as she tried to relax. "So, we're putting on a show because...?"

"It's important not to make a scene—it destroys the illusion of the place, upsets the guests." Wills bent and swayed down to the floor until his face was near her crotch—all the more impressive considering how tight his gown was—and then worked his way back up her body until they were grinding again. "The staff noticed my distress, and considering I do not have a lily in my hair and are therefore off-limits, I believe they're just going to slip him a mickey and dump him at the curb—Serena has no patience for that kind of thing. So, we'll give him some girl-on-girl action to watch until the drug kicks in, which shouldn't take long."

Lizzy looked over and smiled provocatively at the idiot. "He's already had about five shots just sitting there. He may just pass out on his own." She turned around and leaned back against Wills' chest; he leaned his pelvis forward against her and ground himself against her bustle. Lizzy now noticed that pretty much the entire room was watching them; she grinned. "We're apparently quite a show, boss—maybe we should make an act out of this."

Wills made a very unladylike snort.

The song was almost at an end—Lizzy hoped the guy would drop soon. She spun back around. "Dip me," she instructed.

He did, running his palm down the center of her chest between her breasts and along her stomach. He straightened her up just as the band played their finishing notes, and she thought she may have heard a *thud* somewhere as she gave him a swift kiss on the mouth for effect. As the crowd whooped and applauded, they both turned to look.

Mission accomplished. Wills and Lizzy looked at each other and grinned.

"Um...excuse me?" Justin was behind them, dressed in khakis and a black button-down shirt and looking a little...angry? "What was all that about?"

Lizzy burst out laughing. *I have such a strange life...*

"I'll let her explain," she answered. "I need a drink. Thanks for the dance, Mistress Guinevere."

"Anytime, my dear." The Gwen persona had re-emerged. She linked her arm with her husband's. "Buy me a drink, my love, and I'll explain everything..."

Lizzy shook her head as she walked back to her table. Neither of the men said a word—they just stared at her, stunned. She grabbed Gunther's untouched shot of something amber-colored and swigged it; it was liquid fire.

"YEEG!" she proclaimed, making a face. "Thanks, Gunther. See you guys tomorrow!" She set down the shot glass and walked towards the door: the perfect ending for an incredible night.

The next morning, she made her way down to the dining room. There was the usual amount of guest traffic—people taking a short cut, getting a quick drink at the bar—and Justin was sitting at the piano, practicing. He saw her coming towards him and stopped playing mid-measure.

"She told you, right?" Lizzy asked cautiously as she stopped within safe escaping distance.

He grinned at her as he stood and walked across the dance floor.

"Yes, she did," he said as he closed in, picked her up, and spun her around in his arms; her feet flew off the ground in a wide arc. In addition to being a tree-huggy pianist, he was evidently person-huggy, too, when he decided to be. He placed her back on the floor, but not before he gave her one more brief squeeze.

"That must have been uncomfortable, Pet," he said as he guided her towards the piano. "Thank you so much for doing that."

"What, the dancing?"

He nodded as he sat back down at the piano bench.

"No, it was fine," she assured him as she leaned forward onto the side of the piano. "It was just Wills. It was fun—exciting, even—but it was just a scene."

264

Justin started to play a rolling, beautiful melody as he smiled. "Life is never boring when my husband is around—he makes sure of that."

She paused. "Justin, can I ask you something?"

"Sure."

She felt uncomfortable, but she figured he had been asked this before. "How do you square it with yourself, when Wills is Gwen? You look at him...her...the same way."

From his knowing smirk, it was clear that Justin had been asked the question many times before, but he answered it respectfully.

"Still Wills," he simply replied. He played a dramatic crescendo, and then went back to the original composition as he continued the conversation. "Think of your Brian in drag. You'd still love him, right?"

"Brian?"

He gave her a dry look. "Brian, the one who didn't like to dance with you...though I can't imagine why."

"Oh," she said, smiling. That happened a lot, folks misunderstanding his name. "Bry-*dan*." She paused, wondering if she wanted to share this or not. Then she decided, what the hell.

"Brydan was my husband. He had two left feet, but he made up for it in other ways." Then she told him the same basic information that she had given John in the woods the previous year. When she was done, Justin seemed to mull over her story as his music became more bittersweet, more poignant.

"That's awful," he finally said. "At least when Wills and I have to hide our affections we're still together; I can't imagine being separated from your spouse like that and then never seeing him again. I'm sorry." No one said anything for several measures; the music was still beautiful, but melancholy. Then Justin asked a question.

"No one else since then?" His voice was kind.

She shook her head. "There were no opportunities where I was...stationed...and since then..." She shrugged. "I guess there hasn't been much opportunity here, either. I don't want to get involved with anyone in the troupe—that seems like sleeping with your shipmates to me, and that almost never works out well—and..." She shrugged again.

"We're really not settled in a place long enough, are we?" he observed. "We see people briefly, just here and there..." His eyes sparkled as he looked off into the distance. The music grew joyful again.

"I'm very OK with that," she assured him, confused by the happy melody. "My life here with the troupe has been amazing, and the couple of lonely nights here and there is well worth it to me. I wouldn't change a thing."

"Hmmm," was his only reply.

She was involved in several performances at the Jersey Lily Resort. She played the trumpet during the "Dinner and Dancing" set, which happened every night from 5:00 p.m. to 7:30 p.m.; she sat in on "An Evening with Bill and Paul," which was a guitar/violin cabaret show that ran Mondays, Wednesdays, and Fridays from 8:00 p.m. to 9:30 p.m.; she also played trumpet for the "Jump and Jive" swing show on the first Saturday and Sunday nights after 10:00 p.m. and assisted with *The Canterbury Tales* for the Sunday matinee.

Though it wasn't mandatory, she also went to as many midnight improv shows as she could manage, and she *never* missed "The Mistress Guinevere and Lancesalot Cabaret Show" on Tuesdays and Thursdays from 8:00 p.m. to 9:30 p.m., just sitting in the audience.

The trumpet-playing was pretty straightforward—she just had to follow the sheet music. Cabaret, however, was much more challenging. The audience was always limited to about thirty people, so it was an intimate affair. Bill and Paul would mix songs with patter to include the audience and frame the next song. What made cabaret tricky was that it almost completely demolished the fourth wall, so the audience became part of the show. She was a little intimidated about that at first, but Bill and Paul had a rapport between them that was substantial enough to include any audience. She also, for the most part, did not get involved in the patter—she was only there to accompany them.

She heard their patter during rehearsals, and while they did improvise from show to show, it was basically the same themes: Bill would tell a story about growing up in Michigan before singing Stan Rogers' "The Mary Ellen Carter," Paul would talk about going to cabarets in New York City before singing Simon and Garfunkel's "The Only Living Boy in New York." But then, on the first Friday performance, Paul improvised some patter with her.

"So, Pet," he said, picking casually, "You've been spending a lot of time with Max."

"Sure—he's a lot of fun." She played along and grinned for the crowd but wondered where this was going. She turned to the audience. "Max is one of the other trumpet players in the troupe, maybe you've seen him: medium height, dark hair..." She stared into space for a moment. "Very...talented embouchure." She looked back at Paul and twitched her nose at him, smiling. The audience chuckled, and a few people assented that they did know who she was talking about.

"Is it serious?" he asked.

"No—he hasn't even asked me out on an official date yet." She turned back to the crowd. "Do you think he should?" she asked them. The audience whistled and clapped their approval. Paul stopped picking his guitar, so she started to play.

"Y'know, he won't last," he told her. He froze, and then his eyes widened as if to say, *did I just say that?*

Paul had broken a cardinal rule in improv: never say *no, can't,* or *won't.*

Plus...he just made *his* opinion known, hadn't he? She stopped playing and went a little blue.

"That's not what *I've* heard," she said with her most suggestive smile. She made a *Twang!* with her guitar string for emphasis and kept on playing. The crowd laughed and hooted. Paul looked relieved.

Just then, one of his guitar strings broke; the tension of the moment broke, too. He looked at Bill.

"Damn, we were just getting to the good part, too!" He stood up and looked at Lizzy. "Mind singing something while I take care of this?"

"Not at all, boss." She smiled at him: in that one question he indirectly apologized for being an ass while also throwing her a bone. She picked her strings a little, and then looked at the audience, grinning wickedly. "At last, I have my moment!" The audience chuckled in response.

Bill sat next to her. "What are you playing for them?" He addressed both her and the spectators.

Lizzy thought, playing some successive chords. "Ever hear of 'Miss Celie's Blues?'"

"I think so. Start playing; I'll catch up."

"OK." She looked at the audience. "This was a favorite where I come from, where good men are...hard to find." She geared up the introduction and belted out Shug's song from *The Color Purple*. It was saucy and quick, and Lizzy put a little English on it to make it playful. Bill chose not to accompany her, but just listened with the audience. When she was done, he slapped his leg in applause.

"Forget Max; take me," he quipped after the clapping had died down; everyone laughed.

"Miss Petya, everyone!" he announced, gesturing to her. She bowed slightly as Bill got up and Paul took his seat again, and then they continued with the show as usual.

She was winding down at the bar after the show, sloe gin fizz in hand, wondering who the hell Paul thought *he* was when she sensed someone approaching her from behind. She first felt large hands on her shoulders, and then each hand followed their corresponding arm in a long, slow stroke down to her hands, so that by the end she could feel the warmth of Max's front against her back, his body surrounding hers. He leaned down and kissed her neck.

"So... I hear I should ask you out?" he asked in a smooth rumble.

She closed her eyes and enjoyed the feel of him. *He is so good at this...* "That would be an excellent idea."

Abruptly, he released her and sat on the bar stool next to her. He looked directly at into her eyes. "Would you like to go out with me?"

"Yes, yes I would," she replied, smiling.

That formality out of the way, Max got the bartender's attention and ordered a lager. He turned back to Lizzy. "When?"

She thought about when they both had off. "Sunday morning?"

"Sounds good—maybe a hike? We could take one of the trails."

"OK," she took a sip of her drink. "How did you find out about it?"

"A couple of the guests mentioned it to me. The one woman said that we would make a cute couple." He took her hand and kissed it, and then he held onto it as they talked for the rest of the evening.

The Caesar Room
June 1st
8:28 p.m.

The two weeks went by in a blur. Before she knew it, it was the last performance of Bill and Paul's show. Justin sat in as himself to mess around on the piano and add some of his own stories about coming to New York City as a young, pimply-faced pianist from Maryland, fresh from the university. He described how he had delivered for almost every Chinese take-out place in Queens at one point or another while trying to get music work, and that they all seemed to have the exact same menu.

"It was like McDonald's," he said over a mild, pleasant tune. "You could call any of those restaurants at random and order a 14 and a 58, and you'd always get the exact same thing. It was unintentional but very efficient."

"So, what was 14 and 58?" Paul asked him.

Justin thought for a moment. "Shrimp Lo Mein and the General Zhao's combination platter." He smirked at Paul, winked at the audience with a quick shake of his head, and then changed the subject.

"So, one day I saw an ad looking a pianist for a cabaret show," he began one story as he played "Spring in Manhattan." "The ad specifically wanted a blonde man with prior experience. The pay wasn't great, I'm not blonde, and I had no experience, but I decided, what the hell.

"I get to the address, and it is the worst flea-bag of a place you've ever seen. I mean, this building should have been condemned. But I go inside and knock on the given apartment door, and the most beautiful woman I've ever seen opens it, wearing this thigh-high green beaded dress. But not only was she gorgeous beyond measure, she had a certain...mystique...that I found absolutely irresistible. I fell in love with her immediately.

269

"So, she just stands there in the doorway and stares at me for a moment, and then she smiles and says..." He stopped playing and looked out into the audience.

"It's you." Justin paused, and then started playing again. "It was love at first sight for both of us."

"So, I guess you got the job?" Paul asked.

"Sure did," he replied, his eyes welling up a little. Lizzy's eyes got moist, too, just watching him. "That was almost twenty years ago. The pay still isn't great..."

The audience chuckled.

"But, what a ride it's been." He looked into the audience. "Let me perform one of the songs from our very first show. Gwen would sing it better, but she's having girl time with Madame Serena this evening, so we'll make do."

"Manicures?" Bill joked.

"I don't even want to know," he muttered with the look of a slightly exasperated husband. He played a few chords, and then sang and played a heart-melting rendition of Sinatra's "When Somebody Loves You." After the applause and the collective sniffling, Paul turned to Lizzy.

"So, Pet, you got anything for us?" he asked in his stage voice.

She stared at him for a moment, swallowing the lump in her throat. "I can't follow that!" she protested in her stage voice.

"*I* can't follow that," he told her, to the amusement of the audience. "And I'm too choked up right now."

"OK, boss." They had told her beforehand to prepare something, and she had. She had made up some patter to introduce the selection, but decided to skip it and go right into the song, which was "Leaving on a Jet Plane."

She considered the lyrics as she sang. She completely skipped the second verse—completely inappropriate and a little pathetic, frankly—and concentrated on the rest of the words, the yearning and the wanting to stay and the travelling anyway. She now felt that way about the Jersey Lily—she didn't want to leave. None of the Players did, either—it was a wonderful venue, and they all hoped it would become a regular gig on the yearly route.

And what would it be like, she thought, to have someone waiting for her to come home to Valhalla? She glanced over at Paul during the guitar solo and smiled at him, knowing that he had that relationship with his wife, Jen. It was a little like the relationship she had with her own husband long ago.

He smiled back, his expression bittersweet and maybe a little teary.

Justin began to accompany her during the second verse, as if they had rehearsed it that way, and the audience sang along during the final chorus. When she finished, Paul came up to her and hugged her as the crowd clapped and snuffled all over again.

"Dammit, Pet," he said just to her, obviously choked up, "you were supposed to *lighten* the mood!"

"Sorry, boss," she said, pulling away and grinning at him. "I knew you'd like it."

"I did—well done." He turned to acknowledge her one last time to the crowd. In forty-five minutes, the show would be over. In eighteen hours, their time at the Jersey Lily would be at an end, and they'd be packing up their bags, ready to go home.

Dining Room
June 2nd
0745

OK, it was true—she *was* deliberately trying to avoid Max by sitting in the almost empty dining room that morning: she didn't like the idea of being on a shopping list of women for him to say goodbye to. As she sipped her mug of sweetened chicory coffee, she wondered glumly where she had been in the list's pecking order. It didn't matter at that point, anyway—the supplemental musicians were scheduled to leave fifteen minutes ago, and she had made it a point to say her farewells to everyone the previous evening.

He didn't have her heart—she wasn't *that* stupid—but she would miss his sexually-charged companionship and their nightly dinners. There were just so damn few people in her life that weren't Players or peers—it was nice to be able to flirt and tease someone without worrying about propriety or potential break-up awkwardness.

And, yes, his embouchure was *amazingly* talented. *Damn his eyes...*

271

"*There* you are!" she heard from the main doorway as Max ran into the dining room and towards her table.

She jumped to her feet, irked with herself at the thrill of seeing him. "Weren't you supposed to have left by now?"

"Yes—the others are about to tear me a new one. I need to make this quick." He used his momentum to lift her, wrapping her in his arms as he asked, "You don't like goodbyes, do you?"

Lizzy shook her head, breathing in his warmth and his scent. God help her, she was tearing up. "I'll miss you," she said, kissing his cheek.

"I know I'll miss you," Max replied softly, his lips on her neck and working his way up. "When do I see you again?"

"Sunflower Festival?" He needed to get going—she did *not* want this scene interrupted by angry musicians who just wanted to get home. As she took his face in her hands and kissed him, he opened their mouths with his tongue and swept it inside to meet hers, tightening his arms around her to hold them steady.

God, this is so much better when you can mean it. After several mind-numbing seconds, they gently released each other, breathing unsteadily.

"I'll see you in two months, then," Max said, giving her one more gentle kiss. He grinned at her as he ran out from whence he came.

She stared at the doorway after him for a few moments, her insides dissolving and roiling. Then she raised her mug and swallowed the remainder of her coffee in one gulp.

Reality check, Townsend, she thought to herself. *How many times do you think he did* that *last night?* She considered the possibilities...and sighed.

Yup, roger that: sense reacquired, reality check sat. Her guts calmed down as she took a moment to mentally pack up all that she was feeling and put it away. It was fun while it lasted, but...

Back to being the cautious and reserved military deserter. She took her leave of the dining room to secure her gear and make final preparations to depart.

It was so good to see Murray and Dr. Goldberg waiting for them at the crossroads. When Murray saw her, he waved her over.

"Hi, Pet! Want to ride for a while?" He patted an empty spot on the wagon's bench. She climbed aboard.

"Thanks! Damn, it's great to see you both," she said, clapping Murray on the shoulder and waving at Doc as his apprentice snapped the reins to move the horses forward. "How was your trip?"

His lips curved upwards. "It was really nice, actually. Good patients, nothing that we couldn't handle, and I took a half-hour hot shower every day." He leaned in a little and whispered, "Did you get any?"

She glanced over across Murray to Dr. Goldberg, who was staring straight ahead and doing his best not to eavesdrop on the conversation. She smiled.

"No," she replied, "but it was still a lot of fun—we were told they're going to invite us back next year."

"That's good—I wouldn't mind going back to the monastery every year. Hey, have you ever heard of the *Sandman* series?"

"No. What's it about?"

"It was a comic book series by this guy named Neil Gaiman, and the series was put together into graphic novels. One of the monks saw me reading *Watchmen* and thought I'd like it." He paused, looking a little star-struck. "I spent a whole week reading it."

"OK—what's it about?"

"Well, it's about this god, Dream, and his family called the Endless. His sister, Death, is this skinny goth chick..."

Murray just kept going over the course of their journey, telling Lizzy story after story about Morpheus of the Dreaming and his adventures, until they all arrived back at Fiddler's Green.

Zaki

As the two of them sat cross-legged in his father's tent and drank honey-laced chicory coffee, Rohan listened quietly to his son's report.

"If we agree to this," he said when Zaki was finished, "we'll be out of the transportation trade for a while."

"Yes," Zaki agreed. "But we can contract out most of our routes, I think."

"What about the mothers and the children?"

"The Force has agreed to let them homestead up there, on their lands. They'll be safe enough until we can come for them."

"So," his father said with a frown, "we've just fought all of these years to be unencumbered and free, and now you're suggesting that we permanently settle down?"

"Only until we secure the fields," Zaki replied. "Only for the summer, early fall at the latest." He paused. "But, it's about more than the pay, you know."

His father stroked his beard, considering this. "There is revenge."

"Yes, but not just for us: there's also something bigger than that." He sat his cup on the floor beside him and took a breath. "The Barony of the Brandywine is corrupt, not just because of what that slut did to us, but because of her stranglehold on the SCAdians and the Known World." He paused to gauge his father's reaction.

As a second-generation SCAdian, it was clear that his father was interested in this line of logic. "Go on."

"The SCAdians, the *true* SCAdians, would never have shunned us if Isabella didn't have the barons by their ball sacks—we both know that. She runs the barony, specifically Cornwall, like a mundane would, with her own appointed board and under-the-table political deals. In ten years, there will be nothing left of the SCAdian lifestyle in the Known World, believe me—no peers, no traditions, no Orders—she'll make the entire World comply to her standards." He leaned forward a little. "The SCAdians that survived the demon apocalypse deserve better than that, Father: they deserve to be liberated. We will take back those lands in their name, drive out Isabella and her politicians, and reclaim the lifestyle that was *earned* by our blood and tears all those years ago."

Rohan stared slack-jawed at his son for a long moment—and then smiled broadly.

"I had no idea you were so eloquent!" he told his son with pride in his voice.

Zaki smiled slightly. The words were mostly Pete's, but he silently took credit for the convincing delivery.

"With that reasoning," Rohan continued, "we'll not only have justification to do what we're about to do, but we'll be welcomed as conquering heroes!" He looked down at the ground in thought for a moment and then back up at Zaki, beaming.

"Hell, I'm almost convinced that we really *are* going on a crusade!" He stood, and then helped his son to his feet.

"Tell the Patriot's Defense Force that we're in." He clapped his son on the shoulder. "We'll start mobilizing immediately."

Chapter Ten

Red

Dr. Brian Jackson stepped out of Elspeth's room, draping his stethoscope around his neck. In the SCA he was known as Master Chirurgeon Wolfgang of Frankfurt, but before Infusion he had been a general practitioner for several years. He walked over to Red's office and knocked on the door frame.

"Come on in, Doc," Red called out.

Brian stepped inside the office. He moved some papers off a chair and sat down, and then took measure of Red's face. "You look awful. Shall I give you a work-up, too?"

Red didn't even pause. "What's wrong with Elspeth?"

Brian frowned. "I'm sorry, your Excellency, I wish I had better news. Empirically, she has cancer. If I had to guess, that lump in her right breast is the source. It's fairly small, I don't think it's metastasized yet, but it's hard to tell."

"Can you operate?"

"No," Brian replied. "I'm not a surgeon—I'm not even comfortable doing a biopsy—and I don't know of anyone that I would trust to do this. We can make her comfortable, Red, but that's all.

Brian paused, weighing out his next suggestions before speaking them. "I know you have...connections...but even if you were to get medicines for chemotherapy, I'm not really qualified to adminster them. You need a specialist, and I'm not sure where you would find one that would be willing to come out here."

Red sat back in his chair and looked at a point on the wall. After several moments, Brian started to wonder if Red was still cognizant. Finally, Red blinked a few times and looked at him.

"Thanks for coming out, Wolfgang," Red said. "I think I know someone who can help, but they live far from here; I'll send a dispatch. In the meantime, what do you suggest?"

Brian shrugged. "What you've been doing: painkillers, rest, lots of liquids. I also feel that I should warn you, Red: she was already weak from the flu she had a couple of months ago—I don't know how this will play out. If you are going to do something, you should probably do it fast.

"I'm sorry, Your Excellency," he said, rising to his feet. "I wish the situation was different."

Red stood, as well, and extended his hand. "Elspeth is a strong woman, Wolfgang. If there's any way, she'll pull through."

Brian shook Red's hand. "Send for me if I can do anything for you." He bowed and left the room.

Red waited a few minutes, staring at his Known World map. When he was sure the doctor had left, he walked across the hall to his bedroom and peeked in.

Elspeth was propped up on pillows in their bed, her hair in a braid. Her eyes were red and teary. "Did Wolfgang tell you, Caleb?"

Red walked over and sat on the edge of the bed. He took Elspeth's hand. "Yes, sweetheart, he did."

Elspeth looked down. "It doesn't sound, good, does it?"

"No, it sure doesn't." Red squeezed her hand. "But, I have some markers to call in. I'm going to see if I can get some help."

Elspeth looked up into Red's face. "I'd like to tell you to save them for times when the barony needs medical supplies, Caleb, but..." Tears fell down her sunken cheeks. "I am so tired of being tired, and I hurt, and I just want the pain to go away. I'm not even sixty-five yet, and I was hoping to spend some more of your retirement with you." Elspeth smiled at that last statement.

"OK," Red replied. "It might not be responsible of me as a baron, but I am not ready to let you go yet. I have some letters to write." Red kissed Elspeth on the forehead and then left the room.

When he got back to his office, Red immediately went to the farthest filing cabinet to the left and opened the top drawer. He fished through the file folders until he found the standard size, cream-colored card stock. Stagger Lee had given him ten pieces in the beginning; he had eight left. It was understood that he was to use this paper only in the most dire of life-and-death situations, and he had respected that: one was used to get the pertussis vaccines and the antibiotics, the other time was six years ago when an entire hydroponic crop failed because of contaminated water, and they needed a shipment of food to get by. Now Red took all eight pages out of their folder and walked back to his desk. Before he sat down, he reached over the top of the Known World map and felt along the top of the frame. When he felt the pen, he took it from its secret hiding place and examined it.

No one, not even Elspeth, knew about this pen. It was especially created for this type of coorespondence: though it wrote out in blue, the ink would turn black when a certain chemical was added, and a then bright red. It only did that with this pen's ink written on this paper, he had been told. He now sat at his desk, popped open the pen, and began to write.

Alpha Laboratory
District Tango
Location Classified
12 JUL
1245

<u>Bea</u>

Dr. Beatrice Gilbert frowned at the e-mail on her screen. Stella Goddard wanted to see her about "the other business." It was in code, of course, but the message was clear that she needed to come to Stella's office *now*. Bea deleted the e-mail from all three layers of the server's infrastructure and the archives before heading over to the administrative offices. Stella's door was slightly ajar when she arrived; she knocked on it.

"Is now a good time?" she called.

"Sure," Stella replied from behind the door. Bea walked through the doorway and quickly closed the door behind her. Stella was seated behind her desk, the white-noise machine/bug jammer already turned on and humming. She was dressed, as usual, in a crisp, white lab coat. She looked angry, which Bea had seen before, but she also looked frightened...which Bea had never seen, not *ever.*

Uh-oh...

"What's going on?" Bea asked. "What happened?"

Stella paused. "Before I get into that, let me ask you something. If you needed surgery, who would you want to do the operation?"

Bea thought about all of the doctors at the lab and the few she knew at Headquarters. No matter who she considered, however, she kept coming back to the same man. Bea sighed.

"If I could either be unconscious through the whole procedure, or if we could duct tape his mouth shut, I'd say Mike Donovan. He drives me crazy, but he's the best surgeon I know. He could be the best surgeon *left.*"

Stella nodded, frowning. "Yeah, I came to that same conclusion, too." She reached into her top desk drawer and pulled out a piece of cream-colored card stock. Bright red ink blazed from the paper.

"This is from a man I know as Karl the Red," Stella began. "Do you remember him?"

"Sure, we gave him those homemade antibiotics and the pertussis vaccines that time. What does he need now?"

Stella handed her two papers. One was the original message, and the other was the translation. "Read it yourself."

Bea looked at the card stock—the ink was very bright, a little runny, and the message was in an unfamiliar code—and then read the translation on the following page:

To the Honorable Stagger Lee,

I hope this missive finds you well. Unfortunately, I am in a situation that I am requesting your help yet again. I have appreciated all of your assistance in the past: you have saved many lives, you have asked for little in return, and please know that I have always been grateful for your interest in the sake of my people. I must now ask for help again, and it will be my last request—as you see, the rest of the cream card stock is attached.

After this last favor, one way or the other, you will hear from me no more.

My wife has been diagnosed with breast cancer by one of our doctors. As you are aware, we do not have even the minimum of treatments here to administer to her; we do not even know of a surgeon that is capable of possibly removing the growth safely. I am now asking you to provide a surgeon that can treat her to the best outcome under our less-than-favorable conditions. It goes without saying that you will also have to provide the anaesthetics, chemotherapy, antibiotics, and anything else the doctor needs.

I understand that this is risky for you. It endangers valuable members of your staff and, to my knowledge, you have never done anything like this for anyone. You will also be sending a large amount of equipment and supplies, I would imagine. However, I must insist that you do.

I am a straight-forward man, as I know you are straight-forward, as well, so I will be plain. If you do not comply with my request, I shall expose you and your entire system to both worlds: yours and mine. I have known for some time about a settlement of females not too far from here, with children, and another of families near a militia town—I'm sure the government would find it very interesting to hear what you have been doing. I also understand that those in government settlements do not know about the civilian populations—and wouldn't that upturn the apple cart?

My wife was already weakened by the last round of influenza, and now she is getting steadily worse. If she dies before you arrive, or if I do not have a surgeon here within three weeks, I shall tell everyone about us. If you do provide what I am requesting, your secret will remain safe, and I shall be forevermore silent. Please choose wisely. I shall miss our friendship.

Karl

"Shit," Bea breathed as she finished the letter, feeling her face go numb with shock. "Did he go nuts?"

"Grief-stricken, I think." Stella replied. "Elspeth is his world. I do believe he would expose us if she died, because he thinks he has nothing else to lose. He has no children, no family ties, just his barony, and apparently that's not enough for him."

"OK," Bea said, blowing out a breath and handing the letter back to Stella, "What do you want to do?"

"I don't want to use Mike. In addition to his...issues...we've never used him before, but he is the best guy for the job. He does regular rotations at Headquarters to keep his skills up, and he's a master at improvisation." Stella sighed and rolled her eyes. "Just ask him." She looked out the window, and then back at Bea. "I'll need you to go with him, Bea, to babysit."

Bea frowned; she was afraid Stella was going to say that. "But, why me? Why not take a chance and recruit Jessica to go? She could even help talk Karl down or something."

Stella shook her head. "I considered that, but having both of them go would look suspicious—someone might think the married couple decided to run.

"And," Stella got a strange look on her face, "Jessica had said you would be the right choice. I'm not sure why, but I'm willing to go with her judgment."

"OK," Bea said. It was news to her that Jessica knew about their operations, but she supposed it didn't matter now. "When are you going to tell Mike?"

"Today," Stella said as she ripped the note into little pieces. "We need to figure out what he wants to take, how he's going to transport his supplies, that sort of thing. I'm thinking by Friday we should be ready, and then I'll fabricate the message traffic calling the two of you to Headquarters.

"I want you back by next Wednesday though, no matter what happens. I mean it, Bea. Screw him if this isn't enough." She stuffed the paper bits in a tall flask and then lit a match from a box on her desk to throw in after them; the two women watched the paper burn to ash. A small amount of metallic-smelling smoke wafted through the room.

Stella then stood up and turned to a large file cabinet behind her desk. She wiggled her fingers between the top of the cabinet and the rigid plastic sheet that covered it and pulled out a blank green postcard. "I'll send word that you're coming and request he get an attending physician on his end for follow-up." Stella sat back down and began to dig in the back of her top desk drawer. "I'm sorry I ever agreed to help the civilians. Now we all are in danger."

Bea shrugged. "We all knew what we were getting into, Stella, and we've saved a lot of lives over the years. This isn't your fault."

For the first time that afternoon, Stella smiled. "Thanks, Bea. By the way," she called as Bea turned to leave, "if you come back, your seat at the poker table is reinstated."

Bea smiled sadly. "I think my free pass out of here is the least of my concerns, but thanks."

Middle Kingdom Crown Tournament
Montréal
Barony of the Three Trees
July 14th
11:36 a.m.

Lizzy

She decided to be proactive this time and just find John on the field to arrange a time to spar; maybe after that they could catch lunch or something. To her surprise, however, she found Little John in Caradoc's tent, sitting on a folding chair by himself, looking a little down.

"Hi, Little John," she greeted, stepping into the tent. "What's up?"

He threw a wave in her general direction. "Hi, Pet. Dad and Cuthbert are on some sort of mission, and Mistress Elspeth isn't feeling well, so Baron Duke Red invited me to come along instead. It's been OK so far, but there's not much to do."

"Hmm." Little John wasn't fourteen yet, so he wasn't ready to fight in the heavy list, even to spar. "No boffer at Crown?"

"No. I've been waterbearing and stuff, but it's really not the same without Dad here."

Serious teenage brooding, Lizzy thought. Neither John nor his friends were here, and he was bored—he needed a distraction. "We could always use some help at the troupe camp—do you think they'd mind if you came with me for a while?"

Little John smiled a little. "Sure, I could ask." He got up and walked over to one of the fighters standing in a cluster nearby. He began a dialogue, occasionally pointing in her direction. Eventually, the fighter looked over at her, blinked, and then turned back to Little John, nodding his head and smiling. As Little John walked back over to the tent, the fighter smiled and waved at her; she waved back.

"I can stay and help you until the end of the tournament," Little John told her, picking up his knapsack.

"Wow," Lizzy replied. She gestured in the direction they were going, and they both started walking. "What did you tell them?"

"That you were the woman my dad escorted down the aisle at Odin's Challenge, and I wanted to get to know you before you guys started dating."

"I'm sorry...what?" *Dating?* Lizzy was stunned for a few moments, and then she cleared her throat.

"I'm getting the impression," she said carefully, "that walking me back down the aisle meant something."

Little John looked at her, confused. "Yeah, sure it does! Single people go back down the aisle alone. Dating and married people are always escorted by the people they're dating or married to, like when people get their Spousal AoA. You didn't know?"

"No—I thought it was for show, like a dramatic gesture or something." Looking back at previous courts, though, she now realized the pattern. She felt a sinking feeling in her stomach. "Does it always mean that?"

"Yeah."

"Huh," was all she could think of to say. They walked in silence for several steps.

"So, do you want to date my dad?" Little John finally asked her.

Lizzy closed her eyes as she felt herself flush. She really was fine with having this conversation, and she wanted to treat it with all the respect it was due, but she couldn't help but consider for a moment how her love life had sunk to a new low, because she was discussing it in the hypothetical with a thirteen-year-old boy. She took a breath and looked at him critically.

"I want to be honest with you," she began. "Is that OK?"

He nodded.

"Thanks." She paused, forming the words she wanted to say in her head. "This is all news to me, so I don't know what to think. I like your dad, and we're friends, sure, but he's never given me any indication that he wanted more than that. So, maybe you can see why this is confusing for me?"

"What about the massage you gave him at last Crown?"

She arched an eyebrow. How did he know about *that?*

"Your dad had a back spasm, Little John—I knew I could help him. It was nothing but professional, I assure you."

Lizzy looked over at Little John; he didn't look convinced at all. She tried again.

"This is like..." She suddenly had an inspiration.

"OK...you're walking in the jungle, right? And, you see trees and vines and it's blazing hot and humid. Then, all of the sudden, you see an igloo." She paused. "You know what an igloo is, right?"

He nodded. "A house made of ice blocks."

"Right. So, it makes no sense why there's an igloo in the middle of this jungle. So, the only conclusion...is that it's not really an igloo. It's a prop, made of foam blocks or something; it's the only way something like that could exist. Wonderful igloo," she reassured him, because it was his dad they were talking about. "Swooning, romantic igloo. But unless it's just for show, it's out of place."

Little John paused, considering what she was telling him. "But, Dad knew what the escort meant. I don't think it was just 'for show' to him."

"Tell you what," Lizzy interjected with a sigh, because she could already see this going in circles with no conclusion. "Let's table this for now. We really don't know what your father's intentions are, and he's not here to ask. The next time I see him, I promise I'll ask what he meant." As she spoke, she thought Max's ardent attention to her at the Jersey Lily—there was absolutely no question in her mind what *his* sinful objectives were for her.

That was seduction done right, Sir John, not this vague court ritual stuff, even if Little John was right—which, he wasn't.

And, even if he *was* right—what in the hell kind of a way was that to court a woman, that the fucking Known World knew before she did? Did he just *assume* she'd just say, "OK, Sir John, we can be an item now, kiss me?"

She grimaced to herself at the thought. All right, to be totally honest, she would have at the time. But after Max...

No—now he would have to do a lot better than that. Screw John and his assumptions, if Little John was correct.

Which, he wasn't.

"OK," Little John agreed, drawing her back into the

conversation. "We'll both ask him."

"Fair enough," Lizzy agreed, calming down. She paused. "Still want to come back to the troupe camp?"

"Absolutely," Little John told her. "Because I know I'm right."

She chuckled at that, and allowed him to have the last word on the matter.

As it turned out, Lizzy and Little John spent very little time together that Crown Tournament, because Little John fell in love with dentistry. After letting Justin know that Little John would be hanging out until teardown, Lizzy took him to meet Dr. Goldberg and Murray. Dr. Goldberg was busy filling a tooth when they came into the trailer, and Murray was making additional filling paste. The boy's eyes widened with curiosity.

"What's the paste made of?" he asked Murray.

"Come on over..." Murray looked at Lizzy. "What's his name?"

"This is Little John," Lizzy introduced. "He's Sir John the Younger's son, the knight that's always bugging me to spar with him."

"Oh, yeah," Murray replied, nodding. "Come on over, Little John, and I'll show you."

Little John pretty much lived in the trailer for the next three days. On the morning of the second day, Lizzy got up early and went to the morning devotional.

"Is this really OK, Little John being here?" she asked Dr. Goldberg afterwards. "I can have him do something else, if he's being a bother..."

"He's no trouble at all!" Dr. Goldberg replied. "He's been very helpful to Murray and me! It's nice having a second assistant again. Thank you so much for bringing him."

"You're welcome," Lizzy said with a smile. Dr. Goldberg was a hell of a guy; he really was.

At the end of Crown, Little John gave Lizzy a genuine hug. "This was so cool, Pet, thank you!"

"You're welcome," she replied. "I'm glad it all worked out. Oh, hey, by the way..." She leaned over and whispered in his ear, and then straightened up again.

"Remember?" she asked when he looked confused. "Two years

ago you asked me a question, on the way out of Caradoc."

It took a moment, but then he grinned. "That's your real name?"

She nodded. "And, where I'm from. Is my secret safe with you?"

"You bet." He turned to go, but then turned back around and gave her a serious look. "I meant what I said before. I really think he likes you."

Lizzy nodded in acknowledgement. "We'll see. Boring trip home."

He nodded and waved in return, and then walked down the hill towards the fighting fields.

Chapter Eleven

The Town of Winter's Peak
Barony of Split Rock
July 19th
10:03 a.m.

John

He had only been here one other time before, when Anne, the baron's first wife, had died of diabetes; he had made the trip on Red's behalf to give condolences. That had happened five years ago, when the all the modern medications had run out in the Known World. Scores of people had died during the next two years, and John had been constantly on the road offering sympathy. It was a long trip up to Winter's Peak and back—the town was at the very edge of the Known World, butted up against militia country—and he never had an occasion to return since that time. He remembered being surprised that the SCAdians and their militiamen neighbors had such good ties. He wondered if that was still true. Baron Augustine's new wife, Dinah, welcomed them as they came through the gate.

"Thank you for greeting us, my lady," Cuthbert said with a bow. "I am Master Cuthbert from the Barony of Vagabond Haven. May I present Sirs Reginald and Ian from the Barony of the Brandywine, and Sir John from Vagabond Haven."

John was a little annoyed to be here. As much as he enjoyed travelling around as a representative for Baron Duke Red, he was starting to become acutely aware that this job might be interfering too much with his personal life.

For example, he missed seeing Petya at Crown.

But then... He sighed to himself in exasperation. If there was even a shred of truth to the rumors that sent them up here in the first place, then he should absolutely be here, and he shouldn't be so snarky.

But, if not...then this was a waste of valuable time; he had some serious courting to do.

Maybe he was due for a vacation—he'd never taken one. It would be easy to find out where Star-Crossed was camped when they got back. Then he could head over, claim "baronial business," and steal her away for a few days. They could find another local event and have some fun, just the two of them. They could sleep under the stars at night...share a tent when it rained...come up with ways to entertain themselves while it rained...

No! No, John, focus...focus... He could enjoy the hours of planning *that* out later.

Augustine was sitting at a table in the center of his great room as they entered. Introductions were made, and then they all sat down together. Food and drink were already laid out for them. As they ate, their host got right to the point.

"It's an invasion force, pure and simple," he began. "Rumors had been spreading over the past couple of months about El Hajj and the Patriot's Defense Force being in cahoots with each other, trading and such, but we didn't think much of it; El Hajj does most of its trading in militia country now. But then, one of my storekeepers kept seeing the El Hajj guys with holsters under their shirts—the bulges, he said, were unmistakable—so we began to pay attention.

"Then, one of my farmers found their camp two months ago when he was looking for some lost sheep—scared the shit out of him. They moved since then, but we found them. I've made arrangements with another farmer, Claude, to have dinner at his house—he's closest to their camp now. Then, tonight, my men and I will show you what they're doing."

"Forgive me, Your Excellency," Cuthbert interjected. "But, how are you so sure they're coming down to us?"

Augustine stood and went to a desk that was sitting in a corner. He grabbed some sheets of paper and carried them back to the table, spreading them out in front of them. They looked like maps of some kind.

"They're sloppy," the baron explained. "They left these behind at their last camp. Either they have no idea we're on to them, or they just don't care. I'm betting on 'don't care.'"

Sure enough, they were looking at topographic maps. The name on the map was the state park they had settled in, and there was a large red "X" on the map and the name, "Cornwall."

"Well," Cuthbert observed. "Nothing subtle about that, is there?"

The mood was mixed for the rest of the afternoon and into the evening. Dinner was good at Claude's house, and the group swapped stories and gossiped, but there was always a subtle, underlying tension. At twilight, the baron announced that it was time to go.

"Most of the way, we can take a path. They're camped in a large ravine, and the path we're taking will lead to an overhang. You'll be able to see their camp clearly from there."

The men made their way along the path. Their eyes adjusted to the night as they went, and the quarter moon allowed them to just make out where to walk. It was the perfect night for reconnoitering.

As they approached the hills where the camp lay, John noticed a faint glow from deep inside the formations. It was white...and consistent.

"Those... Is that artificial light?" John asked aloud.

"Yes," Ian confirmed.

"That's new," Claude said. "The last time we saw the camp two weeks ago, they were still using torches."

"And, we can see them from here," John observed. "We're not even close yet—that's a lot of light."

They continued on in silence. Finally, the path began to grade up and along a large embankment. The light pollution from their camp was now so bright that John could start to make out the other men's faces.

"The scenic overview is at the top," Claude told the group. "We're far enough away that they shouldn't see or notice us, but with that light...just keep a look out."

The men nodded, and then began to climb.

Claude and the baron got to the top first; there was an audible gasp from one of them. John brought up the rear, so the rest of the men saw the camp before he did. None of them said a word— they just looked over the edge, not moving. John finally got to the top and peered over.

All he could do was stare at first—his mind literally went blank at the sight. After a while, however, he was somehow able to speak.

"You didn't say—" he began.

"They didn't have all that two weeks ago," Augustine interrupted as he crouched back down away from the edge, sounding a little panicked. "That's new. That's all new. God—I'm sorry, guys."

The rest of the men were still looking at the camp, not saying a word.

"Oh, god," Cuthbert finally said. "We are so fucked."

En Route to Caradoc
20 JUL
1116

<u>Mike and Bea</u>

"I'm taking this blindfold off!"

"The hell you are!" Bea scowled as she tried to concentrate on the road. The stripped-out fifteen passenger van was filled to the brim with medical equipment, machinery, and supplies, and it was difficult to drive with all the additional weight, especially when she had to manuever around a pothole in the road or slow down to go over a bump. It was clear that road maintenance had not been a government priority. "You really don't want to see this, anyway!"

Mike Donovan grimaced as Bea hit a bump and everything lurched to the right; both Mike and Bea were jostled in their seats. "I'm getting car sick—it'd be better if I could see." Mike reached up to pull off his blindfold.

Bea reached over and slapped his hand down. "Don't make me duct tape your arms to the seat, Mike."

"Why can't I see where we're going? I'm not going to recognize any of it, anyway. It will be...desert! And then...more desert! For fuck's sake." Mike grabbed onto his shoulder harness as the van rolled to the right again.

"Look, I'm supposed to get you there in one piece, not grant your every wish and make you happy. We have about another half-hour or so and then we'll be there, and then you can stop your whining! Now shut up and let me drive, please!"

Bea was well beyond regretting that she agreed to this assignment. For one thing, Mike was an obnoxious, muscle-bound geek who always seemed to care more about the actual diseases and conditions than the patients—his bedside manners were atrocious. But, he was legendary for his calm and clear-thinking under pressure when practicing medicine, and Bea had always respected him for that.

In this situation, however, he wasn't in control, and he was an absolute *mess*. Watching this tall, handsome bodybuilder throw one temper tantrum after another was eroding her patience.

Fortunately, though, the roads did get better, Mike did shut up, and the rest of the trip was uneventful. When Bea saw the familiar wall of earth-packed cars, she almost broke out into song.

"OK, Mike, you can take off the blindfold now."

Mike whipped off the blindfold and blinked his eyes a few times to adjust to the light. He looked at the wall overshadowing them. "Wow, it's hillbilly hell!"

Bea shook her head in silence. When they arrived at the wall, she rolled down her window and called for the autocrat of the day. A minute later, a man peered over the top of the wall.

"Hail and well met!" the man yelled. "Are you here on Baron's business?"

"Yes," Bea yelled back. "Red is expecting us!"

"OK!" The man disappeared behind the wall. A few seconds later, another man waved them through, and Bea drove into the village.

She had been here during the pettusis epidemic. Back then, there was never anyone in the streets except for a nurse or caregiver hurrying from one house to another; the entire town was quiet and still with the anticipation of yet another meaningless death. This morning, however, there were people everywhere—tons of children playing in the streets, women drawing water from spickets into large plastic containers, and men tending their gardens and talking amongst themselves. It made Bea feel good that she helped this town come alive again. As she manuevered down the main path, she was glad they were about to unload—she could hear a faint scraping coming from underneath the bottomed-out van.

"Mike," Bea began, "What did Stella tell you about this case?"

"That it was probably cancer, and that I may have to operate in this hell-hole," Mike replied. "Why?"

Bea paused—she had to say this just right. "Mike, you are probably the best surgeon I have ever seen, living or dead."

"Yes, I am," Mike agreed.

"But they don't know that. This is a very tense situation, and if you don't present yourself well, they won't even let you through the front door. Actually, you need to put these people at ease immediately, or this could really blow up in our faces. Do you understand?"

Mike looked annoyed and confused. "So, what do you want me to do?"

"You need to pretend that Elspeth is Jessica. You are also the biggest asshole I've ever seen, living or dead, but you always treat your wife with deference and respect. You need to treat this patient the same way, please."

Mike frowned. "OK. I will be as...respectful...as I can. But if it starts to interfere with what I'm doing, or if someone is getting in my way, I'm not fucking around. I'm not going to fall all over people at the risk of myself or my patient."

"Fine, fair enough. Thank you." Bea slowed down as she approached the large house at the opposite end of the village. In front of the house stood a cluster of people surrounding a large man with grey hair and glasses. Bea stopped the van and shifted it into park; the engine died.

"Fuckin' swell," Bea muttered. She turned the key, and the engine roared to life again. She turned it off and said a prayer of thanksgiving while she unbuckled her seatbelt. She looked up and saw that Mike was already out of the van and talking to the group. Muttering another prayer, Bea jumped out and make her way to join Mike.

"...Johns Hopkins and Yale," she heard Mike say to Red as she approached, "and further fellowships around the country."

The baron looked pleased. He turned towards Bea. "And you were here during the epidemic. You helped distribute the vaccines and the antibiotics."

"Yes, Your Excellency." Bea gave a small bow and then took his offered hand. "Miss Mabel, at your service again."

Mike whirled around. "'*Miss Mabel?!*' How come *I* didn't get a code name?"

Bea rolled her eyes. "We didn't have time to come up with a good one, sorry."

Mike seemed to accept that; he nodded. "It's true, it would have to be pretty good one. So," he said, turning back to Red. "May I meet your wife?"

Red stepped to the side and made a gesture towards the door. "This way, please, Dr. Donovan." Red led the procession through the great room and up the stairs to Elspeth's bedroom.

Bea had worked alongside Mistress Elspeth before, so she was shocked at how pale and thin she had become since then. Her hair was stringy, and she looked jaundiced. When she saw Bea, however, she grinned.

"Miss Mabel!" Elspeth said, holding out a trembling hand. "What a wonderful surprise."

Bea reached over and took Elspeth's hand. "It's been a long time, Elspeth. Are you in a lot of pain?"

"Yes," Elspeth replied. "And I'm scared." She looked around at the group. "Did you bring someone else?"

"Hi," Mike stepped forward. "I'm Dr. Michael Donovan. I'm here to help you, if I can."

Elspeth looked up and smiled. "Oh, my." She seemed quite taken by Mike. "It's very nice to meet you, Dr. Donovan. Do you have much experience with cancer?"

"My specialties are contagions and neurointerventional surgery," Mike explained, preening a bit under Elspeth's obvious scrutiny, "but I have been performing surgeries of all kinds since Infusion. I completed my initial residency under Dr. Stanley Bower at Johns Hopkins, who perfected laserscopic cancer surgery for the breast and the thyroid. While we were unable to bring that particular type of laser system here, I do have many other instruments at my disposal that should prove very helpful." Mike smiled and looked around the room. "Now, if you will excuse me and my patient, I would like to give her a once-over before we do anything else.

"Oh, Miss May-bell," Mike said, giving Bea a wide smile, "would you fetch my black bag from behind my seat, please?"

An hour later, Mike walked across the hallway and knocked on the closed door; Elspeth had told him that Bea was staying there. His room was next door on the right, just before the baron's office.

"Come in," Bea called from behind the door.

Mike opened the door and walked in. He looked grim as he closed the door behind him.

"I don't know what kind of shit that general practitioner told Elspeth and her husband," Mike began, "but that lump is *not* small, if that is the cancer. Elspeth is very sick, and she's circling the bowl." He sagged down onto a overstuffed chair in exhaustion and covered his eyes with his hand.

Bea stiffened. "You didn't actually say that to her, did you?"

Mike uncovered his eyes and glared at Bea. "No—you told me to be nice, so I was nice. Not that what I say to her matters, though. If I can't figure out what's wrong with her and treat it, her husband Red is going to draw and quarter us; I've seen his type before. He expects me to fix his wife like she was a leaky pipe or something and medicine, especially in this environment, just doesn't work that way. And he's going to get very angry when he finds that out.

"Before Infusion, Red and his ilk would sue me at the first sign that things weren't going their way, sometimes even before the patient died. But out here," Mike spread his arms wide, "there is no legal system. Hell, that guy *is* the legal system. What's going to happen to us if she doesn't get well?"

"I was told that nothing bad would happen, as long as we made the effort," Bea replied. "Besides, we'll be long gone before her course of chemo is over, right?"

Mike shook his head. "My gut tells me that the cancer has already spread, and there's just no way to tell to what extent. Elspeth confided to me that she's been seeing blood in her feces and urine. She hasn't told Red that yet." He sighed. "I'll be telling him *that* good news, no doubt.

"And I wouldn't put too much confidence in our best efforts meaning shit when this is over. I'll fight it to the bitter end, and I can put on a good show, but I only hope we can get out of town and back to the lab before she finally passes away and all hell breaks loose."

Bea felt sick. "So, are you saying there's nothing to be done?"

"No, I'm not saying that exactly," Mike sighed. "I can remove the lump if it's cancer, and I have tons of drugs and chemotherapy to pump into her—I can make this last for weeks after we're gone. But I don't know if anything will be effective, and don't think Red or Elspeth have the guts to tell us to stop treatment before it gets really ugly. Would he still keep his promise to keep quiet then?"

Bea shrugged. "I don't know. How about you let me know by Tuesday if, in your professional opinion, Elspeth has settled into the bowl?" She grimaced at the phrase, but it seemed very appropriate somehow. "I'll see what I can do at that point to persuade them to accept hospice, and then we can get the hell out of here? The doctor here should be able to manage that, right?"

Mike snorted. "At that point—hospice—there really isn't 'overdosing,' is there? Yeah, he'd be fine." Mike stood up and looked down at Bea. "Why did you agree to do this, anyway?"

"Other than Red threatening to rat us out? Because Stella asked me to. You?"

"For the challenge." Mike opened the door. "But, I think I am finally losing my taste for it. All I want to do now is go home to my wife." He paused; it looked like he wanted to say something else, but wasn't sure.

"What?" Bea asked.

"Biopsy set-up after breakfast," he finally said. "It's not as bad in this house as I anticipated, so we should be able to make a good, sterile field. See you later."

Bea could relate to his wanting to go home, but said nothing more as Mike left the room.

The Village of Caradoc
21 JUL
1621

"How's our patient doing, Miss Mabel?"

Bea pumped up the blood pressure cuff encircling Elspeth's arm. She watched the gauge needle pulse as she heard Elspeth's blood thump through the stetheoscope and then heard nothing again.

"One hundred over sixty-two."

"OK—steady as she goes." Mike looked over at Brian. "I'm almost done with the clean-up—I'll be closing up in a minute. Would you start counting the instruments and sponges, please?"

The tissue samples that Mike had taken that morning from Elspeth's lump were cancerous. Mike had decided that, while Elspeth was under anyway, he would take a quick look at her colon and bladder as well as remove the growth. He performed the investigative procedures with the fiber optic cable camera first, and he verified that Elspeth had a few polyps along her colon and managed to take a few samples. The bladder, however, seemed clean.

The breast tumor was now laying in a steel pan: flesh-colored, globular, and streaked with blood. Mike was sure he had gotten all of it, and was now making sure that there were no blood vessel leaks. His surgical mask billowed out from his exhausted sigh.

"All right," Mike finally said. "I'll start with the smallest needle with the silk, please."

"I don't want to open her up again," Mike told Red later as they sat in Red's office. "She did fine this time, but even if the polyps come back positive I'd like to try less invasive treatments."

Red nodded. "When will you know about the polyps?"

"Later tonight, early tomorrow morning at the latest. I think I can radiate those locally, though. We'll also take some X-rays tomorrow to see if I can see anything in her liver and lungs."

Red's eyes widened. "You brought an X-ray machine?"

Mike nodded. "It's very small, but it does the job. I'd rather have an MRI machine, but that wouldn't fit in the van, not to mention the power issues."

Red stared at the wall behind Mike for several moments. "What would be the odds of you and Mabel taking Elspeth back with you? Then you could treat her properly." He looked back to Mike for his response.

Mike raised his eyebrows, but then thought about it for a minute. "Maybe if we claimed she was Infected, or post-Infected, we could keep her there for a while. But we don't have the right equipment at our lab, and getting her to Headquarters would be a trick, if not impossible.

"Besides, I wouldn't want to transport her right now. She would have to wait at least two weeks before she could go anywhere, and we need to leave by Wednesday."

Red frowned and stared into space again. "If I could arrange it, how about we try for a week from today?"

"I don't think you understand, sir." Mike replied. "We cannot stay past Wednesday. Our superiors would begin to ask questions, and we could all be exposed. Then your wife would definitely stay put. And, I think a week would be too soon—I truly believe she could die on the way."

Red propped his chin up with his hand as he thought. "Everything is negotiable," he muttered. Finally his eyes lit up, and he looked at Mike.

"I helped a military refugee once, for Stagger Lee," Red said. "She's been on the run for two years now. If you arrange for Elspeth to be transferred to a government facility for treatment, I will continue to keep her secret. If not..." Red shrugged.

Mike ignored that his heart was now threatening to push out of his chest and that he wanted to whoop for joy.

Could it be?

Instead, he put on his best unaffected-doctor face and tried to look annoyed. "What military refugee? What are you talking about?"

"She came to me in a Coast Guard uniform, and she requested asylum—Stagger Lee sent a letter of introduction. I sent her to a travelling theater company. She goes by the name of Petya now, but her real name is Elizabeth Townsend."

Mike swallowed. "OK, so what?" *Oh-my-god-oh-my-god-oh-my-god...*

"She knows about our two different worlds, and I know where she is—the next barony over, actually—until Monday or so. If you arrange this for me, she will go on her way with the troupe. Otherwise, I'll arrange for her to be picked up and dropped off at the nearest government facility."

Red leaned in. "I know what she can do. I know how valuable she is."

Mike gave him a questioning look.

"She can make holy water," Red said.

Mike's eyebrows shot up. *Wow...not the last time I saw her, she couldn't...*

"OK," Mike said, allowing his surprise to come into his voice. "We'll have to check out your story first. If she is a refugee, and she can make holy water, I will take Elspeth back to the lab next Sunday and treat her as best as I can. If not, no deals, and we leave Wednesday as planned. Agreed?"

Red smiled. "Agreed. I'll tell you exactly how to get to Hamilton, and how you can find her."

Now Mike leaned forward. "You had better be telling the truth. I don't like to have my time wasted, sir."

Red smiled, unaffected. "Neither do I."

It was only when Mike was in Bea's room and had closed the door behind him that he allowed his face to grin. Within three steps he had reached Bea, picked her up, and embraced her a crushing bear hug.

"What the...what the *hell* are you doing!?" Bea spluttered, trying to breathe.

Mike lowered her down and then looked into her eyes. He just couldn't stop smiling.

"Liz is alive, Bea," he told her. "Elizabeth Townsend is *alive*. And we're going to see her tomorrow!"

Chapter Twelve

<u>Lizzy</u>

The evening had gone normally enough at first. This was the dozenth or so performance of *A Midsummer Night's Dream* that season, so the play wasn't wrung out and overdone yet, and the Players found it comfortable to perform. It was Sweet Bess that first noticed the shadowy figures lingering behind the crowd. Lizzy was changing into her fairy costume in the back of the prompt when she overheard Sweet Bess quietly tell Justin about it. Lizzy finished strapping on her wings before walking around the sheet to the tent opening.

"What's up?" she asked Justin softly. Sweet Bess had already returned to the stage.

"There're three cloaked people in the back of the tent; their hoods are up." He didn't look at her as he spoke but stared straight ahead, watching the play.

She wanted to look herself, but refrained. "Do you expect trouble?"

"We'll see," he replied. "If they're here for us, we'll know soon enough." Then Lizzy heard her cue and climbed up onto the stage. She couldn't see in the back from the stage, so she decided to follow Justin's lead and concentrate on her performance.

After the show, she was packing up the costumes in the prompt when there was a knock against a tent post.

"Enter," Wills called from his desk. As usual after a show, he was busy tallying up receipts and waiting for the baronial representative to arrive for territory's cut.

Instead of Driscoll Baili, however, the three robed figures came through the tent door and stood in a line in front of the desk. Almost in unison, the people raised their hands to their hoods and lowered them.

Two men and a woman stood before them, all of them weather-beaten, their faces leathery. The man in the center looked the worst for wear, his hair long and stringy against the sides of his head and secured in the back with a leather tie. His beard was long enough that it dominated his face, but she could still see his wrinkles and broken blood vessels clearly beneath the patchy growth. His scent of stale sweat and alcohol pervaded throughout the tent. The man on his left had cropped his greying hair into a military-style buzz cut; the woman on his right wore her hair in a long braid down her back. They all wore road dust on their faces, and they all looked tired—Lizzy figured that they had only just arrived.

Wills didn't seem concerned, but just leaned back in his chair. Lizzy quietly walked up and stood next to Wills, where Justin would have stood if he had been there instead of tearing down the stage. She was glad she had thought to strap a mace to her belt after curtain call...just in case.

"Why do I have the feeling," Wills said, his gaze travelling from one stranger to another, "that I'm about to be arrested?"

Lizzy's eyebrows rose involuntarily; so did theirs. The middle man cleared his throat.

"Well, sir," he said in a thick drawl, lingering a little on each syllable, "I wasn't plannin' on it." He looked up at Lizzy, and then back to Wills. "You *are* William Plantagenet?"

Wills nodded.

"I'm Marshal Andrew Bennett of the Northern Militia region, New Wyoming." He stretched out his right hand towards Wills; the SCAdian stood and shook it. "These are my deputies, Matthew Huxley and Sophie Connors." He gestured towards each deputy as he introduced them; they nodded in turn. "If I could have a few minutes of your time, Mr. Plantagenet, I have an official matter to discuss with you. We're not here to arrest anyone or cause trouble," he said, nodding at Lizzy.

"That's reassuring," Wills said. "But, I'll just keep her here—I enjoy her company."

Lizzy put her hand on Wills' chair and looked the marshal in the eye. She smiled slightly and nodded, trying to look firm but nonthreatening.

"Up to you," the marshal replied, returning her nod. He looked over his shoulder to a row of folded chairs that were leaning against a side of the tent. "May we?"

"Please," Wills offered with a wave of his hand.

The militiamen unfolded the chairs and sat down. Their cloaks were not fastened in the front, so as they sat their robes parted to reveal western clothing and gear. Both Wills and Lizzy's eyes were drawn, however, to the sawed-off shotguns that were strapped to each stranger's right thigh and the two pistols that each officer carried on gun belts. Bennett noticed them noticing.

"Now," he said, palms up, "we just got here an hour ago—we didn't have a chance to disarm, just came straight here."

Wills also raised his hands in reassurance. "You're marshals—of course you carry weapons appropriate to your station. How can we help you, Marshal Bennett?"

Bennett leaned back in his chair; it creaked under his weight. "In the past four months, four of the pregnant women in one of our towns, Zion, and its surrounding areas have died. To the best of our knowledge, there was no medical reason for them to die: no illness, no miscarriage, they just...died. The only commonality was that one of the local canaries detected a slight residue of demon Infection, though the women themselves were not Infected, and no one else felt anything unusual."

"I'm sorry," Wills interrupted. "Canary?"

"It's a government term for someone who can sense demons—they also call them Sensors. They often use them outside their bases as an early-warning measure, like canaries in coal mine shafts." He paused. "To be honest, Mr. Plantagenet, we're out of ideas about our dyin' women. We don't know what to do."

Wills looked genuinely sympathetic—babies were an important commodity in a post-apocalyptic world. "I'm sorry for your loss, but how can we help? Why come to us?"

Bennett glanced around the tent before addressing the questions. "About two years ago, a merchant was arrested in a town called Diablo's Keep for Possession of Infected Material with Intent to Sell."

Lizzy took a deep breath and ordered herself to remain calm, though she could feel her heart beginning to pound in her chest.

Wills, on the other hand, yawned. "Sure, I remember the incident. He had a mason jar full of ears."

"The accused," Bennett continued, "after he had been found guilty, was exiled from SCAdian territory and eventually ended up in one of our settlements. When he heard about Zion, he contacted one of my deputies and told him about your statement that had been read into the record at his trial. According to court testimony, his...goods...were discovered by a woman that could Sense his wares from about thirty yards." He absently reached under his cloak and pulled out a small metal flask. "I think that's unlikely, but someone who could Sense the ears from even half that distance could be of a use. We'd like to hire her to help us figure all this out."

Just then, there was a sharp rapping at the door; everyone jumped.

"Wills?" It was Baili. "I'm here for the proceeds."

Wills hissed through his teeth as he stood. "Excuse me," he said to the law officers. "I'll tell him to come back tomorrow." He strode around Huxley and stepped through the tent flap.

The atmosphere in the tent quickly grew uncomfortable as everyone waited for Wills to return. Lizzy didn't know what to say, so she just stared at the tent door and waited. After a few seconds, the three strangers began to whisper amongst themselves, though she couldn't hear what they were saying. Wills returned a minute later, looking agitated and rolling his eyes. As the tent flap billowed in his wake, Lizzy saw Baili standing outside, staring into the tent. She saw him take in the sight of the militiamen just before the flap settled back into place, blocking any further speculation.

Nosy bastard...

"I apologize," Wills growled as he sat back at his desk. "You were saying, Marshal Bennett?"

"We hoped you could tell us the woman's whereabouts." Bennett unscrewed the flask in his hand and took a short pull. "The baron of Dragonsfyre Port is a friend of mine, and he gave me your flyer. Maybe you remember Jochi Maral? He said y'all met once."

"We did, for their first baronial investiture—was it four years ago?" He leaned back in his chair. "It was a good stop; we just haven't made it back up that way since."

"Well, Jochi told me you were a straight-shooter, and he told me to give you this." He reached into his pants pocket and pulled out a folded piece of blue paper. He leaned over across the desk and handed it to Wills. "He also drew me a map to get here off a larger map in his office."

Just enough of the right information to verify his story, Lizzy thought. *Nice...*

There was a pause as Wills unfolded the note and read it.

"Never been this far south," the marshal said after a few moments, scanning the tent as if he could see the landscape through its walls. "Y'all did pick some nice country."

"We like it." Wills' voice was dry as he folded the paper and looked up at Bennett. "You are correct that I could help you find your canary. What are you proposing?"

"We would take her with us to Zion to help us in any way she could. As collateral, I would be willing to leave Huxley with whomever—we brought enough tradable goods for three weeks upkeep, and I would trust that his custodian would keep him well. In exchange for her help, we would offer compensation." He reached into his shirt and drew out a pouch. He handed it to Wills. "Some jewelry, some cut stones, a couple of pearls, and gold coins. More when we return and I have my man back."

Wills spilled the contents onto his desk. Traded correctly, Lizzy figured they would easily pay for a month's worth of food for the troupe. He turned and looked into her face, asking a silent question.

She met his eyes and gave him the slightest of nods and blinked. To anyone else, it was just a movement. To Wills, though, it was confirmed affirmation. He looked into her eyes for a moment as his brows furrowed in concern; then he plastered on a smile.

"Pet," he said in a bright voice. "Please find our canary, and explain the terms."

"Yes, boss." She bowed to the group and left the tent. She looked around for someone she knew, but the courtyard was empty. She found a hay bale and sat down to think.

The appearance of the militiamen was unprecedented, as far as she knew. After the initial land treaties were negotiated and signed seven years ago, the citizens of the mundane territories only entered SCAdian realms for the occasional event or minor trading. That they would enlist a SCAdian to assist them in their business, especially of this nature, was in direct conflict with their xenophobic nature.

If they even *were* militia; they could also be government. They could have found her at last.

But, if that was true, why the façade? Though the story was fantastic, it seemed almost *too* fantastic, almost too fucked up not to be true. And, she sensed no deception from Bennett. Wills hadn't, either, or he wouldn't have indicated to her that she could choose to go—she was sure he would have blown the law officers off and moved on.

Diplomatically, it was good for SCA/militia relations. The Players would have some unexpected, additional lining for their purse. And...if they *were* government...

Then I'm fucked, she decided, *and better to get them far away from the SCAdians, the sooner the better.* She stood and went back to the tent.

"...never heard of them," she heard Wills say as she opened the flap. "What do they do?"

"Mostly re-enactments of movies," Sophie explained as Lizzy positioned herself between Wills and the militiamen so they could all comfortably talk to each other. "They did *True Grit* last year, *The Empire Strikes Back* the year before. They always sell out."

"Huh," Wills said thoughtfully. He looked over at Lizzy. "Well, Pet? What did she say?"

"She had some questions, boss." She turned to Bennett. "She told me to use my best judgment. How many are in your group?"

"Six."

"How many are men?"

"Four." His eyes narrowed. "They're all my deputies, ma'am— trained 'em myself. If rape is what you're concerned about, let me assure you that if any of them tried to lay a hand on her, I'd rip his balls off myself before anything happened."

She glanced at Wills; he nodded. She fingered the pommel of her mace. "Can she carry her own weapons?"

Bennett nodded.

"Feed and shelter her?"

"Yes."

"How long will she be gone?"

"Hard to say. Maybe a month, with travel time?" He took another swig from his flask.

"As payment, she'd like a bolt-action rifle with 100 rounds."

Bennett looked at Wills, who shrugged.

"I'm not the one who's going," the actor pointed out. "The pouch is compensation for lost work. She is my apprentice, and I was just planning to have her lead in our next production."

Lizzy raised a skeptical eyebrow at him.

Bennett looked annoyed, glancing from Wills to Lizzy. "Generally speaking, folk up there only have one rifle for each adult."

"Grandma stays home," she suggested, not unkindly. "You're asking her to take a chance that you are who you say you are, asking her to leave SCAdian territory, all to help you. You can't give her nothing for her trouble."

Bennett's mouth thinned. "The rifle and fifty rounds."

"Eighty."

"Seventy."

"Seventy-five."

"Done," Bennett confirmed. "When can she be ready?"

Lizzy looked at Wills. "Monday morning, when the troupe pulls out?"

Wills nodded. He had a strange emotion on his face that she couldn't identify.

"OK, then," Bennett said as he and his deputies stood up. "Tell your Sensor that we'll meet her Monday morning after breakfast. We'll be a quarter mile outside the north gate by a cluster of boulders by the main path. We brought a horse for her—will she be using it?"

"Yes," Lizzy replied. "Thank you, that was thoughtful."

"Well, it would take a while to get up there walkin'." Bennett smirked slightly at his sarcasm. "Bring someone to collect Huxley." He looked at the SCAdians. "Thank you for your time— see y'all in a month or so."

The group all exchanged handshakes, and then the three officers pulled their hoods back over their heads and walked out into the night. When the militiamen's footsteps could no longer be heard, both Wills and Lizzy sagged into chairs. They just looked at each other for a moment before Wills spoke.

"Are you *actively* trying to get yourself killed," he began softly, "or do you just take opportunities as they come along?"

She couldn't help herself—she chuckled. "No, Master Wills." She exhaled slowly. "The pay is good."

"Fuck the pay," he snapped. "We don't even know who they really are."

"Did you sense any deceit?" she asked him.

He paused. "No." He looked down at the pile of valuables and the folded paper still on the desk. "And, his Writ was authentic— Joshi mentioned something that had happened at that event, something only I would know. I don't think the government would send a drunk, either."

"Neither do I." She gave him a pointed look. "Innocent women are dying."

Wills didn't answer her. He started putting the jewelry and coins back into the pouch.

"And, you and I both know I might be able to help them."

He stopped picking up a pearl and slumped back into his seat, staring into space.

"Because of the holy water," he sighed. He shook his head as he reached for the pearl again. "When I first met you, I dreamt of the day when your gift would be profitable—I knew it could be. Now that it's here, though..." He scooped up the last brooch and placed it in the bag before he rose from his chair. He met her gaze, his face now fully showing his worry. "Are you sure?"

"I'm sure." She smiled at him as he closed the drawstrings on the pouch. She stood up. "Miss me?"

Wills took three strides to reach her and secured Lizzy in a hard embrace, surprising her.

"Of course I will, you haughty government bitch," he muttered softly.

She choked back a laugh as she hugged him in return. "Me, too—you and your fucking freakshow." They held each other for another moment, and then she gently pulled herself away and stepped back. "Who's telling Justin about the trip?"

He grimaced. "I will, tomorrow morning, though you will see him before you go?"

"Of course I will."

He nodded in approval. "I don't want to see you at all tomorrow. Get out of camp, do something fun." He paused, as if he were trying to remember something. Then he frowned.

"Max Wrightson is from around here, isn't he?" he asked sourly as he walked back to his desk.

"Yes."

When Wills picked up the lamp and turned back to her, his face was absolutely, carefully blank.

"Looks like you'll have your distraction, then," he said coolly, making a poor attempt at a smile. "I'll walk you back to your tent."

July 22
6:14 a.m.

Lizzy woke up early, dressed quickly, and stopped in the chow tent to pick up some cucumbers and cheese to munch on as she made her way out of the camp. She didn't head directly for the Melinda's house, though—she had another errand to do first. They were already outside the back gate, so she only had to go a short distance before she found the path in the woods that lead to Caradoc.

This is stupid, she thought as she walked in the morning mist and listened to the chirpings of the songbirds. She knew exactly what was going to happen: she was going to get there, and John would be home, and she would ask about the AoA ceremony, and then it would get awkward as he said something like,

"No, that was really just for show, Pet...why do you ask?"

And then she would have to laugh it off and say,

"Oh, OK—I thought so. Just asking."

And then it *really* would get uncomfortable as he said,

"I hope you didn't get the wrong idea..."

"No! No, Sir John, I just wanted to clear things up..."

And then, if she didn't die of embarrassment first, she would have to offer to spar or something to change the subject.

But then...some questions are worth asking, even when the answer is uncertain. It could very well go the other way, she told herself. He *could* declare his desire and affection for her, and she could end up having a mind-blowing, lost weekend kind of day in the very capable hands of Sir John the Younger. Or, she hoped they were capable—there was only one way to find out.

She walked down his street and found his house. It was cold, dark, and quiet.

Not good, she thought as she knocked on the door. No answer. She knocked a bit louder, just in case, but got the same result.

She brushed her fingers against his coat of arms before she turned around and started back to Hamilton. Even if he wasn't interested in her romantically, she considered the idea that she might have been willing to split the day between frivolous antics with Max and any activity with John, even if it was a working day.

But...that wasn't an option today: frivolous antics for the win. There was always next time.

By the time she reached Melinda's house, the town was wide-awake and moving. Melinda answered the door when she knocked and looked pleased to see her.

"Pet!" she exclaimed as she wrapped Lizzy in a hug. "We wondered if you were going to visit!"

"It's good to see you, too."

"Come in, come in," Melinda said, pulling Lizzy into the kitchen. "I'll put on some tea—I don't have to be in today until noon."

Lizzy sat down on a wooden bench while Melinda got two mugs off a shelf. "Has Max seen you yet?"

"No," she replied. "But he promised me a trip to a waterfall near here—something about a tombstone, too? Do you think he could go today? I know it's short notice, but..."

"Hold on," Melinda interrupted. She went to the doorway leading to the staircase and leaned inside. "Robert Bruce!" She straightened up as loud footfalls thundered down the stairs; Robert Bruce's head emerged from the doorway.

"Yeah, Mom?" he asked.

"Would you go run and tell your Uncle Max that Pet's here, please?"

He looked around the room until he saw Lizzy. "Oh, hi, Pet!" he said, grinning. "I'll go get him!" Then he ran past his mother and jogged out the front door.

Melinda returned to the kitchen and opened a canister sitting on the counter. "By the five-hundredth count," she predicted, depositing a heaping spoonful of herbs in each mug. By the time the water had been poured and the tea had steeped for about a minute, Max barreled through the front door.

"I heard..." Max stopped as he saw Lizzy sitting at the kitchen table. His corresponding smile was wide with pleasure. "Hi."

"Hi," Lizzy replied. No longer in the bold environment of The Jersey Lily, she suddenly felt a little shy. She did manage to grin back at him. "I came for my waterfall tour. Are you free today?"

He put his hands on his hips as he looked down at the ground and thought for a moment.

"Yeah, I think so," he finally said, looking at her. "I'll be right back—let me talk to Ed, see if he'll switch shifts with me at the mill, he owes me one."

"I'll be here." She smiled warmly at him.

He blinked, smiled back, and then walked out to find Ed. As they were talking, Melinda had strained their tea; she placed Lizzy's mug in front of her.

"You two must have had a good time at the resort," she commented, blowing into her own mug as she sat down. "He came back with quite the spring in his step."

Lizzy shrugged. "A good time was had by all. What did he tell you about it?"

"Not much—just that you all were invited back again next year." She took a sip of her drink. "I think he's looking to come back every year at least, maybe arrange more gigs."

"Doesn't he have things to do here, like help at the inn?"

"As the kids get older, he'll be able to do other things to a point. But Max, Eileen, and I are equal partners in the inn, and we've made it clear to him that we expect him to buy himself out before he can go back to being a professional musician."

They both swallowed some tea; Lizzy wasn't sure what to say to that. Just then, Max came back through the front door.

"We're all set," he announced. He walked over and sat on the other side of Lizzy. "So, what's on the agenda?"

"I'd like to finish my tea," Lizzy told him. "Visit a little. Then...do you want to pack a picnic or something, go to the falls, and then see the festival?"

"Sounds good."

A couple of hours later, Lizzy and Max walked out the back gate and into the woods. They went past the rocks where she and John had talked the previous year and continued away from both Caradoc and Hamilton, far into the brush. The path was fairly straightforward, though there was a last-minute fork in the road; Max led her towards the left. Finally, they reached a large, grassy clearing, and she could hear water splashing on rocks in the distance.

"This way," Max said, leading her by the hand across a meadow of tall grass. They soon reached the edge of the overhang, and Lizzy could see the waterfall clearly, spilling out freely from the cliff face and down to a creek below.

"It's beautiful," she said.

"It's more impressive in the spring," Max commented, setting down the basket. They both stared at it in silence for a minute or two.

"You mentioned a tombstone, I think?"

"This way." Max led them to a large tree near the overhang. There, at its base, was a stone with a carved inscription:

Lord Bayard de Montoya, SCA
Douglas A. Santiago
Died as he lived
In Humble Service

"That's lovely," Lizzy commented. "It's been a while since I've seen..."

A mundane name, she was going to say, but the thought was forgotten as he slowly turned her around, raised his hands to either side of her face, and kissed her with warm, open caresses and teasing strokes of his tongue. She immediately responded, wrapping her arms around his waist and pressing herself against him. After several seconds they came up for air, panting for breath.

"God, I missed you," he told her, looking into her eyes. His gaze was hot and sharp and incredibly seductive.

"I missed you, too," she breathed. She leaned over and began nuzzling the side of his neck along his jawline. He groaned in response and gently pushed her backwards until she was leaning against the tree, his body quickly following to cover hers, the bark of the tree biting into her skin. He nudged her legs apart with his knee and began moving in a slow rhythm between her thighs, gently riding against her as he took her mouth again. By the time they paused again, she decided that maybe sex with Max—casual and unpretentious—was the best thing for her right now. Her circumstances altogether were too damn uncertain, and all she wanted now was one distracting afternoon—and hopefully a fun one. She vaguely recalled that the direct approach with men was often best.

"I want you," she told him.

Max blinked—he was genuinely surprised for a moment. "Are you sure?"

"Yes." She nodded, and then looked at him questioningly. *Well?*

He smiled at her then, almost gratefully. At her assent, he slowed down his enticement to an almost leisurely pace, as if she were a special experience to take delight in. He wasn't a hurry-up-and-get-to-the-fucking kind of lover, but seemed to appreciate foreplay as something to be relished with an almost worshipful application of strokes, licks, and playful bites. She could very much appreciate that.

Finally, after a long span of exquisite torture, he sank her down into the grass and spent the afternoon skillfully answering her unspoken question, both in utterances and in deeds.

On the road to Hamilton
22 JUL
1120

Mike and Bea

Mike insisted on driving, so Bea had to put up with listening to the AC/DC disc that Mike had found in the glove compartment. Most of the trip he had it turned up to full volume, but now he turned it down once again to talk about Lizzy.

"So, did *everyone* at the lab but me know what happened to Liz when she disappeared?" Mike demanded. "Did Jessica?"

"No, Mike," Bea answered with a sigh. "Just Stella and me. Maybe Larry the gate guard, only because he made her van disappear when the thugs showed up."

"I can't believe she's alive, and we're going to see her," he said for the umpteenth time. "I wonder if she looks any different."

"Mike..." Bea wanted to ask him something, but was afraid of the answer. "You and Lizzy...y'know...didn't have an affair or something, right?"

Mike stared at the road blankly for a moment, and then scowled.

"No! Good god, no. Well, not that I didn't think about three-ways sometimes..." Mike's face melted into a dreamy look.

"Ew," Bea muttered, trying to get that visual out of her own head. "It just seems weird that you're obsessing about this so much. I mean, I missed her, too, but you seem like a kid at Christmas about it."

Mike glanced over at her. "You knew she got out OK. All this time, you didn't know how she was doing, but at least you knew Stella got her out safely, and we both know that Liz can handle herself.

"I didn't know anything. After Jessica I considered Liz my best friend, even though I know she didn't understand a damn thing I said when I would talk about my work. And then one day all I hear is that there was an accident at Headquarters, and that I won't ever see her again. I know everyone thinks I'm an inhuman monster or something, but that really got to me. I missed her."

Bea was touched. "Wow, Mike, I'm sorry. I didn't know you were that close."

"That's OK. If you really feel that badly about it, you can give me a blow job later." With that, Mike reached over and turned the music back up full blast. He grinned at her while he began to sing along to "You Shook Me All Night Long."

Bea rolled her eyes and went back to looking out the window.

The camp for the Star-Crossed Travelling Players outside Hamilton was huge and filled will all the colors of the rainbow. Bea had never seen so many tents in one place in her life, and they were all painted with bright patterns and happy scenes from fairy tales and folklore. Each tent and pavillion pole had a flag fluttering at the top, and pretty banners were spanned between the tents. Hamilton was apparently another SCA town, because all of the performers were in medieval costumes, though there were a few, more dirty members of the troupe that were wearing jeans, T-shirts, and boots. She approached two guys that looked like they had just mucked out horse stalls or something and asked if they knew Petya.

"Sure," one of them said, giving Bea and Mike the once-over; they were both in jeans and T-shirts, too. "Who are you? You don't look familiar."

"We're from Milltown," Bea explained, sticking to the cover story Red had suggested. "We met Pet a year ago at the A&S Festival, and we had a jam that Saturday night. We were hoping to arrange something here."

"Oh, OK," the man said. "I saw her going into town early this morning—she usually goes to the Coach and Four near the Cornwall gate."

"With that Max dude, right?" the other man asked his companion.

"Yeah—I think he owns the place. Anyway," the first man looked back at Bea and pointed, "just go down that path and ask someone where the Coach and Four Inn is. It's a small town, someone should know."

"Thanks!" Bea waved as they walked towards the town. When they had gotten far enough away that no one could hear Bea asked, "Max? I wonder who he is."

"Who knows," Mike replied. Then he got a glassy look in his eye. "Maybe I'll get that three-way after all!"

Bea punched him on the arm. "Asshole," she grumbled.

Sure enough, the first person they asked when they went through the gates directed them to a larger building down along the main street. There was a beer barrel attached to a pole by two chains off the side of the building, with a sign underneath that the barrel that said "The Coach and Four Inn." A stage coach and four horses were painted on either side of the beer barrel. Bea and Mike stepped inside the opened door.

The main room was dark and empty save for a woman sitting at a table, writing on a well-worn legal tablet by the light coming through the door. She looked up as they came in.

"We're not opened for lunch yet," she said, smiling at Mike.

"Maybe later," Bea said. "We're actually looking for Petya of Vagabond Haven. We met her at an A&S festival a year ago, and we heard she was in town."

"She sure is," the woman said, now smiling at Bea. "She came with Star-Crossed Players for the Sunflower Festival. She and my brother-in-law, Max, are out and about somewhere. I think they were going to Bayard's Falls for a picnic at some point."

"Where's that?" Mike asked. "We haven't met Max yet; does he play an instrument?"

"Trumpet, mostly, but he plays all kinds of brass instruments. So," the woman said as she thought, "the best way to go would be to go out through the back gate and into the woods. Go down the main path about fifteen minutes—you're walking, right? The path will come to a T, and you'll want to take the left one. Then just stay on the path through the woods until you come to an overhang. The falls are there."

"Thanks!" Bea said. "If we don't catch up with her there, we'll wait at the camp and chat with Wills or something." That last part was a total fabrication, but it sounded good.

"OK," the woman said, fiddling with her pencil stub. "If you do see Pet and Max, could you ask him to stop in and see Terry the Wiser and borrow his solar calculator? I'm trying to do my books for the month." The woman gave them a sheepish grin.

"No problem!" Bea told her. "Who are you, again?"

"Oh," the woman stood and held out her hand. "Ellen Wrightson. I'm the owner of the Coach and Four."

"I'm Mabel, and this is Mike." Both Bea and Mike took their turns shaking her hand. "It was nice to meet you. If we have time, we'll try to catch a meal here."

"Just tell Francis at the door that you are my guests—he'll take care of you. Any friend of Pet's is a friend of mine." She grinned and sat back down.

"Thanks again," Mike said as they walked towards the door. When they got outside, Bea and Mike started walking towards the back gate.

"That went well," Bea said. "Friendly folks around here."

"Yeah," Mike replied, looking distracted. "I'll be happier when we get to Liz, though. I feel a bit out of sorts around here."

Ellen's directions turned out to be spot-on until they got about five minutes down the left path—there was a fork in the trail, splitting it in two directions.

"Crap," Bea said. "I'll go left, you go right. We'll go up the paths and come back in...ten minutes?"

"OK," Mike said. He starting walking around, searching for something.

"What are you doing?" Bea asked.

"Looking for a stick, for a weapon," Mike replied. He bent down and picked up a stick about as thick as a quarter and about three feet long.

"Mike," Bea began, "You can bench press...what?"

"250," Mike replied, swinging the stick like a bat onto a tree trunk; the stick did not break and made a deep *thwack*-ing sound.

"Are you *really* that concerned with someone fucking with you?" she asked. "Do you see *me* getting a stick?"

Mike shrugged. "Someone may need a beat-down. See you later." He started down the right-hand path.

Bea turned around and made her way down the left path. About five minutes later the brush thinned, and she saw a large grassy clearing with two half-naked people on a blanket underneath a tree.

Fucking each other.

"Oh, *shit*," Bea muttered as she crouched down into the foilage. She recognized Lizzy immediately, though she was facing away from her and the grass was tall—same dark head of hair, same distinctive, multi-colored mushroom tattoo on her left side. It only took Bea a second to conclude that the encounter was mutually desired, and that maybe this was not the best time for a reunion. She turned around as quietly as she could and made her way back down the path. Mike was waiting for her at the fork.

"Hey, that way just goes to a refuse dump of some kind, broken electrical stuff and...hey, where are we going?" Bea had grabbed his hand and was starting to drag him back down the main path.

"We'll get some lunch at the Coach and Four, and then wait at the troupe camp."

"What do you mean?" Mike stopped them both in their tracks. He turned and looked back at the path Bea took. "Was Liz back there?"

"Yes," Bea replied as she tried to lead Mike by the hand again. "We'll wait at the camp."

"I don't understand," Mike said, looking behind them as he became an immovable object. "We came all this way...did you talk to her?"

Bea stopped pulling on Mike and sighed in frustration. "She's *busy*, Mike. Now will you come on?"

Bea could almost see the wheels in Mike's head turning. Finally, his eyes grew as wide as saucers. He turned back to Bea.

"*Biz-y?*" Mike pronounced, asking a silent question. When Bea nodded slightly in the affirmative, Mike turned around and began running down the path. Bea leaped up, grabbed his right earlobe, and twisted.

"OUCH!" Mike yelled as she led him the opposite way by his ear, his body almost folded in half. "C'mon, Bea! I just want to peek! You got one!"

"Forget it, Donovan!" Bea shouted as she marched. "She's having a private moment, and we can wait until she's done!"

"Hey wait a minute, WAIT A MINUTE!" Mike said. Bea stopped walking and looked up at Mike.

"*What?*"

"How do we know that it's not a sexual assault or something? She could be in trouble."

Bea felt herself blush in spite of herself. She rolled her eyes and decided to answer the question, as embarrassing as it was to even think about. "She was on top, Mike. It was mutual on both sides. Can we go now?"

Mike froze as he took in this new information. Then she saw a gleam in Mike's eyes as he whispered, "Jessica *never* gets on top..." He jerked his head back, trying to escape her grasp; Bea managed to hang on and started marching again.

"C'mon, Bea! I'll be as quiet as a mouse! *God*, what an opportunity..."

"Am I really going to have to drag you all the way back to town?"

Mike sighed as he stumbled on a root. "*No,*" he grumbled. "OK, it was a stupid idea. You can let go now. Please, Bea, this is really uncomfortable, being hunched over like this..."

At that moment, Bea heard a *whizz* sound, right next to her ear. She stopped and let go of Mike's earlobe.

"Shut up," she said, looking around. "What was that?"

Mike looked around, too, raising the stick that was still in his hand. "What was wha—OW!" Mike slapped the back of his neck. He plucked something out and held it up to see what it was.

"Is that...a tranqilizer dart?" Mike asked Bea as his neck and shoulders started to numb.

"Run, Bea," he managed to say before he sagged to the ground, paralyzed. As he lay there, he noted that he was still conscious and that he could still see and hear, which told him that the drug in the dart was most likely Orpheoran.

Too bad he was allergic to the entire TRN drug family, which included Orpheoran. His respiratory passages would swell closed in three minutes or less. Mike already was struggling to breathe.

Laying there, he watched as Bea began to run back towards the falls. As she passed one particular tree, however, he saw a man in fatigues step out from behind the tree and slam the butt of his rifle against the back of Bea's skull. He heard a sickening wet *crunch* and watched Bea fall hard onto the ground. She did not move.

"Oops," he thought he heard someone say as the black spots of asphyxiation swam and grew before his eyes.

A brain injury...Mike thought just before he lost consciousness. *How ironic...*

Lizzy

It was almost evening before Lizzy and Max made their way back to Hamilton. As they walked back, hand in hand, she was debating whether she was grateful or indignant that he had brought a variety of prophylactics with him that morning, obviously taken from the Jersey Lily. Considering what they had just spent the afternoon doing, she decided on grateful.

She was glad she had indulged that day—she *did* need the exuberant, well-executed distraction, stopping only on occasion to eat something—but this was not an arrangement that she'd wish to do for the long-term. For Max, she was fairly certain, sex was an intense recreational activity to satisfy certain drives, like hours of windsurfing or motocross, except that there were happy endings scattered here and there.

For Lizzy, though, the sex marathon with Max was like eating great Chinese food after a long fast. It was *fantastic* going down, but not long after she ate her fill she was hungry again, and not in a particularly good way—it just wasn't quite satisfying enough to ever get the job done. Max was a good-for-now, but unless he decided to settle down—and there were no guarantees that it would be with her or if she even wanted that—he wasn't a permanent solution. She supposed this was the difference between being 22 years old, when she would have eaten Max for breakfast, lunch, and dinner, and 34, having already been married once and knowing what sex could be like with a loved one. Still, she couldn't have asked for a more considerate lover, and she hadn't felt this good in a very, very long time.

He invited her into his house, and when she came through the doorway he closed the door behind them. There were no lamps lit in the house, but she could see his playful grin in the moonlight as he leaned her against the door and kissed her, pressing her in between him and the cold metal. They just stood there for a while, tasting and fondling each other, their restricted breathing and short gasps the only sounds in the room. Eventually, though, she broke off their embrace with a sound of frustration.

"I have to get back," she said, putting on her best apologetic face. "I have an early start tomorrow. And, I'm too damn sore to do anything else today," she added with a sheepish smile.

"OK," he agreed, stepping back away from her. He took both her hands in his and looked into her eyes. "When will I see you again?"

She had to think about it. "Paradiso, most likely, so...next month?"

He gave her a wide grin. "I'll watch for you." He gave her one last, lingering kiss before he reached for the door latch. "Be safe."

She gave him a quick kiss on the mouth goodbye. "I will. See you around." She walked through the door and heard it *click* behind her as she made her way back to the troupe camp. As she walked through the darkening streets, she hoped Max had worn her out enough that she could sleep tonight: another big, new adventure lay ahead, and it began in just hours.

Chapter Thirteen

<u>Lizzy</u>

Wills had told Justin about the trip, and he was not happy about the circumstances.

"Take someone with you," he entreated as he watched her saddle Iago. "Gunther would go, or maybe Malcolm..."

"That wasn't the deal," Lizzy pointed out. "Besides, you'll need all hands for the next few performances. As it is, you'll have to double up for my parts."

Justin sighed, scrubbing his hand through his hair.

"All right," he finally agreed.

It was time to change the subject. "What are you telling the troupe?"

"Almost the truth. You're going on a side-job for a month— none of their business doing what—and the man Wills is bringing back is an injured guitar player from the King's Men, who will be convalescing with relatives nearby." He glanced over at Wills, who was on the other side of the livery saddling Falstaff. "The troupe will infer that you're on loan—no one knows the truth but Wills and me."

"Where's the deputy really going?"

"Better you didn't know. He'll be well tended to, though."

Lizzy nodded as she tied the last of the saddlebags. "You're right—best I didn't know. Hopefully, I'll be back in time for Paradiso."

"That's good—no one else fits into that jester's costume."

She snorted as she turned around to hug him. "Have fun this month—I'll be fine."

"Good luck; be safe," he replied, kissing her cheek. "Thanks for doing this."

"You're welcome—I hope you find some good buyers."

Justin gave her a confused look, and then shook his head, smiling. "No, Pet, thank you for taking the job—it's a very noble thing you're doing."

"Eh," she grunted as she turned back around. "I haven't done anything yet—we'll see."

As she swung herself into the saddle, she felt a sharp stab of pain run along her lower pelvis. She couldn't help but wince when she was fully seated—she *really* overdid it with Max the previous afternoon. Maybe she should have considered that she would be spending several days on horseback before she agreed to try that last position...or the one before that...

Ow.

"Are you OK?" Justin asked, noticing her discomfort.

"Muscle cramp," she said through slightly gritted teeth. "It'll pass." Lizzy adjusted herself in the saddle until the pain was only mildly annoying. She looked down at Justin and smiled. "See you in a month."

He nodded, and then Lizzy trotted Iago over to Wills, who was already on Falstaff and ready to go. He blew a kiss and waved at Justin before he turned his horse around and cantered alongside Lizzy as they made their way to the north gate. He slid her a knowing look.

"Sore this morning, are we?"

She forced a half-smirk onto her face through the discomfort. "What? You told me to go have some fun."

He glowered into the distance. "Humph."

"With all due respect, Master Wills, what did he ever do to you?"

He paused for a moment, concentration etched on his face, as if he were searching for the correct words. He finally shook his head, shrugged, and then looked at her.

"He wastes his time," he finally said. "And, he wastes yours."

Lizzy didn't know how to respond to that without starting a fight—*there's not exactly a line of eligible men at my doorstep, asshole*—so she didn't try.

They rode in silence after that.

The marshal and his deputies were waiting on horseback at a large deposit of boulders, as described. Bennett walked his mount up to meet them. The corners of his mouth twitched when he saw Lizzy.

"I thought it might have been you," he told her.

"How so?"

He leaned back in his saddle. "For one thing, you seemed to know what a canary was, even before I explained the term."

She nodded, but said nothing. She kept her face poker-neutral.

"And, only a goddamn fool would allow someone to speak on their behalf in a situation like this. So either it was you, or I would have had to turn away whoever showed up and asked for my payment back, because the last thing I need on this investigation is another fool."

She smiled at that. Wills cleared his throat.

"I need to put a bandage on your deputy's hand," the actor said. "He's going to be an injured guitar player, so no one will question the trade. She's on loan while he recuperates."

"No problem." Bennett motioned for Huxley to come forward, and then turned to Lizzy. "You play guitar?"

"A little," she admitted.

Huxley stopped next to Bennett and dismounted. He began to untie and unbuckle his two saddlebags, along with a canteen and a bedroll.

"You'll be taking my horse," Huxley explained to Lizzy as he worked. "His name is Ariel, and he's a good horse—my ten-year-old takes him out all the time."

Lizzy also got down off her horse and began taking off her bags. "Is your family OK with you leaving for a month?"

Huxley shrugged. "No, but we need to get to the bottom of this. Going for the rest of our lives without carnal knowledge or babies doesn't seem feasible to me, and there's nothing sayin' that this sickness can't spread to other places."

"Fair enough."

They finished up exchanging gear. Lizzy raised a flat hand up to Ariel's nose so he could get a whiff of her, and then scratched him behind the ears; the horse accepted her attentions amicably. She giggled as Ariel nudged his nose into her jacket, most likely looking for a treat. By the time she felt she and the horse had reached an understanding, Wills had wrapped Huxley's hand in a large white bandage and the deputy was already on Iago, waiting to depart. Wills came over to her for one last hug farewell.

"Good luck," he said as he held her, and then released her. "Happy hunting."

"Thank you," she replied. "I'll see you by Paradiso, hopefully."

"You bet." They both turned away, and then everyone saddled up. The marshal and his deputies shook hands with Huxley before regrouping their convoy, their mounts facing north.

Huxley was correct—just sitting on Ariel, Lizzy could tell that he was an easy-going horse. She smiled and waved at Wills as she turned to follow the law officers, listening to Iago's and Falstaff's hoofbeats grow softer behind her, until they finally disappeared altogether.

Andy

He looked over at the woman who now rode Matt's horse and claimed to be a canary. She was a tiny thing, attractive enough, but she carried herself like a man would. She could handle herself on a horse, though it was clear that something was bothering her—she squirmed a little in her saddle every so often— maybe she had an old injury or something. She didn't complain or draw attention, however.

The more he thought about it, the more he realized that she reminded him of Sophie and Akeisha: she had a very military or para-military feel about her. Where she came from had no bearing on this job, however—there was more important information to find out about her first.

And they would find out, in the next mile or so.

"We'll make introductions when we stop for lunch," he told her. "You can call me Andy, though, since we'll all be workin' together. I noticed you travel light."

"Being with the troupe, you have to," she replied.

There was a pause; she apparently wasn't much of a talker. "Been with the troupe long?"

"A little more than two years." The delivery of the information was clipped and felt a bit rote. "I'm originally from a place called Vagabond Haven. I auditioned for the troupe and was accepted as a guitar player. I also play the trumpet and do some acting here and there." She looked at him. "What did you do before Infusion, if you don't mind me asking?"

"I was a US Marshal, just like now," he replied.

She didn't respond, but just waited for him to continue. She was comfortable with silence and pauses, he observed. He decided to be candid as he took out his flask.

"I was at the end of my career," he began, undoing the stopper. "Been all over the country, even the White House once. They were hidin' me away in the Cheyenne office until I could retire, keepin' me on a desk." He took a sip from the flask. The moonshine burned his tongue and continued its siege all the way down his throat—this was a particularly potent batch. He'd have to tell Pat to ease off next time, don't let it brew so long.

"Anyhow, I was in Jackson for a hearing when the demons came. We tried to secure the town, but the outbreak was too much and we had to withdraw—we were runnin' for our lives at the end.

"Like most folk, the first two years was just trying to get my bearin's, but then it became clear the folk left needed law and order. So, I put my badge back on and volunteered to be the law 'round there. I was elected proper the following year." He paused to look at the woman, who had a strange look on her face. "You all right?"

She frowned, placing a hand on her stomach. "Yeah," she said distractedly, "go on."

He looked around the landscape. They were getting close, but...way too soon. Something else must be wrong with her.

"When I was growing up," he continued, "I always admired Wyatt Earp, Bat Masterson, and the other old-time western marshals. Never thought in a million years I'd be steppin' into their shoes, but here I am." He stopped again as he saw the alleged canary turning green and swallowing constantly. She looked at him, panic-stricken.

"You're testing me, right?" she asked. "There's Infected material around here, please tell me you planted it."

Shock ripped through his alcoholic haze like a rifle crack through a canyon.

No...it can't be! Looking around, he got his physical bearings again.

"Yes," he admitted, allowing his surprise to show. "But...we're not there yet." He nodded up the path. "It's right up there, by those trees." His deputies were now paying attention, staring at her.

She stopped her horse and began digging into one of her belt pouches. The woman pulled out a paper wrapper and opened it next to her lips, dumping its contents into her mouth. She made a horrible face and gagged.

"God, that's awful!" she exclaimed. She reached into another pouch and pulled out another wrapper, repeating the process. Finally, she opened her canteen and took a long drink. As she screwed the lid back on her water container she concentrated on the horn of her saddle, like she was waiting for something to happen. Finally, she breathed a sigh of relief.

"Thank you, Doc!" she crowed to the air. She turned to Bennett. "We have a dentist who travels around with us, and he has a fix for just about anything. I still might throw up, but I don't think I'll pass out on you. Can we go around, please?"

He heard her question, but he was still processing her reaction to the pickled hand he brought from his office, which was currently sitting in yonder tree trunk. He had confiscated it not long after he took this job, but he hadn't destroyed it. Since then, as con artists would come in to peddle wares or services, the body part was of a use sometimes to discount their claims. This was the first instance in recent memory that the hand *confirmed* an assertion. He turned to Sophie.

"How far away would you say we were from that tree?"

She gauged the distance. "Twenty yards? We were about thirty yards when she started getting sick."

"Yup, that's what I'd say, too." He looked at the stranger. "What's your name again?"

"Petya of Vagabond Haven."

He nodded; Joshi warned him not to expect typical names. Her color was returning to normal—that must have been some good medicine.

"Well, Miss Petya, I'd say you passed the test. Sorry to had to have done it, but I had to be sure." He studied her for a moment. "Are you goin' to be OK doin' this job? You're no use to me sick all the time."

"Actually," she said, her eyes widening and a small smile stretching on her face, "I'm feeling pretty good." She looked over at the trees. "Can we experiment, see how close I can get? What is it over there?"

"A hand."

She grimaced, but she started walking Ariel towards the trees; Andy and the deputies followed her. She managed to get about five feet from the tree before she stopped, visibly swallowing again.

"It's definitely in there," she told Andy with a gasp, pointing to the tree. "I could get closer, but I think I'd yak." She suddenly looked worried. "It has to come back with us, doesn't it?"

Shit... He hadn't thought about that when he brought the object. "Well, it's a valuable piece of property—no demon activities to speak of for a long time, so pieces like that are hard to come by.

"Tell you what—I'll give it to Akeisha and Thom over there, and they'll keep it at a comfortable distance, hide it far away when we make a stop. Will that work for you?"

"Yes, thank you," she said, nodding. She looked at the deputies. "Thank you."

They nodded in acknowledgement. Thom reached in and carefully pulled the jar out of the trunk.

Inside the glass, the masculine hand was grey and a bit disintegrated; a wedding band was still sitting against the ring finger's gristled knuckle. Greenish brine sloshed in the jar, disturbing the tiny bits of flesh and fat tissue that had pulled away over the years and were now suspended within the solution. Andy noticed that Petya's demeanor hadn't changed—seeing the decomposing body part didn't affect her at all.

This little girl is getting more interesting by the second. He tipped back his flask for another drink. "Well, this is as good a spot as any to sit a while, let Petya recover a bit. Thom, you and

Akeisha take that up the road a piece; we'll start up again in about twenty minutes. We'll meet you at that campsite by the road—the one with the shit-covered campsite in the back."

He watched Petya smile in recognition: she apparently was familiar with the site.

"OK, Andy," Akeisha said. "We'll see you later." She and Thom rode off down the path as the rest of the group dismounted.

"The creek is just over there," Petya told him, pointing to the east.

He then realized another potential use of this SCAdian. "You know this area pretty well, don't you?" he asked as they walked their horses towards the water.

She shrugged. "Fairly well. I could probably manage to get you to Diablo's Keep from here, in the Barony of Winter's Gate. I'm not sure where that is in relation to Dragonsfyre Port, though."

"It's next door a bit, to the east and south."

"At the very least, I know the campsites along this road until the edge of the Middle Kingdom, if that's a help."

He smiled. "It might be at that."

The Village of Caradoc
The Barony of Vagabond Haven
July 23rd
5:28 p.m.

Red

Baron Red was sitting at his wife's bedside when the reconniscance party returned. He had been watching her sleep for maybe an hour now, relieved that Elspeth could finally go into a deep slumber for the first time in weeks. The drugs Dr. Donovan brought were far, far superior to the homeopathic tonics that the apothocares had, and Red knew that, once Elspeth was receiving treatment at an actual government facility, she would only get better and better. He was sorry that he had to sink to betraying a member of his village to arrange this—though, to be fair, one that was forced upon him—but he was not sorry that he was giving his wife every opportunity to recover.

He was starting to wonder where Mabel and Mike were, but he figured that they were either having trouble finding Townsend or had decided to stay in town and enjoy the festival. Since Brian had assured Red that he could manage Elspeth's care without them for a few days, Red had told them they wouldn't be missed until Tuesday morning. Still, Red had sent a few men to Hamilton earlier that day, just to check up on their two guests and ensure they hadn't skipped out on him. He was confident, however, that they would keep their word: Stagger was very skittish about having her operations revealed, and Dr. Donovan seemed no different.

A knock on the door interrupted his thoughts. He stood up, walked over to the door, and opened it. Tex was standing alone in the hall.

"I need to see you in your office, Baron Duke," he said. He looked grim.

"Of course," Red said, trying not to panic immediately—it *was* Tex, of course. He walked with Tex into his office and shut the door behind them.

"What's up, Tex?" Red asked.

Tex looked down and swallowed. Then he looked up and met Red's eyes full on; Red had never seen him so grave. "We went to Hamilton, sir. Wills' people sent us to a place called the Coach and Four. The lady there verified that Miss Mabel and Dr. Donovan had been there, but no one saw them after that. She had sent them to the waterfall near town, 'cause that's where her brother and Petya were going.

"But Max, the brother, told us they hadn't seen them. We circled back around to where you told them to hide the van, and it was still there." He paused.

"I had the other guys stand guard while I searched the van. I found this." He reached into his side coat pocket and pulled out an envelope; he handed it to Red. "No one else saw it."

Red looked down at the envelope. It was addressed to him. Specifically, it was addressed to Caleb Issac Nestle, BMCS. He felt faint.

"That's your mundane name, sir," Tex said. "Why would someone address the envelope like that? What does the 'BMCS' mean?"

"It stands for Senior Chief Boatswain's Mate; it was my rank in the Navy. Not that it was a secret, but..." He couldn't say anything more as he felt a swelling tide of dread and fear beginning to peak in his chest. He was starting to have trouble breathing.

"I'm sorry, sir," Tex said, getting back to the subject at hand. "We couldn't find them anywhere. Is there anything else you'd like us to do?"

"No," Red said, feeling older by the second. "No, go get some supper, Tex. Thank you."

Tex bowed and left the room, looking concerned.

Red sank into his desk chair and stared at the envelope for several seconds. Finally, he ripped open the side of the envelope and fished out the single sheet of paper folded inside. It was white and woven in appearance, and when Red held it up to the dying sunlight from the window he could see that its watermark was shaped like an eagle with a laurel branch in one talon and a cluster of arrows in the other. The paper was embossed at the top with the old, familiar seal of the United States of America. There was no formal address and no return address; there wasn't even a salutation. The message only contained these words, hand-written in block print:

BLACKMAIL IS BEHAVIOR UNBECOMING, SENIOR CHIEF—YOU WILL CEASE AND DESIST.
SORRY ABOUT EILEEN.

COL/15 ROBERT J. PICKERING, USMC
RETRIVAL TEAM GOLF

Checkmate, Red thought, as he felt tears falling down his cheeks and felt himself finally giving up. *God damn them all...*

Stella

Where the hell are *they?* Stella wondered as she tried for the tenth time that morning to work on a purchase order for more live Infected cell cultures. She figured that Mike and Bea would be later than Wednesday—Murphy was always in charge during these runs, and her people almost always returned a day or two later than anticipated—but she thought Bea would send a note telling Stella not to worry, or something. Her train of thought was interrupted by the ringing of her telephone.

"Dr. Goddard," she said into the receiver.

"Hello, Dr. Goddard," a voice said into her ear. "Do you have a moment for a quick meeting?"

"Sure—I'm sorry, who is this?"

"We have never met, Dr. Goddard. I'm from Headquarters; I'll introduce myself when I arrive. See you in a minute."

Dr. Goddard waited until she saw a man appear at her door. He was average height, average build, with brown hair and eyes, wearing a beige suit and tie. There was absolutely nothing noteworthy about the man except the absolute absence of noteworthiness. If she had passed him on the street, she doubted she would even have noticed him.

"Please come in, Mr....?"

The man came forward. "Mr. Jake Berlin. Forgive me if I don't shake hands, I have a slight cold."

"Of course," she replied, though she noted that Mr. Berlin did not look the least bit sick. "Would you please sit down?"

"Thank you." Mr. Berlin closed the door behind him, and then sat in the offered chair. "You are probably wondering why I'm here."

"Yes," Stella replied. "I am. This is all very irregular."

"You're right," Mr. Berlin told her, "And irregular in many, many ways. My first question for you, Dr. Goddard, is why were two members of your staff found in the middle of the Wilderness, well off the main road?"

Stella took a breath. *Oh, shit...*

"We received message traffic that Drs. Gilbert and Donovan were to report to Headquarters for a few days of training seminars," she explained. "They left Saturday morning. What happened to them? Are they all right?"

"No," he said, leaning back in his chair. "First of all, there was no message traffic sent like that."

"I have copies," Stella protested. "They seemed authentic. What is going on here?"

"They were not authentic, Dr. Goddard. Furthermore, Drs. Gilbert and Donovan were found quite off the beaten path. Do you have any idea why they would have deviated from their original course? I'm afraid they didn't even make it to Headquarters."

Stella shook her head. "The only thing that I can think of that might make them leave the main road would be if they saw, or thought there might be, Infected people nearby. Live Infected specimens are impossible to come by these days—Dr. Donovan especially might have thrown caution to the wind if there was a chance to capture an Infected individual.

"Now, I have answered your question, sir, please answer mine. Are Mike and Bea all right?"

Mr. Berlin straightened up in his chair. His eyes were dead and cold. "Dr. Donovan received extensive injuries, I'm afraid, but we managed to get him stabilized. He will need to rehabilitate at Headquarters for several more days, but he will be returned to this facility in time."

Stella waited. "And Bea?"

Mr. Berlin's eyes somehow grew even colder. "I'm afraid Dr. Gilbert will not be returning to the lab."

Stella sat back in her chair, not wanting to understand—to believe—his cryptic statement. "You mean she's dead."

"Yes. I'm sorry, Dr. Goddard. She received a blow to the head, and there was nothing that could be done."

Stella turned her head away and stared out the window. "May we have the body?"

"I'm afraid that will not be possible; the body has already been interred. She was buried with honors, I can assure you, considering her ultimate sacrifice for her country."

Stella nodded, closing her eyes.

Oh, Bea, I'm so sorry...

Mr. Berlin stood up. "May I recommend, Dr. Goddard, that you inform your staff not to entertain such...potentially dangerous situations in the future? Let this be a cautionary tale not to stray from the established path, as it were. We have so few people as it is, and such errands are foolish, even if the intentions are noble."

Stella nodded, not looking at him. She got the message loud and clear. She wondered how long the government had known about their operations. She wondered why they hadn't just come out before and said that the jig was up. Then maybe Bea would still be alive.

All those resources...all that time sneaking around...all wasted. I thought I was being so damned clever...

Mr. Berlin turned to leave, and then stopped to address Stella again. "And, one more point, Dr. Goddard."

Stella turned and looked at him, determined not to cry until this asshole left the room, though that was becoming more difficult to achieve by the second.

"We've secured the area where Drs. Gilbert and Donovan were found. The individuals that caused the harm will cause no further problems to you or to your staff."

"Really?" Stella replied, only showing the best poker face she could muster, refusing to yield. "We were told that there was no one left in the Wilderness."

"Just...letting you know, Dr. Goddard. Good day." His mouth was in the shape of a smirk as he walked out the door.

1534

This was the hardest thing Stella had to do in her life, and not just because she had to inform Jessica that her husband was badly injured: she also had to decide whether Jessica was going to live past sunset. There seemed to be a traitor in their midst, and she thought she had a pretty good idea who it was. She

332

approached Jessica's apartment door and knocked—she had already checked her office.

"Come in," Jessica said from behind the door. "It's opened."

Stella pushed opened the door and walked in; the automatic door closer pulled the door shut behind her. The apartment was tastefully decorated in a cream-and-white, modern motif, with simple furniture and wide-open space in the main room. Jessica was sitting on a white couch, legs tucked up underneath her, staring out the patio door. She didn't turn around, so all that Stella could see was the back of her head and her long brown hair.

"What's happened, Stella?" Jessica asked.

Stella took a breath. Maybe she could see Stella in the reflection of the window; that's how she knew it was her. "Mike's at Headquarters. He was hurt badly, but they think he'll be back in a few days."

Jessica nodded. "Bea?"

Stella felt anger well up inside of her. *Not yet, not yet...*

"She didn't make it. She was murdered."

Jessica only nodded again. Stella walked around so she could see Jessica's face. She saw that her eyes were red and swollen from crying, and her face was pale. She wouldn't meet Stella's gaze.

"You have a lot to explain," Stella said. "I don't want to hear any bullshit, or you trying to snow me. I need you to tell me how you could tell me to send Mike and Bea on a mission *two years* before it happened, and how apparently the government knew about our operations the entire time."

Jessica shook her head. "I didn't tell the government anything; I didn't need to. If you thought that a lack of response on their part meant that they were ignorant about what you were doing, then you don't know them very well. The government is perfectly content to allow people to believe that they are autonomous—until you step out of line, of course, and they never say where the line is—and then they clamp down and show you what they really are. That happened earlier today, I'm guessing. Any freedom you think you have is just a façade."

Stella stared at her. "Who the hell are you?"

Jessica smiled a little. She finally looked up. "Many years ago, a woman and I had the exact same nightmare, even though we lived across the country from each other. I was naïve, and I posted my experience on the Internet. Not even twelve hours later, I was taken from all that I knew and found myself at a processing center, being poked and prodded and tested. They didn't find anything out of the ordinary, but more dreams came. Later, I discovered that some of them were coming true, that they were premonitions."

Jessica stopped talking and furrowed her eyebrows. "You'd better sit down, Stella, you look ill."

Stella sagged down onto an ajoining chair; the fight had temporarily gone out of her. "Thank you. Please continue," she managed.

"Some are very inconsequential—a glass of water falling over, something like that. But then sometimes I see events...I never know at the time when they will happen, but I usually can guess—maybe someone gets their hair cut a certain way and I recognize it, or I realize that all of the players are assembled and the place is correct. That happened two years ago when Liz Townsend first made holy water at Headquarters. That event was my very first nightmare, all those years ago, and it was only when the DJ started playing "Louie, Louie" that I knew what was about to happen. I had been in that pool room many times before, I had known Liz and her OINC for years, but..." Jessica shrugged. "After my one attempt to change a vision, I can't rely on my earlier visions to be 100% accurate."

"What do you mean?" Stella asked.

"Once, I recognized a certain chain of events as they were progressing, and I tried to alter their course. After about three months in the processing center, I made a bargain with my handlers that if they would allow me to finish my education and become a psychiatrist, I would cooperate freely and voluntarily when they requested information or tests. Just that once they were as good as their word, and before I knew it I had finished my BA in psychology—at a different university under a new identity, of course—and I was in my first year of medical school in Hawaii. I met another student there, and I recognized him from one of my dreams. In the dream, he had drowned while surfing in some sort of competition.

"As it turned out we really hit it off, and we started dating. Within a few months we had moved in together. We loved each other, Stella, but this vision hung over me, and I was nervous every time Kalani surfed. But he only surfed for fun, so it was OK.

"Then one day, he told me he was entering a surfing competition for a local charity. I freaked out, and I thought about just telling him what I knew. But he didn't believe in the supernatural, and I was afraid that he would just do it anyway to prove me wrong. So I lied and told him he had agreed to do something else that day—he tended to be forgetful—and he didn't go. I was so relieved, and it *was* the competition that he was supposed to die in—we drove past, and it was exactly as I had seen it in my dream. He would have died that day for sure." She paused.

"Three months later, he pushed a kid out from in front of an oncoming car and got struck instead—instant vegetable." More tears fell from Jessica's eyes. "The last time I saw him, after I had graduated and was about to come back stateside, he was still attached to the respirators and feeding tubes—his father was considering removing them, though I'm not sure if he ever did.

"I know that for Kalani that fate was worse than death. So not only didn't I save my boyfriend, but I changed the course of my reality, too, so all of the dreams I had before the car accident are now inaccurate to various degrees.

"So when Lizzy was at that pool party with me, I really couldn't warn her, because I wasn't sure *what* was going to happen. Though, that event went exactly as I had seen it, which was unusual. Thank god that Phillips was the only person who died that day, it could have been so much worse." Jessica grimaced and absently wiped her nose with her sleeve.

"I had seen Mike and Bea getting attacked two years ago. But I knew that, if I didn't interfere, Mike would eventually recover and come back to me. I'm sorry, Stella, but there are much bigger things coming than one woman losing her life, even Bea's, and I have to pick my battles. When I interfere in a prophesied vision again, and there is one dream that I will do everything in my power to stop from happening, it has to be worth flying blind again."

Stella shook her head. "What is the vision that is scaring you so much? What is worth Bea's life?"

Jessica paused for several moments. "I have never told anyone—not the government, not Mike—about this one. It is so...monsterous...that I hesitate to get anyone else involved. But I cannot begin to change this alone and maybe, if we use your connections and we are careful, we can stop it somehow. Or, we have to try.

"I had this prediction seven years ago, not long after we came to the laboratory. In this vision, in a time I do not recognize yet, the government mobilizes and marches during one night to every female and family commune. They take the children, Stella. They take every one of them, from the babies to the teenagers, and they put them in cattle cars, and they murder everyone else."

Jessica began to cry in earnest. "All the females, all of the mothers and the fathers, and anyone else over twenty or so they mowed down like grass, and the greasy smoke from the cremation fires blotted out the sun, and the ash looked like snow. And I saw every invasion over the course of that night, down to the last detail. All of the communes were destroyed, and I was their witness.

"It was a holocaust, Stella, executed by our own government. And somehow, *somehow*, it has to be stopped."

Stella felt sick; she couldn't explain it, but Jessica's voice had the ring of truth to it. As implausible as it all was, she believed her. There was just too many traumatic, fucked-up events going on that afternoon; she needed a drink...no, screw that, she needed to be oblivious on a two-week-long morphine cocktail. "You haven't recognized anything yet?"

"Well," Jessica said. "Joe, the new guy from Commune Ruth, is working here now; I didn't see him dying at Ruth, and I would have noticed that. I recently went to Family Commune Joe of Am, and the new OINC there is the one that perishes in the holocaust. She was very brave, trying to fight off the army with her one pistol.

"But I haven't seen any of the other players yet, so we probably still have some time. I think, though, that with something that extreme there will be signs that it's coming; some pretty significant events would occur, I would think, to make that happen."

"You're probably right," Stella agreed. She patted Jessica's knee and stood up.

"Say nothing," Stella advised. "I'm not sure what to do yet, but we won't let this stand without a fight." She started for the door, and then turned around. "Are you going to be OK?"

Jessica nodded. "I'll be better when Mike is back, but I'll be all right."

"Have..." Stella paused. "Have you ever had a dream about me?"

Jessica smiled at her question. "Yes. A good one, actually—I have those, too. Just wait and see."

Chapter Fourteen

Lizzy

"I feel like I should be calling you Sacajawea," Andy commented as they rode towards the barony's northern border. "The trip back was much better than the trip down, thanks to you."

The deputies nodded in agreement.

"You're welcome." Lizzy was pleased that she could be helpful to the expedition in some way, considering the uncertainty of the mission's true success.

She found herself very comfortable around the officers—she liked them. They were a very grounded, unpresumptuous kind of people, and they seemed to reason through situations as she might. There was a pleasant camaraderie among the men and women in the group that she recognized from her time on her first cutter, the *Buzzard Bay,* but never found on the *Surveyor.* After a couple of days they seemed to quasi-accept Lizzy into their group, though not into their confidence, which she could understand.

It also didn't hurt that she took her share of the less desirable grunt work on the road, she supposed, like digging latrines and splitting firewood. Though, Lizzy sometimes wondered if there were any soft women left—it seemed that anyone who didn't pull their load, male or female, in this post-Infusion world would be quickly left behind. She was sure even Baroness Isabella had to work the hydroponic fields in the beginning along with everyone else—at least at first.

They had been riding in militia country for over an hour before they came to their first settlement. When the group could just begin to see a collection of shacks and buildings, Andy pulled alongside her.

"The folks in this town can be a bit—touchy," he told her, but not with real concern. "Just stick with me."

The town was very quiet as they rode in, even though it was near midday. They stopped at a sturdy-looking wooden structure with the words "Inn/Livery Stable" painted on the front in black. A short, stocky woman came out from the front.

"Marshal," she greeted. She looked over the group as she went up to Andy and handed up a metal flask much like the one he always carried. "Travelling kinda heavy, aren't you?" She looked at Lizzy. "Who's she?"

"This is Pet—she's a new recruit." Andy shrugged dismissively as he handed her his old flask. "We're having some trouble up north, but nothin' anyone 'round here needs to worry about." He looked around as he unscrewed his new flask. "Danny in?"

"Yeah," she sighed. "He's in the back with a prisoner—she's waiting for trial."

"Oh," Andy said, surprised. He took a pull of whatever was in the flask and swallowed. "I'm glad I stopped in, then." He dismounted; everyone followed suit. He turned to his deputies as he untied a saddlebag. "While you get the horses settled, Pet and I'll find out what Danny's up to. Go ahead and start lunch without us." He looked at the woman. "What's on the menu, Jen?"

"Ham hock stew with sourdough bread. I even have some fresh goat milk today, but that'll be extra."

Andy made a face and shuttered slightly. "I'll pass on the goat's milk. C'mon, Pet, let's see what the charges are." He threw his saddlebag over his shoulder and made his way inside the building, Lizzy following close behind.

It was dark inside the inn—the only light source was the sunlight coming in from the dusty windows. The table and chairs were fairly clean, but the place had an unused, desolate feeling.

"Could we be the only customers today?" she asked Andy quietly.

"They'll be some folks who'll come in tonight, after dark," he explained. "Everyone's in the fields or on their farms right now—nothin' but farmers 'round here."

In the back half of the building was a large room with two jail cells made of wrought iron bars against the inside wall. A stringy man was sitting at a desk next to the cells, writing in a large bound journal. He looked up when Andy made a floor board creak and grinned—his smile was thinly made like the rest of him, but it was pleasant enough.

"Hey, Andy." He stood up and walked around his desk to shake the marshal's hand.

"Danny," Andy replied. "Danny, this is Pet—she's helping us out on the Zion case. Pet, this is the local sheriff, Danny Piscopo."

"Pleasure," Lizzy said as they shook hands.

Danny gave her the once-over. "So, can you really Sense from thirty yards?"

She shrugged. "I also tend to puke and pass out without medication—I'm not sure how much help I'll be."

"Well, anything you can do 'll be a help." He looked at Andy. "I heard they lost another one while you were gone."

The marshal sighed. "OK." He glanced over at the cells. One was empty, but the other one held a sleeping woman in a calico dress and black, thick boots. "Isn't that Lynne?"

"Yeah," Danny said with a sigh. "She had to shoot another intruder dead."

Andy reached up and rubbed the back of his neck wearily. "I thought you convinced her to move into town."

"She doesn't want to move," the sheriff replied. "She figures she's doing a public service, shooting dead all the vagrants that come into the area and try to break into her place."

"That's right, Marshal!" Their talking must have woken up Lynne; she now joined in the conversation. "And, it's not like I go *lookin'* for people to shoot—they just show up!"

"Lynne, aren't you afraid they'll get the jump on you someday?" Andy asked.

"Nah—they just see me and my kids in town, and they think I'm easy pickin's—they don't know what they're getting' into." She paused. "I'm surprised word hasn't gotten around yet to stay clear of my place!"

"Lynne, it's not like the drifters have an online forum or somethin'," Danny pointed out.

"How long has she been in custody?" Andy asked as he placed his saddlebag down and worked on opening the buckles.

"This is the second day—she turned herself in Friday morning, first thing."

"Where are your kids, Lynne?" Andy pulled a wooden gavel set out of the saddlebag.

"They're with Bobby and Stacy—just like the last two times."

Lynne was standing up now, each hand gripping a bar as she spoke. Lizzy could now see that she was shorter than she was, pretty, and had a full head of fiery-red hair. She didn't seem to be physically sturdy enough to stand up against a large gust of wind, let alone a home intruder.

"All right, let's get this done." The marshal placed a carved block of hardwood on Danny's desk and banged the gavel on it.

"Oye-yea, oye-yea, oye-yea," Andy began in his slow, careful draw. "The First District Court of the Confederation of New Wyoming is now in session, the honorable me presidin'. All who have cause to plead draw near." He looked at Danny. "Sheriff, please present the case."

Danny reached over and picked up a legal pad from his desk. He referred to it as he addressed the court. "Marshal Bennett, the accused, Lynne Thompson, is charged with first-degree manslaughter of one Jake Lemmon. Mr. Lemmon was identified by an expired driver's license on his person."

"OK." Andy looked at Lynne. "How do you plead?"

"Not Guilty, 'cause it was self-defense!" Lynne answered defiantly.

"So noted. What are the circumstances, Sheriff Piscopo?"

"Sometime during the early morning of July 27th the victim, identified as Jake Lemmon, entered Ms. Thompson's home through the front door. Upon hearing sounds of a home invasion downstairs, the accused took her shotgun from the floor of her bedroom and made her way out of the room to investigate. She surprised the victim on the stairs and shot him once in the chest with a 20-gauge shotgun, killing him instantly. The blood trail down the steps confirms that part of the story, as well as the placement of the body, face-up, at the bottom of the steps."

Andy nodded. "Lynne, is that how it happened?"

"Yes, Marshal Bennett."

"Did you know this man?"

"I've seen him in town a couple of times, but I've never met him."

"Danny, what do we know about Mr. Lemmon?"

341

"He's a known drifter—he'd been making the circuit around the territory for years, looking for day work. He's been jailed before for drunk and disorderly, but nothing like this before."

"Hmm." Andy considered the information for a moment. "Lynne, are you sure you didn't lead Mr. Lemmon on, or invite him into your home at any point?"

"Hell, no, Marshal!" Lynne looked indignant. "I don't invite strange men into my house, not with my kids there!"

So, you don't invite them into your home to 'protect your kids,' but you voluntarily stay in a place after you've been broke into twice? Lizzy wasn't sure what to make of Lynne—she seemed a bit...off.

"All right, then. Danny, does Mr. Lemmon have any kin that we know of?"

"No—both times I processed him for the drunk tank he gave no next of kin, no one to contact to post bail. He served his time and left." Danny paused for a moment in thought. "That's all I have, Andy—I rest my case."

Andy nodded. "Anything else, Lynne?"

"He was going up the stairs to my kids' bedrooms—I had to shoot him!"

"Oh...well, that tears it." Andy walked over to the cell and looked the woman in the eyes. "I'm going to rule in your favor, Lynne, but we need to figure out somethin' different here—you can't be shooting people dead all the time."

"I can't move, Marshal—I've got a chicken farm to run," Lynne said. "If you got a suggestion, I'm all ears—buckshot costs money, y'know. Plus, it sticks into the woodwork—you can't dig those pellets out easy, you have to putty them."

Andy nodded as he went back to the desk. "Well, that would be a bother. We'll work on something everyone can agree to. But in the meantime..." He raised his gavel. "I find in favor of the defendant." He slammed the gavel on the wood block, placed it on the desk, and then immediately reached for his flask. Danny walked over to the cell and unlocked the door. Lynne stepped out and smiled at Andy.

"Thank you, Marshal!"

"You're welcome." Andy said after taking his drink and screwing the flask closed. He watched Lynne leave the room and walk out the front door of the inn before turning to Lizzy. "Well, Pet, what did you think?"

Lizzy thought about the case for a moment. "Is Lynne new to the area?"

Andy looked at Danny, who shrugged. "She moved into the area about three years ago."

She twitched her mouth. "Do we know where she's from, originally?"

"No way to tell—it's not like we have an electronic database anymore and we can run her social." Danny's eyes narrowed at her. "Are you in law enforcement or somethin'?"

"No—Andy asked me, I'm just speculating. I also don't know how often home invasions happen around here—maybe it's common, I don't know."

"Eh, it happens," Andy told her. "Especially when there's a drought or some such and folks can't find work." He looked at Danny. "You hungry?"

"Sure—let's get some stew." He shot a brief glare at Lizzy before they all left the room.

Three hours later, after they restocked on supplies and the settlement was at their backs, Andy sidled up to her again. "So, what did you really think of the trial?"

She gave him a sideways look. "I'm not sure it's my place to say—he's your sheriff."

Andy snorted. "He's not under my jurisdiction—they just use me as a circuit judge for felony cases. As a judge, I can only rule on the evidence provided—if the officer presents a shit case, then I have no choice but to rule in favor of the defendant. Tell me what you think."

Fine—she'd give it to him with the bark on. "After the second time, a mother worth a shit at all would have picked up and moved. Chickens can be portable: they move the coops where I winter all the time to give the chickens fresh places to scratch and use the poop for fertilizer, so that's a bullshit excuse. Couldn't tell you why she wants to be alone and isolated, but it seems to be that way—maybe there's more to how she makes a living than chickens.

"And, did Danny ask around to see if there was no work, if Jake Lemmon *was* that desperate? If Lemmon had been in the area for a while, he should have had *some* sort of inkling that Lynne Thompson had killed before—that kind of news gets around.

"She doesn't have a man—what happened to him, or them?" She shouldn't assume all the kids had the same father. "The only thing I can't figure out is, if she's so isolated, why bother turning yourself in—why not just bury the body in the backyard? Unless…she wasn't entirely sure he wouldn't be missed? The whole situation is weird.

"And, if you really want to know, I think the sheriff's banging her."

Andy's eyebrows shot up. "What makes you think that?"

"For one thing, she was asleep when we came in—she didn't seem worried about her *third* manslaughter trial—I think that'd worry most people, even if it was self-defense; it just doesn't look good. I'm guessing all of her trials have been the same way: crappy evidence, no questioning, self-defense?"

Andy nodded.

"And," she blushed in spite of herself, "she smelled especially…musky…when she walked out the door. It could be that she hasn't washed in a couple of days, but…" She trailed off, not sure what else to say on the matter.

Andy unscrewed his flask and took a swig. "All good questions and observations." He looked at her with a degree of admiration. "Sorry I had to shut you up back there, but considerin' I don't have official jurisdiction, I didn't want you to piss off Danny and for him to do somethin' I couldn't stop—that would have been the 'touchy' I was warning you about."

Lizzy nodded. "I'll know that *touchy* means *keep my opinions to myself* from now on."

He smirked at that. "Well, you can tell me afterwards, unless it's somethin' that'll get us all killed." He blew out a breath. "Again, I'm just a circuit judge. Until the townfolk get tired of the shitty police work and throw him out—most of his trials are like that, actually, unless the victim has local kin—I just call 'em as I see 'em."

Lizzy thought about Sheriff Piscopo. "How many sheriffs are like him?"

"Not too many—we have shitbags alongside the good people, same as before. The demons changed the world, but they didn't change that."

John

"It looked like a military base before Infusion," John told the group of baronial officers that were sitting in Red's great room. "They had transport vehicles, deuce and a halves, and crates and crates of weapons just lying around. It's not an invasion force—it's a force of annihilation. If they come our way, there's just no way we can stop them."

No one spoke.

"Are we sure they're coming for us, too?" Ivan, the baronial exchequer, finally asked. "They have every reason to attack Cornwall, but we're really small potatoes compared to them."

"We're right next door," Cuthbert pointed out, "And we were one of the first baronies to bar trading with them. I see no reason why they wouldn't take us out, too. I don't think they'd even break a sweat."

Red was quiet as the conversation buzzed around him. In fact, he hadn't said a complete sentence to anyone, including John, since Miss Mabel and Dr. Donovan disappeared.

John and Cuthbert were told about the two government people's visit and Elspeth's prognosis. All of the medical equipment was still in this house, hidden in the basement. Only the pain-controlling drugs remained in Elspeth's room now, and Wolfgang had to keep increasing their dosage almost constantly to have an effect. When she somehow got word that the two strangers had vanished, it seemed as though she made up her mind that she was done fighting and began deteriorating. Wolfgang, at this point, was just concentrating on making her comfortable. John hadn't managed to catch her awake since they

345

returned—he hoped he would soon.

For him, Elspeth wasn't only his knight's wife: she had been a bedrock of support during those first horrible years after Regina had died when he was plunged into the unfamiliar abyss of parenting a young child alone. She, along with the other women in the village, helped him fill in the blanks when he didn't have a clue, and on more than one occasion Elspeth just showed up at the house and took Johnny for an afternoon so he could get some chores done and maybe catch a nap. He stopped this train of thought, though, when he realized that the voices in the room were now shouting.

"Whoa, Whoa!" he yelled over the other officers; he got their attention. "Sorry, I zoned out for a second—what's the problem?"

"I am *not* sending Melody and Angus away from here, John. You can all forget that!" Baroness Morgan said. Melody and Angus were her children.

John paused, thinking through that possibility. "I'm not sure we're at that point yet, Morgan, but we may be soon. That's like...Step 7, and we're not even at Step 1 yet. That's...just not our priority right now.

"The first thing we need to do is send out the recall letters, so folks have time to get back here." He turned to the knight marshal, a squire named Antonio. "How many folks are out of the barony, officially?"

Antonio thought for a moment. "About twenty, maybe? Most are in Cornwall or Hamilton; Master Daniel's in Carpathia. Then there's Lady Petya, of course, sir..." He looked at John a bit apologetically.

The heavy weight of gravity that was already pushing on John's chest leaned in deeper. Unlike Petya, Antonio knew full well what an escort after an AoA ceremony meant—at least in Vagabond Haven.

God, I wish I had said something sooner to her... But, deal with it later—back to business.

"OK, let's get those going—I want them out the door by August 1st." He turned to Red. "What else should we be doing, Red?"

Red was staring into space, in another world.

"Red!"

Red blinked a few times, and shook his head as if to clear it.

"I need to talk to you out on the back porch, John," he

suddenly announced, standing up. "The rest of you carry on—try not to wreck the place while we're gone."

John followed Red out the back screen door. They both found a chair and sat down, facing the barn. For a minute, they both just listened to the quiet and the occasional animal noise. Finally, Red spoke.

"I'm going to Cornwall, to offer my diplomatic services to Isabella." He paused, looking into the night. "Maybe we can talk our way out of this one, offer concessions."

John couldn't believe what he was hearing. "Maybe I didn't make myself clear, sir. They are not interested in diplomacy; I can promise you that."

Red stood up and walked to the porch railing. He leaned forward against it, still watching the blackness.

"I've fucked us up but good, John," he said, his voice thick with emotion. "I gave away the rest of our boons to bring those people to help Elspeth. Now we are truly alone out here, and it's my fault."

John was surprised—he never considered that there was a limit to the government assistance they received from time to time. It always felt like...humanitarian aid or something. "They always gave medical supplies, sir, or food—never weapons. I'm not sure they could have helped."

"Still...I'm no good here. You can lead these people just as well as I can, but I have some experience with dealing with hostile groups like those. I don't think I'll be able to do much, either, but too many lives are at stake not to try.

"Besides, Elspeth's going to die, and there's nothing I can do about that now. I really would prefer to die with my boots on, I think, than just sit around and watch my wife slowly waste away only to die myself. She felt bad, too, that we wasted our largesse on such a foolish endeavor—she would want me to try and stop this." He turned and looked at John.

"You're responsible for the barony until I return. Good luck." He opened the screen door and walked back into the house. By the time John had stood and returned inside to the great room, Red had already gone upstairs. The baronial officers were looking at him and each other in confusion.

"What was that about?" Cuthbert asked.

"Red's going to Cornwall," John replied. "Looks like it's just us now."

The recall letters were ready by Wednesday morning. Most of them were local deliveries, and they were done by noon. It was more of a formality, really—once those trucks started arriving, John was sure they'd come running. Antonio volunteered to go to Carpathia to deliver Daniel's letter. Only one letter remained.

John picked up Petya's sealed letter from the table in Red's great room. Red had already left the day before for Isabella's mansion; he had said goodbye to Elspeth privately. John knew he should let someone else deliver it...he was officially in charge now...

"Why don't you take it, John?" Cuthbert interrupted his thoughts; John hadn't even heard him come in. "I've got this. There's not much left to do until they're actually here, anyway. I've already looked it up—they'll be in Freeport until next Sunday."

John smiled at his friend with sadness and gratitude. He placed the letter inside his shirt.

"Thanks, Ben."

Little John was reading Cuthbert's copy of *The Anarchist's Cookbook* when John walked in the door. "Hi, Dad."

John stopped short when he saw what Little John was reading about. "Molotov cocktails?"

Little John shrugged. "Why not? You said they were mostly ground troops. You didn't see tanks—maybe we could make a dent."

John nodded and sat across from him. "It's a good idea—we'll have to see how much flammable liquid we have around here. The brewers should have plenty of bottles." He watched Little John take notes for a minute before speaking again.

"I'll be taking Petya's recall letter to Freehold—I'll be back as soon as I can. I'd ask you to come with me, but..."

Little John stopped writing and looked at his father. "You and Pet have a lot to talk about." Little John had told his father about their conversation at Crown; John's almost-worst fear was confirmed.

His *worst* fear was that Petya would reject the idea of him

348

courting her outright—that didn't happen. The *confirmed* fear was that she wasn't clear about what he wanted, so she didn't know how to react—she even made a very interesting analogy about the situation. He could work with that, but he wondered if there was a point now.

A few incredible nights of bliss, perhaps, before they went to their deaths?

"When are you leaving?" Little John asked.

"Tomorrow morning. Do you want to stay here, or go to a friend's house? Cuthbert's staying to mind the store; you two could swap anarchist recipes."

"I'll think about it. I'll be working the co-op tomorrow with Kit—maybe I'll stay at his house. I'll let Cuthbert know where I am."

At that, John just stared at his son, his heart swelling with delight. "I'm so proud of you—you know that?"

Little John made a face. "If I didn't behave, someone in the village would snitch."

"Maybe...but you're getting to the age where you could sow some seriously wild oats on the sly, but you don't: you get your homework done, you do your chores when I'm out, you keep up with your shifts at the co-op—*I* don't even do that. You're going to be a hell of a man someday." He leaned down and kissed Little John on the cheek. "Thank you, and I love you."

"I love you too, Dad." Little John replied, smiling at him.

"I'm going upstairs to do some packing. Think about what you want for dinner."

"OK." Little John bent his head and began writing again. John started towards the stairwell.

"Dad?" Little John called.

"Yes?"

"When you see Pet...tell her that I told her so."

John was confused. "Told her about what?"

"She'll understand."

Chapter Fifteen

The Town of Zion
Confederation of New Wyoming
July 29th
5:29 p.m.

Lizzy

The town of Zion, she was told, was the largest in the marshal's jurisdiction; it was about one and a half the size of Caradoc. It had no wall or notable defenses to speak of, which surprised her: even the smallest of SCAdian villages at least had a barbed wire fence. Lizzy asked Sophie about it, who was the town's deputy and had been around when Zion was formed seven years ago.

"This is flat land," she explained. "If mobs show up, we have plenty of time to see them coming and make a run for it. If they start up within the town, folks can escape freely. As far as actual people coming in our town..." She shrugged. "Everyone carries guns, and they know how to use them."

Lizzy nodded, but thought to herself that the antagonist in Robert Frost's poem was correct, that "good fences make good neighbors."

The group's final stop was in front of the marshal office's livery stable. A boy who was about ten years old came out of the stable carrying a metal flask, which he exchanged with Andy after the marshal dismounted.

"Thanks, Kevin," he said, smiling at the boy. "What's new?"

"Ingrid's foal, Thunderbolt, is doing well," Kevin replied with some excitement as Andy unscrewed the lid on his new flask. Then the boy's expression grew serious. "Everyone is still worried about the mommas. Ms. Fisher died a couple of days ago, Suzanne said she felt weird."

"Yeah." Andy sighed as took a swig from the flask and grimaced, gritting his teeth. "Dang! I need to speak to Pat about his brewin'—this'll take off paint!" He gestured with his flask in Lizzy's direction. "Kevin, this is Petya, she's here to help us out with the mommas. Petya, this is Kevin, he runs things 'round here."

"Hi." Lizzy waved at the boy.

"Hi," he replied, glancing at her but not really interested. "Marshal, I have to get started tending the horses; excuse me, please."

"Sure thing, thank you." Andy paused a moment. "Go ahead and get Pete to help you, tell his mother I'll send something by for payment."

"OK, Marshal." Kevin sped off towards the center of town.

Andy turned to Lizzy. "Well, let's get you settled in, and then we'll get some chow at the tavern. We can talk about how to do this over supper." He helped her unstrap and untie her saddlebags and carry them in the direction that Kevin ran.

The town had several buildings from before Infusion, but it was obvious that those houses had been refitted with fireplaces or cooking hearths. Lizzy noticed they were walking towards a large, three-story building with a porch and double doors in the front.

"Fancy," Lizzy observed.

"That's Mrs. Simpson's Boardin' House and Tavern—that's where you're stayin'. It was already here when the town was formed—historically preserved and registered. It was built in 1893, and it was a museum by the time the demons came. You'll notice that most of the museum pieces are still there, but now it's a workin' boardin' house again. We had to open up the chimneys and rebuild the cookin' hearths but, if you ask me, I think the ol' girl appreciates having a real use again."

"Does Mrs. Simpson own the place?"

"Yup—we changed the name when she took the place over, felt that way we'd had more of a claim to it, somehow."

They walked up the wooden steps and onto the porch. The cut-glass windows of the front doors sparkled with the glow of the interior lamplight. She could hear laughter and talking coming from inside with piano music barely heard underneath the auditory traffic. Andy opened one of the doors and held it for her as she stepped inside.

The lobby was fairly small in proportion to the rest of the building. A large desk sat to the left of the doors with several wooden cubby holes behind it, and two Victorian-style couches and upholstered chairs were at the other end, next to the unlit fireplace. A large fan was mounted on the ceiling that was turned by a large brass pendulum on a chain, much like an old-fashioned clock. The weight of the pendulum turned a gear that rotated the fan in a slow, lazy spin. Lizzy was impressed by the ingenuity of the device.

Andy walked up to the desk and pressed the plunger on a small, silver bell; it *tinged*. A few moments later a tall, older woman in a tie-dyed wrap dress and sandals came out of a door next to the desk. She had multiple piercings in her left ear, a nose ring, and sleeves of tattoos on both arms. She grinned at the marshal.

"Hey, Andy!" She gave him a hug. "Welcome back!" She turned to Lizzy. "Who's your friend?"

"Joan, this is Petya—she's helping us with the pregnant women. Petya, this is Joan Simpson, owner and operator of the boarding house."

Lizzy stuck her hand out. "Nice to meet you."

"Pleasure's mine," Joan replied, shaking her hand, her face now sober. "The town will be happy to see *you*—god, it's been horrible, Allie and Lisa and the rest." She walked around behind the desk and opened a large, bound book. "I have a room on the third floor—will that be OK? We have no working elevators, so you'll have to hoof it up and down the steps."

"Sure," Lizzy replied. "I'm just glad for the roof and the bed— I'm used to travelling around and sleeping on camping cots."

The woman gave her an apologetic look. "Well, the beds on the third floor aren't great, but I had a bedbug infestation not too long ago, and I had to make do with what I could find. Sign the book here, please." She turned around and grabbed a key fob as Lizzy registered as her SCAdian persona.

"'Petya of Vagabond Haven'?" Joan read aloud, upside-down, as she handed her the key. She looked at Lizzy. "What's Vagabond Haven? Don't you have a last name?"

Lizzy gave her an uncomfortable look. "No one uses their real names down in SCAdian country, where I'm from. It's the name they gave me, so it's the one I use."

Joan looked at Andy, surprised, and then back to Lizzy. "So, what I've heard about you guys dressing in medieval costumes and having weird names and even having knights and stuff—that's all *true?*"

"All true. I'm not originally from there, so it took me a while to get used to it, too. But, they knew what they were doing when they settled there, and it suits them."

"Huh...I suppose whatever floats their boat. God knows we got our types around here." Joan shook her head as she turned back to Andy. "Y'all staying for supper?"

"We'd like to," Andy replied. "What are you servin'?"

"We got fish chowder or chicken pot pie—I'd go for the fish chowder—and green beans. Peach cobbler for dessert—I'm really pleased how this last batch turned out, you'll want to save room for that." She turned to Lizzy. "We have three beers on tap and a house wine—first glass is free with the meal."

"Thank you." Lizzy looked at her key fob for her room number, then at Andy. "I'll drop off my bags and wash up a little, if that's OK, Andy. See you in ten minutes?"

"OK, come grab me at the bar when you're ready."

As they ate their meal, Lizzy asked about the Sensor that thought the mothers felt Infected. She had tried to ask about the situation during the trip, but for whatever reason Andy didn't seem to want to talk about it on the road.

Now, however, Andy seemed more than willing to talk. "Her name is Suzanne, and she's been here since the beginnin'; in fact, she lived in the town before Infusion. She was their only canary for a long time, though she can only sense Infected material from maybe five or ten yards.

"We have two other Sensors in the jurisdiction—Henry and Katie—but they don't agree with her. They're all about equal in their Sensin', so you can see how Suzanne's a bit annoyed that they can't feel it."

"You paid Wills a lot of money for the confirmation of a minority report," she observed.

"Well...Suzanne can be very persuasive, and I wasn't the one doin' the payin'. And like I told you both down there, we're out of ideas."

"Can we see her tonight? And the women?"

"I think that would be a good idea. Suzanne lives near here with a couple of other women. One of the remainin' pregnant women is local, the other ones we'll have to travel around—we'll see them after breakfast tomorrow."

Lizzy fiddled with her peach cobbler. It was good, but she didn't have much of an appetite.

"Andy?" she began softly. She thought she knew the answer, but she still needed to ask. "Why don't the women...terminate?"

The marshal sat quietly for a moment, watching the bubbles rise in his third beer. "It's not their way 'round here."

"They've gotta have ways of doing it—better than dying."

He paused again. "Pet, we don't know what we're dealin' with," he said after a sip of beer. "Most of the women 'round here couldn't live with themselves if they got rid of a baby and found out later there was nothing wrong with it. We don't even know for sure if it's demon-related—that's why you're here. Doesn't do us any good at this point to jump to conclusions. It could be something simple, like an illness we haven't seen before.

"And, besides, it's not their MO. They're raging monsters with no minds of their own except to kill in mobs—it doesn't make sense." He swigged down the rest of his beer.

She didn't answer him. After a long pause, she asked, "You done eating?"

"Yup," he replied, wiping his face with his napkin before rising. "Let's go see what Suzanne is up to."

The house next to the old post office was pretty enough: gingerbread trim, gables, and all the other accoutrements of a fine Victorian house. There were three women sitting on the porch: two were on a wide wooden porch swing, the other one was on a rocking chair next to the swing. From the looks of them they were all in their fifties, and they all were casually dressed in shorts, t-shirts, and sneakers. Glasses of tea sat on small wicker tables, and the Wyoming sky surrounding the house was especially pretty that night.

If it wasn't for the fact they were all toking up, the scene would have been almost quaint.

Lizzy glanced at Andy, who was looking at the trio with some amusement. She concluded that perhaps some federal laws were more important than others in Marshal Bennett's jurisdiction.

Hell, she wasn't military anymore—maybe *she'd* ask for one.

Lizzy and Andy walked up the porch steps and into the hemp-scented haze surrounding the women. Andy made a small cough when they arrived within the thick of it.

"Evenin', ladies," he said. "Y'know, I always feel pretty good when I come around visitin' here, but I can never figure why."

The woman in the rocking chair took a long drag of her joint and blew the smoke out of the side of her mouth. "Must be our company, Marshal. It certainly isn't the fine tobacco cigarettes we're enjoying. Would you like one?"

"Uh, no thanks."

Lizzy enjoyed the smoke from a good tobacco cigar. In college and in the Coast Guard, she had smoked cigars and cigarettes alike. There was no way in hell that *this* cloud was tobacco smoke. In fact, she suddenly wanted another stab of that peach cobbler back at the boarding house...

"So, Andy, is this the Sensor I paid for?" one of the women on the swing asked.

"Yes, ma'am," he replied. "Petya, this is Becky, Suzanne, and Kim. Ladies, this is Petya, and she indeed can Sense from thirty yards: Johnny confirmed it."

Three pairs of slightly glazed eyes stared at her.

"Well," Becky finally said, "I'm glad I got my money's worth."

"Thank you for coming," Kim said from her rocking chair. "How was your trip?"

"It was good," Lizzy replied. She looked around for a chair.

"Oh, we'll go inside," Suzanne said as she stood up. She carefully pinched the lit end off of her blunt. "We shouldn't be talking about this in the open." She looked at her companions. "Y'all be in soon?"

"Sure," Becky replied. "I've only got a few more puffs left, and then I'd like to hear all about our new friend here." She gave Lizzy a friendly look. "By the way, what did you do with the payment?"

"I'm an apprentice, so it went to my master," she explained. "Thank you for being so generous, that'll cover our food for a while."

The woman frowned, and then looked at Andy. "My intention was for the money to go to *her*, not to her boss."

"Pet did some horse-trading of her own," Andy told her. "She's getting a bolt-action rifle and rounds out of the deal."

Becky looked at Pet. "You OK with that?"

"Yes, ma'am."

"Becky, the woman is tired, stop yappin' at her!" Suzanne called from the doorway. "C'mon Pet, Andy, we're lettin' all the bugs in."

Suzanne led them through an entryway and into a small parlor already lit with two oil lamps. The furniture was upholstered with pure white material and was tightly covered by thick, clear plastic. The chairs and the couch squeaked and rustled as they sat down. Suzanne rolled her eyes as she tried to get comfortable.

"I've been trying to get Becky to take off this damn plastic for years, but she insists on it." She sighed. "So, Andy, where'd you find her?"

"Down in the SCAdian territories, in a place called the New Middle Kingdom." He glanced at Lizzy. "Petya is a guitar player with a theater troupe down there."

Suzanne grinned at her. "Do you all really dress in medieval clothing and sword fight? Do you say *thee*s and *thou*s and stuff?"

Lizzy arched an eyebrow. "No, though I can break your kneecap with a wooden sword." She didn't smile back. Granted, a lot of what the SCAdians did was strange, but she didn't come all the way up here to be ridiculed. Besides, day garb was much more comfortable than mundane clothing, fuck her very much...

Suzanne didn't seem threatened at all. "Really? I'd like to see you do that sometime. Not actually break my kneecap, but maybe a pot or something."

Lizzy nodded. It would be interesting to see if this was the marijuana talking or whether this was Suzanne's true personality. She heard Andy clear his throat.

"Suzanne, are you up to talking about the pregnant women, or should we come back in the morning?"

"No, it's OK, Andy." She looked at Lizzy.

"It started about five months ago. The last baby was born two months before that, and he and the mother were fine, but then the first woman, Allie Bates, just...died twenty-seven weeks into her pregnancy. She was ill, but she had no real symptoms except that she seemed sickly and was running a fever. When I went to her viewing—me and the girls often help out with weddings and funerals at the church—something felt strange about her. She felt

Infected to me, sort of, but her husband Randy insisted that she was talking and was herself right to the end.

"I really didn't think much else of it until three weeks later, when Jackie Myers died—same circumstances. I went to *her* viewing, and I felt the same way. I even paid a visit to Johnny to make sure I was remembering the feeling right—I was."

Lizzy looked at Andy. "Johnny is the hand, right?" she muttered under her breath.

Andy nodded. "You remember Señor Wences?"

"Who?"

"Before your time, I'll explain later."

"So," Suzanne was saying, "when Lisa Garrett died, I asked Henry and Katie to come over for a whiff. Nothin'—they both said they didn't feel anything, but I *knew* I felt Infected material. So, that's when I started bugging Andy to find a stronger Sensor than all of us. A month later, Troy Vargas suggested Andy look up that woman that got him banished from SCAdian territory, and here you are!"

"So, what do you think is going on?" Lizzy asked her.

Suzanne paused. "I don't know. I always thought being Infected was like being pregnant: either you are or you're not, that there wasn't a *kind of.* But, that the women were themselves until they died—I can't explain that. Hell, if I'm wrong about this, I'm wrong, but I don't think I'm wrong."

Lizzy considered this for a moment, and then turned to Andy. "You said there was a pregnant woman close by?"

"Yeah—Amber Johnson is down the street. We'll go there next."

"Suzanne, have you seen her yet?"

"Yes—I can't Sense anything from her yet, but she isn't very far along—maybe twelve weeks?"

"OK." She looked at Andy. "Is it pretty well known why I'm here? Will the pregnant women know what I can do?"

"Those in town will—word spread pretty quick in Zion where I was going and why." He glared at Suzanne.

"Hey, don't look at me," she said, raising her hands in a defensive gesture. "Troy Vargas blabbed about it from here to Nazareth. People were asking *me* about it."

Andy shook his head and reached for his flask. "What were you thinkin', Pet?"

"That I'm a fairly good actress, but I might not be good enough if I walk in and they're Infected. I can take the stuff that Doc gave me if I need to, but if it's that subtle I'd rather not. I'll try to keep a good poker face, Andy, but it sucks that I'm suddenly the angel of death or something."

"Well, cat's out of the bag now," the marshal drawled, taking a swig from his flask. "We'll just make do."

Within thirty yards of the Johnson house, Lizzy felt ill. Without saying a word, she reached into her pouches and took the powders Doc had made; she took them dry and just worked through the awful taste. Andy watched her with a grim expression. Suzanne looked puzzled.

"If it's Amber that I'm Sensing, she's Infected," Lizzy told her. She took a deep breath. "Let's go."

The Johnson house was a small, cozy place that had a fairly new-looking chimney on the side. Sure enough, the closer they got to the house, the worse Lizzy felt. Around the porch, Suzanne touched her arm.

"I feel it too, now," she said, looking ill.

"Do you puke?" Lizzy asked her.

"No—I just get really nauseous. I'll be fine." She got to the door first and knocked.

A pretty young woman no older than twenty answered the door, her body just showing the first signs of expecting under her long skirts. She looked pale, but she smiled at the visitors.

"Hi, Suzanne, Andy." She blinked at Lizzy, and then looked as though she had just remembered something unpleasant. Her eyes grew wide. "Are you the Sensor?"

God, here we go... She decided to try soft evasion. "Yes, but I'm also a prenatal masseuse. Back home, I used to help the doctor deliver babies. My name's Pet." She held out her hand and watched the woman take it gingerly.

"I'm Amber, nice to meet you. Do you Sense anything?"

Lizzy swallowed—it was hard being right next to Amber, even medicated, and she had to really focus on not vomiting. "Nothing worth mentioning, but I think Andy's rotgut's getting to me." She managed a weak smile at Andy. "You shouldn't have let me drink that stuff." She turned back to Amber. "How are you feeling? Rough first trimester?"

"Please come in." Amber stepped back into the house and allowed the group through the doorway. "Ryan, we have guests!"

A rather large man about Amber's age came in from the kitchen in the back, a dish towel in his hands. "Hey, Marshal, Suzanne." He stared at Lizzy. "Is this the Sensor?"

Tomorrow, Lizzy was going to get a long black mustache to twirl as she leered at people with dastardly glee. "I am, but as I was explaining to Amber, I also can help with aches and pains." She looked at the woman. "Do you have any?"

She eyed Lizzy warily. "The back of my leg hurts something awful, especially when I sleep."

"That's probably your sciatic nerve. That's not uncommon— did you tell your midwife about it?"

"Yeah, she said to just stay off my feet."

"Well, if you want to try therapeutic massage, just let me know—I'll be around for a while, I have one hundred women who could testify that I do good work."

"OK." Amber didn't look convinced at all. She held her stomach gently, guarding it from the stranger that could only bring death.

"Well, that went well," Lizzy commented dryly as they walked back to the boarding house. They had dropped Suzanne off at her house with the agreement that they'd visit the other mothers in the morning. "She didn't buy the bad moonshine excuse for a second."

"She did, though," Andy said. "She allowed herself to believe what you told her, even though somewhere in her mind she knew it most likely was a lie; people do that. Leon Festinger called that *cognitive dissonance.*" He took a swig from his flask. "As long as we tell her that her baby's fine, she'll believe it—for now. When she gets sicker, though, we'll have to tell her the truth."

Lizzy decided to just say aloud what everyone was thinking. "The fetuses are Infected."

Andy nodded. "Looks that way, though I can't see how."

Time to lay down my hand. "I can." She looked Andy in the eyes. "Is your office close by?"

"Sure," he pointed forward and over to the right a bit. "It's right next to the stables, why?"

"I need to tell you a few things about me—and why I can help more than you think."

A Beetle in Andy's Office

"Bullshit!" the insect heard but didn't understand from the far corner of the room.

"It's not bullshit." A higher-pitched vibration came from the other one. "Get a container of water and I'll prove it to you. Where do you keep the hand?"

"Upstairs—don't move from that spot, I'll be back! I sure as fuck hope I didn't go through all of this to be conned…" The voice trailed off as the sound of ascending heavy steps reverberated throughout the room.

The beetle skittered away from the corner in jumps and jerks, dragging a large, stuck ball of dust behind it. A minute later the footsteps grew louder again, and the man returned; the beetle kept going.

"Are you sure you want to waste a whole finger?" the female asked.

"It's not goin' anywhere!" There was the sound of a splash.

"OK, Andy…"

Whoomph!

There were several long moments of silence, followed by the sound of thin metal grinding on metal. The beetle finally detached itself from the dustball and scurried faster.

"My god…" An audible swallow could be heard. "Where the hell have you been hidin'? The only people that can do this the government hauled off…"

There was a long pause, followed by another loud swallow. The man screwed the top back onto his flask. "Oh…I get it." The room went quiet as the beetle turned and crawled even faster towards the doorway to the outside. The man finally took an audible breath.

"OK, then—they can plan, and you can make holy water. That's absolutely terrifyin'; I'm convinced. What now?"

"I don't know. Get a good night's sleep and see what happens in the morning?"

He sighed. "Yeah. I'll walk you back to your room." The humans started towards the door.

"Sorry about the finger, Andy. I tried to warn you."

"Hell, that's OK—I've got four mo—"

Crunch.

Lizzy

There were four expecting women who lived near Zion proper; two were Infected. The other woman had naturally miscarried six days before.

"This is terrible!" Suzanne exclaimed as they rode back to town. "All these poor women—what the hell are we supposed to do?"

The word hadn't spread to the women in the surrounding communities what Lizzy's true purpose was—or, at least not yet. She even convinced one of the women to allow her to rub her feet as they talked. The woman, Dana, insisted that Lizzy come back later in the week for another treatment.

Suzanne shook her head. "I can't see abortions. These women are into their second trimester—I can't imagine it would be easy to force a miscarriage. And, I don't know if the...practitioners... have a limit." She looked at Andy. "You ever run into folks who do abortions?"

Andy's mouth twitched. "Considerin' the current population problem, and the fact that we can't screen for abnormalities like we used to, there's really not much of a need right now for that kinda thing. There are two that I've heard about second-hand, one in my jurisdiction and another fella out by Schnecksville, but I have no idea how they operate. They haven't killed anyone that I know of, at least. But, by the time we track those folks down and figure out if they're on the up and up, the women will be dead."

"OK, so that's out." Lizzy finally gave up on that option. "We should get the midwife onboard—don't you think?"

Andy and Suzanne exchanged glances.

"What?"

"She's kind of...quit." Andy muttered.

"She blamed herself for the deaths, and she lost her confidence." Suzanne added.

"Well, this would vindicate her, right?" Lizzy paused for a moment, frowning. "What, there's no one to deliver babies right now?"

Suzanne shrugged. "She has apprentices, sure, and they've been minding the store, but the women won't let Kristin come near them."

"Oh, for Christ's sake—childbirth is dangerous!" Lizzy exclaimed. "Even in the best of conditions, babies and mothers don't always make it! Was she a good midwife before all this happened?"

Suzanne pondered this for a moment. "I suppose so—I never needed her services, so I can't say for sure. She'd lose one once in a while, but I suppose that'll happen."

Andy cleared his throat. "Keep in mind, Pet, that there *is* a rash of expectin' women dyin' all at once for no particular reason: that would spook anyone. Even Kristin thinks she did somethin' wrong." He paused to spit onto the ground. "Might be helpful not to be so judgmental."

Lizzy glared into the distance, though he was right. "Yes, sir."

"We'll see Kristin after lunch." Andy glanced at her, assessing if there were sore feelings.

She gave him a half-smile to reassure him, and then asked him the question she had been avoiding since they arrived in Zion.

"So...how difficult would it be to exhume one of the deceased mothers?"

Andy grimaced, but didn't look surprised by the inquiry. "I think Sean Garrett could be convinced—he wanted an autopsy, even though there's no one really qualified in this jurisdiction to do that. I think he'd let you have a *look*." He gave her a sideways glance.

Look, don't vaporize, he implied. Lizzy understood, but it might have to come to that. *Speaking of vaporizing...* "When do you want to start talking about Plan B, Andy?"

Andy reached into his vest pocket. "Whenever you're ready."

Lizzy looked at Suzanne. "How good are you at keeping secrets?"

Suzanne's eyes widened. "Why?"

"Because I know of another way to help these women. But if it got out what I want to do, it could be very dangerous not only for me, but for the town, too."

Suzanne thought about it for a moment. "I suppose so. Depending on what you're telling me, if it's that dangerous, I may want to tell my roommates—they're like family, and they're all I have."

"How are they about keeping their mouths shut?"

"Between the three of us, I think we could keep a confidence—god knows they know some pretty gnarly things about me, and nothing I've said to them has come back around."

"All right—I'll tell you all at once, because I'll need your help eventually."

By the time they got back to Zion, Lizzy's stomach was grumbling. Suzanne heard it and smiled at her.

"Let's all talk over lunch—the girls should be in." They all dismounted by Suzanne's house and tied up their horses.

"What do you all do for a living?" Lizzy asked Suzanne as they went up the porch steps.

"We work for the local dairy, milking the cows and goats and taking care of them. A lot of the townsfolk work there. The girls and I work early mornings and late afternoons."

The group walked into the house, went past the ground floor rooms, and into the kitchen. It was a large, open space with enough room for a table and four chairs. The cooking hearth on the side was obviously added recently—the paint on the wall was mismatched where they had removed some cabinetry. Becky and Kim were on the far end of the kitchen by the sink, doing the dishes.

For whatever reason, seeing them there reminded Lizzy of washing dishes with John on the first morning of Odin's Challenge. She smiled at the memory and wondered what he was doing at that moment. Probably on the road, negotiating another contract or something...

"Hey," Suzanne greeted, interrupting her thoughts. "Is there something to eat around here?"

Kim nodded at a trapdoor in the floor. "The ham's still down there and the baked beans. Pull bread in the breadbox."

Suzanne went over, bent down, and pulled on the ring attached to the trapdoor. Lizzy could barely see the top of a ladder just below the opening. "Is that going to work for everyone?"

Lizzy wasn't a fan of baked beans, but she'd try them or just manage on ham and bread. "Thanks, that'll do fine."

"Thank you," Andy said.

When everyone had sat down with plates of food—the baked beans weren't actually that bad—Lizzy began her story.

"I'm telling you all this because Suzanne wasn't comfortable keeping secrets from you," she began, looking at Kim and Becky. "What I'm about to share can't leave this room, please. Can everyone do that?"

The three women looked puzzled, but nodded in agreement.

She took a deep breath. "Before I lived in SCAdian territory, I was working for a place west of here that was trying to make vaccines, things like that."

"Really?" Becky asked. "That would be *great*—kids die from childhood diseases now, it'd be nice to have them vaccinated."

"Well, they weren't very successful when I was there—not yet—but they were trying. So, one day I was in the lab, fixing a piece of equipment the best I could, and one of the guys became Infected and got the jump on me. He tried to kill me."

"Wait," Suzanne interrupted. "Why didn't you feel him coming?"

Lizzy turned red, but she figured these women wouldn't judge. "It was my birthday, and I was high."

"Ah," the women said in unison, nodding with understanding.

"So, it wasn't that I was attacked that made it notable, it was how: he fired an entire vial of stimulant into me with a hypogun, just...*pow*. No ripping of flesh, no eating, just cold, calculated murder. If one of the workers hadn't Sensed him, and one of the scientists hadn't figured out what had happened and had given me the antidote, I would have died." She pulled down her t-shirt and pointed at the diamond-shaped scar that the second hypogun had left in the center of her chest. The needle had looked like an ice pick from her perspective, and Mike had driven it right into her heart. He had saved her life that day.

Well, and he had also given her Jeff's Cocktail to turn her skin bluish-green, just for fun, but that was Mike all the way.

The women nodded. Their faces were hard to read—Lizzy wasn't sure if they believed her or not.

"The Infected man didn't survive, but I'm surprised the information hasn't gotten around." She looked at Andy. "Andy didn't know anything about it when I told him."

The women looked at each other, and then they all shook their heads.

"That's big news," Kim commented. "And scary as hell—if it's true."

Suzanne looked thoughtful. "It would explain why the alive pregnant women feel Infected, but that they aren't demon-like." She studied Lizzy. "Do you think they're actually Infected, and the demons are doing a good job acting, or do you think it's the fetuses?"

"That's why I want to examine a corpse," Lizzy replied. "To get that *kinda* feeling you were describing. My hunch is that it's the fetuses."

Everyone in the room sat in silence for several moments.

"Why did you leave the lab, Pet?" Becky finally asked her.

"There was an accident that could have been prevented, and I didn't want to be there anymore." She would tell them about the holy water later, when she confirmed for sure whether it was the fetuses or the mothers themselves that were possessed. "So, what do you think?"

No one said anything for several moments. Finally, Becky cleared her throat.

"If they can plan...if they are intelligent..." she said slowly. "Why aren't they more active? Why are they fooling around with pregnant women?"

"I don't know," Lizzy replied honestly. "I think we'd all like to know the answer to that question.

"But for now, let's see what we can do about these women." She took a bite of pull bread.

"Worry about the demon horde later," Kim finished with a frown.

As it turned out, Kristin Palmer was a quiet, shy woman that wore large-framed glasses and thick greying hair pulled into a bun. She was very intelligent and knew midwifery inside and out. As they sat in her living room, she listened to Lizzy and Suzanne with interest and concern, looking at Andy every so often for a non-verbal confirmation of what was being said.

"For once," she said after they were finished and had paused for several moments of contemplation, "I wish those women's deaths *were* caused by something I did." She looked out the window as she stroked a large ginger cat that was curled up in her lap. "At least then we could correct the mistake. This..." She shook her head. "After all of these years..." She looked at Suzanne and asked, "What do we do now?"

"Until we have a solution," Suzanne suggested. "Nothing for now, just keep doing what we're doing."

"Well, do you have a plan?"

Lizzy and Suzanne exchanged glances.

"We're working on that," Lizzy replied. "But, no, we just confirmed that the women are strangely Infected this morning. We're going to exhume Lisa Garrett later on for further investigation." She paused for a moment. "You're office is in town, I understand."

"Yes. Do you want to use it?"

"Please."

"Sure."

"I also understand you have a birthing tub, too. Could we use that?"

Kristin narrowed her eyes. "I have one, but why on earth would you need one?"

"Ummm..." Lizzy swallowed uncomfortably, thinking on the fly, "for collection purposes. We're not sure...what the body will be like."

"Oh, I guess that makes sense," the midwife said, grimacing. "Sure, whatever you need. Just... thoroughly clean it when you're done."

Lizzy had no desire to be at the gravesite when Andy and the deputies dug up Lisa Garrett's body that afternoon or when they transported the coffin to the midwife's examining and birthing room. She was present in the room when the deputies set the long wooden box on the floor next to the examination table. She felt a little ill as she looked at Andy, but it was a good old-fashioned revulsion of having to see a decomposing body rather than being near Infected material. That was good news, at least.

"What am going to see?" she asked the marshal as Thom and Jim began pulling nails out of the top of the casket.

"Hard to say," Andy replied over the *screek*ing complaints of the nails. "Decomposition is a tricky thing to predict—there are a lot of factors. Advanced decomposition isn't really my thing—I usually saw bodies first thing, and then I only had to make a guestimate. That was all forensic stuff." He paused and wrinkled his nose as they were hit with a putrid, nauseating smell. "She shouldn't be dried out yet, though."

The two remaining nails were pulled off with the lid. Thom and Jim looked inside. Jim visibly swallowed.

"She's still intact," Thom reported. Andy and Lizzy went up to the foot of the coffin and looked down.

The body was in some sort of patterned dress, though it was hard to tell what the original colors were—the garment was now a mottled, dingy mix of greys and browns with greasy-looking stains splotched throughout. Lisa Barrett's body was mostly skeletal, but there were still some fairly large bits and pieces of her face remaining. Surprisingly, there were very few insects or flies around the body. Lizzy asked Andy about that.

"There's a point in the decomposition process that insect activity diminishes significantly—guess this is the time." He sniffed the air. "The body is past the bloating stage, at least. That makes things easier to work with." He looked at Lizzy. "Anything?"

She twitched her head to the side and shrugged. "It's a *kinda* feeling, like Suzanne said. I can tell you that Lisa Garrett was not possessed, though. I'll know more when we get her into the birthing tub." Surprisingly, she wasn't grossed out at looking at the body. It smelled a little, and it was gruesome, but it was at a point in its putrefaction that it was almost an abstract form, that she could almost pretend that it hadn't been a real person.

Or, she had finally snapped, and she was permanently damaged and detached from the world. She supposed time would tell.

"OK, then," Andy said with a large sigh. "Let's get the plastic sheeting under her, and then we'll lift her into the tub. You still OK helpin'?"

She nodded as the four of them pulled on latex gloves and started to gently maneuver the body onto the sheeting. The right arm came off the shoulder, but other than that they managed to keep the corpse intact.

Thom gave the count over the crackling of the thick plastic. "On three: one, two, *three...*"

The body was surprising light as the four of them lifted it into the air. When it was about chest level, Andy gestured with his head to go down to the other end of the box and then around. When they arrived at the tub, Thom gave the three count to lower the body into the dry birthing tub, which was the size of a medium-sized wading pool. As the body sagged down into the vessel, the head suddenly snapped downward and the chin *thunk*ed against the bony chest. Everyone paused and looked to see if the head would come off: it didn't. When the body was more or less settled and mostly lying on the bottom, everyone stood and stretched a little. Jim looked at Andy.

"How much water do you want?"

Andy looked at Lizzy.

"I think half-covered should do it," she said. "We just need to make sure the pelvic region is totally covered."

The next ten minutes were spent filling pails of water from sink in the examination room and ever-so-carefully pouring the water into the birthing tub. They did a good job not disturbing the body—there were only a few pieces of chum floating in the water when Lizzy called it good. Without invitation or fanfare, Lizzy stripped off her right glove, knelt by the tub, and placed her hand in the water.

It was a very strange experience. The geyser of light burst forward like usual, but the current narrowed as it left her hand, becoming very, very small. She traced the energy, feeling its current as it ran through the water and into the body's vaginal opening. She didn't hear or see anything directly, but she could indirectly sense the energy doing its work, purifying the cavity inside the corpse. As it worked, she imagined a valve within herself, and an invisible hand turning the valve, reducing the flow.

She might as well have tried to turn off Niagara Falls. The energy cheerfully finished its work without pause or interruption, and it only ceased when the Infected material was gone. The whole event took about five seconds. There were a few bubbles and some wisps of smoke coming from the water right above her pelvis, but the body itself didn't look affected.

"Damn," she muttered as she stood up. She reached for a towel on the counter. "I can't control it. Let's check for damage."

Andy pulled the plug on the side of the tub. The water spilled out from the opening and then directly into a grate in the floor. When the birthing tub was clear of water, Lizzy crouched down, lifted the upper leg with her gloved hand, and then peered between the legs of the body. The corpse was completely charred around the vaginal area, and the damage seemed to continue up into the body. Andy and the two deputies bent down next to her to look, as well.

"Shit," Thom breathed.

"Well, I'm not doing *that* to live subjects," she said, annoyed. She gently lowered the upper leg back onto the lower one and stood back up. "You're not going to like this, Andy, but I need more practice."

The Office of Marshal Bennett
The Town of Zion
Confederation of New Wyoming
August 1st
11:23 a.m.

Whoomph!

"FUCK!" Lizzy hollered as she jerked her hand out of the water. She looked up and saw Suzanne in the doorway of Andy's office.

Suzanne looked at the jar next to Lizzy and winced; Andy must have told her about Lisa Garrett and what Lizzy was trying to do. "You're running out of Johnny."

"I know!" She was beyond exasperated. She had to figure out how to dial this down, but it was like trying to ground a lightning bolt with a coat hanger. She told Suzanne as much.

"I refuse to believe that I can't do anything with this except passively receive it—I'm not a goddamn radio tower."

"Have you tried using other parts of your body?"

"*Yes*—same effect."

"What happens if you touch the material directly?"

Lizzy held up her bandaged right hand. "I touched a piece with the back of my hand. I got a chemical burn and the piece exploded. When I make holy water my wounds heal quicker than usual, but this one's still a little ouchy." She carried the basin of water to the sink, dumped it, and then refilled the container with fresh water. "It was wet with formaldehyde, though, so maybe that wouldn't happen with a dry sample." When she got it back onto the worktable, Lizzy unscrewed the jar and pulled out a chunk of hand with a pair of long tweezers. She flicked it into the basin.

"How are you feeling?" Suzanne asked her.

"I haven't eaten all day, so that helps. I also doubled up on Doc's powders, and that helps, too." She looked down at the pickled glob of flesh that was floating in the water. "I can't stop it. I can't reduce it. What the *hell* is it good for when all it can do is destroy things?"

Suzanne seemed to consider her statement. "Does it *always* do that? Every time you've done this, the material turns to ash?"

Lizzy paused. "No. The first time I did this, there were multiple people in a swimming pool, all Infected. Most of them were OK enough to get out of the pool on their own once I started and they were exorcised, but I didn't see what kind of damage I did in the long-term." She ran her fingers through her hair. "I was focusing on one person." She paused again. "I'm always focusing on the energy and what I want to do with it."

Where I want the energy to go... She unscrewed the jar again and pulled out another specimen with the tweezers, shaking off the excess formaldehyde before totally removing it from the jar.

She placed the skin on Andy's desk. She then screwed the lid back on and handed it to Suzanne.

"Take this outside, please—I don't want to know where," Lizzy said.

Suzanne turned a little green, but she did as she was told. Thirty seconds later, she was back in the room. "OK, now what?"

"Experiment." Lizzy took a deep breath and stretched out her hand towards the flesh on the table. She visualized opening channels through her body and out of the palm of her hand and the sole of her foot, channels that would lead the energy to the desk. Not even considering the piece of hand in the water, she touched the water with her fingertips.

The geyser appeared, warm and dazzling with its white light, but just as it started to erupt into her body she focused all of her will upon it and told it, *There!*, directing all of her attention to the chunk of Infected matter next to her.

The energy did as it was told...sort of. It pulsed down through her arm and leg and then did its best to push through the air and wood of the floor, but these elements apparently were not nearly the good conductors water was—the geyser could only go about a foot past Lizzy, and then it just...dispersed into the ether.

"Suzanne? What's happening in the basin?" she asked through clenched teeth. Lizzy didn't want to break her concentration and look herself. Trying to guide the energy was trying to ride a bucking bronco—she wasn't sure if she was really the one in control. Focusing so hard to direct this much energy was making her body shake violently.

"Nothing," she heard the woman breathe. "No bubbles, no smoke. It's fine."

"OK." Lizzy glanced over at a spare hat hanging on a hook on the closest wall. She focused on the hat and told the energy to zap it, shifting her body in that direction.

Instantly, the energy flowed back into her and redirected itself into the basin of water.

Foomph!

She sagged in relief—it was so much easier, and felt so much better, when the energy just did what it wanted. Her body continued to tremble as she fell into a chair with a thud.

"What happened?" Suzanne frowned at the ash floating in the water.

371

"I told it to zap the hat. It needs a viable target, I guess." Lizzy exhaled sharply and wrapped her arms around herself, trying to stop it from vibrating. The experience actually left her feeling a little cold. "I need to eat something and rest. I'll try again this evening, but I think we're onto something." She grinned, her teeth chattering slightly. "Fuckin' ass, there's hope yet!"

Suzanne

By the time Suzanne was done with her evening milking shift and checked in on Pet again in Andy's office, Pet was able to focus on Johnny and bleed off just a trickle of energy from her "geyser" to dissolve the Infected material in the basin very, very slowly. The SCAdian looked exhausted, and she was pale to the point of ghostly.

Has it only been three days since she's been here? It seemed like much longer than that, just with so much going on and the pace of the investigation. This SCAdian didn't fool around, though Suzanne wondered if she was too reckless with things she didn't understand.

"You should take a break," Suzanne suggested. Pet wasn't going to be able to help anyone passed out on the floor, which looked imminent.

Pet nodded, and then lifted her hand out of the basin and lowered the other one. She sank down into a chair, her arms hanging limply at her sides. She was shaking all over.

"C'mon, I'll walk you down to the boarding house for dinner." Suzanne was curious about this amazing new skill Pet was learning, and she doubted she could lift Pet's dead weight on her own. "I'll even eat with you."

"Let me wash my hands first." Pet staggered over to the sink and lunged at the faucet.

"Has Andy been checking in?" Suzanne asked as the SCAdian washed up.

"No—he had some business to take care of. Sophie was by a little while ago." As Pet rinsed her hands and then dried them on a towel, Suzanne noticed that her right hand was no longer bandaged. There was just a small, puckered scar left on the back of her hand. "She helped me get a gauge of how far the indirect Infected material can be for this to work."

That wasn't the most coherent statement, but Suzanne got the gist. "So, how far is far?"

Pet gave her a slightly bewildered, unfocused look. "Pretty far, actually. We had Johnny at about ten yards before the energy became uncontrollable." She smiled wearily. "Even better, I don't even have to have a visual of it, I just have to know it's around there somewhere, and the energy does the rest of the work. Or, tries to." The SCAdian's expression turned sardonic. "It really is useless in the air or through solid matter. It likes liquids." She held her stomach, looking uncomfortable as it audibly growled.

"Let's get you out of here before you fall down." Suzanne grabbed her elbow and led her out of the office and onto the street.

Joan Simpson was at the door, greeting guests when Suzanne half-carried Pet into the boarding house lobby. Joan took one look at Pet and grabbed the other elbow.

"What the hell happened to you?" Joan asked her as they all walked into the dining room. "You look terrible."

"I've been working on a project," Pet replied. "It's very tiring."

"I guess so." Joan's eyes met Suzanne's, but Suzanne just shrugged; a secret was a secret. "What's for dinner, Joan?"

"Brats or shepherd's pie, either one with brussel sprouts," she said as they eased Lizzy into a seat by a dining table. "You, young lady, are having the brats—you look like you could use some iron."

"Yes, ma'am." Pet reached over and lifted her water glass to her mouth, draining it in one sitting.

"And, I'll get you more water." Joan gave Suzanne a pointed, questioning look as she took Pet's water glass out of her hand.

Suzanne ignored her. "I'll have the brats, too, Joan. Is it the usual mix?"

Joan pulled her mouth into a thin line: Suzanne knew that she hated being left out of the loop. She still managed to keep her voice light, though. "Sure is—venison, pork, beef, and my special mix of spices, of course."

"Sounds great, thanks, with the house wine."

Joan turned back to Pet. "Usual ale for you?"

"Yes, please," she replied as she slouched back into her chair. Joan nodded and walked away to place the order.

Suzanne took a sip from her own glass as she gave her dinner companion the once-over. She noted that Pet was already looking better—not being next to the Infected material and not channelling whatever the hell made holy water was doing her a world of good.

Which brought up an interesting question: if it was "Holy Water" with a capital "H," suggesting that everything about it was divine, why did it tire and strain Pet so? Shouldn't it *always* be soothing, a reflection of God's love or of heaven?

Looking over at Pet, though, she decided not to ask that particular question...it was a mystery that was beyond their understanding, anyway. She would rather learn about other things tonight. "How long have you been doing this?"

The SCAdian's eyes were still a little glazed as she answered her. "I first did it a little more than two years ago. It never came up before that, and my life was in danger. One of my friends died that day. She just had too many...demon issues."

"I'm sorry." Suzanne paused. "What does it feel like?"

"When I let things go naturally, it feels wonderful," Pet replied with a smile. "It's warm and soothing. When you try and force it, though, it kind of burns a little, though it still feels good—it's hard to explain." She stopped talking as Joan came back with their drinks.

"Have you seen Andy this evening?" Pet asked Joan as she set glasses of various liquids on their table.

"Not yet—do you know what he was up to? I might be able to guess."

"He said something about going to...Cooperstown? Some militia group up there?"

"That'd be Washington's Brigade—the marshal goes up there to hold trials for them. It's kinda far, I wouldn't expect him until after dark."

"OK, thanks." The SCAdian smiled at her and took a sip of her ale. When it was clear that she wasn't going to say anything else, Joan twitched her mouth and walked back to the kitchen.

Pet's smile turned mischievous. "Andy's going to shit a brick when he finds out what I've been doing." The sip of ale must of helped, because her eyes were clearing up as she looked back at

Suzanne. "I wanted to ask you—I'd like to try and teach you to do this, too."

"What?"

"I can't stay here forever—I need to get back home eventually. If you could learn what I know, you could screen women when they became pregnant. Or, if things get active again, you could help defend the town. What do you think?"

Suzanne's first thought was, *I want no part of this.* It was bad enough feeling like a freak sometimes because demons made her sick. She also thought it extremely unlikely that she could do it. "How would you do that?"

"I don't know—I've never tried to do it before. I was going to start with you putting your hand in the water, see if you could get anything out of that."

Suzanne shuttered at the thought of sticking her hand in anything that had dead flesh in it. "No."

Joan came back with their meals and, sensing the growing tension between them, just set the plates and mumbled, "Enjoy," before walking away.

Suzanne looked at Pet. "Do you want to say grace, or shall I?"

"You go ahead—I'm a little tired."

After a brief prayer, the two women ate in silence for several minutes. As she was working on her second brat, Pet broke the silence. "What about the other two Sensors? Do you think they'd do it?"

"They're idiots," Suzanne said quickly. "Henry and Katie couldn't Sense what I could. They'd be useless, believe me."

"I don't see how I have a choice, though, if you won't do it." Pet took a sip of water. "Otherwise, what's the alternative—let more women die? Is that what you want?"

"No, that's not what I want!" Suzanne caught herself and lowered her voice. "It's just disgusting!"

"Yeah, I know!" The SCAdian looked angry now; she barely managed to keep her voice at a whisper. "This isn't exactly my idea of fun, but at least I can maybe help these women now, and that's worth all the nastiness of dealing with cadavers and rotting flesh. Not to mention trying to contain the damn whirlwind all the time—I won't lie to you, it's no picnic." She speared a brussel sprout and shoved it in her mouth.

"But, this is the *needing your help* part I was telling you about earlier," she said, talking around her food. "This is not my home— it's yours. Maybe you should think about defending it, and not have a stranger do all your dirty work for you."

Screw her! Who the hell did she think she was? This town wouldn't even be here if Suzanne hadn't been such a competent canary in the beginning. She glared at Pet, not saying anything.

Pet didn't seem to care, just went back to eating.

They silently chewed their food and their thoughts until their plates were empty. Joan noticed they were finished with their dinner and came over.

"Dessert, ladies? It's shoo-fly pie."

"Yes, thank you," Pet answered. "Do you have chickory coffee?"

"Sure do. Sweetened, of course?"

"Thank you."

"Suzanne?" Joan turned to her.

"No, thanks, not tonight." She wiped her mouth on her napkin and stood up. "I'll see you in the morning, Pet." She nodded at Joan. "I'll settle up tomorrow, OK?"

"Sure thing," Joan said, looking from one woman to the other. "I'll see you then."

Suzanne stormed out of the room and out into the street. She managed to contain herself until she arrived at home. Kim and Becky were sitting at the kitchen table, playing cards by lamplight. Becky noticed her stormy expression first.

"What the hell's wrong with you?" her friend asked casually.

"That SCAdian is asking too much!" She pulled out an empty chair and sat between them. "She wants me to stick my hand in that Infected crap and try to make holy water!"

There was a pause as the two women looked at her.

"Well, where did you *think* this was going?" Kim asked her with a puzzled look as she took a card from the draw pile. "She can't stay here forever."

"Why the hell not?" Suzanne muttered, reaching for the salt shaker. "She's getting free room and board."

"That *I'm* paying for," Becky reminded her. Her parents had been vacationing in the Carribean when the demons came, leaving their only daughter with the house and a *lot* of liquid assets of mostly gold and precious gems. Fortunately for Becky, they hadn't trusted banks. "She can't stay indefinately."

"No, but..." Suzanne sighed. "I don't *want* to do it. You should have seen her when we went to dinner—she looked like she was about to pass out. There's no guarantee that I can even do it, which means I could be sticking my hand in demon crap for nothing!"

"Why does she want you to learn, anyway? I thought she could only disintergrate stuff," Kim said as she placed a queen of spades in the discard pile.

"She's...gotten better at it," Suzanne said begrudgingly. "She can make it work slowly now."

Becky picked up the queen of spades and then placed three queens down on the table in a neat spread. "So, it's possible that the pregnant women could be saved, even though the unborn babies are toast?" She made a disgusted face. "God, I didn't mean to say it like that. Sorry, girls."

"She *might* be able to help them," Suzanne admitted. "It depends if she can convince a woman to do it, I suppose."

"Well, what choice do they have?" Kim asked as she drew a fresh card. "Once you confirm that the baby's Infected, it's either risking the fetus or they both die." She placed three sevens on the table, and then discarded a two of hearts.

"There's always Henry or Katie," Becky observed, drawing a card. She glanced at the ace of clubs and placed immediately it on the discard pile. "I don't know them well, but I think Henry would absolutely cream himself to learn something like that."

"Yeah, he would, and that's the problem." Suzanne grimaced at the thought of Henry Douglas. "He'd be even more impossible to deal with than he is now, and I think he'd charge women to do it. Besides, do you see him crouching next to women with them exposed like that?"

All three women shuttered at *that* thought.

"And, Katie falls apart at the sight of *anything*—I can't think of a worse person to be a canary. Remember how she freaked out at Lisa Garrett's funeral, and it was *closed casket?* It amazes me she's survived this long—how does she deal with plucking chickens, preparing meat, stuff like that?"

"I asked her that at a revival meeting once, when we were wringing turkey necks," Kim said. "She's OK with animal meat, it's sick or dead humans she can't deal with. Something about a bad experience during childhood—I didn't get into details with her."

There was silence for a few moments.

"So, I'm screwed, aren't I?" Suzanne asked her friends.

Everyone was quiet as Becky drew a card.

"You don't even know if you can do it," Kim finally said, "but I think you should try."

"This is about the species, Suzanne, pure and simple," Becky added, laying down an ace-two-three straight and then discarding a nine of diamonds. "The demons are trying to Infect babies, and you might be able to stop them. Isn't that worth some effort?"

"And, what about those women?" Kim added. "They're going to be scared to death when you or Andy or Kristin finally tell them. Wouldn't it be nice to be able to offer something more than your condolences?"

Suzanne stared at the salt shaker she had been turning in her hand as she sulked. "Yeah."

Kim drew a card, placed a trio of jacks on the table, and then discarded her last card. "I'm out."

Becky threw down her hand with a muttered curse, and then she looked Suzanne directly in the eyes. "I'd do it if I could, if only to give those hellspawn a big *fuck you,* just for once."

Suzanne stared at her admiringly. *Leave it to Becky to put me in my place.* She knew that her prickly roommate had said that out of love, which was how they had managed to remain good friends over the years, even though Becky was mostly a cantankerous grump. After all the lives they had ruined and the world being powerless to stop them, it *would* be nice to send a big *fuck you* to the demons...just for once.

"All right," Suzanne said with a sigh. All three of the women had lost every relative and loved one they knew during Infusion. "For our families."

Kim placed her hand over Suzanne's. "Thank you."

<u>Lizzy</u>

Chelsea Scott would only agree to come to the midwife's office if another pregnant woman, Dana Owens, came with her. Dana Owens would only come if Lizzy promised a full body massage.

"Dana, after this is over and we're successful, I'll give *everyone* a full body massage," Lizzy replied. She looked at Andy. "Even you."

Andy raised his eyebrows at the offer. "Uh...that's OK, Pet. I'm good."

She smiled at the marshal as everyone else chuckled at his discomfort. She was actually nauseated beyond belief and scared shitless about what they were about to do, but she didn't want to upset the women. Live Infected material was a lot stronger than exorcised dead material, and she wasn't sure how much juice it would take to release the fetuses, or if she was going to fry them trying. Then there were the mothers, and what if she damaged *them?* The more she considered this evolution, the more she realized that this was probably not going to end well.

She was extraordinarily glad Andy, Sophie, and Thom were there, along with Suzanne and Kristin. When Suzanne had first walked into the room, she had just shrugged at Lizzy and said, "Sorry."

Lizzy had nodded at the Sensor. "It's OK—I'm glad you're here." With that, all had been forgiven and forgotten, thank god, because she didn't want to do this alone.

She now looked at Chelsea and her husband, Scott, as they sat on the two cushioned chairs in Kristin's office. "I'm just going to go over this again, in front of these folks, just so everyone understands the protocols we agreed upon, OK?"

Chelsea and Scott nodded. They both looked scared and nervous about what was to come, but Lizzy couldn't sugar-coat this—too much could go wrong.

Lizzy took a breath. "My first priority is Chelsea, and making sure there is no permanent damage—we did agree to that?"

The couple nodded.

"Yes, we agreed to that," Scott said.

"I will do the best I can to release the fetus unharmed, but it will be a long shot at best. Understood?"

They nodded.

"I've never done this before specifically," she glanced at Andy, "So I have no idea of the outcome. I *have* made holy water and have had people released and walk away, which is the only reason I'm trying this. But, no guarantees, OK?"

"We understand," Chelsea said, tears in her eyes as she caressed her stomach gently. "I'm dead, anyway, if we don't do this."

Lizzy looked at Andy. "Can you think of anything else?"

Andy paused, and then shook his head. "Nope. We know how insane the demons are, and now we know they can be unpredictable, so everyone keep that in mind." He turned to the couple. "Whenever you're ready, we'll start."

Scott kissed his wife, got to his feet, and then helped Chelsea to hers. He led her to the birthing tub, which was already halfway filled with clean water. She stepped in and carefully lowered herself until she was sitting.

"It's cold!" she complained.

"I'm sorry about that," Kristin replied. "If this lasts a while, I'll heat some water for you."

Sophie stepped next to the tub with a padded two-by-four and some white strips of cloth. "Please hold out your arms, Chelsea."

The woman held out her right arm. Sophie set the board behind her, resting it on the edge of the tub and against Chelsea's shoulders, and began to tie her wrist to one side. Thom came over to hold the board steady.

"I hate this," Scott said aloud as Thom secured the other arm.

"Us too, Scott," Sophie replied. "But there will be less injury to her with us pressing on the board rather than pressing down on her." When Chelsea's arms were secured, Sophie tied the woman's feet together.

"Are you sure you'll be able to do what you need to do with her legs closed, Pet?" Sophie asked.

"The energy doesn't care—it'll get where it needs to go. If I'm wrong, just be ready to pull her knees apart."

"OK."

Lizzy looked at the last of Johnny sitting in his jar on Kristin's examination table, right behind Chelsea so she could keep line of sight on both the hand and the patient. There was still a goodly amount left in the jar, actually, but she wished there was another source of Infected flesh in case it was back to the drawing board after this procedure. She looked at Suzanne. "Ready for this?"

Suzanne nodded, her jaw clenched. "OK."

Lizzy looked at Kristin. "Are you ready?"

Kristin nodded. "I'll be monitoring the baby's heartbeat the best I can and Chelsea's vitals. I'll let you know if things go south."

She finally looked at Chelsea. "You're being very brave—thank you."

Chelsea nodded, and then looked over at her husband, who was holding her tied hand. "I love you, Scott."

"I love you, Chelsea."

"*My baby, forgive me,*" Lizzy heard Chelsea whisper.

Lizzy chose to push that one aside. "Here we go." She knelt at the tub's edge and raised her right hand, concentrating on Johnny. "Suzanne."

Suzanne placed her left hand in the water.

Lizzy took a deep breath and placed her own left hand in the water. Like countless times the previous day, the geyser blasted out of the abyss, and she forced it to her will.

There! she thought, and the energy flowed across her right arm and through her legs and tried to get at Johnny.

Chelsea let out a shriek, surprising her.

"What?" Lizzy asked, trying to get her body under control. "I haven't done anything!"

"I...felt something, just then." Chelsea said, panicked. "The baby...moved...or something."

Sophie and Thom quietly pushed down on the board, steadying it.

"Just try to relax," Kristin told her, taking her other hand.

"OK, I'm going to focus the juice slowly, just a little," Lizzy said. She started a small trickle of energy back into herself and down and through her left hand. She sensed the energy go right between Chelsea's legs.

"OW!" the woman screamed. "Oh, my god!"

"It's OK, Chelsea, we said this would happen, just breathe..." Kristin was speaking in soft tones as she checked the patient's pulse. She glanced at Lizzy and nodded.

Lizzy didn't feel any progress. "I'm going to wait a few moments, and then turn it up a bit more."

For those few agonizing moments, the only sounds in the room were Chelsea's controlled breathing and Kristin's muttered words of encouragement. Finally, Lizzy drew just a bit more energy and sent it into the tub.

Then, all hell broke loose. The energy changed shape in the water, and suddenly it surrounded Chelsea entirely. Instead of just a few bubbles here and there, the whole tub began to boil.

"*Oh, shit!*" Lizzy shouted. "Chelsea's hot! Hold onto her!"

Lizzy was expecting wild flailing and gnashing of teeth, but that didn't happen. Instead, the patient just sat there for a moment, calmly staring into space, like she was catatonic. Then, she turned to Lizzy...and just *looked* at her.

Lizzy could only stare back, not able to move or speak. The thing was...*cataloguing* her, noting who she was as if to remember her later.

Oh, this can't be good...

She felt a hiccup in the geyser, and she went back to concentrating, refocusing on what she was doing. The demon remained passive, sitting in the water.

"Chelsea?" she heard Scott ask.

Then, Lizzy understood what the hiccup was about. She was losing control of the geyser because more demons were coming. She only had a few seconds at best.

"Pet?" Suzanne asked, her voice rising in pitch. She must have felt company coming, too.

"What is it?" Kristin asked.

"More are on the way!" Lizzy growled. "I'm losing control!" She frantically searched her mind for a solution, anything, because she was *not* going to disintegrate anyone today...

"Andy!" she shouted. "Get your asp ready—I might need it! Suzanne, open up the jar and throw Johnny in there—*now!*"

Two seconds later, Johnny and all the brine splashed into the tub with a *throp!*, sending foul-smelling liquid sloshing over the sides of the tub and onto Chelsea's bare legs. Lizzy steered the energy to the hand, only allowing a little to envelop Chelsea.

Phoomph! Because of the mass and the age of the Infected material, it didn't disintegrate right away—it boiled for a good seven seconds before it became ash. Around the fifth second, Chelsea let out a scream, and the energy drew back from the woman and finished its job with Johnny before completely dissipating from existence. Lizzy removed her hand from the water and sank to the ground, slowly falling onto her back, feeling completely lifeless. Her body was too spent even to shake.

"Are you OK, Chelsea?" she managed to call from the floor.

"What the hell happened?" she heard Chelsea ask over the tub. "I blacked out for a minute, and now I feel like I'm sunburned all over!"

Lizzy swallowed. "You were Infected for a minute—the demon transferred from the fetus to you. You're both clean now, though. You can untie her, guys.

"Kristin, what's the status?"

From the floor, she watched Kristin untie Chelsea's feet and lean into the tub. The midwife reached down, made some searching and prodding motions, and then looked incredibly sad as she gazed in Chelsea's direction.

"I'm sorry, Chelsea, Scott. *You* are fine, I think—I don't see any burns or scorch marks—but there's blood and bits of tissue coming out. I think we've lost the fetus." She focused in Scott's direction. "Let's get her out of the tub and onto the table—I'll clean her up."

Lizzy just laid there motionless, her eyes closed, and listened to Chelsea's heartbreaking wail of anguish and the sloshing of the contaminated water as people helped the woman out of the tub. She felt water droplets and bits of residue splash onto her arms and chest, but she didn't care or try to move. She felt absolutely defeated as hot streaks of tears ran unchecked down her face and into her neck. This was bringing up a lot of bad memories—things she didn't want to think about, not ever.

Then she heard heavy bootsteps approach her and stop next to her head. She opened her eyes and looked up into Andy's face.

"You OK?" he asked gently, his haggard face kind. He offered her a hand.

She grabbed it and allowed the marshal to haul her to her feet. "I will be," she said, sniffling. "Miscarriages are the worst, next to stillborns."

He put his arm around her shoulder in a fatherly way and squeezed. "Let's go outside for some air." He led her out the door of the birthing room, through the waiting room, and onto the porch outside. He pushed her down onto an Adirondack chair, and then sat down onto an ottoman next to it.

"That mother is alive," Andy pointed out. "You did the best you could, don't you think? It sure looked that way from where I was sittin'. You did some quick thinkin', too, with Johnny."

She exhaled sharply and looked Andy in the eyes. "Next time, if the demon goes into the mother, we're taking out the kneecap. I should have done that sooner, the baby might be alive."

He paused, swallowing. "Well, let's just list that among the possible options when we talk to the next mother, let her decide if that's what she wants." He gave her a half-smile. "Right now, Chelsea can walk *and* can probably have another child eventually. Once she's had some time, she'll probably realize results could have been worse."

"Yeah," she sighed. "I just hate flying blind like this."

"No," he looked at her pointedly. "If lives weren't at stake, you'd be lovin' this."

She made a short chortle and gave him a shadow of a smile. "Yeah, I would." She took a couple of breaths. "Sorry about Johnny."

"Yeah, he'll be hard to replace," Andy sighed. Just then, Suzanne came through the doorway, Dana right behind her. They stood next to the Adirondack chair.

"You OK?" Suzanne asked.

"I will be," Lizzy replied. She looked at Dana. "How about you?"

"I'm terrified now," Dana admitted. "That was absolutely the most horrible thing I have ever seen, and I'll be spending every waking moment praying to Jesus and all the saints that I won't have to go through that.

"But, I think you did the best you could—it was clear you did your damnedest. Chelsea might not feel like saying thank you right now, but I will—thank you." She looked at Suzanne, and then back to Lizzy.

"Suzanne's going to escort me home." She suddenly looked embarrassed. "I'm not going to ask for that massage today, but..." She smiled sheepishly. "Later, maybe?"

That Dana would allow Lizzy to touch her after what she just saw made her smile at the expectant mother in relief. "You bet. I'll try for Friday."

Lizzy turned to Suzanne. "Did you get any of that?"

Suzanne paused, and then shook her head sadly. "Maybe I felt something towards the end there, just at the end when the demon left? But it was hard to tell if it was the energy or just the agitation of everyone moving around."

Lizzy twitched her mouth. "That's too bad." She paused, and then half-smiled at the Sensor. "I'm glad you tried—thank you. We'll figure something out."

"You bet." Suzanne turned to Dana. "Ready?"

Just then, Thom and Sophie stepped out onto the porch.

"I heard Kristin tell Chelsea that she didn't see any permanent damage," Sophie told the group. "They'll have to wait and see, but Kristin doesn't give false hope—I think she really thinks it'll be all right."

Everyone nodded. Andy got to his feet and reached into his vest pocket.

"Well, I'm going to take Pet back to her room to wash up and rest a bit," he announced as he unscrewed his flask. "Sophie, I'll meet you back at the office in a while—there's some other business we need to discuss."

"OK, Andy."

After taking a swig of moonshine and securing his flask, Andy helped Lizzy to her feet. As they both waved and took off towards the center of town, the rest of the group walked towards the horses that were tied up to the left of the building. The marshal and Lizzy walked in silence for a minute or two before Andy cleared his throat.

"I'm...guessin' you're going to need more Infected material."

"Yes, sir."

"That's not going to be easy. Possessing Infected material is technically illegal in these parts."

She thought for a moment. "Could you spread the word about what we're doing, offer an amnesty program or something?"

Andy nodded, staring straight ahead. "I'll also pay Troy Vargas a call after I drop you off, see if he can be of a help. If we can't get anything here, maybe some of his old SCAdian contacts can help us."

"That's a good idea," Lizzy said. When they arrived at the entrance to the boarding house Andy paused at the door, looking uncomfortable.

"Y'know, Pet," Andy began hesitantly, talking even slower than usual. "I really don't think I'd like it if you gave me one of those...massages. I, uh, appreciate the offer and all..."

"Marshal," Lizzy interrupted, looking into his bloodshot, wizened face and smiling. "I think everyone knows, including me, that I'm not your type. I was just trying to lighten the mood in there."

"Oh...OK, that's good." Andy reached for his flask again, looking relieved. "'Cause it's just, y'know, there *are* marshal groupies out there..."

If Andy was trying to distract her with the ultimate in awkward situations, it worked: as tired as she was, she was almost percolating with amusement now. She smiled broadly. "We're good, Andy. We really are OK, no hard feelings." She slapped him on the arm to hide a quick chuckle. "I'll put in a wake-up call for dinner—catch you later."

She quickly turned and went into the boarding house. She allowed herself to laugh out loud only when she reached the second landing.

Professionally speaking, would she give Andy a full-body massage if he asked her to? Sure.

Would she *want* to...? She would leave that kind of massage to the marshal groupies.

She had scared folks a bit when Joan's daughter Mitzy couldn't wake her up the previous evening for dinner. She was told later that people had been in and out of her room all night, taking turns checking in on her to make sure she was still breathing. She hadn't regained full consciousness until that morning, right in the middle of Thom checking her pulse while Andy stood in the doorway.

"Damn, Pet!" the deputy had exclaimed when she sat up with a start. "You've been out all night—you scared the living shit out of us!"

Andy, on the other hand, had just said calmly, "Well, now we know not to expect you for a while after you do your...thing. Meet us at my office about 10-ish, Sleepin' Beauty, after you've eaten. C'mon, Thom."

Lizzy cleaned herself up—she had literally fallen into bed fully dressed with bits of ash and chum still on her clothes—and after a hearty breakfast headed over to Andy's office. Suzanne, Sophie, and Kristin were waiting for her.

"Hi! It's good to see you among the living," Suzanne said when she walked through the door.

"Hey, everyone, and thanks—I appreciate folks making sure I wasn't dead."

"Well, Becky wanted to play a prank on you—Sharpie your face, I think—but I wouldn't let her." She smiled. "You might hear some grousing from her the next time you see her—I told her you might be here for another couple of weeks, and she wasn't happy."

"Well, jeez, I could do other things around here, if money's an issue." Lizzy said with frown.

"Nope," Suzanne said, raising a hand. "I mean, do other things in the meantime if you want to, but she has *plenty* of money— what good is it doing in her safe? And, as much as she gripes

387

about the expense, I think she likes the attention, of being able to fund something so notable."

"OK," Lizzy said. "But until we get more Infected material, I can't just sit around all day doing nothing."

There was the sound of footsteps walking across the porch, and then Andy and Thom came through the door.

"Hey, all, thanks for comin'," Andy said as he hung his hat on a wall hook. "Let's get this meetin' started—I know folks got things to do." Andy took his seat behind his desk, and Thom grabbed a chair from the cell room.

"So, Thom and I just got back from a visit with Tony Vargas," Andy began. "I explained to him how valuable his tip was to us, and how any further assistance would be much appreciated." He looked at Lizzy. "He wants to meet you, is that OK?"

Lizzy knitted her brows in skepticism. "It depends. Does he want to shoot me for getting him exiled?"

"No...I think you're just an interest to him. I wanted to ask you first...didn't want you to think of yourself as a sideshow or somethin'."

She smiled: this was the exact situation that she and Wills got into their first fight about. "Y'know, Andy, I don't want to start a precedent. If he happens to be in town and he wants to meet me, fine, but this is already starting to sound like something to charge admission for."

"Fair enough." He took a swig from his flask. "He thinks he may have some leads, and they may offer a fair price or even *gratis*, considering the circumstances.

"It looks like you'll be hanging around for a little while, Pet, until we can re-prime the pump, so to speak." He paused for her reaction.

"Well, I could tag along with Kristin, if she doesn't mind." She looked at the midwife, who nodded. "I have a mechanical background—I did maintenance at the lab I told y'all about—but I don't know if that's something that's needed here."

Thom looked thoughtful. "We might—I'll have to ask around, but maybe that'd be a use."

"Otherwise, I guess I'm 'As Directed' for now." She shrugged.

"Well," Andy said as he put his flask back in his vest, "we'll work somethin' out."

For the next two weeks, until an anonymous donor ponied up a mummified demon corpse that was so well-preserved Lizzy almost cried for joy before she puked, she was busy doing odd jobs. Kristin did let her come along to some of her visits, and she had time to give Dana *two* weekly massages. After the first one, both Dana and her husband, Saul, begged her to stay until the baby was born in March. She did not visit the Infected women—massaging their feet, and then later killing their babies just seemed too fucked up for words. She knew there was a risk that would happen with Dana, too, but the woman was just too damn likable to say no to.

There were a surprising number of machines in the area that were still utilized on the regular basis, though gasoline and electricity were scarce to non-existent. A lot of enterprising individuals had rigged up solar panels to power small equipment or pedaled wheels, not unlike Doc Goldberg's drill, to generate enough juice to charge a car battery and power things that way. She managed to fix a couple of generators and a wind turbine, and one of the villages had a portable stick welder, but no one who knew how to weld. It had been more than four years since she had welded something together, but after a couple hours of practicing a lot of plows and other farm equipment got repaired until the gas ran out.

Andy even took her up into the northern end of his jurisdiction for a couple of days so she could see more circuit trials. Sure enough, most of the cases presented by his deputies were well-presented and thorough, and the couple of trials that weren't the marshal took the reins of and redirected the questions until he was satisfied. She wondered if this was similar to a Court of Chivalry trial, which she had heard of during that first week with John, Cuthbert, and Little John, but really knew nothing about.

She *knew* this was different from baronial hearings, where the baron or baroness was the judge, jury, and prosecution for any charged citizen that was not a peer. The accused could hire a peer for his or her defense, but Lizzy had been lead to understand that, if the defendant got to the point of a baronial hearing, they were as good as guilty in the eyes of the law. Most cases were settled out of court with fines, extra community service, or favors, like what happened between Red and Wills that led to her apprenticeship.

If someone was to ask her opinion, she preferred the militiamen's form of justice better: there was still the potential for corruption, but at least there was the illusion, if not the actuality, of balance. In Andy's jurisdiction, at least, not one of the defendants complained about their trials—they all seemed to think they were getting a fair deal, even when they were found guilty.

Lizzy had no idea why the militiamen and the SCAdians didn't interact more. They were both...off...but they both had survivability and sense of community in common. Both groups were resourceful, and both had no love whatsoever for the former government—she was pretty sure she'd be strung up for being military just as quickly here as in the Known World if someone held a strong-enough grudge. There were only two big differences that she could see: most of the SCAdian communities preferred cooperative farming to working privately owned lands, and the SCAdian towns and baronies had more longevity. Militia towns and settlements were known to dry up and just disappear off the face of the earth, while the Known World hadn't changed in almost six years.

Overall, Lizzy concluded, the two groups of people seemed more alike than different. Maybe in a few years they'd see that, too.

Chapter Sixteen

<u>Wills</u>

Wills was working on the bid for New Meridies' Coronation next spring when there was a tapping on the beam of his tent. He frowned.

Who the hell? Even Justin's in bed by now... "Enter."

Sir John the Younger of Vagabond Haven stepped into the tent. He looked a bit haggard, like he just completed a long ride.

"Sir John." Wills smiled and stood. "It's a little late for a visit. But for you, I'll make an exception. Please, sit down."

John crossed through the tent and sagged into a folding chair. He stretched out his legs. "Thank you, Master Wills. You'll forgive me if I forgo the usual pleasantries—I'm a bit worn out."

"Not at all—I believe pleasantries are best before the witching hour, not well after it. Can I offer you something? Water? Maybe something stronger?"

John pondered the offer. "I think both. I'm here to bring Petya back to Caradoc, and not under the best of circumstances."

Wills stopped pouring John's glass of hooch and looked at him. "Why?"

John shrugged. "We understand that El Hajj is mobilizing. We're not expecting trouble, but we are next door to Barony of the Brandywine." He paused while Wills handed him his tumbler filled with one inch of clear liquid. He sniffed it, reacted violently, and then took a sip. He exhaled sharply.

"Damn!" He took another sip. "It's good, just strong."

Wills poured himself two fingers of hooch and sat back down at his desk. He leaned back and studied John. "I suppose it's prudent to do a recall, but she's not here."

"What do you mean, she's not here?" He looked around, as if Pet might step out of a corner at any minute and prove Wills wrong.

Wills took a sip of hooch; he didn't even flinch. "She's on an errand."

"Oh," John looked around again. "I could use some water now, please. When will she be back?"

Wills poured water into another tumbler and handed it to him. "I don't know. She's on an unusual case, it could take a while."

John's eyes narrowed as he swallowed some water. "Could you be more specific?"

Wills shrugged. "Sorry." As he took another sip, he watched the knight's eyes flash with anger as he stood up.

Well...isn't that interesting. Some previously observed behaviors were beginning to fit into place...maybe. His husband was convinced already—he was about to find out. It was time to play out a scene; the night just got entertaining.

"Where did you send her?" John demanded.

"I'm sorry, I really can't tell you—I'm not going to have you traipsing all over creation so you can deliver your stupid recall letter. Leave it here with me, and I'll be sure to give it to her when she returns."

"I wouldn't be 'traipsing all over creation'—I've been all over the Known World, just tell me where she is!"

"She's not *in* the Known World!"

John paled. "My god...is she all right? What is she doing out of the kingdoms? Why didn't you stop her?"

More interesting. "First of all, she is no longer indentured, as you well know, so I couldn't just stop her; she seemed pretty determined to take the job. Secondly, she can take care of herself. Finally, I took a man of theirs in trade for her safe return, and he's been nothing but cooperative—I believe that he believes that they will come back for him.

"And, no," he added, seeing John's face beginning to flush, "you can't speak to him—he wouldn't know where she is, either. She isn't doing anything illegal or breaking any treaties or agreements; she's merely on a fact-finding mission. It's a straight job, scout's honor.

"So, please," Wills said as he held out his hand, "I'll take the recall letter. Feel free to grab a bunk somewhere to sleep for the night; you're our guest. I think you're tired, and you'll feel better in the morning."

John shook his head as drained the rest of the hooch, and then the tumbler of water. "She might come back while I'm here— I'd prefer to deliver it myself. May I stay for a day or two? If she's not back in two days, I'd appreciate it if you would give the letter to her in my absence. In the meantime," he stretched and reached for the ceiling, "where can I crash?"

Wills wasn't fooled: he saw that look of worry. He couldn't help but smile. "Come with me—I need to go to bed myself. We'll set up Pet's tent for you; I'm sure she won't mind."

True to his word, John approached Wills and Justin after lunch on the second day. He handed the parchment to Wills. "Thank you."

"Sir John," Justin began, glancing at Wills, "we've grown rather fond of Pet around here. You do understand that if we believe that she is in danger, or she does not wish to go, we will not force the issue."

A gambit of emotional reactions passed over John's face. He paused a few seconds before answering, "You are men of honor— you will do the right thing." He gave Justin a hard, pointed look.

Justin nodded. "We shall." He bowed to John. John returned the bow, and also bowed to Master Wills. Wills reached over and clapped John on the shoulder.

"Safe trip home."

"Thank you. I shall convey your regards to Baron Red." He walked over to his horse, which was already saddled and ready to ride. After he mounted, he took a minute to scan all the sides of the horizon. Then he tugged on the reins and started south towards Caradoc.

Justin sighed as he and Wills watched the knight fade into the distance. "I knew it!" he said in triumph; he was grinning from ear to ear. "It's so romantic!"

Wills took Justin's hand and squeezed it. "Yes, it is. But I'm worried, love. There's a lot he isn't telling us about the El Hajj situation." Wills turned to look at Justin. "We need to keep an ear out. Maybe this year, we should bug out early to Asgard."

It only took a moment before a look of comprehension dawned over his husband's face. He grew somber as he looked over Wills' shoulder at John. "He wasn't going to give her the letter, was he?"

"Oh, he was going to give her the letter. And then I'd like to think that he was going to beg her to stay, which is exactly what we are going to do.

"No, love, the real reason he came here...is because he doesn't think they're going to make it out of this alive. He came to see her one last time, and to tell her goodbye."

The City of Cornwall
The Barony of the Brandywine
August 10th
12:42 a.m.

<u>Max</u>

Fuck this noise! he thought as he ran back to his house. There was no way in hell any of them were going to survive *that.* Max had to get out of there.

Thank god he was able to convince the rest of his family to head out to Bad Ischl, where they were using the town hall as a distribution point for single mothers with children. They might not be able to stay together at first, but Ellen and Melinda were wily—they'd get back on their feet again, maybe even reopen the Coach and Four.

If there was a Coach and Four, or a barony, after this...

He had every intention of honoring his oath—he really had. But he had been on the north wall when he saw the headlights of the military convoy coming, heard the diesel engines and the *singing* of hundreds of troops as they came over the ridge, and witnessed the line of vehicles that just *didn't end.* The singing was supposed to demoralize them, and it had worked on Max.

Hell, yeah—as soon as his watch was over, he couldn't get down off the wall fast enough.

There was no doubt in Max's mind that every man and woman out there felt the same way he did, except everyone knew there was nowhere to run. Someone could *try* to forge a Writ, but those documents would be extra-scrutinized now, and peerese was a sophisticated language. Every baron had their own unique interpretation that was only known to other barons and select peers. Getting caught during times of war carrying forged documents would often mean exile if you were lucky or, if it was a baroness like Isabella, you would just be thrown into a deep hole to rot.

He was in a cold sweat by the time he arrived at his house. Once he was inside the quiet and stillness of his great room, he collapsed on his couch and sat to think.

There *was* somewhere he could go, actually, and he didn't think they would ask any questions. In fact, as Pet had so wonderfully put it, it was his own personal idea of heaven. But if he was going there, he knew in his bones that he had to leave *right now,* or he would never get out of the city.

For all of that, it might already be too late, and the call had already been made to make the gates too secured and guarded to escape. Spurned by desperation and the will to live, he went upstairs and began to pack a knapsack.

As he was thrusting shirts into the bag, his racing mind considered Pet again—she would have also received a recall letter as a citizen of Vagabond Haven. As he considered this, another thought occurred to him. It made him pause, his arm suspended in mid-shove.

That would be an interesting scenario: would Wills have sent her there? He was a SCAdian, sure, but Max was pretty certain that he kept himself and his troupe well above local SCAdian politics. It was also clear that both Wills and Justin had a great affection for her—surely they would want her safe.

And, Pet was no fool—she was a sensible woman who seemed to love life as much as he did. Her loyalties—and rightly so—would be to the troupe. He'd bet a barrel of champagne that she was already there, acclimating herself as a temporary member of the performance staff.

Max reminisced for a moment about how she had looked in her costume last May, and how much fun she had been at the waterfall. He also considered how...accommodating...she was about his dalliances at the Jersey Lily.

Yup—he hadn't needed any further motivation to leave, but that had sure sweetened the deal. He finished packing, walked out the front door, and blended into the night, heading for the south gate.

<u>Eloise</u>

Wearily, she walked up the stairs of the baron's house to settle in for her shift at Elspeth's bedside. It wouldn't be much longer now, she thought—Elspeth had stopped eating and drinking altogether about three days ago. They began rubbing lotion into her skin to make her more comfortable, and Wolfgang had upped her dosage of pain medication again last night. She was no longer lucid anymore, but just breathed and slept. Eloise knocked gently on the doorframe.

"Come on in," Adelaide said, almost inaudibly. She was Elspeth's other apprentice and a fellow household member. She rose from her chair when she saw Eloise.

"How is it out there?" she asked her.

Eloise took a breath. "John announced that they're going to go ahead and release the children tomorrow morning for safe refuge. As you can imagine, everyone's a wreck tonight—a lot of crying and worrying going on." She paused and sighed.

"The scouts returned an hour ago, and they say Cornwall is still holding, though they think the city is running out of ammunition and artillery: they aren't returning fire as often as they had been."

Adelaide nodded sadly. "Are there still fires in the city?"

"I didn't hear, but I'm sure there are." She looked at Elspeth. "How is she?"

"Very cooperative, as always," Adelaide replied with a look of affection towards her mistress. "She hasn't said a word all day. I

396

just changed her, so she should be good for a while. With Mistress Elspeth not eating or drinking, there's just not been much to do. I've gotten more sewing done this afternoon than I have in the past month." She looked back at Eloise. "Did you bring something to do?"

Eloise held up the books she had been carrying. "*The Little Book* by Selden Edwards. It's complicated and romantic—perfect for keeping one's mind off of things for a while. I also brought *Two from Galilee* to read to her when she's awake. It's one of her favorite books, remember?"

"Oh, yes." Adelaide bent down and kissed Elspeth's dry cheek.

"I'll see you tomorrow, Mistress," she whispered. The apprentice straightened up and looked at Eloise. "Come get me if anything changes."

"Of course I will. Good night, Adelaide."

"Good night—see you tomorrow."

After Adelaide left, Eloise checked Elspeth's vital signs—her pulse was thready but definitely there, she was cool to the touch—and adjusted her mistress's pillow so her head was higher off the bed. Then she sat on her chair and waited to see if Tex would come in again tonight.

She was still uncomfortable with him coming in Elspeth's room when she had the watch, and she didn't understand why he was there. Since his failed attempt to ask her out over a year ago, he had avoided her whenever possible. She didn't *mean* to hurt him that evening, but Tex was just too—ridiculous. Though, *ridiculous* would not describe the Tex that came in that past Sunday night.

He had knocked first but hadn't waited for a response, just came into the room. He had brought a chair from downstairs.

"Hi," he had said softly, holding the chair in front of him. "May I sit a spell? Visit?"

At first she was going to object that Elspeth needed peace and quiet, but then she had seen the gravity of his countenance. He had looked...diminished somehow. "Sure." She gestured to a space next to the bed.

He had walked over, placed the chair next to hers, and then sat down. She had waited for a fountain of news and boasting, but it hadn't come. Rather, he had leaned back in his chair, covered his eyes with his hand, and just sat there, not saying a word. Several minutes passed; he hadn't moved. Eloise finally decided to say something.

"Are you all right?" she asked him.

He had removed his hand from his face and looked at her. He hadn't been crying, but his eyes had been red.

"No." He had said, looking down into his lap. "There's some...horrible things being done to people over there."

She knew he was on one of the scouting teams. "Do you want to talk about it?"

"No."

And that had been it. She had continued to read her book, and he had mostly stared into space. Around midnight, he told her good night and left with his chair. Pretty much the same thing had happened the following night, but there had been even less conversation. It was very confusing.

Sure enough, around nine o'clock Tex came into the room—he didn't knock. After he settled himself into the chair he had brought he reached into his pocket, pulled out an apple, and then handed it to her.

"In case you get hungry."

"Thank you," she said, taking it from him. She put it on the nightstand for later.

He nodded at Elspeth's prone form. "How's Mistress Elspeth tonight?"

She told him what she knew. He nodded, but said nothing more. They sat in silence for a while.

"Tex," she began gently. "Why are you here?"

He hesitated, and then reached over and took Elspeth's hand. He didn't look at Eloise at all, but watched his thumb gently stroke the back of her Mistress's hand as he spoke aloud.

"They're some cocky bastards over there," he said hoarsely. She noticed that his drawl was more pronounced when he was tired. "It's almost like watchin' a cat playin' with a mouse, tormentin' the poor thing before he eats it—batterin' it around to death. We understand that they're tryin' to keep the hydroponic fields intact, so they're avoiding a full-out assault, but that would almost be a mercy compared to what's happenin' now." He swallowed.

"So, when I'm done watchin' that for the day, every day, I think about where I want to be," he continued, "if there is any place that I could find some peace." He stopped rubbing Elspeth's hand and closed his eyes.

"Even just sitting in the quiet here with you—that's peace enough." He straightened up in his chair and met her gaze. "And, it really is enough—it's all I want."

She felt tears in the back of her eyes. She nodded. "OK."

The City of Cornwall
Barony of the Brandywine
August 16th
9:25 p.m.

King Mattheson of Berkenshire

Well, I certainly didn't sign up for this, Mattheson thought, not for the first time, as he looked out over the balcony at the wreckage that had once been Cornwall. He had been thoroughly prepared to defend the kingdom when he won Crown last year, but he was expecting to ride against bandits, mediate disputes in the Court of Chivalry, or even ride with his brothers-in-arms onto a fighting field.

Shit, in those scenarios he would have *help*, not simply stand in the middle of a burning city and get bombarded to death with this twat and her advisors. As much of a bastard as he felt for thinking it, he almost wished he hadn't rhino-hided John the Younger in their bout last year—then maybe John would be the one sitting here shell-shocked, and Mattheson would be enjoying his evening with his wife and children on their farm, far away from here.

But, then...John had a kid, too, and no wife to care for his son if John should die. It was also possible that, when Cornwall fell, it was only a matter of time before these same troops would march on *his* lands. And a neither a king nor a knight could choose his enemies in these times—he could only defend against them.

Uneasy lies the head that wears a crown... He heard someone step onto the balcony with him.

399

"Your Majesty," Baron Duke Karl the Red greeted as he joined Mattheson on the balcony. They both looked over the city in silence.

"What do you think this meeting is about?" Mattheson finally asked.

"Exit strategy," Red replied, not taking his eyes off the fires. "It was over when the north wall was breached on Tuesday, even though we got it back. That action severely depleted our forces. I think Isabella wants to cut her losses and surrender the city."

Mattheson snorted. "She's wanted to do that since they've arrived. What's different now?"

"She thought she could get out of this alive before now." Mattheson could see the ironic smirk under Red's mustache; it was comforting somehow. "Did you see the look on her face when they refused a majority cut of the fields, if they would only withdraw?" He paused. "I think she's also planning to destroy the fields before she'll let them have them."

"*Fuck,*" the king swore under his breath. "That's unacceptable. Even if El Hajj takes over the fields, there's still a very good possibility they'll maintain current trading with the Kingdoms. We're not established enough yet, people would starve."

"Don't worry," Red assured him. "I'm going to persuade Her Excellency not to do it."

9:39 p.m.

"I believe our cause is lost," Isabella said from the head of the table in her conference-turned-war room. She looked drawn and haggard, and it was obvious that the night bombings precluded much sleep. "We must withdraw."

"Good luck with that," Baili said bitterly. "How do we leave the city? They have it sealed up tight. Even if we were to get out, where would we go?"

She took a shaky breath. "I...trust in the Lord and his mercy. I know he will protect us." She didn't look very convinced of her spoken convictions.

"In the meantime," she continued, "it is my primary desire now to *not* allow the invaders to have the hydroponic fields. I am

400

going to order them burned and salted tomorrow morning, or just as the city falls, whichever comes first."

Red stood up and stood next to Isabella. He was placid, even casual in his bearing. "Isabella, think about what you are saying. The Known World relies on those fields—it would be a great hardship if they were destroyed. The people of Cornwall that survive this will need those fields to work, to justify El Hajj sparing their lives.

"Besides, there will be other battles—others will take up arms to retake the city, if they so choose it."

"So, why didn't they come to *our* aid?" the Baroness snapped.

"Not the proper strategic moment," Red suggested. "It doesn't matter now. I'm beseeching you, Your Excellency, do not order this—"

"They are *my* fields!" Isabella was well on her way to a rage. They were an almost twice-daily occurrence now, and they were gaining in frequency. "I will *not* allow those barbarians to take one leaf from that farm! I will burn it first, and the SCAdians can pray for their own salvation, as they should have done—"

Mattheson hadn't even seen Red move. One second he was watching Isabella tantrum, not even a second later he had her pinned up against the wall, her feet dangling, and a beefy forearm pressed against her throat.

Damn...the old Duke's still got it...

"That's enough," Red said quietly as Isabella struggled for air. "I am entreating you, your sense of Christian charity, and your responsibility to your people that the fields are left undamaged." He looked at her face, which was working on bright red. She still looked defiant, though, even choking to death.

"Very well," he said. Red turned his head and looked at Mattheson. "Your Majesty, in accordance with the guidelines of our charter, I officially declare that Baroness Isabella is unfit to rule, and I am hearby relieveing her of her title. What say you?"

Mattheson looked around the room. None of the knights stood in her defense; none of her advisors made any objections. Baili, her strongest supporter throughout the crisis, only looked as though he was about to shit himself.

"Very well, Baron Duke von Worms, I concur. You shall take over the role of Baron of the Barony of the Brandywine as to such time as a special election can be held, or the barony falls."

The knights muttered an agreement as Isabella turned purple. She was about to pass out.

"That's enough, Red," Mattheson suggested.

Red released her suddenly, and Isabella fell to the floor like a sack of potatoes. She lay on the ground, gasping for air.

"Sir Charles," Red said, turning to the closest knight to him. "You and Ishim take Isabella to her room and confine her there." He turned back to the former baroness, who was still holding her throat, breathing heavily.

"This is the final negotiation I shall make," he told her. "You behave yourself and don't give the knights any trouble, I shall do all I can to enable safe passage for you and your niece, with or without the consent of El Hajj." He crouched down until his face was inches from hers.

"If I hear one word of treachery, one suggestion that you are scheming anything, I'll kill you myself. Do you understand, and agree to the terms?"

Isabella looked him in the eyes, her entire body shaking with rage, but gave him one shallow nod of assent.

"Take her away," he ordered, straightening up. The two knights got Isabella to her feet and lead her away. Red turned back to the group.

"And now for something I've wanted to do from the minute I got here." He smirked, the old Senior Chief once more, just for that moment. "The knights of the realm can stay. Everyone else, you worthless pieces of political shit, you're fired! Get the fuck out, and good luck saving your worthless hides!"

After the hasty exodus of Isabella's former staff, Red sank down into one of the chairs and looked at Mattheson.

"I hope you approved, Your Majesty," he said.

"Oh, yes," he told Red with a sigh. "For all the good it will do."

<u>Isabella</u>

It was déjà vu: she was packing one bag, grabbing her niece, and running for her life, just as before when she left Austin during the Rapture. She also presently enjoyed the same feeling of calm as before, the calm that came with the absolute determination to survive, no matter what the cost.

She did not believe Baron von Worms when he promised her escape. If the fool could have arranged their salvation from persecution, he would have done it long before this. She realized at the last negotiation meeting with El Hajj that they would settle for nothing less than her head on a pike, like the infidels during the Holy Crusades.

Isabella could almost appreciate that, however—if the roles were reversed, she would not show mercy, either, even though *she* had done nothing wrong. And, being a prophet of God, the Godless wishing for her destruction just came with the calling.

Grabbing her bag, she leaned far out of her window and threw it into the one beneath her, having faith in Christ that it would not cause alarm. Hearing nothing, Isabella snuck out of her window and eased herself down to the windowsill below. There was a quick moment of panic as she let go of her window and freefell, but she stuck her landing on the sill with both feet and crawled into the room. The room was empty, and she wasn't sure whose it was, but the hallway outside of it was void of people. She walked swiftly down the hallway towards Christina's chambers. There must have been a rumor of another attack tonight—the mansion felt empty.

Isabella was shocked when Christina opened her door. She hadn't really had time to see her niece since the first reports of the invaders mobilizing in the north, but...God have mercy.

"Have you been eating?" she asked, stepping into Christina's chambers. The room was pristine and in perfect order, which was

an unusual practice for her niece. It might have even been...
clean?

"As little as possible," she admitted. "I've really let myself go over the past year, but since Zaki is coming for me, I want to look my best."

Astonishment came first, followed almost instantaneously by rage. "What *are* you talking about, little girl?" she hissed.

"I am *not* a little girl!" Christina snarled back in reply. "I am almost twenty years old, and I will be treated as such! I've seen him from the wall, leading the troops like the leader he was born to be, and I know he will come for me!" She paused, smiling at her aunt in triumph. "Tonight, I think...don't you?"

"Christina," Isabella tried to calm down, tried to sound reasonable. "This...has nothing to do with you, dear. He is not coming for you. They are here for the fields and to punish me—that's all. And, while they may take my fields, they will not take *me.*

"Now we need to leave—pack a bag and let's go." She dropped her own bag and started towards Christina's bedroom.

"I'm not going," she heard her niece say quietly behind her.

She whirled around. "What did you say to me?"

"I'm not going, Aunt Maryanne."

Christina hadn't called her that since she started living with Rothbert. "My name," she said in her chilliest parental voice, "is Isabella."

"No, it isn't—not anymore," the girl replied softly, shaking her head. Christina actually looked *sorry* for her, which only enflamed her rage again.

"Fine," Isabella growled, giving up on her once and for all. "Suit yourself. I will pray for your soul, Christina. Good luck with El Hajj." She walked past her niece, picked her bag up off the floor, and then walked out into the hallway. She considered telling Christina that she loved her, but the words stuck in her throat.

She will only believe what she wants, anyway: belligerent, wicked, sinful girl.

It was a time for new beginnings, it seemed—she would see what wonders God had in store for His ever-faithful, but lonesome servant.

From the Journals of Maryanne Weber
(Her Excellency Baroness Isabella de Castilla)
August 17th
Ninth Year of the Tribulation

I have found refuge in an abandoned house near the southern gate—I'm going to wait until the confusion and battery of El Hajj's assault and make my escape. I can hear the men on the walls, shouting to each other, making preparations for what they say will be the final attack on Cornwall. I think they're right—it's been very quiet since nightfall, like the calm before the storm.

Good—let these miserable, Godless people fall, devour each other.

Perhaps this is God's wrath upon them...that I have brought about? Was this my true purpose here—to execute the Lord's vengeance on these non-believers? How strange, how mysterious the Lord is in His ways.

I shall begin again, spreading His will to wherever he sends me. I will wait for the still, small voice after I leave here, like Sa—

And then the bitch whore Isabella went to hell, and El Hajj lived happily ever after. Rohan says hi. ☺

2347

Zaki

In the end, it was so easy—while a few platoons gave a flashy artillery and gunfire show at the north gate, the rest of the forces climbed over the south and west walls and silently took out all resistance like an encasing shadow of death. Overall, they met very little opposition: if his troops hadn't knocked down the remaining threads of Cornwall's forces that night, they probably would have simply fallen down within a day or two. It was an easy walk to the baroness' mansion.

To his surprise, there were still a few people remaining within the residence. The defending knights and the others that were left were dealt with after only a few minutes of resistance—a few well-thrown grenades finished them off. Zaki and his men walked over the bodies lying in a heap at the door and began their sweep.

"Wipe your feet," he told his men. "Don't get blood on the rugs—they're nice."

The mansion was clear until the second floor. As they were checking rooms, one of the female militia fighters called his name.

"We found a woman," Rose told him. "I think it's the niece, Christina. She's asking for you."

At those words, he felt a stirring in his loins. She had waited for him to come.

"Which room?"

Rose pointed to the last door on the left.

"I'll see to her alone," he said. "Tell the others to secure the rest of the building and to ignore anything they hear coming from that room." He strode over to the door and walked into the chamber, closing it behind him.

The first room was empty. He looked around. "Christina?"

"In here!" he heard a woman call from the back. He saw a doorway to the right with light spilling out.

There, sitting on a large bed, was a thinner Christina then he remembered, dressed in a silk nightgown and a flimsy robe. She looked him up and down and smiled happily.

"Zaki," she said, her intonation flirtatious. "You look wonderful."

He stood and allowed her to take him in. He had gained at least twenty pounds of muscle since she saw him last, and the BDUs the militiamen had issued them looked particularly good on him.

"Have you come for me?" she asked as she rose from the bed and strolled towards him, slightly swaying her hips. She stopped in front of him and looked at the front of his pants, then back up to his face, pleased.

"You've missed me." She placed the palms of her hands on his chest and leaned in to kiss him.

He gently stopped her, placing a hand on her shoulder. "Before we're interrupted, where's your aunt?"

"Gone—she ran off a little before nightfall."

His erection suddenly went limp.

Motherfucker! The first fucking time he managed to get hard since the barn—*painfully* hard, even—and he had lost it. It was the real reason *he* had come here: not for the fields, not for revolution, but to find his manhood again.

Nobody else would do—he had to find the bitch whore.

Christina noticed the expression on his face change. "What's wrong?"

He wasted no more time with the niece, but pushed her onto the bed and pulled his trigger. Blood sprayed and bloomed over her chest and gown, killing her instantly.

Isabella still had to be in the city. They would find her, he would end this, and maybe he could get on with his fucking life and actually have *sex* with a woman.

Hell, maybe he could even get it up with Fidelma.

He turned and left the room, closing the door behind him as he shouted, "Clear!"

The Village of Caradoc
Barony of Vagabond Haven
August 18th
12:01 a.m.

<u>Eloise</u>

She was dozing in her chair when she suddenly became aware of someone else in the room, but no one had come through the door. She looked over at Tex, who was still sitting in his chair and looking intently at Elspeth. Eloise turned to see what was going on.

Elspeth was wide awake, looking at the opposite wall. She looked radiant, almost like her old self. Eloise reached over and took her hand. "Mistress Elspeth?"

Elspeth looked at Eloise—her eyes were unfocused, but they sparkled in the lamplight. "Do you hear him?"

Eloise glanced at Tex, and then back at her mistress. "No, who do you hear?"

"Caleb," she replied with a wondrous smile. "He's almost here, I think."

Oh, god... Eloise felt hot tears rolling down her cheeks. She dashed them away with her free hand. "Are you in pain, Elspeth?"

"No—not anymore." Then Elspeth's eyes widened as she turned and focused on a spot on the opposite wall to the left of the window. It didn't get colder in the room—Eloise had heard that happened when spirits were in a room—but she *definitely* felt a presence now.

Tex must have felt something, too, because he reached over and took her other hand in both of his.

"*Caleb!*" Elspeth suddenly exclaimed. Her smile was dazzling, her face jubilant for one beautiful moment.

Then her face went slack as the air left her chest; her eyes remained fixed on the wall. Her chest did not rise again. The presence vanished.

Eloise and Tex just sat in silence for a few minutes, with Eloise holding Elspeth's hand and Tex holding hers. Finally, Eloise stood up, freeing her hands.

What good people they both were. Red and Elspeth had saved all of their lives during Infusion, helped them make a new start, and were such invaluable friends to her and to the barony. There was no eulogy that could begin to address all they had done for so many people throughout the Known World. Her only comfort was that they left this world together in such a moving, extraordinary way. She would expect nothing less than that Baron Duke Karl the Red would come for his beloved Mistress Wife, even from beyond the grave.

In spite of this, she felt empty inside—nothing would be the same again after this. Then she realized what Red's death probably meant for all of them.

There might be nothing *after this...*

"We should tell the others," she said to Tex, "about both of them."

Tex nodded his head, his eyes glistening with tears. "Yeah... but we can tell 'em in a minute." He stretched out his arms to her.

Eloise choked back a sob as she finally felt her heart crack with sorrow. She sank down into his lap, buried her face into his shoulder as his arms gently surrounded and sheltered her, and cried.

Chapter Seventeen

The Office of Kristin Palmer
The Town of Zion
Confederation of New Wyoming
August 18th
10:20 a.m.

Lizzy

The first lesson Imhotep the mummy taught Lizzy was that the energy *really* didn't like dry, solid materials. She still got chemical-like burns on her skin if she made direct contact with his flesh—*she* was nice and hydrated—but the untreated bits and pieces of the mummy remained wholly unaffected.

So, before each experiment, every dried sample had to sit in a sealed plastic container of damp sand for hours and hours to plump it up before it could be used. The good news was that this made a viable Imhotep sample last a lot longer than a wetly preserved contemporary. The bad news was that some pieces, like toes, just weren't usable—there wasn't enough tissue to plump.

Suzanne and Lizzy had been working on making holy water for two days, and while Lizzy was getting better at channeling the energy, even to the point that she didn't shake anymore, Suzanne was getting nowhere.

"I'm running out of ideas," Lizzy complained. "You touching the water, you touching me, you touching the water *and* me, getting right next to the sample." She paused, running through everything they had tried in her mind. "Yeah, I'm out."

Suzanne looked at Imhotep, who was laid out on Kristin's examination table. "What if we tried different liquids? Maybe it would work better with something different?"

"Like what?" Lizzy thought for a moment. "Blood, maybe? What other liquids are organic?"

"Well, there's fruit juice...or milk?" Suzanne suggested.

"Hmm." That didn't sound right. Blood, though... She looked at Suzanne. "Want to try something crazy?"

Suzanne gave her a sideways look. "What?"

"Do you have any blood-borne diseases?"

"So, why don't you try cutting yourselves and putting the cuts in the water first?" Sophie asked over lunch. She had seen Lizzy and Suzanne in the boarding house dining room, and she had joined them. The two women told the deputy about their plan over dessert.

"Well first off, I'm not comfortable putting an open wound into demon chum," Lizzy explained. "It might do something unexpected, make us sicker. Second of all, just...*ew.*"

Sophie smiled. "OK, I'll grab Andy after lunch, and we'll try this."

An hour later, Sophie and Andy watched Lizzy pick up a freshly rehydrated piece of calf muscle from the plastic container with a pair of tweezers and place it carefully in the water-filled basin. Then she picked up a scalpel, dipped it in rubbing alcohol, and then used her Zippo lighter to fully sanitize the blade.

"Are you OK with our arms being tied together?" She asked Suzanne. "I figure that would be one less thing to worry about."

"Yeah, that'll be fine."

Lizzy made a one-inch, deepish scratch on Suzanne's inner forearm, and then made a similar cut on her own upper forearm. Then Sophie tied the two arms together with strips of cloth.

"Let's get this done before the wounds cauterize," Lizzy suggested. She held out her free arm to focus on Imhotep, and then placed both of their hands in the water.

In an instant, Lizzy knew this time was different: she could feel Suzanne's energy, too, somehow. It wasn't wonderfully soothing like the geyser energy, nor was it harmful like demon energy, but rather it was...neutral? Familiar?

"*Oh!*" she heard Suzanne say immediately. "Wow, this...this is what's it's like?"

"Are you OK? What are you feeling?" she asked, keeping all the geyser energy focused on the mummy for the moment.

"Yes, I feel fine." She paused, and then said, "It's like being on the other side of a closed door during a windstorm—you feel little puffs every so often coming through the cracks, but you know that the storm outside is fierce. The puffs, though, feel wonderful."

"OK, I'm going to start redirecting the energy to the sample. Let me know if you feel anything dangerous." She gathered a wisp of current and sent it into the water. Suzanne gasped.

"Oh!" Suzanne said again. "That's so nice!"

"Now," Lizzy instructed, "Try to focus on that energy, on that feeling of pure rightness, and see if you can manifest it."

There were a few moments of silence. "No, I can't get it."

What Lizzy did next was completely unconscious: she thought about getting Suzanne closer, somehow, so she could feel this more directly. Then, the strangest feeling came over her, like her body was being...*crowded*. It didn't hurt, it was just...

She wasn't alone in her body anymore.

"Oh, *fuck!*" She felt Suzanne's body start to free-fall next to her, their arms still attached.

"Shit—grab her!" she screamed. Her body jostled as someone caught Suzanne and held her up. It was a little hard to breathe, as it turned out, being inhabited by a second soul. She didn't dare stop the holy water or disconnect, but rather *pushed* Suzanne back into her own body, hoping to hell that it worked. She visualized forcibly making Suzanne's energy go back where it belonged.

To her intense relief she suddenly felt alone again, and she heard Suzanne's gasp for breath a moment later. The whole event couldn't have lasted more than five seconds, but it was one of the most terrifying things she had ever experienced.

"Fuck!" she gasped. "Are you OK, Suzanne?"

"Yeah," the woman answered calmly after a pause. "Sophie, get me untied, please."

Lizzy felt the straps loosen, and then Suzanne's arm pull away. She quickly finished disintegrating the sample and turned towards the Sensor. Sophie had made her sit down on a folding chair, but Suzanne looked fine.

"Shit, Suzanne, I am so sorry!" Lizzy exclaimed. "I didn't know that was going to happen!"

Suzanne just smiled at Lizzy serenely. "It really is OK, Pet."

"Uh, excuse me?" Andy interrupted.

Lizzy had forgotten he was there. She looked over and saw that Andy had drawn his revolver, though he now had it pointed at the floor.

"Could someone tell me what just happened? 'Cause... Suzanne fell down, and she looked dead. And then Pet swore, and then Suzanne started gasping for air, and then everyone was fine." He kept looking at the two women, one to the other.

"I...think I might have sucked Suzanne's soul into my body...accidentally." Lizzy finally offered. She turned to Suzanne. "Is that what you think happened?"

"Yeah, I think so," the woman replied. "I felt...*pulled*...and then I was looking through your eyes, Pet, and I could hear you shouting. I couldn't read your mind or anything, but it felt like stepping into a Pet skin or something.

Though, I felt your energy work—I felt it *all*, like I was doing it." She paused, grinning broadly. "I felt the connection, just for that instant, that you had with the geyser. I saw it; I felt it.

"Then, I felt pushed back into my body, felt a sort of...snapping in, like fitting a key into a lock, and then I was back." She smiled at Lizzy again. "I'm not angry, it just... happened."

Everyone just stood and watched as Suzanne stood up and prepared the basin for a fresh sample. She walked over to the plastic container sitting on the windowsill, opened the lid, took the tweezers from the table to secure a sample, and then dropped it into the water. After closing the lid and placing the container back on the windowsill, she placed her fingers in the water and closed her eyes.

The water began to boil around the sample. Lizzy's eyes widened, but she half-expected it, considering how confident Suzanne seemed.

"Wow, this feels good," Suzanne commented.

What made Lizzy's breath catch, though, was that after the water stopped boiling and smoking, the sample remained intact.

Both women looked at each other in surprise. Lizzy reached down and touched the dead flesh with the back of her hand.

Nothing happened.

"How did you do that?" Lizzy breathed, looking at Suzanne.

"I don't know!"

Everyone in the room just stared silently at the basin.

"Did...you just cleanse that sample without hurtin' it?" Andy finally asked.

"She sure did," Lizzy said with a grin. She looked at Suzanne. "I'd love to know how you did that!"

"It just...happened that way," the woman answered. "I just did what you did." She held up her scratched arm. "Want to try again, see if I can bring you to me this time?"

"No," Lizzy said quickly. "That was too fucking dangerous for me—you could have gotten killed, or worse...been trapped." She gulped at the thought. "I'm good leaving well enough alone."

"OK." Suzanne emptied the basin into the sink to prepare another run.

Even after what had just happened, though, Lizzy just couldn't stop smiling. Suzanne was a goddamn miracle, and that meant that she could go home.

And just in time for Paradiso...life couldn't be better.

August 19th
3:45 p.m.

Lizzy was pretty sure that Kristin wouldn't wait until after church to deliver a baby, or that a doctor wouldn't wait until after church to resuscitate a patient, but all of the Infected mothers had to wait until after church that Sunday to get cleansed.

Whatever. She would be *so glad* to get back to the Known World, if for no other reason that she didn't have to pretend to be a believer anymore. The Infected women were still in good shape, she supposed, so it *really* wasn't that much of an emergency. She still thought exorcising demons was the perfect excuse to skip church, though...

They took one additional precaution for that afternoon's procedures: none of the mothers knew Suzanne could make holy water. Kristin had told them that Lizzy had just gotten better at making holy water, and that she would be doing the exorcising. Andy and the others had agreed that, since the demon got a good look at Lizzy in action, let them think it was still her.

Suzanne had successfully freed the other fetuses from possession, and now Amber Johnson was the only one left. She walked into the room with her husband, Ryan. Chelsea, Dana, and the recently treated women were surrounding the tub, smiling encouragingly at her. Ryan helped his wife into the birthing tub, and then Sophie and Thom tied her arms to the padded plank of wood.

"We're getting too efficient at this," Thom commented.

"Well, it's the last one," Sophie replied. "We'll be out of practice soon enough." She glanced at Lizzy and smiled.

Performing her role, Lizzy looked at Amber. "Are you ready?"

Amber nodded as Ryan took her hand and squeezed it.

"Let's get this done," Lizzy sighed. She turned to Suzanne. "Ready?"

Suzanne nodded.

Lizzy raised her hand, focused on Imhotep's left thigh in a wrapped sheet so the civilians didn't freak out, and then both women simultaneously placed their hands in the water. Lizzy kept her energy entirely out of the water, while Suzanne fully allowed her energy geyser to enter the tub. Amber gasped.

"*Whoa,*" she breathed. "It doesn't hurt, just feels...strange."

The treated women behind her nodded silently in agreement.

"OK," Lizzy said to the room and to Amber, "Any second now."

Amber looked confused. "What's happening an—"

Sure enough, like all the other times, Amber's face suddenly went blank, and she became Infected. Just like all the other times, the demon looked around the room, and then focused on Lizzy's face.

She grinned at it.

"Hi," she said quietly. She hadn't addressed the other demons, but since it was the last one, why the hell not? "Please let the rest of the assholes know that this experiment failed—whatever you're trying to do, it's not working. We know about it, and we can stop you now—and we are going spread the word. You guys can go fuck yourselves." Her grin grew wider as she felt the demon leave Amber's body. Amber blinked several times and looked around. Both Lizzy and Suzanne stopped channeling and began to get to their feet.

"What happened?" Amber asked.

"You were Infected," Lizzy explained. "But, only for a few seconds." She turned to Kristin. "What's the status?"

Kristin did a pelvic check as the deputies untied Amber. "Everything's intact." She pressed a Pinard horn to Amber's lower stomach area and listened. A slow grin spread across her face. "We're still in business!"

Amber began to cry as Ryan held her gently for a moment, and then helped her out of the tub. She turned to Lizzy.

"Thank you! Thank you so much!" She reached across the tub and gave Lizzy a drenching hug.

"You're welcome," Lizzy replied, glancing at Suzanne and smiling. She wished Suzanne could get in on this gratitude, since she did all the work, but the fewer people that knew about Suzanne the safer she would be. Suzanne also didn't have to get soaked with contaminated water and ash with every hug—lucky her.

After the mothers and their husbands had left, everyone else helped Kristin scrub down and sanitize all of her equipment and the examination room. Except for his thigh, Imhotep had not been present that afternoon. He was now residing in his new permanent home in Sophie's basement, where he would hopefully just sit quietly and await eternity.

When the last piece of equipment had been dried and put away, Andy turned to Lizzy. "When do you want to go home?"

"Tomorrow?" she asked hopefully.

Andy smiled and nodded. "I figured—I've already sent word to a couple of deputies to come to Zion. We'll treat you to dinner tonight, everyone will get a good night's sleep, and then we'll start headin' back south." He looked around the room, and then back at her. "You did a good job, Pet." He paused and nodded, looking around the room again and smiling. "Yup, that was some fine work."

"Thanks, Andy. I'm just glad I could help," she replied as they all left the office. On the porch, Suzanne poked her in the arm.

"Hey, when's your birthday?"

"It was a few months ago," Lizzy told her, puzzled. "Why?"

The newest known creator of holy water gave her a wide, mischievous grin. "Oh, no, I think it's today. The girls and I have a present for you, right after supper, and we won't take no for an answer."

Kim

She had forgotten how much fun it was to watch someone smoke pot for the first time. Pet was staring at the sunset, a large joint in her hand, absolutely mesmerized by the sky.

"*Wow*," she said, her eyes wide. "Now I know why you guys smoke this stuff! All the colors…"

If there was anyone on earth tonight that needed to kick back and relax, it was this SCAdian. She had worked so hard, from the moment she arrived in Zion to this afternoon, and even during her down times she seemed…tense. They knew absolutely nothing about her, really, except that she needed an evening to get high. Kim and her friends had even discussed getting Pet laid somehow, but even the male deputies thought she was a little scary, and she didn't seem the one-night-stand type, anyhow. Smoking her own joint, Kim wondered who her type was.

"Do you have a man back home?" she asked Pet, because if there was one thing weed was good for, it was relaxing inhibitions. In Kim's case, it made her bold enough to ask new people personal questions, which she never did off the marijuana.

Pet chuckled at the question and took a drag. "Oh, I've got a fuck buddy in one town." She sat up, concerned, and looked at the women. "Oh, shit, can I say that here, that I have a fuck buddy? Is someone going to jump out and condemn me to hell?" She glanced around the porch.

Becky leaned over and patted the SCAdian on the knee. "No, Pet. Hypocrisy is the homage vice pays to virtue—I think even the most virtuous among us has had a fuck buddy at one point or another…at least in this town."

"That's good," Pet said. She was looking at the sunset again. "That's something that surprised me about Zion—y'all seem pretty understanding about things."

"Well, we're probably one of the more liberal towns out here," Kim said. "You go up past Washington's Brigade territory, though, and folks would pray for your immortal soul with violence if you fornicated outside of marriage."

"Then again," Becky observed, taking a drag, "they wouldn't have had the balls to go down to SCAdian territory to hire a heathen SCAdian, either, and they'd had dying women all over the place, wondering why prayer wasn't working."

"But, we still believe in Jesus, go to church, things like that," Suzanne added. "We'll just pray for your immortal soul *after* you leave."

Pet thought this was extraordinarily funny.

"So, how good of a buddy is he?" Becky asked after the cackling had died down.

Pet shrugged. "He actually takes sex to an art form, but he's all form, no substance. He has three or four girls in every port, if you know what I mean."

The women nodded. No one spoke for a few moments, watching the sun as it started to disappear into the horizon.

"There...might be a man at Paradiso, though." Pet volunteered slowly. She didn't look very sure about that.

"What do you mean, *might* be?" Becky asked.

Pet grinned. "It's...kinda complicated. He's a knight and the seneschal of my home barony. He's like a deputy mayor or something."

"A real knight?" Suzanne asked. "Armor and everything?"

"Oh, yes." Pet's look got dreamy. "He looks *phenomenal* in armor." She took a puff of her joint. "He looks good in everything, actually. He's a great guy, too."

"So, what's the problem?" Kim asked.

Pet sighed as her expression sobered. "He hasn't ever come out and said he was interested in me. I know he dates, but he's never asked me out." She paused, looking perplexed. "His *son* thinks he's interested, but I haven't gotten the chance to ask Sir John what he wants."

"That's his name—Sir John?" Becky asked.

Pet nodded. "Sir John the Younger."

Suzanne giggled. "Younger than who?"

Now it was Pet's turn to giggle. "I don't know—I've never asked. His son is called John the Youngest, though."

"So, he'll be at this Paradiso thing?" Kim wanted to know.

"Well, I hope so—he wasn't at Crown Tournament, so maybe he'll still be out on baronial business again, but I hope I can see him there." Suddenly Pet sat up, excited, and turned to the women.

"Oh, you should *so* come with me to Paradiso!" she exclaimed. "Lots of mundanes come down for that. It's a week-long music festival at the end of this month, and there're games and workshops and performances and a lot of alcohol—wow, that would be great! There're even *bagpipes!*"

The women smiled at her. Who knew Pet could be so exuberant?

"Not this year, dear," Suzanne said. "It would be too late to get time off. But next year...?" She looked at Becky and Kim, who both shrugged and nodded in agreement. They never left Zion except for the occasional revival meeting because there really wasn't anything interesting around. A music festival, however...that might be something worth travelling for.

And, Kim reflected, maybe they were too isolated up here—maybe going down to SCAdian territory to visit would be fun, especially now that they were friends with one of them. Pet had said that they could be geeky, but she also described SCAdians as kind, fun-loving folks, too. It would be nice to get to know more people like that.

"So, when will *you* be coming back *here?*" Kim asked her.

Pet took the last remaining puff of her joint and awkwardly snubbed it out in the ashtray. "I've been thinking about that. I'm going to try and talk Master Wills into making our way up here sometime soon. We've been starting some socially-minded programs, and maybe we could do some workshops up here or something.

"Or, if he's not interested, I could try and visit myself, maybe in the off-season." The sun had finally set, and the glow of lamps and candles could be seen up and down the street.

"But, I'll work on it!" she promised, standing up. "For now, let's *do something!*"

Kim smiled—this was typical buzzed behavior.

"Let's have a sing-along!" the SCAdian continued. "Who has a guitar around here?"

Suzanne stood, as well. "Let's go see Mark down the street—I think he has one." She looked at her roommates. "We'll be right back."

"Oh, this'll be *so cool!*" Pet told Suzanne as they stepped off the porch and down the street. "I know a ton of bawdy songs, like this one about fucking a dead whore by the roadside..."

As they walked down the street, Kim could hear her continuing to describe the evening's proposed repertoire, all of the songs involving some form of fornication or criminal activity.

This should be interesting...

"Hey...didn't you say you wanted me to break some pots?" was the last thing Kim heard Pet say as they disappeared into the night.

Chapter Eighteen

<u>Wills</u>

"Pet's back, Wills."

Wills looked up from the plank in the stage he was ripping up; a new board was sitting next to him. "How does she look?"

"A little tired, but OK," Justin replied. "She and the caravan just stepped into camp. No one's approached them yet, as per your orders. She looks confused that no one's greeting her, but the militiamen don't."

Wills sighed. "Grab Pet and that marshal guy and bring them to the prompt. Make something up—explain that there's been an accident and everyone's twitchy, but that the injured person will recover. Offer the militiamen some late lunch, and tell the marshal that I will send for his man immediately."

As his husband jogged away, Wills hoisted himself to his feet and sighed again. This was not going to be a pretty scene, but it was better to just get it over with. He made his way to the prompt and walked back around his desk to the shelves, where he grabbed four tumblers and the rest of his hooch. He was pouring equal amounts of liquid into each cup when Pet and Bennett came in. Pet was dressed in her favorite day garb of breeches, a white shirt, and a jerkin—it warmed his heart to see her alive and well in SCAdian garb. His apprentice looked washed out, though—it must have been a hard time up there—and concerned. He walked over to her and gave her a brief hug in greeting. "Welcome back."

420

"Wills? There was an accident?" he heard her ask. He could hear the fatigue in her voice.

He gave her a reassuring smile as he released her. "No, my dear. I have an important matter to discuss with you, and I didn't want the troupe to blab about it before I had a chance to talk to you." He distributed the tumblers. Bennett waited until Wills took a swallow from his tumbler before he sniffed into his cup and then took a sip of his. He inhaled sharply, and then looked impressed.

"Potatoes?" he asked.

Wills smiled. "I'm not entirely sure. One of our performers, Gunther, is the resident stillmaster. Before you leave, I'll make sure that you get the recipe."

"Thanks," Bennett replied before he finished his drink.

Pet set her drink down on the desk without a sip. "What's going on?"

"First, old business. Were you successful?"

Pet exchanged a look with Bennett before frowning at Wills. "Yes. The fetuses were Infected—the mothers were not."

Wills wasn't expecting to hear that. "How on earth did you figure that out?"

"It's a long story—I'll tell you later. But, I did manage to teach one of their Sensors to make holy water—don't ask me how—and she's going to screen the pregnant women from now on.

"But, I don't think there will be any more—I think the demons figured out that the experiments weren't working and quit."

Wills squinted at her. "Demons don't plan like that."

Pet rolled her eyes. "They do now. I knew that from...another episode with them. I thought everyone did." She glanced at Bennett, who shrugged.

Wills did not like this new camaraderie between the militiaman and his guitar player, nor that his apprentice apparently had a more interesting past than he had ever suspected. "So, Marshal Bennett, are you satisfied with the results?"

"Very satisfied; thank you, sir." Bennett stared at Pet's tumbler. She pushed it over to him. He took it from the desk and raised it to his mouth. "Thank you," he mumbled around the tumbler lip.

Oh, that's enough of that. "So, I assume our transaction is complete?"

Bennett nodded as he swallowed the last of Pet's hooch. "Yes—Pet has the rest of the payment. We'd be much obliged if you would sell us some supplies to get us back to Zion, and then we'll be on our way."

"Please, do join us for lunch first—on the house—and then we can barter. It's going to take about two hours for your man to come back—you and your people might as well be comfortable. And, I think you'll find that my troupe is very hospitable. Please."

Bennett smiled. "You had me at 'free lunch,' Mr. Plantagenet." He turned to Pet and offered his hand. Pet shook it.

"Thanks again, Pet."

"Good luck, Andy. I'll try to see you all before you go."

Andy? Wills gave Justin a quiet signal. Justin stepped forward.

"If you will, Marshal Bennett, I'll show you where you can wash up." Justin led Bennett out of the tent.

When he was sure *Andy* was gone, Wills arched an eyebrow at Pet. "So...you got pretty comfortable with the militiaman. Would you like to make it an extended stay?"

Pet grinned at his grumbling as she reached in her jerkin and pulled out a pouch. She dropped it on the desk. "You don't need to be jealous—you know you're the only man for me."

He ignored the payment. "I'll feel better when they're out of my camp."

"Y'know, they aren't that bad," she told him with a frown. "They just don't like medieval cosplay."

Oh, I'm about to change your mind in a minute... Wills wished he had more hooch. "I do have something to talk to you about. Sitting or standing?"

"I've been sitting on a horse for four days—I'll stand."

"OK," Wills took a breath. "I suppose I'll start with your recall."

She blinked. "My what?"

Wills reached into his desk drawer and removed the parchment. He handed it to Pet. "Sir John dropped it off three weeks ago." He paused to watch her reaction.

Her face showed only curiosity as she unrolled the scroll. "Oh, that's too bad. It would have been nice to see him." She started to read.

Ouch...swing and a miss for the stick-jock...

When Pet was finished reading, she looked at Wills, confused. "OK, this tells me that I'm supposed to report to Caradoc for further orders. Unless the reason is written in some really obscure peer code, that's all it says."

"Yes—recalls are usually straightforward. The usual procedure is to report to the baronial seat, and then the knights let people know what's going on, what they are to do, that sort of thing. But..." He reached down and pulled out another piece of paper. This one was thin, like copy paper, and a light cream color. He handed it to her to read.

"This is a request from Baroness Isabella for aid against...El Hajj and the Patriot's Defense Force?" Pet looked shocked, and then paused in thought. "I've never heard of them, and I heard a lot of names being thrown around when I was in Zion. I guess we could ask Andy. Are we sure they're legit?"

"Regardless if they are...legit...or not, Isabella seems to think they are. The mayor of New Swampkeype gave this to me. He received it from three children who were sent from Cornwall with a request to foster them until the conflict is resolved. All the baronies in the neighboring kingdoms received children from the barony and this notice; it's unprecedented. To my knowledge, no child was turned away."

Pet grew pale. "Barony of the Brandywine is going to be attacked?"

Wills took a careful breath. "Was attacked, about three weeks ago. The militia brought an army's worth of military-grade weaponry and artillery, so it's only a matter of time before the city falls." He paused as Justin came back into the tent. "I was just getting to the bad part, dear."

Justin gave Pet a side hug. "It will be all right, no matter what happens."

"Thanks." She turned back to Wills as Justin took his usual place at Wills' side. "So, what now? It seems pretty clear that I need to go."

"See...that's the thing. Vagabond Haven is probably piles of rubble by now. There's probably nothing left to report to."

She stared at Wills. "What do you mean, 'probably'? Is it piles of rubble or not?"

He shrugged. "We've been told the attacking forces are focused on Cornwall. Once they overrun the seat, however, it is expected that they will spread to sack the barony and move onward to Vagabond Haven, maybe further."

"Why would they do that? I thought Maalik was this benevolent leader, anyway? I can see why they'd want payback from Isabella, but why now?"

"Maalik is dead. His brother Rohan is in charge of the tribe now, and he apparently made some sort of deal. If he's crazy enough to pull this off, why would he stop at Brandywine?"

"Then, I need to go, while there's still time." Lizzy ran her fingers through her hair as she thought—things were happening way too fast. "I'll need a horse..."

"Pet, no one is expecting you to go," Wills interrupted. "One fighter isn't going to make a difference."

What? She couldn't believe this statement was coming from Master William Plantagenet, Double Peer and SCAdian Poster Boy.

"That's not the point!" she exclaimed. "I took an oath to defend the barony. They gave me an AoA!"

"Oh, so all it takes for you to stay is to give you an award?" He smiled at her. "Hell, we could do that. And, it would be so much grander than that scroll they gave you." He turned to Justin. "Couldn't we, dear?"

"Absolutely. We probably should have some sort of formal order for the troupe, anyway, since we can't issue our own AoAs..."

"I swore to defend the barony," Lizzy interrupted. They were offering her something she wanted very badly—formal acknowledgement that she belonged with the Players, maybe even that she was family—but it was too late for that now. "What the hell's the point of an oath if you don't honor it?"

"You swore an oath to the government," Wills pointed out, "and you ran away from that."

"They were trying to kill me!"

"HOW IS THIS ANY DIFFERENT?!" Wills' voice boomed throughout the tent.

Lizzy was exasperated; she took a breath and tried a different tact. "Do you think I *want* to go? I *want* to stay here, with you and the troupe, and be bored out of my mind in Fiddler's Green this winter. But, this is how service works. An old-salt coastie once told me that, 'You have to go out; you don't have to come back.'"

She must have been more tired than she thought, because tears were starting to well up in her eyes. All the people she knew at Caradoc—they could already be dead or even dying at that very moment while she and Wills stood around arguing. Fighters in armor wouldn't have a chance against bullets...especially one particular knight who she was sure would feel compelled to lead the charge...

Nope—not going there, she thought as her heart squeezed painfully; she forced herself to quickly and completely push the reaction aside. It was foolish to feel something so unrequited now, and it only made matters worse.

Tamp it down, Petty Officer Townsend—you have a job to do. To her dismay, the pep talk didn't help much.

"Please don't fight me on this," she pleaded. "It might not be certain death, you know. They may not come, or maybe we can fight them off. It may be over by the time I arrive.

"But I have to go. Just tell me I can I come back here, please, when it's over?" Her throat closed up; she didn't trust herself to say anything else.

Justin maneuvered around the desk and embraced her in a very Justin kind of way. Suddenly Lizzy just couldn't stop herself anymore, and she allowed herself to cry in earnest against his chest. Then she smelled the familiar, comforting scents of vanilla, sandalwood, and sawdust as two more arms came around them, embracing them both.

"Of course you can," she heard Wills say above her. "Just be sure to come back."

She couldn't leave right away: she was exhausted, hungry, and some arrangements had to be made before she could depart. After hugging each member of the troupe, she joined the militiamen to finish the remains of the salted chicken and barley rice.

She ate in silence while she thought about the Wrightsons, who were literally right next door to Cornwall. Would Ellen and Melinda have left Hamilton with Robert Bruce and Eugenia? Lizzy wasn't sure if the women would have just left their business standing empty—their entire livelihood was there.

Or, if they had sent away the children, then what: stay at the Coach and Four to try and defend it, or would they continue on with business as usual? Lizzy supposed that invading armies liked hot meals, too, and they *would* be right on the front lines... Christ, no matter how it was sliced, it would truly be an awful situation.

And, what about Max? He would have been recalled to serve like she had been. Did he even *know* how to fight, to handle *any* kind of weapon? Just "finding a peer" to sign off on an AoA application didn't exactly invoke confidence about his potential skills in combat.

Against her better judgment, her heart squeezed a little for him, too.

All in all, the situation reeked worse than shit. She needed to find out, at the first available opportunity, what happened to them. She just hoped there would be friends alive left to find.

After they ate, she pulled Andy aside and showed him the aid request from Isabella. He whistled.

"Shit," he growled. "These crazy fuckers."

Considering the source, they must have been some crazy fuckers, indeed. "What can you tell me about them?"

He scratched at his beard as he read the request again. "They're way, way up north. They do the government's dirty work—they have close ties. No one'll deal with them except other mercenary groups. They're shit-eatin', nasty pieces of work."

"So, they'll have government people there?"

"No, probably not—maybe an advisor or somethin'. The government just supplies their gear and weapons." He looked at her. "Are you going there?"

She sighed. "Yeah, after I've rested up a bit. This isn't my town, but we're right next door—I have to go help defend it."

"Good luck with that," Andy said, frowning. "I have some grenades I could let you have, and you have your rifle and your shot, but I don't have to tell you that you'll get your head blown off if you get in their way, right?"

"No, you don't, but I gotta go, Andy. You know how this shit works."

He nodded and sighed. "Yeah, I do." He paused. "Y'know, I could go with you and give you a hand—it'd be like old times for me. The deputies could handle things up north for a while."

Lizzy smiled gently. "It's not your fight, Andy, but thanks."

"No...I reckon it ain't." He reached into his vest and pulled out his flask. "But, if you do manage to get up next to one of them," he said with one of his admiring looks, unscrewing the lid, "shove a grenade up their ass and pull the pin for me."

9:15 pm

Wills

By the time Pet was done with her nap, the militiamen were long gone. It was well after dark when she went into the prompt. On stage, the troupe was performing a break-in of *Lysistrata*. Justin was sitting by the tent flap, watching the performance and waiting for something to go wrong. Wills was at his desk, writing. He looked up and smiled when he saw her.

"Come in," he whispered, gesturing her inside. She squeezed Justin's shoulder as she walked past his chair. When she arrived at the desk, Wills shoved several pieces of paper at her. He spoke quietly.

"You'll need to change out Socks at some point, so here are two vouchers: one for Richard at the Dunghill Keep Livery Stable, and the other for Gwen at Bad Ischl. Both are along the way."

"Socks?" Pet stopped sorting through the papers and looked at Wills. "Sir John's horse?"

"Yes, he left him for you." *C'mon, Miss Pet, put it together. Survey says...!*

"Oh, that was thoughtful. He must have borrowed Wind Walker from Master Cuthbert."

BZZT! Wills desperately wanted to bash his head into the desk in frustration but managed to control the urge. *He comes up*

427

specifically to see you; he leaves you his OWN PERSONAL HORSE, GODDAMN IT...

"What else is here?" Pet was back to looking at paperwork.

"Some referrals along the way, if you need them, and a pocket map of the area. It's very crude—Justin just copied down your main route and some back roads—but it should get you where you want to go." His stomach was cramping just looking at her. "Are you sure there isn't anything I can say to change your mind?"

Pet shook her head as she folded each paper carefully and placed them in her pouch. "No." She leaned down and kissed his cheek. "Don't worry—I'll find you when it's over." She walked over to Justin, gave him a kiss on the cheek, whispered something in his ear, and then walked past the stage and into the night. Justin kept watching the performance—no matter what, the show must go on—but Wills knew that his husband was just as scared for Pet as he was.

At noon the following day, hours after Pet had left, the herald from New Swampkeype arrived to talk to Wills in private. Right after the meeting, Wills assembled the troupe and announced that there would be no Paradiso this year—and probably not ever again. The rest of the season would have to be played by ear, but he expected that they would be in Avalon by the harvest, if not before.

Odin's Challenge in the spring: still undetermined.

August 27th
4:00 p.m.

"Wills? We have a situation."

Wills looked up from his desk to see Raul standing inside the tent flap. "What's the problem?"

"There are three kids here, and the oldest one says that they are from Caradoc, and that they came for asylum. They're looking for Pet."

"*What?*" Wills jumped from his chair and ran out of the tent.

Sure enough, there were three boys huddled together in the center of their courtyard, already being tended to by Sweet Bess.

428

Fortunately, there were still cookies from last night, and all three were munching away. Wills recognized one of them immediately. "Little John?"

The boy looked up. He was taller—he almost came to Wills' shoulder now—but his face was still pudgy with youth. The boy walked up to him and bowed.

"Good afternoon, Master Plantagenet. My father, Sir John the Younger, sent me and Stewart and Ian to stay with Lady Petya until it's safe to come home." He handed Wills a large, thick envelope.

Shit. "Little John, Pet isn't here—she went to Caradoc."

"Oh, no." Little John instantly lost his formal demeanor and now looked genuinely frightened. "She was supposed to stay here! Dad said she was going to be here! We came all this way—what am I going to do with these kids?" Tears started to well in his eyes.

Wills put an arm around the boy's shoulder and gave it a little squeeze. Damned if he hadn't had his share of consoling crying people this week...

"You and your companions will stay with us," he said. He looked up and smiled as he saw Justin approach. "We have company, sweetheart!"

A few minutes later, Wills and Justin were at the prompt, going through Little John's envelope. It contained the boys' Writs for Safe Passage, a letter addressed to John the Youngest, and three halves of individual documents, each cut and colored uniquely; anyone who came to claim a child would have to present the other half of their sheet, in case the parent or guardian was not able to make the trip. There was also an envelope addressed to Pet. Wills and Justin stared at it.

"We shouldn't," Justin said.

"It's none of our business," Wills agreed.

There was a pause.

"Fuck that—is it sealed shut?"

Wills checked the envelope flap. "Yes, but it's a gum envelope."

"Where's a kettle?"

Twenty minutes later, the envelope was steamed opened and they were reading the letter between them. It was a short letter, but they each read it twice before looking up at each other.

"This is a goddamn Greek tragedy!" Wills exclaimed. He shook the letter. "Really, you stupid stick-jock? He writes the sweetest love letter I've ever laid eyes on, and she isn't even here to read it. Goddamn it!"

"It's beautiful." Justin eyes were moist as he took the letter and carefully placed it back in the envelope. "She doesn't even *know*—you just can't make this shit up. God, I hope they get out of this OK."

"Me, too." Wills put his arms around his husband and held him. "I want the Happily Ever After for them, too, love." And then he held him tighter, because there was nothing else left to be done.

Military Liaison Base Camp
Cornwall, WY
29 AUG
1110

General Edison

BG/10 Zachary Edison of the US Army was not pleased with what he saw on the field. "Get me Clemens—now!"

Five minutes later, a middle-aged man in full fatigues ran up the hill. He saluted. "Yes, General?"

Edison gestured at the valley with his binoculars. "What the hell is going on down there? Why is El Hajj mobilizing for another attack? We've secured Cornwall—they're supposed to finish cleaning up and call for transport, end of story."

Clemens squirmed a little. "Rohan is concerned that we may have flank opposition from Vagabond Haven. I advised against it, but..."

Edison got right into Clemens' face. "Who did I assign the weapons to?"

Clemens gulped. "Us, sir."

"So why is El Hajj still mobilizing when you told them not to?"

There was a pause. "Rohan is...more unstable...than I thought, sir. His people have become a mob; they feel they can take more..."

"Goddamn it!" Edison handed his binoculars to one of his aides and started walking back towards his field tent, Clemens on his heels. "We agreed to the hydroponic fields, and that was it! We still have a shortage of breedable people; we can't go around randomly killing off livestock for a vendetta." He pushed through the opening of the tent. His radioman was sitting next to his equipment. "Get me HQ."

Clemens stood at the opening of the tent. "Let me try again, there's still time to stop them."

Edison whirled around. "You're still here?"

Clemens ran down the hill.

"HQ on the line, sir."

Edison rolled his eyes as he picked up the receiver. "HQ, this is Farmer Ben. I need to speak to Ground Control, over."

"Farmer Ben, HQ. Roger that, stand by for Ground Control, over."

As he was waiting, Edison turned to yet another aide. "Get a read of the situation. Give me an update in three minutes."

"Yes, sir."

He handed the receiver back to the radioman. "When you get Ground Control, ask for a secure channel, and then let me talk to them."

"Yes, sir."

Edison paced while he waited. A minute later, the radioman handed him back the receiver.

"Ground Control on charlie-delta, sir."

"Thanks." He pushed the transmission button. "Ground Control, Farmer Ben on channel charlie-delta, standing by, over."

"Farmer Ben, Ground Control on channel charlie-delta. OK, Zach, we're secured, what's the problem, over?"

"Goddamn Patriot's Defense Force can't control El Hajj, and they're about to attack the next area down—Vagabond Haven. This is a clusterfuck—we may have to bust up the party ourselves, over."

"Roger that—we can have birds in the air in five minutes, ground-pounders in fifteen. What's your status, over?"

431

"I'm fine—I'm well away from the situation..." There was an alarm at the far end of the tent.

"Stand by, Miles." He released the transmission button. "What the hell is that?"

"There's an unauthorized transponder signal on the field," the radioman explained. "We have a friendly party crasher, sir."

"That's just great. Get a verification of the code."

"Yes, sir."

"Hey, Miles, we have a Renegade, Unknown on our field. Know anything about it, over?"

"Negative, over."

"Sir?" the radioman interrupted. "It's a local, sir. It's Deep Fryer."

Edison stared at the radioman for a moment. "What the hell is she doing out there? She was up in militia country...oh, never mind!" He pushed in the transmission button. "Miles, Deep Fryer is out there—make that a Renegade, Extremely Unfriendly. Do you know who I'm talking about—Deep Fryer—over?"

"Negative, over."

"Ever hear of Petty Officer Townsend of Commune Ruth, over?"

There was a pause. "Negative. Why? Should I have, over?"

"She's been out there a while, keeping quiet, but now she's steering herself into harm's way. She's supposed to be hands-off, but advise HQ that we may have to pull her liberty pass, over."

"Understood, over."

The aide returned from his errand. "It's like watching the ocean, sir—they're moving and churning in waves, both El Hajj and the militia. I think they're going to cut loose any second now."

"Damn it." He pushed the transmission button. "They're about to break. I recommend engagement; I say again, engage—requesting suppression fire."

"Roger that. Stand by for confirmation of suppression fire, over." Edison waited, pacing around the tent. After about a minute, he heard his name over the radio.

"Go ahead, Miles."

"Suppression fire approved—they're on their way, over."

"Helos' ETA, over?"

"Stand by for their ETA—they're mobilizing now. The ground troops might not make it for this round, but they're on the way, over."

Edison turned to an aide. "Get your gear and the deuce and a half; take Washington with you. Pinpoint our Renegade, see what she does. Do not engage her unless it looks like she's going to get herself killed. If things go south, yank her. Understood?"

"Yes, sir."

"Good luck."

Chapter Nineteen

<u>John</u>

He could just make out the compound in the distance when he saw someone running towards him on the path. John could tell by the way the person moved, and by his general outline, that it was his son. He had seen a lot of astonishing, mostly terrible things over the past month, but his son running towards him, healthy and whole, was the most amazing sight of all.

"Dad!" Little John called; John waved. When Little John finally reached him, John dismounted to throw his arms around him and hold him close. He kissed him on the cheek.

"Thank god," he said, not wanting to let go. After several seconds, he released the boy to look at him. "You've grown since I last saw you." They began to walk towards the main gate, Little John leading his father's horse. "Did you have any trouble with the towns along the way?"

"No, all the towns were great to us—we mostly stayed with mayors and barons at night, and then travelled with escorts during the day. The kids were no trouble. When we got to Wills' camp, he gave us a tent to live in."

"How about the troupe? Have you been treated well?"

"They've been taking really good care of us—we eat as much as we want, and Sweet Bess always has cookies or something. We've been helping with the harvesting, mostly, but Murray— that's Dr. Goldberg's apprentice—has been letting me help in their laboratory, making medicines and stuff. It's really interesting." He suddenly looked alarmed.

"What happened to the barony? Where's Pet? Did she make it to Caradoc?" Then he stopped and really looked at his father. "You look terrible, Dad. Were you injured?"

John smiled sadly. "No, I'm all right—it's just been a very long six weeks. Both the barony and Caradoc are safe and sound. And, yes, Petya did make it to Caradoc. Did you see her before she left?"

"No—I missed her by a day. Is she OK?"

It took a few moments for John to answer. He quickly processed through that Petya didn't know Johnny was coming to her when she left. John could almost forgive her now for leaving the safety of the troupe and steering into harm's way. Almost.

"Sort of," he finally replied. "I'll tell you all about it, but let's find Wills and Justin first—I don't want to tell the story twice." They continued towards Avalon.

It wasn't hard to find Wills and Justin—the same border scout that had told Little John that John had arrived had also told them, so they were waiting at the main gate. To John's great surprise, they each gave him a huge bear hug when he arrived.

"Aren't you a sight for sore eyes?" Wills exclaimed as he embraced him to the point of asphyxiation.

"We thought you were dead for sure!" Justin added during his hug.

"So did we—it was a close thing."

"Where's Pet?" Wills asked.

John looked down at the ground. "She isn't dead, and she's probably all right, but it's complicated. Can we go somewhere?"

"Of course," Justin said. They walked down the main street to the first enclosure on the right, where Wills and Justin lived. As John stepped inside, he was amazed at all of the books and manuscripts that they had in their living room. They covered all the walls, floor to ceiling. He could see more filled shelves in the next room.

"You did loot the Library of Congress, didn't you?"

Wills chuckled. "That is a story for another time. Now, your audience demands to hear your soliloquy." He gestured to a thick sofa. "Relax here. Anything to drink?"

"Do you have any of that hooch?"

"God, no—that's strictly for the road." He poured an amber-colored liquid into a glass and handed it to the knight. "Try this."

435

John sniffed it, and then took a sip. "This is marvelous."

"It was merely good when I bought it years ago, back in New York. Now, compared to what we're left with, it is beyond quintessence." He sat down in a love seat; Justin sat next to him. Little John sat next to his father.

"So what happened, and where is Pet?"

John took another sip; he already felt his eyes getting moist, and he hadn't even started to tell the story. The warmth and the numbing properties of the liquor helped him begin his tale.

"We thought we were dead," he began. "After the fall of Cornwall, representatives from the militia and El Hajj came and assured us that they were just after the hydroponic fields. Of course, we didn't believe that for a second, and we kept watching them. For almost two weeks, all was quiet.

"Then, on the 29th of August, our scouts reported that the occupying forces were swarming towards us—they had all but abandoned the city. When we first saw the mob, it was clear that they had whipped themselves into a frenzy. They were pumping their rifles in the air, and the way they moved..." He swallowed. "It was clear that they wanted to sack Caradoc, too, so we all took our positions along the walls. We wouldn't have been a match for their forces, though: they were going to rip right through us.

"Then, just as they were starting to charge—it was the most incredible thing—we heard military aircraft approaching."

There was a pause.

"Excuse me?" Justin asked.

"Yeah—we were approached by a detachment of army helicopters, no shit. They looked like Cobras, but they had some modifications I didn't recognize. They came in fast, and then they just opened up on the mob. I think they were trying to lay down some suppression fire, but the people didn't seem to know to take cover, and they started firing on the helicopters. That's when the helos shot to kill; it was all over pretty quickly. Who would have expected that?" He stared into space for a moment.

"What we didn't notice, though, was that a large piece of the mob had splintered off and was approaching the west side—we were all so distracted watching the helicopters that no one saw them coming. I was at the main gate; Tex, one of our squires, was at the west side, up in one of the towers. It wasn't a large enough force to take over the town, but there would have been heavy casualties if they had gotten in.

"So...so then Tex tells me..." A nervous giggle bubbled up as he thought about what happened next. Then he remembered the end of the story and choked out a sob. Finally he just lost control of himself as a tidal wave of emotion crashed over him, leaving him hysterically laughing and crying at the same time.

It still surpassed his understanding why his heart had to be broken for the people of Caradoc to be saved, and he felt selfish and ashamed about the spite he felt whenever he considered it. It also didn't help that he hadn't slept much in the past two months. He kept waking up in the night shouting, often after dreaming about the indescribable fear that gripped him when heard the runner's message...*No, please...*sprinting towards the west wall, heart pounding out of his chest...*She's going to get herself killed!*...never getting there in time, finding her already gone...the dream then dissolving into him stoking the burning bodies...the piles and piles of corpses...

God, the smell...

"Umm...do you need to take a break?" Justin finally asked.

"No, no..." John forced himself to deeply inhale. "I have to get this out." After some calming breaths and a couple more sips of alcohol, he was able to continue.

"So, Tex told me that he heard a woman outside the wall yell 'Incoming!'", and the next thing he sees is a *grenade* in mid-air— he yelled for everyone to hit the deck. The grenade exploded, right in the center of the splinter group.

"It was Petya." He swallowed the lump in his throat. "Tex recognized her, hiding behind some rocks." He couldn't help but smile at this next part, because it was so Coast Guard of her. "It was clear that she had never thrown one before, because she apparently forgot to duck after throwing the first one. She watched it explode," he quickly sobered again, "and she caught some of it. When Tex looked up, he saw her wiping dirt out of her face, and there was a small gash on her forehead. She wrapped her head in something and threw some more." He paused, looking directly at Wills through narrowed eyes.

"Petya had...*grenades*...Wills." He impatiently watched Wills for a response, who was intently watching him. Then his mind was overwhelmed with the sickening image of Petya bleeding and alone on the ground, saving their asses, while he and the others were cheering for themselves along the front wall. Guilt overcame him, and his composure snapped again.

"WHERE IN THE *FUCK* DOES A SCADIAN GUITAR PLAYER GET GODDAMN GRENADES, WILLS?!" His voice cracked at the end.

Wills' face was carefully blank as he spoke. "She made some friends in militia country when she was up there—they probably gave her some before they left."

"God," John looked up, blinking back tears. "So, eventually I guess she ran out of grenades, because then she started shooting at them." He started to giggle again. "Tex told me...that her first shots were wild, but then her groupings got much better." He began to laugh all over again, but he recovered quickly—he was just too exhausted for another outburst. "By this time, anyone in the splinter group that was left had taken cover in a ditch and was returning fire. Tex and the west group were picking off people as they could." John took a shaky breath—he could imagine the scene clearly in his mind's eye as he relayed the rest of the story.

"Then, Tex thinks her rifle must have jammed. She was trying to clear it, but she left her shoulder exposed, and someone got the shot.

"She went down....Tex said blood started streaming..." He closed his eyes; he forced himself to take a breath and keep talking.

"Then, a deuce and a half comes flying out of nowhere; it stopped right in front of her position. The guy in the cab covered for another guy, who dove behind the rocks and grabbed her. They were both in camo BDUs, flack gear—all of it. She struggled, but Tex said that he jabbed her with this pen-looking thing, and she went unconscious. He dragged her to the back of the truck and got her inside. Then the truck drove away, and that was it. I got there maybe three minutes later." He felt bleak. Little John placed a hand on his shoulder.

"Anyone that was left of the attacking forces that could run away, did. Those that couldn't, the government left for us to clean up. That's why it took me some time to come up here—I wanted to make sure all of the dead were buried or burned before I took Johnny back with me." He was starting to feel very fatigued, like the story had been his sole driving force: now that it was spent he was, too.

"So, they took her back?" Wills asked gently.

John nodded. "She was alive when they took her, and I don't think they would have gone through all that trouble if they had

438

wanted her dead." He took a sip of his drink; he noticed that his hand was shaking. "She wasn't supposed to be there. In fact," he suddenly became angry again, "I'm sorry I didn't come right out and say 'Keep her with you,' but I thought we had an understanding! Why didn't you keep her here?"

"We tried," Wills replied calmly. "We did. But she insisted she took an oath to defend the barony, and that's what she was going to do. She also told us that she wasn't going to do anything stupid." He looked at Justin. "So much for that."

"She probably was intending to stay clear when she saw the helicopters," Justin suggested, "but then she saw that other group, and that you were all distracted. She was in a good position, so she took advantage of it."

"Yeah," John sighed. *My formidable lady*, he thought, though he no longer felt worthy of such a claim. "God, that was so brave of her."

"Something I've noticed about our Pet," Wills observed with a hint of a smile, "is that when she is set on something, she'll listen very carefully about why it's not a good idea, and then she'll go ahead and do what she wants, anyway. I suppose we could have locked her up..."

"No, no—knowing her, she would have gotten away somehow." Now that he had told them what had happened, John just wanted to curl up somewhere and cry himself to sleep. "But, she did defend Caradoc, and she was captured—that makes her a prisoner of war. That doesn't sit well with me. She got in harm's way for us, and now I want to get her back." He leaned forward and buried his head in his hands. "I just don't know where to start."

"There's always a way," he heard Wills reply. "She came to Red, so Red must know the story..."

"Red's dead," John interrupted as he looked up at him. "He died in Cornwall."

"Oh." Wills frowned. "That's too bad; that does make things more difficult. She didn't mention much about her life to us, but I'm sure we can piece together a trail back, see where it leads. You also might want to search Red's files—I'm sure there's something to go on. But, that will all come in time." Wills leaned over and placed his hand on John's shoulder.

"She's our family now as well as yours, John, and we'll do what we can to help you," he said, looking him full in the eyes. "We're going to find her. We're going to get her back."

Justin nodded in agreement.

As John looked at Wills, he felt the tiniest sliver of hope starting to form. Everyone in Caradoc spoke in admiration of Petya and what she did for them, even over the incredible stench of the bodies and the groans of the wounded. There was even some talk of searching for her, but the task seemed so daunting, so impossible, that he feared by now most had given her up for dead. She would be remembered as a martyr for the barony, may she rest in peace, and life would go on.

Now this man, who John thought only cared for himself, was telling him they *would* find her, and he said it in a way that John believed it.

He suddenly remembered his induction into the Order of Chivalry, when he had taken his first oath to protect the realm. The king's last act, before he was declared a knight, was to buffet John across his cheek. He still remembered his head whipping back from its impact and its sting.

"That will be the last blow," the king had commanded him, "that you will accept unanswered."

Now he looked at Wills and Justin, his surprising new allies. He thought of friends not yet met, because Wills was right— someone *had* sent her, which meant *she* had friends on the government side, and her friends would become his new best friends...as soon as he found them.

This will not go unanswered, he thought. Not by him, but with others to help him, and with some luck...they *would* get her back. This was far from over.

Upon my honor, he vowed to himself...and to her.

Act Four

Chapter Twenty

Hospital Ward
District Tango Headquarters
Location Classified
30 AUG
1031

<u>Lizzy</u>

The first thing that she noticed, even before the ache in her shoulder, was the softness of the mattress beneath her and the coolness of the sheets. She smelled antiseptic and perfume in the air. She immediately knew what that meant.

It was OK, though—Caradoc was safe, and if she escaped once she could do it again. Being here also meant that she would have the best medical care possible, and that she would be fit for full in no time.

For a minute, though, she decided to lay there and enjoy the feeling—she couldn't remember the last time she was in a soft bed like this, even at the Jersey Lily. She thought about finding her way back to Caradoc and seeing John before she went back to Asgard.

So, John, what did *you mean at the AoA?*

Or, even better, maybe she'd just kiss him passionately on sight and just get it the fuck over with. After the time she just had—riding almost non-stop for three days, ducking flying shrapnel and bullets, getting wounded and captured—she owed it to herself.

She tried to nestle in a little, but then the pounding ache in her shoulder got worse. She became aware of the tubes in her arms and around her legs.

And then she felt the straps.

Oh, fuck me. As she came into full awareness, she heard a voice off to her right.

"You might as well open your eyes—I know you're awake, Lizzy."

Lizzy couldn't remember at first why the voice was familiar. Then she did.

Her cloying, sweet perfume...double fuck me. She opened her eyes and looked over to her right.

There, sitting on a chair next to the bed, was Abigail Burgess. She was buffed and polished as usual, in a light pink ensemble with a pink necklace and earrings to match.

But she looked like absolute shit. The pink was a poor color choice—it completely washed out her already pale face. No amount of makeup could hope to remedy that, though Abby had tried with a very liberal hand. She was much thinner than the last time Lizzy had seen her, and her suit hung...strangely, especially on her left side. The left side of her face sagged. Lizzy tried her voice.

"This is awkward," she croaked.

Abby gave her a wide half-smile; the effect was rather gruesome.

"It's *so* good to see you again, Lizzy!" she said brightly. "You lost a lot of blood during transport; I was worried when I first saw you in the emergency room. Even with your injuries, though, you were in better shape than I was when you tried to kill me two years ago, so I shouldn't have been that concerned.

"You were hit twice; one of the bullets embedded in your shoulder, but they removed it. See?" She held up a little vial and shook it; the pellet inside made a rattling sound. "The other shot right above it was a through-and-through."

Lizzy realized that Abby had to slow down and over-pronounce her words to compensate for her palsied face. "What happened to you?"

Abby crossed her right arm over her body to put the vial on Lizzy's nightstand before she answered. "Oh, when you tased me in my office and force-fed me narcotics? I suffered a massive stroke. I lost the entire left side of my body for a while, but I got it back. Just the left side of my face is useless now, but you take what you can get." The half of a smile she could manage was blindingly cheerful.

Lizzy nodded warily. She knew it would be the decent thing to apologize to Abby —at the very least, the polite thing—but she just couldn't do it. This woman forced her to kill her OINC and hadn't cared a shit about the potential body count. "Are you in pain?" she asked instead.

In response, Abby reached over and tightly squeezed Lizzy's shoulder. Thousands of invisible knives impaled themselves across her chest and arm as she gasped for breath.

"Don't scream," Abby warned. "I'll just press in harder."

Black dots swam across Lizzy's field of vision as she bit down on her bottom lip to keep her voice contained. Abby eased her grip, and Lizzy fought against the nausea and panic that was churning inside her. Through the dots, she saw that the composure on Abby's face was already beginning to slip.

Maybe I should just shut up now. She started to feel around for the nurse call button.

"Now, when did you start being concerned about my well-being?" There was a now a twinge of anger in Abby's mostly sunny voice. "Certainly not when you left me for dead in my own excrement, wedged up under my desk. Why start now?"

"And, no one will be coming, my dear." She let go of Lizzy's shoulder and reached down to show her the plug for the call button. "You're at the other end of the hall from the nurses' station—no one will hear you. Your guard just went for a smoke break. Being as incompetent as they all are, you and I will probably have at least ten minutes together before anyone notices something is awry."

There was a faint buzzing in Lizzy's ears as hundreds of hot needles pricked at her shoulder. Abby could do a lot of bodily damage to her in *one* minute, let alone ten, and Lizzy was powerless to stop her. If she provoked her and was very, very lucky, maybe Abby would slit her throat and be done with it— instantaneous death was better than a ten-minute death. Maybe spitting in her eye...

No, she amended, looking into Abby's face; it wasn't going to be that simple. Abby was settled in—she had an agenda. She was obviously excited about performing this monologue, like she had planned it for a long time.

And the more she talked, the more time for someone to come. Lizzy just looked at her, waiting.

Abby continued in her syrupy-sweet voice, "But, this isn't just about me, you know. It's about you, too! I bet you're wondering how we found you so quickly?"

Lizzy nodded.

Abby leaned forward; Lizzy involuntarily flinched. She thought she saw a glint of metal at Abby's left wrist.

"We knew where you were the whole time," Abby whispered into her ear. She sat back up. "Of *course* we kept track of you, Lizzy—you're valuable property! Once you started travelling with those circus players, we would just send someone to go to a show and see how you were doing. Dr. Hart went himself on a few occasions. I had hoped to go, too, someday, but that wasn't in the cards.

"And, *I* was the one who suggested that we keep you out there. Would you like to know why?"

Lizzy nodded again.

Abby's arm shot out again and clamped down on the wound. This time Lizzy let out a short scream as her shoulder went into spasm around Abby's fingers, sizzling pain racing down her arm.

"I told them that it would be easier to contain you out there, rather than in here. Here, you would never cooperate, and in trying to continuously escape you would have gotten yourself killed. You see, *I* care about *you*, Lizzy—I always have." Abby released her shoulder.

Lizzy blinked her eyes to clear the tears. She wished she would faint.

"But, then," Abby was downright bubbly now, "something else happened that I wasn't expecting: you started to enjoy yourself! You were *happy*, Lizzy! I couldn't have arranged a better life for you if I tried. You had your faggot friends and your guitar and even a brand new boyfriend! Acting on stage...meeting people...I have to admit, I got a little jealous when I read some of the reports. Until you got caught up in that battle and almost got yourself killed, you were having the time of your life!

"And you know what, my dear? That made my plan for you *so much better!*"

Abby pushed herself to her feet and reached for the button on her suit jacket. "Because you were happy...because you had such wonderful adventures..." Her button came undone and she shrugged off her jacket. When she bent her left arm to unbutton her blouse, Lizzy saw that her left appendage was a hook. She watched it open and close by itself as she undid the row of buttons.

Abby noticed her staring. "They told me I'd never walk again, Lizzy. My whole left side was dead to me. But then, new prosthetics were developed that are remotely controlled by brain implants. So I asked to have my dead flesh removed, so my body could work again!"

By this time Abby had removed her blouse, and Lizzy could see that she was almost half machine. Her left arm and leg were completely gone, replaced by metal limbs. The appendage she was standing on actually looked like a human foot, complete with realistic-looking toes, but the rest of the leg and the arm were completely made of green and blue titanium. Her bra strap at her shoulder divided where the person ended and the apparatus began. Her limbs were long, twisted rods, and freakishly unnatural in their movement. What made the sight most unnerving, however, were the multitude of wires and thick metal pieces stitched and fused to various places on her torso—to make the unresponsive left side coordinate with the limbs, she figured. The skin around each entry point was red and puckered—they must have been a constant source of irritation.

It was sending Lizzy into a full-blown anxiety attack, seeing Abby like that. She was unreasonably terrified at the sight—she did recognize that—but between the real danger of the situation and her pain and fatigue, she felt it nonetheless. She was becoming unhinged; she needed to calm down somehow...

"They haven't quite mastered fingers yet," Abby explained, snapping the hook opened and closed in front of her. "But I have gotten quite adept at using my hook, so I'll wait." She leaned over Lizzy again.

"When I woke up from the coma you sent me into, I made myself three promises. I promised myself I would walk again: I have." Abby reached over with her hand and carefully peeled back the shoulder bandage while Lizzy fruitlessly pulled against the straps.

"*Fuck*—somebody help!" Lizzy shouted. "Fire! There's a fucking fire in here!"

"Don't make me gag you, Lizzy—you might suffocate," Abby said. "I promised myself that you would suffer."

There was an audible *thwick* as Abby thrust her hook right through one of the bullet holes in the shoulder, ripping through the already-broken skin. Lizzy felt herself detach from her body for a moment as the woman twisted the claw counter-clockwise, tearing muscle and tissue as blood spurted into the air. Lizzy screamed as her entire arm went into spasm, and she felt the warm stickiness of her blood seep through the gown. Despite everything, she managed one brief moment of clarity and looked at her monitors through blurry eyes: her heart rate and pulse were dangerously high.

"And, you don't even know the half of it yet!" Abby said, half-beaming, pulling her hook away with a sucking *squick*. She raised her voice a little so she could be heard. "You're going to the other side of the continent! Upon my recommendation you will be taken far, far away from here, and you will be confined to your new base—no more field trips for *you*, young lady!"

"You will be experimented upon, made to perform, and you *will* do as you are told," she continued as she wiped her claw on one of the bed sheets. "There is no underground system there— yes, we know about *that*, too—so there will be no escape."

"Shut the fuck up and kill me!" Lizzy gasped, giving up on rescue. *"Bitch!"* It was getting harder to breathe...

"Best of all," Abby continued, ignoring her completely, "the place I have chosen for you, Echo Headquarters, is a real shithole; you should feel right at home there. And you will have *so many* opportunities to impress them with your abilities—they have one of the largest quantities of Infected tissue, living and dead, in the country!"

Lizzy thought she heard voices in the hallway, but she didn't care anymore. Everything was getting fuzzy...slipping...

Abby
=====

Abby heard the voices, too; she began putting her blouse back on.

"But do you know the best part?" she continued, watching Lizzy's eyes roll into the back of her head. "I will get monthly reports about you. I will read, in detail, how desolate you will become. How you will slowly shrivel up and wither under such isolated confinement and unmerciful experimentation. You won't last a year, I doubt. And, what a pity, knowing the whole time that your friends have continued their lives right on without you. And, they will, Lizzy—they already have." She made the saddest half-frowny face she could manage, then half-smiled again.

"But before *that* happens, I will know how many times a day your throat bleeds because of your consistent vomiting from exposure to demon flesh, how many Infected specimens you will be forced to burn. Your psychological evaluations will describe in detail how you're coping with disintegrating live subjects over and over and over again!" She leaned down next to Lizzy's ear, making sure she heard this last part—it was the most important of all.

"You will suffer there, and I will read about it as it happens. That was my third promise to myself: I get to watch."

With that—*right on cue!*—Lizzy finally slumped into unconsciousness, the new wound on her shoulder still pouring out blood.

Abby was very pleased—she *finally* had her say, and her little Sensor had heard all of it. She hoped she didn't just ruin everything by causing a fatal wound, but if Lizzy could survive in the Wilderness for two years...why, she could live under even the most extreme circumstances!

What a strong girl she is, she thought almost admirably. Abby was certain that she would have reading material for a good long time to come. She finished buttoning her blouse and glanced over her shoulder as two nurses rushed through the door.

One nurse walked straight to Lizzy's bedside, took one look at her shoulder, and then ran to the phone next to the bed.

"Get your hand on that!" she yelled to the other nurse. She picked up the receiver and dialed some numbers, talking into the phone urgently.

The other nurse sped over and pressed her hand down over the wound, working frantically with the other hand to push the necessary buttons to lower Lizzy's head and raise her legs.

"Tell them she's unresponsive and in shock!" When the other nurse saw clearly the sopping mess of blood soaking through the patient's dressing and gown, her mouth tightened.

"Ms. Burgess, I'll have to ask you..."

"That's OK, nurse, I was just leaving!" Her hook left a smear of blood on the front of her blouse. Abby picked up her jacket and half-smiled at Lizzy's prone form.

"It was *so* good to talk you again, Lizzy! Enjoy your rehabilitation at Echo." She turned on her heel and walked haltingly out the door.

District Echo Headquarters
Location Classified
12 SEP
1935

<u>Emily</u>

"Now, Dr. Peterson, your presence is requested at the receiving dock. Dr. Peterson, receiving dock."

Emily looked up from her paperwork and checked her wall clock.

Too late at night for a delivery. She rose from her desk and made her way to the receiving dock. When she got outside, however, she was surprised to see two soldiers unloading a gurney from the back of a truck. The person on the gurney—it looked like a woman—was hooked up to IVs, with wide restraint straps spanned across her body.

What the... "What's going on, please?"

"Are you the OOD?" One of the soldiers asked.

"Yes."

The other soldier picked up the thickest medical folder she had ever seen from the gurney and passed it to her. She needed both hands to hold onto it.

"This is Petty Officer Elizabeth Townsend, Extreme Sensor and currently in altered mental status—big time. She's been transferred here."

Emily felt a twinge of alarm at the words *Extreme Sensor* and even more alarm at the phrase *altered mental status* as she looked down at Townsend. The woman was quietly sobbing, slightly hyperventilating, and she didn't seem to be registering what was

449

going on around her. It also looked like she hadn't showered in days. If she was that powerful a Sensor, it was a wonder that she wasn't unconscious—the pain of just being *on the dock* must have been excruciating.

"We are not equipped to handle someone like this!" she protested. "This woman needs to be at a psychiatric facility!"

The soldier that gave her the folder shrugged. "Look," he glanced at her collar device, "Doc, we're just the delivery service. We were told to take her here, and we have. What you do with her from here is your business."

She looked at Townsend's eyes; they were glassy. "What's she on?"

"A minimal amount of Percocet—it's the only thing we brought that keeps her calm, plus she has a really ugly shoulder wound that must hurt like hell. She wants a lot more, but we wouldn't give it to her—we gave her just enough so she wouldn't keep screaming at us."

"When was the last time she ate?"

"We made her drink a protein shake about two hours ago. Look, with all due respect, Doc, we'd really like to start getting back to Tango—where can we put her?"

Tango? She wasn't even sure where that was—west coast, maybe? "OK, let's get her to the infirmary."

Once the paperwork was signed and the soldiers were gone, Emily sat next to the bedside of the newest member of their permanent party. She placed the dictionary-thick file by Townsend's feet and opened it to the first page. Once she confirmed she was indeed an Extreme Sensor, she stopped reading to push the nurse's call button next to the bed and order an IV bag with a 50 mg/hr drip of D-ance.

"I'm sorry, ma'am—did you say a *fifty* milligram drip?"

Emily sighed—she wasn't sure if it was too much, either, but she was flying blind here—she'd never met a Sensor so attuned. "Yes, as soon as it can be made." She continued reading as nurses came and went, occasionally glancing up at Townsend— sometimes to check her status, sometimes in amazement, but mostly in utter disbelief.

They *really* were not equipped to handle someone like this. According to her file, the highlights were that she accidently killed her OINC while making...*an entire pool!*...of holy water, severely injured a member of the senior staff at Tango while somehow escaping the facility, and was on the run for over two *years* before she was shot twice in the shoulder and recaptured several days ago.

How did she survive out there? she wondered. *And, why did they send her* here?

Just then, Townsend seemed to come back to reality. She looked over at Emily.

"Echo?" she asked. Her voice was scratchy.

"Yes, you're at Echo headquarters. I'm Dr. Emily Peterson—I'm a psychologist. How are you feeling?"

Townsend squeezed her eyes shut as she arched her back as much as the straps would allow. "I'm here, in straps, with a ripped shoulder," she gasped. "I'm trying to stay here, Doc, but it's so hard..."

"What do you mean?"

"Pain—hard to concentrate." She choked on a sob. "Please—Demerol helps, I don't care on Demerol, please..." Her face contorted as tears streamed down her face.

Wow, Townsend was a mess. Emily wasn't sure where to begin. "We're giving you D-ance through the IV, which is a demon necrosis medication—is it helping with the nausea?"

"It's...hard to tell. I haven't wanted to eat since Tango." She swallowed. "Don't want anything from here—I want to go home. Wills...Justin..." She started to cry harder.

She stayed with people, apparently... Well, time to start with the basics.

"What would you do if I removed the straps?" Emily asked.

Lizzy

I'm never going to sleep again I'm trapped TRAPPED I can't move can't shift GOD MY SHOULDER pain god the pain I don't want to be here no one to save me SOMEONE PLEASE SAVE ME oh god oh god the wave's coming again no no please NO...

She hung on as best she could through yet another crash of panic and fear. She could almost see the swirls of emotion in her mind as she tried to stay sane.

451

Lizzy had been so wired the past few days on adrenaline and pain that she could only sleep when she passed out from utter exhaustion, and then in her perception she would wake up in agony only a second later never dreaming, never sleeping. Her body felt itchy and hot, and she constantly wanted to crawl out of her skin.

Abby had fucked her perfectly—she had no clue where she was, and she absolutely believed that there was no possible way to get home. And then there was this *fucking* ticker tape...

Like delirium...

Delirium. Dream...like the Endless....

Dream, who controlled the nightmares and the cats and the Fiddler's Green...

Oh, god...Fiddler's Green... She felt new tears roll down her cheeks. She'd never see them again, never see any of them again...

No one can save me no one can help me never sleep no sleeping... The mantra began again as the tide rolled out, gearing up for another push.

"Elizabeth, what would happen if I removed the straps?" Lizzy heard again, coming from somewhere over the ticker tape.

I don't know KILL MYSELF? I want to sleep can't sleep... She forced herself to focus.

"Maybe not a good idea," she managed to say to the woman at her bedside. "Can I try some water?"

"Sure." The woman stood up... *What was her name again?*...and got a cup of water from the sink. She put a straw in the cup and offered it to Lizzy. It tasted good, and it seemed to stay down. The ticker tape droned on in her brain: *someone save me will anyone remember I was ever alive NO THEY'RE GOING TO FORGET YOU THEY'VE FORGOTTEN YOU ALREADY! THEY'VE ALL FORGOTTEN YOU AND YOU NEVER FOUND OUT never sleep never sleep again FUCK THIS SHOULDER!...*

"Who are Wills and Justin?" the woman asked.

To answer the doctor's question, the ticker tape pushed past Lizzy's defenses and did the talking for her.

"NO! No, you can't know my secrets you can't have them THEY'RE MINE because secrets have power but ONLY if you keep them secret, if you speak them aloud they lose their power AND I

CAN'T, I HAVE TO REMEMBER THEM I'VE LOST THEM GOD I
SAID THEIR NAMES ALOUD..."

At that moment, her entire field of vision was filled with this
woman's face. She was scary.

"SNAP OUT OF IT!" the woman screamed into her face. "I
think I've given you too much D-ance, Petty Officer Townsend; I'm
going to dial it back. I'm also making the executive decision to
give you enough Demerol to drop a horse, which will help with the
shoulder pain and the Sensor nausea until you've stabilized and
CALMED THE FUCK DOWN!" The woman straightened up. "I'm
also going to authorize soft belts for your wrists and ankles,
which should also make you more comfortable." She sighed.

Lizzy just stared at her. The ticker tape had diminished to
quiet background noise as the woman spoke...even the ticker tape
was scared of her...

"Try and get some sleep," the woman told her. "I don't know
why you're here, but you're here now, and we'll try to make a fit."
She turned and left the room.

The ticker tape then grew back to its normal volume, and
didn't stop rambling until an hour later, when the Demerol finally
kicked in.

Demerol...my old friend... Lizzy thought as she finally drifted
off to sleep.

District Echo Headquarters
Location Classified
08 OCT
0828

HS2/9 David Lundberg

"You're going to have to hold her hand under the water,
Tavis," David said into the microphone that carried his voice over
to the loudspeaker in the next room.

Tavis reached down and grasped Townsend's wrist, who was
sitting in a chair next to him. David could hear him tell her

453

something like, "Sorry, I don't want to hurt you..." as he pulled her hand towards the basin.

David heaved a sigh. From what he knew about people who could make holy water—all second-hand knowledge from medical journals—they all started out the same way: gung-ho to burn, baby, burn. Then some of them lose the taste for it, and they don't want to do it anymore. Unfortunately, that's when coercion had to come in.

He personally had never seen anyone actually make holy water—he had just watched the standard training videos. He watched in curiosity as Tavis lowered her hand into the water, right next to a cube of rotting skin.

Nothing happened. Everyone, including Townsend, looked surprised.

Tavis raised her hand out of the water and tried again, like he was trying to reconnect a circuit. Not a wisp of smoke or a single bubble was seen.

Tavis let go of her hand. She actually kept it there for a few moments before removing it, the expression on her face one of confused disbelief. The corpsman looked up at the microphone in the ceiling.

"Are we sure this cube is Infected?" he asked the air.

"Oh, it's Infected," Townsend assured the corpsman. They both ignored her.

"It's from a verified batch," David announced to the room. "Shall we try a bigger piece?"

"I guess so," Tavis agreed as Townsend grimaced and visibly swallowed. "Bring a whole finger."

David reached behind him and grabbed a vacuum-sealed, plastic-wrapped male finger and walked to the door, peeling back the edges until half the digit was exposed to the air. He opened the door and passed off the body part to Tavis. David watched him walk back over to the basin, peel the plastic some more, and then dump the finger into the water. A little of it splashed on Townsend.

"Hey, man—what the fuck?" She tried to brush off the water that had landed on her shirt.

"You'll live," Tavis told her. "Let's try again." He didn't even apologize this time, just grabbed her wrist again and placed it into the water. Nothing. After about twenty minutes and three more additional pieces of Infected material, Tavis told her to take a break and knocked on the door to get out of the room.

"I don't get it," he said to David when they were in the observation room. "Didn't the reports say she could do this?"

"Yeah," he said slowly. "Though, it was in a pool with a lot of other people. Are you thinking what I'm thinking?" They watched her stick her hand in the water several times, shaking her head.

"It wasn't her?" Tavis looked as puzzled as Townsend. "But, *she* even thinks she's the one who did it! Has she made any more since then?"

"No. For some reason, they never made her do it when she was being processed—maybe because she's so sensitive—and there was no further attempts until the pool incident. Then they got all hot and bothered about testing her abilities and she ran, I guess."

"OK," David said, opening the door.

"You can stop, Townsend," he called to her. He shut the door again.

"Could it be the meds she's on?" Tavis asked him.

"No—meds have no effect on holy water production."

"Could she be...controlling it, somehow?"

David paused, and then shook his head. "According to all the books and the journals, none of them can control it—once there's Infected material, the juice turns on. When the material is ashes, the juice turns off, end of story. If there was a way to turn it off, one of the resistant ones would have done it by now, I think."

He glanced at Townsend, who was now wiping her hand on her pant leg.

Ew. "Anything is possible, but she's pretty convincing if she's conning us."

"Well, the officers won't be happy about this."

"Nope." David turned around to grab towels and plastic containers. "We can try again in another day, but I think they picked the wrong person at Tango that night."

"So, we're stuck with a grouchy-bitch coastie that gets sick off of demon flesh, but isn't actually *useful* to us in any way?"

"Guess so."

Dr. Donald Hart

Abby isn't going to like this. He knocked on the door of Abigail Burgess' office.

"Come in," he heard her say. He walked in to find her at her desk, typing on her computer with one hand. She smiled that macabre grin at him.

"Donald, hello! What can I help you with?"

He took a breath. "We just got a report from Echo about Lizzy Townsend with some very disappointing news." He handed the file to her. "She can't make holy water."

She stopped mid-motion, the folder in midair between them. "That's impossible." She jerked the folder towards her, opened it, and began to read.

"They tried three different times, with three different batches," he summarized for her. "They even replicated almost the exact conditions in *their* pool with a live subject—nothing. We got the wrong person that night, Abby—our creator is still out there."

Abby ignored him, reading the entire report in silence until she had finished the last page. Donald waited.

"This can't be right," she insisted. "She's...figured out a way to control it, turn it on and off..."

"No Sensor that we know about," he began firmly, "or have ever heard of, can control the energy. They are merely a conduit for whatever energy does the...cleansing." Donald had never been comfortable with that term, but he didn't know what else to call it. "There have been people who have been doing this since the beginning, who have *wanted* to reduce it down, but no one can."

"But..."

"*Plus*," he interrupted, "we have no evidence that she's made holy water since that night. Hell, *she* was even visibly surprised that she couldn't do it. Occam's razor would say that it wasn't her, that someone else was actually doing it that night, and she only *looked* like she was doing it. Convincingly so," he had seen the tapes several times, "but the evidence now rules her out."

"Don't worry," he said, observing the anger and disappointment in her face, "she's staying there—she can still be of assistance to them as an Extreme Sensor, I'm sure."

Half of her mouth scrunched up in thought. "Have they tried it with her unconscious?"

"No, Abby, and I don't think they're going to." *Jesus, woman, would you just drop it?* "We still have plenty of creators around, and she's staying there at your request." He reached over and carefully removed the folder from her hand.

"I'm going to start going back over the list of who was in the room that night, specifically who was in the pool. Don't worry, Abby, we'll get to the bottom of this." He turned and walked out of the room, very glad that *that* was over with.

Room 124
District Echo Headquarters
Location Classified
21 JAN
0935

Lizzy

She was sitting in Emily's office again, talking about cutting her Demerol...again.

Fuck her.

"Why should we?" Lizzy asked her for what seemed like the thousandth time. "It makes life tolerable, I can drink those shakes without throwing up, and I even can do my maintenance job around here..."

"See, you really can't, though," Emily replied. "You space out, and your quality of work is in the toilet. You don't talk to anyone except when you absolutely have to. Plus, Demerol isn't meant for long-term use. We need to try something else to stabilize your condition."

457

"Not interested," Lizzy replied. "We've been through this before. Even with D-ance I feel like ass, and I'll be dead in a year or two." She pulled on her hair, which was cropped to jaw length. "See the grey?" She showed the psychologist her arms. "Slightest hint of yellow, even on that Chtah stuff—I'll be on dialysis eventually. You're stuck with me; I'm stuck here.

"I lived more in those two years than most people live in a lifetime, well-loved, with only one unanswered question. I'm good."

Emily glared at her—she got very frustrated with the indifference shtick. "I could just cut you off."

"I die quicker," Lizzy replied, shrugging, which is what she always said. She waited for the inevitable dismissal with no change in treatment.

Emily just looked at her in silence for a full minute. Then, her eyes filled with mischief.

"*Are* you stuck here?" she asked her.

This isn't how it goes... "What are you talking about?"

The psychologist smiled at her. "C'mon, escape artist, let's play a game. What do you need to bust out of here?"

It was impossible, so what the hell. She thought about it for a minute. "I'd need a vehicle, a means of escape."

"OK. What else?"

"To know where we are in relation to where I'd want to go." An unwelcomed clarification popped into her mind as her eyes suddenly filled with tears: *anywhere on a stage, with the Players...*

Damn it! The sudden emotional response to thinking about them was barely contained by the Demerol, but she managed to secure it back down.

She and Emily spoke in the hypothetical for several minutes about escaping, discussing the finer points of cutting the building's communications and whether or not she could manage to arm herself before she left. Though Lizzy knew deep down that it was useless, she did find herself vaguely interested in playing along, probably because it was the one thing in that place that she gave a shit about.

By now, Emily was *en fuego*. She geared up to drop her shrink bomb. "When you get there, at this place..." She paused for effect. "What is the unanswered question you want to ask?"

Direct hit. She never talked about the SCA—she never talked about anything in her past, even Commune Ruth—but Lizzy decided to say it. It was the only thing that really caused her regret, so maybe admitting it would make her feel better about it.

"The questions cannot be answered *there*...but near there." She paused for several moments...what *would* the question be, exactly? Finally, she had the wording right.

"Do you feel the same way about me...that I feel for you?"

Unfortunately, she did not feel any better about confessing aloud that she cared. In fact, she realized with growing despair, it was now *more* painful, because now she had to finally acknowledge that *was* going to die at Echo, and John would never know how she felt. The one man she was attracted to *and* that she could trust since her husband died, and she'd never see him again.

But then, he never showed an interest in me, anyway. God, this hurts...

Then she suddenly remembered—these sessions went into a file that went to Tango, which is why she was usually very careful about what she said to Emily.

Shit and fuck me! Well, Lizzy was sure Abby would have a grand old time reading about *this* conversation. She felt her anger begin to build as she considered that she was too stupid to be let loose. *Maybe getting off the Demerol* is *a good idea. I'm getting sloppy...*

Emily's ability to pick on non-verbal cues was not good. She was, in practice, a mediocre counselor. She also was wrapped up in her therapeutic *ah-ha!* moment, so she was oblivious to Lizzy's pain as she smiled back, extending the moment, allowing the question to linger in the air.

"That, Petty Officer Townsend," she said with a hint of triumph, "is something worth living for."

Instantly, Lizzy saw nothing but red and glimmering stars as her entire body exploded in rage at the futility of it all. She called Emily every vulgar name she could think of and left.

Lizzy knocked on Emily's opened office door. She wasn't going to apologize, but...

"What is killing me, exactly?" she asked from the doorway.

"The D-ance and the Demerol, directly," Emily replied after a pause. "But if you were off those meds, you wouldn't be able to keep food down, so indirectly the Infected material here would kill you.

"But," she leaned forward on her desk, "with cognitive behavioral therapy and some mindfulness techniques, we may be able to help you deal with the nausea enough to wean you off the Demerol and the D-ance, or at least get you on something else less toxic."

Lizzy considered Emily's words. Her first thought was that, even though Emily was a crap therapist, she was a good-hearted person with a lot of patience, thank god. Her second thought was that it all sounded like complete psychobabble horseshit.

But... She gestured to the chair nearest the door, silently asking to sit. Emily nodded. She sat down and leaned back into the chair.

"If I'm dead, I can't get out," she said simply. "What do you want me to do?"

Chapter Twenty-one

District Echo Headquarters
Location Classified
16 JUN
1445

She wasn't sure what was wrong, but something was definitely up. The technicians were all a little more twitchy than usual over the past two days; the doctors were distracted. She knew better than to ask, so she decided to wait—if it was important, she'd find out eventually.

Sure enough, about fifteen minutes ago HS2/10 Siegel had come into the lab and told her that she was to report to sub-room 22. She quickly put the microscope that she had been working on back in its box and made her way to the grimy underground passages.

As she descended down the stairs to the sub-rooms, she could feel herself getting nauseous, and not just because of the Infused materials: they kept the whole, conscious subjects on the 2 deck, as far away from the general population as could be managed.

This was her first visit to that floor. She had hoped that she never would have to go down there.

She pulled on the fire door at the bottom of the steps and was temporarily blinded by the white walls and bright overhead lights of the passageway behind the door—an intense contrast to the low-watt bulbs and dingy green walls of the stairwell. When her eyes adjusted, she saw a corporal sitting behind a metal desk in front of an electronically-locked door; she noted that the hinges were on her side. The soldier looked up from a log book.

"Are you Townsend?" he asked.

Lizzy nodded.

The corporal stood. "Just a minute." He walked over to a number pad mounted to the right of the door, about chest level.

The pad made several *boop* and *beep* noises as the man keyed in the door's entry code. There was a *click*, and the man pulled on the door handle, swinging it opened. As he did, a stench of shit, puke, and decay washed over them while Lizzy concentrated on her breathing.

"This way," the soldier said. He walked through the door and down an equally pristine white corridor; Lizzy followed. At the third door on the right, he stopped and knocked. A few moments later, Lizzy saw the doorknob turn, and a rather large man that Lizzy had never seen before slipped out. He was disheveled, his curly-brown hair waved about in several directions, and his shabby lab coat sported more than a few stains. There were dark circles under his eyes and about a week's worth of patchy beard growth on his cheeks. Lizzy could say without fear of contradiction that the man looked like hell.

"Townsend?" he asked.

"Yes, sir." Lizzy replied.

"I'm Dr. Patrick Kestenbaum, the lead researcher here." He stuck out a meaty right hand.

Lizzy blinked. She then remembered her manners and took it. "Pleased to meet you." Dr. Kestenbaum's grip felt like a dead fish; she let go.

"How are you feeling?" He looked at her face as he might examine a patient. "Are you overly queasy here?"

Lizzy shook her head. "I was allowed to take my meds this morning, and I've been working on mindfulness techniques with Dr. Paterson. As long as I pay attention, it's tolerable."

Dr. Kestenbaum nodded. "OK." He turned to the soldier. "You can go back to your post. I've got her from here."

The corporal nodded and went back down the hallway.

Dr. Kestenbaum reopened the door. Inside, Lizzy could see that it was an observation room. On the opposite wall there was a large picture window that Lizzy could see through. In the next room there were two figures: one restrained in a reclining chair, the other standing. The standing figure was wearing a lab coat and looked rather ordinary. The seated figure, on the other hand, was the most bloated, disgusting human being that Lizzy had ever seen. She entered the observation room to take a closer look.

The seated man—Lizzy guessed it still could be considered a man—was at least 400 pounds of fat and water weight. There

462

were gaping sores on his arms, legs, and torso that oozed streaks of blood and pus down his marbled limbs and the metric shit-ton of tubes coming in and out of his body. The man wore a simple examination gown, so there wasn't much of his physique left to the imagination. From the vacant look on his face, Lizzy deduced that he was possessed. The tubes were attached to various machines and computers, though he seemed to be breathing on his own. Lizzy wondered how he was able to sit, instead of having to lie down.

"Who is he?" Lizzy asked.

"His name is...was...Juan Molina. I can't tell you much about him, except that he is maybe the fifth Infected person we know of that the demons have been able to make speak."

Lizzy studied the doctor for a long moment, and then turned back to Molina. "No shit? That's scary—and new to me."

Dr. Kestenbaum nodded. "According to the demons, who call themselves 'Chisel,' they number about 10,000 in that one body. The sheer number integrating together makes it possible, apparently."

"What has he...they...said so far?"

"Not much so far. They said their name, how many were in there, and..." he stopped. Lizzy looked back at him.

"And...they asked for you."

Well they would, wouldn't they? Lizzy thought grimly, rolling her eyes. *Why is it always me? What the fuck...*

"No," Lizzy said, "I have no idea why they would ask for me. I was attacked by one of them over three years ago, but I'm not their buddy or anything. Hell, I thought I killed a bunch of them at Tango Headquarters..." She could feel herself getting riled up, which was not helping her manage her nausea. She took a controlled breath and centered herself again.

"So, is this the part where you say that they won't talk to anyone but me?"

Dr. Kestenbaum stared at her. "Yes, that's exactly what they said. How did you know?"

"Because I'm getting the idea that these guys have a sick flair for the dramatic." She crossed her arms and examined Molina through the glass again.

"So, shall I talk to them? Is there anything you want me to say?"

"No—we'll be taping everything. Just get them to talk for now. We have Mr. Molina stabilized for the time being, and we expect that we can keep him viable for at least two months, maybe more."

Lizzy took another controlled breath, let it out, and then reached for the door handle.

The smell inside the inner room was beyond description. It was clear that the man was actively rotting, but Lizzy knew from working at Tango Alpha Laboratory that the doctors had chemicals to keep the blood of the Infected oxygen-rich and hinder the natural bacteria in the body that craved to finish its natural cycle of putrefaction. Surprisingly, Lizzy did not feel any worse for being in the room—maybe past a certain number of demons the Sensor reaction remained constant. She'd have to ask Chisel about that.

She also wasn't at all afraid. The body that the demons possessed was frail and restrained well. And, after all these years, Lizzy figured that if they had wanted to possess her, they would have done it by now.

Juan Molina—Chisel—looked up at her. The eyes were milky-white, but they seemed to still work.

"*You are Elizabeth Townsend.*" Chisel's collective voice was deep, gravelly, and unsteady, but they could be understood. They sounded like the long gasps of a dying man, stretched over time.

"Yes," Lizzy replied. She still wasn't afraid, but the voice made her shiver.

"*You look different from...the last time we met.*"

Lizzy ran her fingers through her cropped hair. "I suppose. You guys sure get around, don't you?"

"*We do.*" Chisel looked at Dr. Kestenbaum and the other man. "*Leave us.*"

Dr. Kestenbaum nodded to Lizzy. "We'll be right outside." The two men left the room, closing the door behind them. There was an extra chair in the room, but Lizzy chose to stand.

"So, what would you like to talk about?"

Chisel gave her what almost looked like a chastising expression. "*Come now, Petty Officer Townsend, you surely have some questions for us first?*"

"OK...why am I not fainting on the floor, if there are 10,000 of you?"

Chisel paused, and then shrugged. Molina's tubes bobbed and shifted. "*We can only guess that, after a point, the numbers become...irrelevant.*"

"Yeah, that's what I thought, too. Nice use of our nonverbal gestures, by the way. Y'all sure do have a good vocabulary for a bunch of sadistic, murdering cocksuckers."

Chisel seemed to ponder that for a moment; the only sounds in the room were the soft *whurrs* and *clicks* of the machines. "*We have evolved since we were first given our chance at redemption. We care very much about the...possibility of living as you do.*"

Lizzy tasted bile in her mouth. "Never going to happen. I saw your little experiments at Zion, assholes—you failed horribly."

"*It is only a matter of time.*"

"What makes you so goddamn sure?"

Chisel sighed; Molina's tubes creaked in reply. "*Have not you ever wondered where we come from?*"

Lizzy considered this for a moment. "Hell?"

"*In a matter of speaking. It is actually a large energy chasm filled—packed—with souls. We all exist there, forced to spend eternity without feeling, without any sensation. It is hell, Petty Officer Townsend.*

"*Since we can remember, however, we have been able to come into your world, to inhabit a body and to feel all of the sensations your race takes for granted. But it takes a lot of energy to break through the barrier, and we were too...primitive...to fully appreciate what we had. Our nature is to seek out sensation, no matter pleasurable or painful, though pain is easier to acquire. Inevitably, the body would die, or a human with the capacity would drive us out, and we would return to our prison.*

"*But something has changed in this place. We discovered, on that day you call 'Infusion,' that we could enter this plane more freely than we ever could before, and that live blood could carry us from body to body. We now could travel freely, and for the first few years we gloried in our new-found independence. We ravished, we rampaged, we felt and experienced until we were drunk with it.*

"*But then, when we were finally sated and we realized that the human race could not impede us in any meaningful manner, we began to consider that perhaps we could stay permanently. We*

465

now seek to make this place our home: to leave the nothingness, integrate with this plane, and become sentient. We feel ourselves grow stronger here with every passing year, even though we conserve our strength and do not frequent here as we did. We instead study the knowledge that was passed to us when we joined with human hosts. We are fluent in every language on the face of the earth, we know the intricacies of the human struggle, and we know many secrets.

"But, most importantly, we are learning that we could be better than you, that you do not deserve, as a race, what you have: your history of warmongering, neglect, and environmental destruction has shown that to us. We have learned from your mistakes, Petty Officer Townsend, and we will make a better go of living. This is Paradise, and we intend to become its devoted stewards."

All at once, Lizzy thought of the movie *Gremlins 2* and the Brain Gremlin, the super-intelligent spokesperson for the otherwise-senseless gremlin population. She pondered asking Chisel if they were familiar with the movie, and wasn't this situation a funny parallel, but then she decided that the situation was really too full of *gravitas* to mention it.

It then also occurred to her that her grasp of reality might finally be slipping, and that engaging an alien-soul population in a conversation about *Gremlins 2* might be compelling evidence of that. She forced herself to focus on the task at hand.

"It sounds like you have it all figured out." Lizzy said to the demons. "In fact, you're scaring me shitless. What do you want?"

Chisel attempted a smirk; it was actually rather convincing.

"*Would you like to know where your husband is?*" Chisel asked.

Chapter Twenty-two

Sub-Room 22
District Echo Headquarters
Location Classified
16 JUN
1526

Lizzy stopped breathing. Of all the things the demons could have said, she couldn't have guessed that. Her face lost feeling. She purposefully took a breath, and eased herself down into the chair.

"What do you mean?" Lizzy asked.

"*We mean,*" the demons replied, "*That we know exactly where your husband is. And, he's alive.*"

"Prove it."

Chisel paused then, and for a moment seemed lost in thought. Then they spoke.

"*Brydan Samuel Townsend, Machinery Technician, Second Class Petty Officer of the United States Coast Guard. You met on-board the Coast Guard Cutter Buzzard Bay. You were married in Newport News, VA, in a civil ceremony.*"

"You're not impressing me," Lizzy interrupted. "There were a ton of people who knew that. I'll ask you a question, something only Brydan would know."

Chisel nodded.

"What was the name of our child?"

Chisel paused for several moments, looking at the floor. Then they spoke. "*You never carried an infant to term...as far as he knew...but you were with child once.*"

Lizzy felt sick; a panic attack was building.

"The unborn child was almost three months into the gestation process when it died. You insisted that you know the gender of the fetus, and you named the child...Shayna."

Lizzy's chest tightened while a cold chill raced through her. It was a good thing that she was seated, because her legs would have failed her, and she would have sunk to the floor.

The demons paused. *"Brydan did not know this, but that word means "beautiful" in the Yiddish language. It is a name for a female."*

"Then...he's Infected."

"Yes."

Lizzy broke down and began to cry. "Yes," she whispered. "It's all true. Oh, god..."

Because her periods were always irregular, she didn't know she was pregnant. She had gone on a southern patrol, and then went to visit Brydan during his dry dock in Savannah. She had woken up early on the third morning with agonizing cramps; the sheets on the hotel bed were already soaked with blood. The anonymous nurse at the contracted civilian clinic told her that the fetus had been ten weeks along, and that she was very sorry. It had been the only time in her life that Lizzy had carried another life inside her, and she had been utterly and completely cheated; they had both mourned for their lost baby. The memories of that day, that at this abomination had spoken her little girl's name aloud, and that Brydan was still alive, but possessed, were all too overwhelming. Plus...

Oh my god—I cheated on him! I didn't know he was still alive! Shit! Lizzy didn't know how to handle all of this. Then she looked up.

Chisel was showing their teeth—it was an attempt at a grin, Lizzy was sure of it. They were watching her cry, and they seemed highly entertained by it. Lizzy's sorrow instantly turned to rage.

That's better. She stuffed her emotions back down for the time being and got back to the issue at hand.

"Yes, then, goatfuckers," Lizzy said, wiping her face with her sleeve and taking a breath. "I would like to know where he is." Then, as soon as she said those words, another thought began to dawn upon her.

"He is occupied," the demons reminded her.

She ignored Chisel for the moment, slowly realizing that the doctors were being very quiet back there, considering what was being said—they should be shooing her out by now. She turned her head and looked back at the two-way mirror.

"They're dead, aren't they?" Lizzy asked. She went over and tapped on the glass. No answer.

Fuck me... she caught herself beginning to hyperventilate; she slowed her breathing. She was trapped with the demons, and now was not the time to succumb to her Sensing.

"*We cannot have any witness to our conversation,*" Chisel explained, "*regardless of the outcome. All tapes will be erased, so please...speak freely.*" The demons swallowed, which looked like it took some doing. "*We have more to say, but this mouth is dry. Would you?*" Chisel motioned with Molina's eyes to a cup on a small table with some plastic sticks poking out.

Lizzy walked to the table and picked out a water-soaked sponge swab from the cup. She then reached over and placed it inside Molina's mouth. The demons closed the mouth over it and sucked a little as she held it. When Chisel asked for more, she complied. It was the most normal event that had happened since she arrived on 2 deck, and at the same time the most fucked up. She did her best to pretend it was Juan Molina she was giving aid to and not the psychopathic monsters inside. When Chisel was finally done, Lizzy stepped back.

"As we were saying," Chisel said, swallowing again, but this time with less effort. "*Your...husband is occupied. Does this change your resolve to see him?*"

Lizzy pondered this, but then made the snap decision that being Infected didn't matter. If he was breathing, and they could read his mind, there was hope. She would find a way to exorcise him—she could make holy water, couldn't she? Maybe she could get him back.

"How long has he been down?"

Chisel twitched; they might have been trying to shake their head. "*A while. We don't know exactly how long.*"

"Fair enough. What now?"

Chisel showed their teeth again. "*We would ask that you kill us.*"

"I don't understand."

"We cannot leave until a body is dead, we have access to a fresh body, or enough pain is inflicted that we are forced to leave. We would do it ourselves, but..." They glanced down at the restraints.

"It seems our captors will be able to keep this body going for some time, and we really have...other things to do."

"All right," she said. "But, how are you going to tell me how to get to Brydan? I don't know my way around; I don't even know where Echo is."

"We can show you."

Lizzy paused. "OK...how?"

"When you kill us," Chisel explained, *"You will make us bleed out, and you will cut yourself, as well. When our blood mingles, one of us shall come into you and implant what you need to know. Then, our brother will leave back through the wound. It will be almost...instantaneous."*

"How do I know you won't just Infect me?"

"You don't," they replied. *"But, you going to your husband suits our purposes, too. Let's just say that, in this case, your government is our common enemy, and..."* Chisel paused, searching.

"The enemy of our enemy is our friend."

An alliance with the demons was not something she thought she'd be doing when she woke up this morning. Lizzy was glad once again she was sitting down—this day was seriously exceeding her weird shit quota.

"How am I supposed to kill you?" she asked. "I have no weapon. Plus, they have me locked down—I can't get out."

"Leave that to us," Chisel said. *"And, you have glasses in your front pocket. That will do the job."*

Lizzy reached down and pulled out her reading glasses; one of the side effects of D-ance was astigmatism.

"Yes, I do." She popped out the left lens and placed it on the floor. She then lifted her chair, aimed one of the back legs over the lens, and fell. Her butt hit the chair with a *thud*, and then she heard the glass snap. She looked down: the two lens halves were sitting on the floor, on either side of the chair leg, with just a hint of glass dust. She picked up the sharper-looking half. She looked at Chisel.

"What about Juan Molina?" Lizzy asked.

Chisel made the body shrug. *"He is here, but we will not let him go. If you kill us now, he will never wake up, and will be spared misery."*

Lizzy raised the lens; she'd take that deal on his behalf. "How big a cut?"

"We can enter a pinprick; a scratch will do. So, Petty Officer Townsend, is it a trade?"

Lizzy positioned the glass on her right arm. She pressed down, and blood welled up—the glass edge was so sharp that she didn't even feel it. The cut was about an inch long, and was more than enough. She turned to Chisel and walked up next to him. She took a deep breath, and in one fluid motion she pulled back his head with her right hand and sliced his carotid artery with her left. Blood poured and pumped from the wound.

"Trade," Lizzy whispered, and pushed her arm into the wound. The room grew darker, there was a flash of light...

...AND THEN EVERY CELL IN HER BODY WAS ON FIRE.

Lizzy couldn't even gasp. Every muscle—*every* muscle—in her body went into spasm as she toppled to the floor. She couldn't even catch herself: she landed on her shoulder hard, and her head bounced on the tiles. She felt the pressure of the impact but didn't register the pain, the burning was so great. She couldn't see, and all she could hear was a dull *buzz* in her ears. She was amazed she was still conscious.

*Positive and negative charges...*she really should have thought this through. She was violently allergic to being even *near* demons; to not consider the reaction of being *Infected* by one was beyond stupid.

But, it was too late for deliberations: now she had to figure out how to uncoil and get her body to respond. She remembered her training, and through the heat of a thousand suns she began to concentrate on breathing.

Find your breath...find your breath...go with the pain...relax your toes...relax your feet...

She couldn't relax much of anything, but she did finally register that she was wet. Mr. Molina's blood was on her, Infected and sticky, and that couldn't be helping her situation, either. Then she had an inspiration.

The blood is fluid...it's a conduit.

But then, why isn't kicking on automatically, like water does?

She managed to twitch the fingers on her right hand. Sure enough, they were resting in a substantial puddle. She found her center, and then she concentrated. Almost immediately she saw her white geyser in her mind, and the power surged through her—not just channeling down her arm, but all over and within her body. It was nothing like Lizzy had ever experienced before: it felt more cleansing and soothing than exorcising with water, and the healing of each individual cell was almost palpable. When the geyser finally receded she didn't feel great, but she felt much, much better.

Though, *now* she could feel her head and shoulder. *Ow...*

And then Lizzy could see, and she was indeed on the floor, covered in steaming blood and piss and shit. The body of Juan Molina was still in the chair, strapped in place, and the blood flow had diminished to nothing. He was dead, and Chisel was gone.

Lizzy then realized that the plan had worked: the demon was inside her just long enough to do its job before the pain kicked in—she supposed—and he was expelled. She knew, somehow, where she was going, and she could see the route clearly in her mind. She got to her feet.

The demon had even left an escape plan. She was getting out of here.

And, she admitted to herself as she reached the door, *it really is a clever plan.*

Chapter Twenty-three

Commune Matthew
Location Unknown
23 JUN
0221

More specifically, Lizzy considered yet again as she watched the Canary Tent, *the parts of the plan they left were clever...*

While Chisel did leave Lizzy most of a good plan—an escape route out of Echo, who to tap for help at Matthew—there were elements that the demons apparently had no knowledge about, so those components of the timeline were literally silent, grey pictures of haze. In Lizzy's mind, the implanted information went along, showing Lizzy images and bits of random data and sounds, and then there was...nothing.

For example, knowing the passcode to the receiving door at Echo was useful, and the subsequent picture of the loading dock. However, then her mind went foggy and only cleared to images of the open road, so Lizzy was left to her own devices to figure out how to get off of the base. She ended up stealing a hybrid and a few plastic containers of gas from the motor pool and then driving for Jesus. Knowing about that German shepherd loose at the gate would have been nice, too—she was glad she didn't have to hit that dog.

Other than the dog, though, there was no resistance—none at all. There weren't even bodies lying around or even blood, the outside perimeter was just...empty. She guessed that the entire base probably went Red Blossom as soon as she and Chisel had begun their conversation—they were very clear about their concerns regarding evidence. The only solace she could offer herself was that her decision to follow their lead wouldn't have changed that—Echo was doomed from the start.

Or, that's what she told herself.

Navigation by demon was interesting. As she was driving, she just knew to make a right turn at a particular intersection, or that up the road by that tunnel she could siphon gas, take a shower, and get something to eat at an abandoned warehouse/self-serve respite station for government truck drivers. It was second-nature, as familiar as a morning commute, though if Lizzy consciously stopped and thought about her actions she would have no idea where to go next. After trying and failing several times to synthesize the information into her active brain, she finally gave up and allowed the demon auto-pilot to do its job.

The other troubling aspect about Chisel's plan was how much they knew about government operations and the territory at large. As careful as the government was about safeguarding information, it seemed, the demons knew an awful lot about how things got done and where things were. Lizzy wondered if the government knew how spotty security really was. It seemed entirely possible that the demons could take down the government infrastructure if they wanted to. For some reason, though, they were biding their time.

She had arrived at Commune Matthew about two days ago, and she had been watching the shifts of the Canary Watch. There was one marine in particular that she observed—a marine she was pretty sure was here because of her. And this man was her best chance, the demons were certain, of getting in undetected.

Great...the guy I unintentionally fucked over is now my new best friend...

Lizzy knew Miller the Tree Trunk's mind from the demons—he had a strange habit of talking to the Infected that he guarded, and internally she could hear his whispers detailing his hatred of Commune Matthew, the government, and for her. But the hellspawn had a strategy for Lizzy about what exactly to say to Miller to get his cooperation. It was a logical argument, she supposed—Lizzy only hoped Miller was feeling logical tonight.

The demon images grew fuzzy when the plan got to the part where she gets Miller's attention and seeks his help, but she had that covered. If Matthew was anything like Ruth, the non-Sensing watchstander always slept during the midwatch while the Sensor stayed awake. This was against regulations, of course, but it was the unwritten, unspoken arrangement: it was understood that it was the Sensor's watch, and the other watchstander was just there on standby to die with the Sensor if the demons attacked. Sure enough, Lizzy noted on the first night, one watchstander curled up in the back of the tent and went to sleep, and the other watchstander read a book.

Fortunately for Lizzy, Miller had the mids the very next night. She waited until Miller's partner was fast asleep in the back of the tent and then went into action.

The other plus that night was that there was no moon. Lizzy had the cover of darkness, especially since Matthew kept the Courtesy Tent well-lit. Leaning behind a large boulder, with just a shaft of light coming from a divot on the top of the rock, Lizzy removed her cover. It was standard issue: a dark navy blue ball cap with "U.S. Coast Guard" embroidered on the front in yellow. A second class collar device was affixed underneath the lettering. Inside the cover, when she had been issued her uniform items at Echo, she had written "Townsend" along the inside of the brim. Now, she pulled out the black marker that she had taken from a self-serve station and wrote next to it "Southwest, large rock, 10 minutes".

Trusting that the night looked pitch-black to Miller and the tower guards, Lizzy slinked from behind the boulder and crept over to the Courtesy Tent. She approached from Miller's rear to minimize her chances of being seen. When she got to about twenty feet, just when she could begin to see the outlines of her hands in the floodlights, she tossed her cover into the tent and made her way back to the rock as quickly as she dared. After a full minute of listening behind the boulder, she peered over the top.

Miller hadn't noticed the hat yet; he was still watching the opposite horizon.

Oh, for fuck's sake! She considered throwing a rock, but then decided to bide her time. Finally, Miller shifted and turned around. It was only when he was almost on top of the cover that he finally saw it. He took several steps back.

At first, Miller just stared at the hat; Lizzy could imagine the gears of his mind churning through the possible reasons a coastie ball cap would be there.

Not mine...not my partner's... Lizzy imagined him saying to himself.

He cocked his head to the side. Lizzy continued the monologue: *Too small to be a man's cover...*

He pulled out his Ka-Bar knife from his ankle holster and chucked it at the cover. The Ka-Bar hit it handle first, and both the knife and the cover skidded across the floor of the tent. Nothing happened. *All right, no incendiary device...*

Miller walked over and picked up the cover and looked inside the brim. *Townsend...? Southwest...oh, shit!!*

In one smooth movement, Miller dropped the cover and drew his sidearm. He released the safety switch, cocked the hammer, and began to walk the perimeter of the tent, scanning the night, his 9 mm at the ready.

This is the dicey moment, Lizzy thought, watching. Miller could elect to do any number of things: wake up his partner, turn off the floodlights and let his eyes adjust, and/or sound the alarm. The comco on the folding table squawked.

"Hey, Miller," a voice said. "Is something going on?"

Miller hesitated, and then lowered his sidearm. He walked over to the table and picked up the comco.

"Sorry, Koch, I thought I heard something. Scared the bejesus out of me."

"I guess so. Are you sure it's nothing?" Lizzy could hear some laughing and comments about "Fuckin' Miller!" in the background.

"Yeah, I'm sure. I'll be taking a piss in a few minutes. Miller out." He set the radio on the table and sat down. He reset the hammer and the safety on his 9 mm and holstered his weapon. He just sat there for a few minutes, looking out into the night a little to the right of Lizzy's position. Then, he walked over and picked up Lizzy's cover and his Ka-Bar. He glanced at a compass he had clipped to his belt loop, looked into the night to get a bearing, and then began to walk. About ten paces out, he paused to get his mini-Maglite out of its holster and then aimed its beam at the ground as he travelled.

When he was about five feet from the boulder, Lizzy whispered his name and said, "I'm behind this rock, Miller. I'm coming out, unarmed and alone." Lizzy stepped directly into Miller's path, her fingers laced behind her head. Miller stopped in his tracks and stared. He kept the beam of light pointed away from her.

"You feel funny," Miller said, holding his Ka-Bar between them, the metal dull in the residual light. "Like you've been Infected, but not quite. Like you've been touched by them, or something."

476

"Yeah," Lizzy admitted. "I had a run-in a week ago. But as it turns out, Sensors can't get Infected—we go into anaphylactic shock or something. I almost died, I think."

Miller nodded slightly, his eyes never leaving her face. "I'm here because of you, you know." He raised the knife an inch or so. "Maybe if I turned you in, they'd send me away from this place, somewhere better."

"You could," Lizzy agreed. "But, I'd like to take you away from the government for good—somewhere better."

Miller twitched. "Bullshit." He gave Lizzy an once-over. "It looks like they found you. How long did you last in the Wilderness? Two days, maybe?"

"Two years. The Wilderness is not empty—there are many, many civilian settlements that are doing well. I got in the middle of a confrontation between two of them." She pulled back her shirt to show Miller the twisted mess of a scar that was clearly visible on her shoulder. Then she reached in her jacket front pocket and pulled out the mutilated but still recognizable homemade bullet that they had extracted—the same one Abby had showed her at the hospital. She held it up for Miller to see. "It isn't military issue, is it?"

Miller took a step closer and looked at it. He didn't lower his blade, so it was now a step closer to her heart. "No, it isn't. But say I believe you. Why are you here?"

She nodded toward Matthew. "I recently found out that my husband is in the lab downstairs, Miller. I'm here to get him out."

Miller stared at her. "There's no way, Townsend."

"I need your help getting in," Lizzy continued. "I've been told he's alive in there, though Infected. You've seen what I can do, Miller—I'm lookin' to get him out of there."

He shook his head and then glanced back at the commune. "This is crazy." He turned back to Lizzy. "Look, I can't stay out here much longer. You obviously got some bad information, but I could just let you find that out for yourself. Tell me why I should help you, rather than gut you now and turn you in."

She swallowed: this was the moment where she finds out if the demons knew humans as well as they thought they did—Miller specifically. She took a breath, and then said what the demons told her to say.

"Because the first time I left, I made a mistake—I should have taken you with me. I didn't know what was out there, so I didn't feel comfortable taking anyone with me. But I've been out there, Miller, and there's a place for you. In fact, you are going to take my place, because I cannot stay where I was anymore, but you will be welcome. They can use someone like you.

"I'm going to correct the mistake I made that day, Miller. This time, you're coming with me, and I swear I can get you clear of this, even if I die trying."

Miller looked at her, not moving. Lizzy began to count to herself: *One-one thousand, two-one thousand, three-one thousand, four-one thousand, five-one thousand, six...*

"You got here," Miller began. "You say your husband is here. I don't know what shit you're pulling, but I'll go along for now.

"But," Miller took one more step forward; the tip of his Ka-Bar lightly brushed the fabric above her breastbone. "If this goes down bad, if I even *think* you'll leave me with my ass in the wind again, I will correct *my* mistake. Do you get me?"

"Yes," Lizzy said, making sure to look at his face and not at the Ka-Bar. "I want to see my husband."

"OK." Miller lowered his knife and sheathed it. "Though I have to say, Townsend, that if your husband is in there, I am very sorry."

"Why?" *What the fuck, demons?* "He's alive, right?"

"After a fashion." Miller tossed Lizzy's cover to her; she caught it. He turned around, stopped, and then turned his head back to speak to Lizzy over his shoulder. "After the watch is relieved, meet me at the fence by the receiving dock on the other side of the commune. I'll get you in. Wait for me."

Miller turned back around and started toward the Courtesy Tent. The last thing Lizzy thought she heard him say was, "It looks like it's time to put my coat back on."

Lizzy didn't know what that meant—he was wearing a coat—but whatever. She backed into the shadows and started walking toward the rear of the compound.

478

It was still dark and early in the morning, so the receiving dock was deserted when Miller walked out to the fence and lit up a rolled cigarette. Lizzy walked up to the fence. She glanced at the closest watchtower.

"How'd you arrange to have the tower empty?" Lizzy asked.

"Mayer's on the down-low." Miller replied, pulling out a pair of dykes from his coat pocket. "Everyone knows he gundecks his watch—he only stands the first hour and the last hour." He started cutting the fence. "He's buggin' his lady at the bottom of the tower." He cut just enough for Lizzy to squeeze through. "Most guards gundeck a little—the general population is scared shitless, so they really don't kick up much."

"Scared of what?" Lizzy asked as she maneuvered through the hole in the fence.

"I'm about to show you," Miller replied, glancing around. "Let's go—no point pushin' it. And no talkin'...your voice is too high, you'll get noticed."

Miller led Lizzy to a door next to the receiving dock. The dock was on the ass-end of a five-story, ugly, stucco-covered construction the size of a typical office building that towered over the tents and shacks; it was the only permanent structure at the commune. Actually, she had never even *heard* of a permanent building in a commune before—how was it that it was never mentioned? Did the other commune OINCs know about it?

When they got to the door, Miller punched a code into the pad next to the door and pulled the handle. He held the door opened for Lizzy, and they both went inside. Miller led her through the receiving bay, through a set of double doors, and down several passageways. Eventually, they arrived at a black-painted door. Lizzy began to feel that familiar, queasy feeling.

Miller looked at her face. "Yeah, there's a lot of Infected down there." He studied her face for a second. "You really don't know what's down there, do you?"

Lizzy shook her head. Miller reached in his coat pocket and pulled out a prescription bottle. He lifted the white cap and shook out a small white pill. He handed it to Lizzy.

"It helps with the nausea."

Lizzy nodded, and then dry-swallowed the pill.

"OK," Miller said as he looked into a box next to the door; a lacy pattern of red laser beams illuminated his face, "Here we go." A second later Lizzy heard a *beep* and a *click*, and Miller pushed the door opened. After a landing only six inches wide, the concrete steps led straight down. Miller began his descent. Lizzy followed.

Finally, Lizzy couldn't help herself. "What is this place?" she whispered. "It's a permanent building in a *commune*, for Christ's sake..."

"It's a lab," Miller replied as he made his way down, the stairwell growing brighter as they descended. "They've called Red Blossom on this place three times, they say, and every time they came right back here. Until McClellon arrived, no one knew why this place was so important. All they have in the building above are offices, storage rooms, things like that."

"There's a lot of Infected down here, aren't there?" Lizzy asked.

"Yup," Miller said. "There surely are." They arrived at the bottom of the stairs, which was almost butt-up against another door. There was a computer screen mounted on the center of the door, along with a keyboard on a horizontal bracket. Miller reached over to the keyboard and hit "Enter."

A question appeared on the screen: "24 divided by ½ is?"

Miller thought for a moment, typed "48," and then pressed "Enter."

The screen went blank, and then another question appeared. "What is your favorite type of soda?"

Miller typed "lemon-lime" and pressed "Enter."

The screen went blank, and finally it asked for Miller's military ID number. Miller typed in nine digits and hit "Enter." The door swung opened. Lizzy was downright nauseous by now—she began to focus on her breathing.

"The first question is a totally random math question, and then the second question is also random and is cross-checked against your ID number." Miller led her through a white room with double doors at the other end. "Not that the hellspawn can type, anyway."

Lizzy didn't dare contradict him. After meeting Chisel, though, she wouldn't put it past them.

When they arrived at the double doors, Miller looked in their windows.

"Strange," Miller said. "They always have at least one person here." He turned to Lizzy. "I thought you came here alone."

"I am alone," Lizzy said. "I don't know what's going on."

"Maybe the tech's in The Farm," Miller muttered as he punched in one last code. He waited for the red light on the pad to go green, and then he opened the door.

Lizzy didn't like the sound of "The Farm." Then she looked through the large, plate-glass window in front of her, just inside the next room.

Chapter Twenty-four

The first thing Lizzy took in were the bald heads—rows upon rows upon rows of bald heads—a football field full. Each bald head seemed to be attached to a scrawny, skeletal body, with each body covered by a thin white sheet. There were hundreds of bodies with thousands of machines monitoring them. They were all in one gigantic room, as large as a cavern, with a grey tiled floor and white acoustic tiles covering the walls and high ceiling. She could hear the droning of the mechanisms, even outside the airtight door.

"What am I looking at, Miller?" Lizzy asked, not able to take her eyes off the rank and file of humanity.

"It's The Farm," Miller replied. "These are mostly soldiers who are milked of their sperm for repopulating purposes. They have qualities that the government likes—their genes and such. They also are used by McClellon to keep the peace, though he made it clear there would be no harvesting if it was one of our guys—just Stasis."

"How long have they been here?" Lizzy whispered. She knew the answer; the room began to spin as she put everything together.

"Most of them since Infusion."

Lizzy finally turned away. She crouched down into a ball.

"A while. We don't know exactly how long," Chisel had said. Chisel had lied. Of course they knew, but they had given her hope—and Lizzy had taken the bait. She started to hear the monotone of the ticker tape begin to murmur in her head again, ever so slightly…

While Lizzy rocked herself back and forth, silently flipping out, Miller typed on a computer keyboard in front of the window.

"Townsend?" Miller looked down. "Townsend? *Townsend!*"

Lizzy tipped herself back and let her butt hit the floor. She looked up at Miller, her face white and pasty.

Miller hesitated, but then continued. "Was your husband's first name Doug or Brydan?"

Lizzy had half-hoped that the demons were wrong, that Brydan wasn't here, but now she had to face the truth—all of it. "Brydan—his name was Brydan."

Miller nodded. "I found his location. I'll take you to him."

As Lizzy stood up, she noticed that Miller had softened towards her a little; his guarded demeanor and cautious approach had been replaced with concern. He believed her now, she supposed—she was acting like someone who just found out her thirty-seven-year-old husband was now a withered bag of bones and flesh. Honestly at this point, though, she was too numb to care anymore what the fuck he thought. She followed him into The Farm.

Every man looked basically the same. No one had hair, and all of their eyes were taped closed. The tape on each man was dingy and dried out, like it had been there for a long time. None of the men appeared to have teeth—their cheeks were sunken; their lips were curled in. Their skin tones were slightly different, but all of the men had a pallid undertone that made even the darkest skin look grey and translucent. Every last man was hooked up to a respirator, and there were tubes coming in and out of the bodies, feeding and medicating and disposing. It was all so *clean*—no bad smells, no odors, and no mess anywhere. No one had bed sores, like they had been carefully maintained beyond reason.

The noise from the ventilators and other machines was noticeable, though the noise-absorbing tiles that covered the walls and ceiling helped with the din quite a bit. Each decrepit creature looked the same to Lizzy, but finally Miller stopped in front of one particular bed.

"Here he is," Miller said above the noise.

Lizzy didn't recognize him at first: the old man lying before her was bald, colorless, and fragile. He didn't move, save the working of the respirator raising and lowering his chest. Lizzy came closer, afraid to touch him. She looked at Miller questioningly.

"You can touch the bodies, just be careful," Miller said. "The skin can rip, but it takes some doing. They wash the bodies and rotate them, that kind of thing."

Lizzy treated the man's right arm as she would a butterfly wing: she picked it up with a careful but firm grip and lifted it to view the underside. There, on man's wrist, were two red hearts intertwined with a smaller red winged heart above them. Brydan had wanted a tattoo to memorialize his miscarried child, and it was small enough to be covered by a wristwatch band. She lowered the arm back onto the bed.

"It's him," was all she could say as she felt a wave of grief and resignation wash over her. She pulled the sheet off the body.

Her field of vision was immediately overwhelmed by the sight of the large stainless steel cylinder that lay between Brydan's spindly legs and on top of his enlarged, distorted testicles: his nuts were at least three times the size she remembered.

"Is that...to *milk* him?" Lizzy asked, looking at Miller.

"Yes," Miller said. "They take the sperm from these men and send them to the female and family communes. If your husband is here, he must have been found to be genetically acceptable—he's probably fathered hundreds of kids, though it's hard to say. They don't keep track of that here, just volume, where it's sent, stuff like that."

Lizzy began to feel anger building up. "So they give him drugs so he's hung like an elephant and puts that...that *thing* on his junk? Oh, *hell*, no..." She began to reach for the cylinder; Miller grabbed her wrist.

"Don't, Townsend." He looked at her pleadingly. "It's been on there too long. I've seen them try to remove them, and...you just don't want to do that. Trust me, please."

Lizzy bowed her head as Miller allowed her to pull her hand away. "Goddamn them," she croaked. "Fuck them all." She gave up and reached over to take Brydan's hand. She tried to remember him as he was—meeting on the *Buzzard Bay*, the first time they had sex, the day they got married, *anything*—but her mind kept pushing her back to the present. This moment was just too stark for anything else.

"I'm here, Brydan, sweetheart," she finally said. "I'm sorry I can't even give you your dignity." Then, suddenly remembering her role in the plan, she leaned in and kissed Brydan's cheek—it felt like dry paper.

"I'm here," she whispered next to his ear. "I will love you forever."

Goddamn the demons, Lizzy thought, closing her eyes. While it was true, and she would have probably said something like that anyway, it cut to the core that they would choose that phrase to be signal to unleash them...and that they knew that Brydan himself would never hear her.

"Goodbye, Brydan," she whispered. As she stood up, she blinked her eyes to clear the tears. She covered Brydan with the sheet and started to follow the electrical cords. She tracked the individual cords to their shared power strips. From the power strips, she followed those cords to outlet banks against the wall.

"Townsend, what are you doing?" Miller asked, following her gaze as she tracked the bank's conduits to their main feed.

She played the strains of "Eternal Father, Strong to Save" in her head as she followed the main conduit back to the control room—it was the only tribute she could give. She noted where the pipe disappeared into the wall.

"I'm releasing these men, Miller." Lizzy replied. "I'm granting them peace." She walked back into the other room, Miller following at her heels.

"As soon as you throw the power switch, the alarms will sound," Miller told her. "We'll be caught in seconds."

Lizzy paused in her inspection of the main breaker box to shoot Miller a dark look. "Did you really think I would come alone?" She turned back around and opened the door of the box—there was one main switch that would cut the power to all the machines.

Miller didn't answer her; he crumpled onto a rolling chair by the control panels and watched her work.

Lizzy saw that her hand was shaking as she reached for the switch. She took one last look at the hundreds of men she was about to kill, including her husband. She allowed her tears to flow freely; her body shivered with silent, anguished sobs.

She didn't want to do this—she didn't want to do this. This might have all been worth it if she could have taken Brydan with her. But he was gone, and her moral obligation was clear: these men—these human souls—needed to be released. Then the hordes would come, she and Miller would make their escape, and so many more people would die today because of her.

But there was nothing she could do about that now. The die was cast, and there was no going back. She still wasn't sure if the demons knew as much about humanity as they thought they did, but they sure did know her.

"Can you sing, Miller?" She didn't wait for an answer. She took a final breath, released it, and then threw the switch.

The main lights went out, the respirators fell; they did not rise again. There were no alarms, there was only silence.

A growing, engulfing silence. An overwhelming silence.

The profound, blasphemous silence.

Then, the catch of a breath.

A whimper.

Now stand by for an excerpt from the third book in the Elizabeth Townsend Triptych, *The Last Religion*:

The Farm
Commune Matthew
Location Unknown
23 JUN
0757

<u>Lizzy</u>

Before she had slit the throat of their host and had Infected herself to get their information, the demons had told Lizzy that there was no such thing as hell—or, at least, not the fire and brimstone kind, with tortured human souls that were forever repenting for their sins. Rather, their world—their chasm filled with souls—was void of any sensation or sound, and they were the only ones who dwelt there.

She wasn't sure if she believed them. There *should* be a place for those who willing to hurt other people. Just for a logical, karmic balance in the universe there should be a hell, and she now deserved to go there.

Not for the hundreds of withered human husks that she just released from their suffering, though if there was a God, and He was overly vengeful, He might think differently.

Instead, she would go to hell for the demon horde that she just unleashed against the men of Commune Matthew. She had brought down the switch that stopped the ventilation of the bodies in The Farm that had ensnared hundreds of demon and human souls alike, and now those freed hellspawn were rioting above them with fountains of blood and explosions of weapon fire.

As she and Miller the Tree Trunk listened, they could hear the rifles' reports, the screaming, and the crashing of large objects above their heads as the soldiers fought and succumbed to the Red Blossom attack. That was exactly according to the demon's plan, but she hadn't cared before now—her only concern was getting her husband back.

But as it turned out, Brydan was one of the living husks, fuck their lying demonic hides. In the end, the only thing she managed to rescue was his soul and the souls of the hundreds of others who had been kept alive only to harvest semen for some fucked-up eugenics program. She believed that the remnants of the United States military were capable of some really psychotic shit, but this was mind-blowing.

She couldn't worry about that now, though: she had to get Miller and herself out of there. Frantically, she searched in her mind for the demon's implanted instructions to tell her how to escape to safety. She had been relying on demon navigation this whole evolution, from finding her way out of Echo to recruiting Miller to breaking in to The Farm.

OK, demons, Lizzy thought. *Escape plan...anytime now...?*

There was nothing.

She took a breath and slowly replayed the last two steps the demons left in her mind, hoping to trigger a response: *say the prearranged words, pull the switch, and...*

Nothing.

She scanned her mind once more as she felt herself slide into panic. Surely, there was something: a door, an escorted escape, *something, goddammit!*

But, no—there were no more images, no more unconscious suggestions, not even the grey haze when the demons didn't have any information and she had to fill in the blanks. For the first time in a week, she was truly on her own.

Which meant she and Miller were in a world of shit.

For a fleeting second, she considered just lying down and letting the demons take her. She was so goddamned tired, and everything she did just seemed to make things worse. Maybe it was time to cut her losses and call it a day. She even searched the floor by the glow of the emergency spotlights, looking for a nice, comfortable place to be ripped to shreds.

*But...*no, she had made a promise to Tree Trunk, and she was going to die trying to get him out of here as she said she would. Though, maybe in a minute he'd just snap her neck in anger, and then she wouldn't have to worry about living anymore. She cleared her throat.

"Um...Miller?"

"Yeah?"

She swallowed. "This," she gestured towards the ceiling, "wasn't part of the plan."

His eyes narrowed. "What the fuck do you mean?" he asked quietly.

They both jumped as they heard a loud *bang!* coming from above and over by the stairwell. If Lizzy had to guess, she'd say it was the ground level door leading to the stairwell being forced opened.

"I mean...this wasn't supposed to be like this. We were supposed to have help by now." She paused as she heard the stomping of feet and the tumbling of bodies down the steps. There was a *thud!* as something hit the door beside them—hard. She looked Miller straight in the eyes.

"I don't know how to get out."

References

This is not the complete list of references that I used in the development of this novel: that list can be found at www.sites.google.com/site/phillipsandmore. Rather, this is an annotated reference list of resources that I used for certain key elements of the story.

Finn of Ynos Mon, Dame Aoife (SCAdian name) (2004). *Masters, mistresses & knights SCA elevation ceremonies SCAtoday_net.* Retrieved April 16, 2011 from www.scatoday.net/node/2401. A clearinghouse of SCAdian information, including induction ceremonies and general information about the Orders and royalty. The entire site (SCAtoday.net) is quite informative.

Gilmore, J. (2011). Using theatre to develop leadership capacity on social issues. (Unpublished undergraduate thesis). Millersville University of Pennsylvania, Millersville, PA. In exchange for reading and reviewing my first novel, *Demons Among Us*, I agreed to assist Justin in editing his thesis. It introduced me to Augusto Boal and his Theater of the Oppressed, and an entire subplot was born.

Hindalong, S. and Dougherty, D. (1992). Beautiful scandalous night [Recorded by The Choir]. On *Flap Your Wings* [CD]. Brentwood, TN: Galaxy21 music. (2000). When I was an awkward, angsty teenager who felt like she didn't belong anywhere, this incredibly talented band set a lot of my soul-searching to music. They still produce albums, they are still not preachy, and they still tour: www.thechoir.net.

Keyser, W. (2009). *Blue ridge entertainment – sideshow collectibles and more.* Retrieved April 16, 2011 from www.goodmagic.com. In addition to the Carny, Circus, and Vaudeville dictionaries that are free and incredibly entertaining, there are also CDs of ballyhoos, design plans to build sideshow attractions, and comprehensive information about Romany, Carny, and Circus cultures.

Lyttelton, T. (1903). *Littleton's tenures* (ed. Wambaugh, E.). Washington, D.C.: John Byrne. The AoA oath (not taken in the current Society) was written using bits of both the oath of homage and the oath of fealty (c. 1480) that was listed on the following website: http://faculty.goucher.edu/eng330/ceremonies_of_homage_and_fealty.htm.

West Kingdom College of Heralds (2011). *SCA – west kingdom college of heralds|court heraldry|ceremony book|west kingdom.* Retrieved May 20, 2012 from http://heralds.westkingdom.org/ceremony/west/chivalry.pdf. I borrowed parts of the Swearing of Fealty Ceremony for knights and barons of the realm for my character's AoA ceremony, including: the oath, the testimonials of spokespeople, and the use of symbolic tokens given to newly inducted members of the three Orders. The tokens that were given to my character are not given in the current AoA ceremony, save for the AoA scroll.

Glossary

advance – in Star-Crossed culture, the group selected to go ahead
of the rest of the troupe to set up the stage and tents (always
with local help) and begin promoting the event's shows and
workshops.

AOD (Autocrat of the Day) – This SCAdian is in charge of the daily
gate and wall watches, logging visitors, and would sound the
alarm in the event of an emergency.

bill – a list of acts.

boatswain's mate (BM) – an enlisted Coast Guard Petty Officer in
charge of most things nautical, from navigation to maintaining
the paint on the ship's surfaces (keeping it "pretty") to being the
default leader in any general evolution on the enlisted level
unless otherwise specified. A BM is thought to work "above
decks," while engineers (MKs, DCs, and EMs) work "below
decks."

CO – Commanding Officer.

coasties – coastguardsmen, otherwise known as Puddle Pirates,
Knee-Deep Sailors, or The Guys Responsible For All the
Especially Cute Navy Children.

comco – two-way radio transmitter.

company commander – The Coast Guard's equivalent of a drill
sergeant; someone who oversees recruits during basic training.

cutter – a Coast Guard ship more than 65 FT long.

damage controlman (DC) – an enlisted Coast Guard Petty Officer
who maintains firefighting and flooding control materials/
equipment, repairs components of grey water and sewage

systems, and fabricates wooden and welded objects afloat; usually maintains housing for families ashore.

despot – tyrannical asshole. *Despotism* is being ruled by a tyrannical asshole.

down-low – "On the down-low," a reference to men engaging in acts of a homosexual nature clandestinely.

flash act – an unscheduled act that can be used as filler in between acts or as an emergency replacement.

FNG – Fucking New Guy.

jump – going from one place to another.

mud show – small-time show playing in country/rural areas.

mundane – Anything or anyone that is not directly involved with the SCA.

OINC – Officer IN Charge. To be perfectly correct, it probably should be Non-Commissioned Officer In Charge (NCOINC), but I never heard a coastguardsman use this term during my years of service.

OCS – Officer Candidate School, which gives civilians with bachelor's degrees and certain enlisted personnel the opportunity to become a commissioned officer.

OOD – Officer of the Day.

palla – a rectangular mantle worn by ancient Roman women.

peplos – a body-length, tubular garment worn by women in ancient Greece.

paper the house – in the circus and vaudeville cultures, it means giving out complementary tickets for a show so that the crowd looks larger, drawing attention and selling more seats. In Star-

Crossed culture, it refers to filling in the empty seats for court, so it looks like there was a large turnout.

Red Blossom – military code word for a demon attack upon a military instillation. It is always transmitted just before the compound is completely overtaken and lost.

seam checker – derogatory name for a SCAdian who is so concerned about authenticity that she will look at the stitching on the inside of someone else's garb to ensure that it was done by hand, rather than sewn on a machine. See despot.

sight act – an act without speech, like a juggler or a contortionist. They are often placed first or last on the bill because the audience makes so much noise filling or emptying a space.

shellback – a sailor attached to a ship that has crossed the equator. There's usually a questionable induction ceremony involved (called Crossing the Line, pun inferred by me).

SNL – Saturday Night Live, a late-night comedy show on the National Broadcasting Company (NBC) television network.

The Society for Creative Anachronism (SCA) – a social organization that re-enacts various aspects of medieval society; its timeframe is approximately from the fall of the Roman Empire to the end of the 16th century.

route – the schedule of towns and baronies to be played during a season.

terminal leave – leave (paid vacation) a serviceman takes just prior to being discharged or retired.

triclinium (pl. *triclinia*) – the ensemble of a dining table with a reclining couch or couches that surround the table on three sides. This arrangement was often used in ancient Rome, so it would be fitting for the Jersey Lily's motif.